THE
PRETTIEST
ONE

ALSO BY JAMES HANKINS

Shady Cross
Brothers and Bones
Jack of Spades
Drawn

THE PRETTIEST ONE

JAMES HANKINS

THOMAS & MERCER

Published by Thomas & Mercer, Seattle

www.apub.com

Amazon, the Amazon logo, and Thomas & Mercer are trademarks of Amazon.com, Inc., or its affiliates.

ISBN-13: 9781477829820
ISBN-10: 1477829822

Cover design by David Drummond

Printed in the United States of America

For Lynne and John, who, in addition to raising the child who would later grow up and become my wonderful wife, are pretty terrific people themselves.

CHAPTER ONE

"MY NAME IS CAITLIN SOMMERS," she said aloud even though she was alone.

Her feet hurt as she walked. Her legs were tired. She wasn't sure why she was walking, but she kept going, her sore feet protesting as they carried her across the cracked pavement.

Though the night was clear, she walked in a fog. What day was it? Did she have to work in the morning? If so, she'd have to be in the office by nine. For a moment, she wasn't certain what office that was, then remembered she was a real-estate agent. She couldn't imagine why that fact had momentarily escaped her. Something bumped against her leg and, looking down, she was mildly surprised to see that she was holding a small canvas bag by its strap. She wondered where she'd gotten it.

She didn't know where she was or how she had ended up there, walking across that pavement. She looked down and saw faded, painted white lines passing under her feet, one after the other, as she walked. She was in a parking lot. An empty one. No idea why. She'd simply woken up and there she was . . . wherever that was.

But no, she hadn't truly woken up, because she hadn't been asleep. That was how it felt, though, like she'd been sound asleep and dreaming for days. Even now, wisps of pale memories shimmered briefly in her mind before disappearing quickly, the way snippets of dreams so often do moments after waking.

I know who I am, she thought, then followed that thought immediately with, *Why wouldn't I?*

The last thing she remembered was . . . well, it was hazy. She recalled . . . going to the gym, maybe? And being in a store, a small one with a bell over the door. She'd bought . . . something yellow.

She kept walking, kept putting one achy foot in front of the other, until she saw a car up ahead illuminated by the wan light falling from a thin sliver of moon. It felt to Caitlin as though she might have been heading toward the car all along without even knowing it, so she held her course.

Moving slowly, she walked all the way to the far corner of the lot, where the car waited in the moonshadow of a big shade tree. She stopped and turned. Far across the expanse of empty asphalt hunkered a big rectangle of a building. It looked like a warehouse. Even from this distance, and despite the dim moonlight, the structure's broken windows and graffiti-decorated cinder-block walls told Caitlin that it was abandoned. She turned back to the car and peered through the passenger's window. There were no keys in the ignition. She reached into a front pocket of her jeans and found a set of keys. She pulled them out, slid one into the keyhole in the door, and unlocked the car. Inside the vehicle, she slid behind the wheel and dropped the bag on the passenger seat beside her.

"My name is Caitlin," she said to no one.

She started the car, then wondered where to go.

Home, she realized. Of *course* she should go home. Her husband must be wondering where she was.

Join the club, Josh, she thought.

"My husband's name is Josh," she told the empty car.

She glanced at the dashboard clock: 1:17 in the morning. Josh must be frantic. She leaned first to one side then the other, patting her back pockets. It felt like she had a thin wallet in one. The other pocket was empty. Strange—she always kept her cell phone in her back pocket.

Okay, no phone. No problem. She'd just drive home and talk to Josh when she got there.

She eased the car across the empty lot until she reached the exit to the street. It was a quiet, wooded road. This warehouse, wherever it was, was located somewhere remote. Caitlin looked left, then right, then chose left because . . . well, because she had to choose a direction.

She drove for a few miles, surrounded by trees, until the trees started to thin and signs of life began to appear—first a few houses, then a few businesses, then a strip mall. On the other side of the street from the mall, she spotted the bright yellow sign of an open Shell station. She was about to pull in, ask where she was, and figure out the fastest route home when she saw a sign for Interstate 91 North.

She nodded to herself. This situation didn't feel right at all, and she was confused about a lot of things, but she suddenly felt strongly that I-91 would take her home. She checked the fuel gauge, saw that it was nearly full, and swung onto the on-ramp. Soon she passed a sign for Holyoke, which she knew was in Massachusetts. Finally, she had an idea where she was, even if she still didn't know how she'd gotten there. More importantly, she knew she'd be home in Bristol, New Hampshire, in a few short hours.

Nothing made sense to her. She had so many questions. But she was suddenly very tired, so she refused to think about anything but the road ahead. She'd be home in a little while. It would be good to get home.

CHAPTER TWO

JOSH SOMMERS DREAMED OF HIS wife, as he often did. Tonight, she was wearing her yellow sundress with the red flowers, the one she'd worn on their first date. They were walking in a non-descript park, surrounded by faceless people enjoying the brilliant sunshine. He and Caitlin were laughing. They used to laugh a lot together. Somewhere, a church bell rang.

"Come on," Caitlin said, "we'll be late."

She turned and started away from him at a trot, the sundress swaying against her slender calves, her blonde hair bouncing against the back of her neck.

"Slow down," Josh called.

She turned her head and smiled but didn't slow her steps. In fact, she began to retreat from him more quickly, even though her legs didn't seem to be moving any faster. Somehow she slipped farther and farther away, despite his having broken into a run.

"Caitlin, wait for me."

She didn't turn around again. And she didn't slow down. She was almost flying across the grass now, moving with an ease and grace that should have been impossible at the speed she was traveling. The sun disappeared behind a dark veil of clouds that hadn't been in the sky just seconds ago. A strong, cold wind blew in Josh's face, slowing him down, though it didn't seem to touch Caitlin at all.

The church bell rang again. Caitlin reached the crest of a hill and stood for the briefest of moments, a bright splash of yellow against a sky as dark and gray as wet concrete.

Josh was running as fast as he could now, his legs pumping, his heart hammering.

The bell rang again and Caitlin sank from sight behind the hill. She was gone.

Josh opened his eyes to the darkness of his bedroom. He'd known it was a dream all along, but his breath was still short and his pulse was still pounding. He blinked at the ceiling, slowed his breathing, and tried to calm his racing heart. His hand reached out and found the cold, empty side of the bed.

The doorbell rang, and he realized it had been ringing for some time, that it had been the church bell of his dream. He turned to the clock by his bed: 3:09 a.m.

What the hell?

He slipped out from under the bedcovers, tugged on a pair of jeans, and headed for the stairs as the doorbell rang yet again.

"Hang on," he called as he neared the bottom step.

He crossed the foyer and peeked through the little curtain beside the door. It took a long moment for his mind to process what he saw. As soon as it did, he fumbled with the dead bolt and yanked open the door.

Caitlin stood on the porch.

It was really her. It didn't seem possible, but there she was.

"I'm sorry, Josh," she said as she slipped past him into the house. "I know it's late. I know I woke you. I would have called, but I must have lost my phone."

How . . . ?

"And I would have let myself in, but I guess I lost my house key, too," she said. "It's probably with my phone, right?"

He could only stare at her.

"I know you must be angry and have a lot of questions," she added. To Josh, she sounded like someone who had recently awakened from a drug-induced sleep. "Believe me," she said, "so do I. But I've been driving for hours and I'm really tired. Can we talk in the morning?"

She did indeed look tired. And a bit . . . lost. She also looked very little like the woman he'd married.

"Caitlin?" he asked. "Is it really you?"

She was heading for the stairs when she stopped and turned back toward him.

"I expected questions," she said, "but that wasn't one of them."

"What were you expecting?"

She gave a small shrug. "Maybe something more like 'Where have you been?'"

He nodded. "Okay, where have you been?"

She said nothing for a moment, looking lost in thought. Finally, she said, "I really can't tell you."

"Seriously?" he asked, his voice rising just a little despite his effort not to let it. "I understand you were upset with me when you left, but you've been gone for seven months, and you can't tell me where you've been?"

Caitlin opened her mouth to reply, then seemed to realize that she had no idea what to say.

CHAPTER THREE

"WAIT," CAITLIN SAID. "WHAT? Seven months?"

That made no sense to her. For a moment, she thought her husband might be putting her on. But he looked so . . . stunned. And serious. Then she wondered if something could be wrong with him, like he'd had a stroke or something. Finally, she had to consider the possibility that there was something wrong with *her* instead.

"What, Caitlin?" Josh said. "You just lost track of time? Somehow seven months just—"

He stopped. His eyes widened.

"Is that blood?" he asked.

Caitlin looked down. Her low-cut, tight-fitting sweater was maroon, so it was hard to see the darker red splotches. But they were there. At her stomach. On her sleeves. She also now saw smaller reddish-brown spots on the thighs of her dark jeans. She looked back up at Josh.

"Jesus, Caitlin," he said, moving quickly to her. "You're hurt."

"I don't . . . feel hurt."

"My God, what the hell happened?"

"I . . . I don't know."

He touched her arm with a quick, comforting hand before slowly, gently lifting her sweater. He was wincing before he even got a glimpse of what lay beneath. Caitlin kept her eyes on his face, not wanting to see whatever wound she'd suffered. Josh's wince disappeared and a frown took its place. Still holding up her shirt, he peered at her sides, then her back.

"There's nothing here," he said. "I don't think it's your blood."

She wasn't all that surprised. She hadn't felt injured. Of course, that begged the question—

"So whose blood is it?" Josh asked.

She wished she knew.

———

The shower seemed to clear Caitlin's mind a bit. She stood with her head down and let the hot water wash over her, allowed the steam to work its way into her. She was tired, but she no longer felt drugged. When she stepped out of the shower, she found that Josh had left her favorite flannel pajamas on the vanity, the ones with drawings of teacups all over them. After she dried off, she slipped into them and they felt wonderful.

She turned to the sink, used a corner of her towel to clear the steam from a little circle in the mirror, and nearly screamed.

The person looking at her from her reflection wasn't Caitlin.

She backed away, bumping into the wall behind her.

After a steadying breath, she stepped forward and looked again at the mirror, but the steam had already reclaimed it. She used the towel to clear another spot, then sucked in another breath, a deeper one, and looked.

Who the heck was that?

Where was her blonde hair? Who had dyed it red?

And if she hadn't still been so confused when she'd washed her hair in the shower moments ago, she likely would have noticed then that it was a good four inches shorter than she'd always kept it. No longer shoulder length, her hair now fell just below her ears.

Caitlin leaned closer to the glass and studied her face. It was thinner. No one would ever have called her overweight in the past, and she still looked healthy, but she could see in her cheeks that she had dropped some weight. She ran her hands down her sides. Five pounds gone, maybe ten, which, when you started at 123, made a difference you could see. Where had the weight gone?

Where had the *time* gone?

Josh said she'd been missing for seven months.

Seven months.

———

When Caitlin walked out of the bathroom, Josh was sitting on the bed, waiting. As soon as the door opened, he came to her, wrapped his arms around her, and hugged her as though he never planned to let her go. She hugged him back and it felt good. He kissed her damp hair. She breathed in his scent.

After the longest, most meaningful embrace of her life, Caitlin said, "I need tea."

Downstairs, she sat at the kitchen table while Josh made her tea with honey and lemon; then he followed her into the living room where she curled up in a corner of the sofa. Josh sat beside her. Not at the other end, but right beside her.

"Feeling okay?" he asked. He looked like he was trying to be casual about it, but Caitlin could sense him studying her. That was natural, she supposed, under the circumstances.

"I'm okay," she said, though it was only partly true. Physically, she felt fine. Mentally? Less so. She took a sip of tea, her hands wrapped around the oversize mug.

"While you were in the shower," Josh said, "I bagged up the clothes you were wearing. I also went out to the car in the driveway and found a gym bag on the front seat."

He nodded to a little black canvas bag on a chair across the room. Caitlin looked at it. It seemed familiar.

"Thanks," she said.

"Ready to talk?" he asked softly, still watching her intently while trying to appear as though he wasn't.

She shrugged. She wasn't sure how much she could say. She didn't know anything.

"Okay," he said, "I'll start. When you left seven months ago . . ."

"Has it really been that long?"

"It has."

My God. "I don't remember it, Josh. Not a moment of it."

He frowned, then smiled uneasily, and it felt to Caitlin as though he were trying to gauge her honesty. *Well, why wouldn't he?* This was crazy. After looking into her eyes for a long moment, he dropped his gaze to the tabletop.

"Honey . . ." he began, his voice different. Sad, maybe. He started to say something else, then stopped.

Her heart sank. He didn't believe her.

Finally, he nodded, seemingly to himself, and said, "You were gone more than half a year." When he looked up again, his eyes were wet. "I thought you were dead, Caitlin. *Everyone* thought you were dead."

He took a big, shuddering breath. Caitlin reached out a hand and held one of his.

"I'm sorry," she said. "I can't imagine what you've been through."

Heck, she couldn't even imagine what she herself had been through.

"You really don't remember any of it?" Josh asked.

She shook her head. "It's terrible. I looked in the mirror upstairs and didn't recognize myself. I came home covered in blood. Whose was it? What the hell happened to me?"

"What's the last thing you remember?"

She tried to focus her thoughts. There was a parking lot. And . . .

"I found a car," she said.

"The one out front? Whose is it?"

"I have no idea. But I found the key in my pocket, and when—" A terrible thought came to her. Her hands shook and she nearly dropped the hot tea in her lap. "Do you think . . . do you think the blood came from whoever's car that is?"

"Caitlin . . ."

"Do you think I could have—"

"No," he said quickly. "Of course not. Not you, Caitlin. No way."

"But—"

"Not you, honey. I don't believe it. I just don't. So let's forget about the car for a second. You got in it; that's all we need to know right now. What then?"

"I saw a sign for I-91 and drove home."

"Where were you? What town?"

"I'm not sure. I . . . don't remember. I feel like I might have known when I started driving, like I'd seen some signs, but some-how I've forgotten them already. My mind is . . . not really clear yet. I know I drove north, though."

He nodded. "Okay, but what about before you found the car? What's the last thing you remember?"

She shook her head. "Nothing."

"Caitlin," Josh said gently, "you remembered where you live. You remembered me. Anything else?"

She nodded. She wasn't thinking straight at all. Of course she remembered things. She remembered almost everything from before, actually. She remembered her mother's singing voice and the fact that her father was never without a roll of peppermint Life Savers in his pocket. She could easily recall various Christmas mornings over the years. She remembered her first and only cigarette, and high school dances, and losing her virginity to Charlie Granger, and getting her driver's license, and meeting her college roommate, and listening to her college boyfriend's horrible rock band. She remembered the terrible day she learned that her parents had died in a car wreck when she was twenty. She remembered meeting Josh at a Starbucks, and him asking her out when they ran into each other two weeks later at a different Starbucks. She had no trouble remembering their first date, their first night in bed, their wedding. She remembered her job in the real-estate office and Josh trying in vain to talk her into buying a spectacularly ugly bulldog puppy when they moved into this house.

She remembered all of that. But the last seven months were apparently just . . . *gone*. It was as though someone had taken the story of her life and torn out an entire chapter.

"What's the very last thing you remember?" Josh asked. "The absolute last thing before you found the car?"

She closed her eyes.

"I bought a new purse. A yellow one."

She opened her eyes.

"That's right," he said. "You showed it to me. That was a week before you went missing."

She closed her eyes again. He was right. She remembered now. She bought the purse on a Wednesday. She'd gone to the gym after work and on the way home stopped at a little boutique she had been meaning to check out. "I remember having an argument with Frank at work. I thought he was trying to get a bit too cozy with one of my clients."

"You told me about that. It was a couple of days before you disappeared."

She kept her eyes closed and concentrated. "I remember falling on a run and cutting my ankle on a rock."

"Yeah, that was a pretty bad cut. I patched you up when you got home. That was the night before you . . . left."

She looked down at her bare ankle and saw a faint scar, all healed. "I remember . . . I remember fighting with you."

He was quiet for a moment. "That's right," he said somberly, nodding. "We argued and you left. You were mad and you left and then you just . . . didn't come home."

"I can't remember what we were fighting about," she said.

He shrugged, smiling sadly. "It was so long ago now. But whatever it was, it got out of hand. I remember that. And when you didn't come home, I had to wonder if . . . if something terrible had happened to you. You were just . . . gone." He shook his head.

He looked so sad that she put down her mug and kissed him. Then she rested her head on his shoulder, closed her eyes, and felt the night begin to fade from her mind.

Where does seven months go?

CHAPTER FOUR

HE WAS LITERALLY TWICE CAITLIN'S size and smelled like rotting garbage. His skin was the pale white of a fish's belly. His bald head was bumpy and scarred. His dark little eyes were too far apart. His hands were freakishly strong. He was the Bogeyman. And he grabbed at her and clawed at her, trying to drag her down into the ground. "I've got you, my pretty Caitlin," he said, and his breath stank like dead things.

It was the same nightmare she'd had since she was little. Only this time, when she awoke, he didn't disappear right away as he always did, as he had for more than two decades. No, this time, though she was awake, she could still see his eyes, feel his hands on her, smell the fetid odors that clung to him.

But morning had come and those things began to fade.

She'd had the nightmare so many times over the years, so very many times, but its frequency didn't diminish its power one iota. His eyes . . . his hands . . . his rotting smell. *Pretty Caitlin.*

She was lying on the living room sofa. She disentangled herself from the furry throw blanket Josh had evidently draped over her sometime during the night, and which she had apparently twisted around herself during her nightmare flight from the Bogeyman. She took a few calm, steadying breaths.

She felt foolish. She felt like a child. But she couldn't deny the terror the dream had instilled in her.

As the last vestiges of the nightmare faded, as the rotting-garbage smell left her nose, Caitlin became aware of a new smell. A fantastic one. Because after all, what smells better than bacon? She rarely ate it but loved it when she did. She also smelled coffee. She'd have been willing to bet there were eggs somewhere nearby, too.

After a quick trip to the bathroom, she followed the wonderful aromas to the kitchen, where she found Josh sliding an omelet out of a frying pan and onto a plate.

"I know, I know," he said. "Bacon is the devil, but it's a special day."

"I love bacon," she said. "It's evil, but I love it."

She sat at the table and he slid the plate in front of her, placed a mug of tea beside it, then sat across from her with a plate of his own.

"This is good," she said.

"No, it's not," he said, smiling. "We both know I'm clueless in the kitchen."

She laughed softly. He was right. The omelet was underdone, and there was too much ham and not enough cheese in it. Seven months on his own hadn't made him a better cook.

"The bacon's good, at least," she said.

Caitlin took a few more bites because, even if the omelet wasn't too terrific, Josh had made it for her. And besides, she was hungry.

"I've been thinking," she said between bites.

"When? You've been sound asleep for hours. You barely moved once you closed your eyes."

"How do you know I was so sound asleep?"

"I checked on you a few times."

She looked him in the eye.

"Okay," he added, "more than a few times. You were dead to the world until two minutes ago." He winced as though regretting his choice of words.

"I was thinking in the bathroom just now."

"Okay . . ."

"I want to go back."

"Go back where?"

"Wherever I was . . . you know, lately."

Josh put down his fork. "How? You said you didn't know where you were."

"I think I can retrace my route back to where I first realized where I was. Then I would . . . figure it out from there. I'm sure I'll recognize something."

Josh hesitated. "I'm not sure that's a great idea."

"I have to."

"Caitlin . . . we don't know where you've been or what happened to you, but you've clearly been through something serious, something traumatic. We need to get you to a hospital, get you checked out—"

"I feel fine," she said.

"You may feel fine, but something's not right if you can't remember seven months of your life."

That was a good point. "I think going there might help me remember."

Josh took a deep breath. "Honey . . . you came home covered in blood, remember? It could be dangerous to go back."

"It wasn't my blood," she reminded him.

"I'm not sure that makes it any less dangerous. *Something* sure as hell happened to you, and it can't have been good. Maybe . . ."

"What?"

"If whatever happened to you was bad enough to make you forget seven months, maybe you *shouldn't* remember."

Caitlin didn't know how to make him understand, but she needed to know what happened, whatever it was. Good or bad, she needed to know . . . where she'd been, what she'd done, whose blood it was. "What if I committed a crime?"

"If you did," he began carefully, "it's over now."

It was her turn to put down her fork. "Seriously? What if I hurt someone?"

"You wouldn't do that."

"How do we know that? Apparently, we don't know me very well. We didn't think I'd go running off somewhere for seven months, but I did. So I don't think we really know what I would do. If I hurt someone, Josh, I need to know."

Josh stared down into his unfinished eggs. "What if the police there are looking for you?"

"If they are, then they should find me. I have no desire to get away with anything. If I did something terrible, I should be punished for it."

"Wait a second. If you did do something—and I'm not saying you did—but if you did, you obviously weren't in your right mind. It's not your fault."

"That would be for a jury to decide, not us."

"Are you serious?"

"I am."

He looked away from her, out the window. When he looked back, she held his eyes with her own.

"I have to know," she said. "I couldn't live with not knowing where I was, what I did, and whether I did something . . . bad. Just a few days to see what we can find out. After that, I'll go to a doctor and let him run every test known to medical science. Unless I'm in prison, of course."

Josh winced at that, but after a moment, he said, "Just a few days?"

"I promise."

He stared down at his half-eaten omelet before meeting her eyes again. "You did a lot of thinking during thirty seconds in the bathroom."

———

After breakfast, Caitlin washed up and got dressed. Her clothes were a tiny bit looser on her than they used to be. Nothing drastic, but she felt it.

As she brushed her teeth, she ran things through in her mind. She thought Josh was probably doing the same thing. She could hear him putting away the dishes downstairs, a little more loudly than necessary. It didn't sound like angry dish-doing—rather, more like distracted dish-doing.

She went downstairs and met him as he walked into the living room, drying his hands on the legs of his pants.

"We have so much to talk about," he said.

"We can talk in the car on the way. Are you sure you can get away from work for a few days?" Caitlin herself certainly didn't have to worry about asking for time off. Her employer and coworkers no doubt thought she had run off with another man or was dead. She doubted her desk was waiting for her, with her notepads all stacked and her pencils sharpened, just the way she always left them at the end of every day.

"They won't even know I'm gone," Josh said. "They didn't fire me after you went missing, but with everything that was going on . . . They said they were looking out for me, giving me a little time, but they started sending out other reps to my clients, forcing me to split the commissions. We rolled out a new data-storage product and I wasn't even invited to the prerelease meetings. So yeah, I think I can get away without the office falling apart."

"God, Josh, I'm so sorry, really—"

He waved off her apology. "Where are we even going?" he asked. "Do you have any idea?"

"I think I can remember where I got on the highway. We'll head there. You look terrible."

"See, that's why I missed you."

She smiled. "I mean, you don't look like you slept well."

"I didn't. There are so many questions. Like I said, so much to talk about."

"And like I said, we can talk in the car."

"Caitlin . . ." His grim expression gave her pause.

"What is it?"

"I thought you were dead."

"I know. I'm sorry."

"Everyone thought you were dead." He paused. "And when a wife disappears, who does everyone suspect?"

Then she understood. *Oh, God.*

"Josh, I'm so, so sorry. I can't believe people would . . . Anyone who knows us . . ."

"They thought I killed you, hon."

"Who would think that?"

"Everyone. The police. Strangers. Friends. Everyone."

"But I'm alive. They'll see that and everyone will know they were wrong. Which friends?"

He shook his head.

"Tell me," she said. "Which of our friends thought you killed me?"

"None of them actually said so, but I could tell they were all thinking it, especially when the first few weeks went by and you didn't come home and you weren't . . . found. At first they stood by me. They were there for me. Soon enough, though, they stopped dropping by. Then they stopped calling. Then they stopped returning my calls."

"Oh, Josh."

"The cops didn't help things any. Or the media."

"The media?"

"They might as well have come right out and said that I killed you."

Tears were threatening. It crushed her to hear what he'd gone through, to imagine how it had been for him. "Well, we'll go to the police right now. Show them I'm alive. Hold a press conference. You can blow kisses to all the jerks who didn't believe you, including our so-called friends."

He didn't say anything for a moment. He was wrestling with something. She could see it in his eyes.

"Caitlin," he finally said, "if we do that, there will be questions. Ones you can't answer."

"Like where I've been."

"For starters. They'll question the hell out of you, for a long time. And they won't just question you. They'll *evaluate* you. Maybe admit you to a hospital or . . ."

"Or some kind of psychiatric unit."

He shrugged. "I have no idea. All I know is that when we make this public, the police will want answers about where you've been and what you've been doing. And God, the media. They'll be all over you. You were a hot story for a few months, at least locally. And there was a little national coverage."

"National coverage? Seriously?"

He nodded. "So if we go public now, you'll be tied up for a long time. And if you are . . . you won't get your answers."

"I thought you didn't want me looking for answers."

"I'm just worried that you might not like what you'll find. Or even worse, that you'll get hurt looking. But I want you whole. And I think you need answers to be whole. So if we have to go back there to get them, to wherever you were, then that's what we'll do."

"Okay," she said. "For just long enough to figure out what I was doing all that time, then we come home and go right to the police, okay?"

"Okay."

She looked at him. "You're a good man."

"I don't know about that. But I love you. And I just thought of something." He crossed the living room and picked up the black gym bag from the armchair. "You had this with you in the car. You brought it back from . . . wherever. I figure it's probably just a change of clothes, but maybe something in here can tell us . . . something."

He put the bag on the sofa and sat next to it. Caitlin sat on the other side of it. He nodded to the bag.

"Well?"

She took a breath and zipped open the bag. Immediately, she wished she hadn't.

"Oh shit, Caitlin, is that a gun?"

It sure was.

"And what are those? Are those . . . human hands?"

It sure looked like they were.

CHAPTER FIVE

INSIDE THE GYM BAG THAT Caitlin had brought back with her from wherever, a black handgun lay on top of what looked for all the world like half a dozen human hands. Five of them had light skin and one was dark brown. There was no blood. The hands were fake, Caitlin realized after a closer look. Prosthetic. She could even see the glint of metal at the wrist opening of one of them.

She did the math, and it wasn't exactly college-level calculus. She had returned home with a gun, covered in blood. Without even factoring the fake hands into the equation, she knew what she must have done.

"I killed someone," she said, getting to her feet. She started pacing.

"Now hold on," Josh said. "We don't know that."

"Okay, even if I didn't kill anyone, I sure as heck shot someone. And why? For a bag of fake hands?" She ran her own hand through hair that was shorter than it should have been, hair she didn't remember cutting . . . or dyeing, for that matter.

"We don't even know that you shot anyone, Caitlin. Try to calm down."

She slid her hand through her hair again and something felt wrong. "Where are my rings?" she asked, looking at her naked third finger.

"They're gone?"

A wave of emotion rippled through her. She remembered Josh holding the engagement ring, down on one knee in the middle of yet another Starbucks—it seemed only fitting, after all—telling her that she'd make him the happiest man in New Hampshire if she agreed to marry him. When she'd asked why just New Hampshire, he'd replied, "Well, I don't know many guys in other states. I have no idea how happy they are." Then he'd winked at her and she had accepted right then. And the Starbucks manager bought them each a caramel macchiato, which weren't cheap.

"I loved those rings," she said.

"Hey, don't worry about it. At least you aren't wearing a different wedding ring, right? We still have no idea what you were doing all that time."

He smiled. She didn't. She wasn't ready yet.

"I can't believe they're gone. I can't believe that, whatever I was doing, I'd let them out of my sight." She shook her head sadly.

"They were probably stolen, honey."

"Maybe," she said. "Or maybe I hocked them in a pawnshop to pay for the gun I used to shoot someone."

She wasn't trying to be funny, but he chuckled. "That's a bit of a reach, don't you think?"

"I don't know what to think."

—— ·——

Josh Sommers hated the idea of his wife going back to wherever she'd disappeared to for so long. He wanted her to stay here, with him, in their home. Frankly, he wanted to hire a marching band and drive Caitlin slowly through the streets of their town on a parade float—taking several trips past the police station—with the event covered by all the same reporters who had essentially accused him of murder. More importantly, he wanted to get her medical attention, both physical and psychiatric, to make sure that she was okay. Maybe Caitlin's disappearance had occurred because she'd suffered an episode of some kind—something symptomatic of a serious, even life-threatening condition. Or perhaps she'd been physically hurt while she was gone in some way that she didn't remember, that she had blocked out because it was too traumatic. God forbid, maybe she'd been assaulted. Or suffered some kind of psychotic break. Though he had no reason to doubt that she was being honest with him, he was ashamed to admit to himself that he *did* doubt her, even if only a tiny bit. Amnesia was the stuff of soap operas, not real life. He had done a little Internet research last night, while Caitlin slept, and read stories about people who seemed to have truly suffered through it. But he'd read just as many stories about how most amnesiacs are fakers. In his heart, though, he believed her, and that was where it mattered. That said, would it even help her to remember what she'd been through, or would it cause more serious mental or emotional issues? Would it really do her good . . . do either of them good . . . if she remembered *everything*?

But she seemed to desperately need whatever closure she thought she could get by returning to wherever she had been. And he couldn't imagine how terrible and frustrating it must be to have such a void in your memory. What would it be like to just lose seven months of your life? More than half a year, gone in a flash? So even though it might cost them both in the end, he intended to follow her wherever she needed to go and find out whatever it was they would find out. And he had an idea where to start.

"I'll be right back," he said.

Caitlin was staring at the handgun lying on the small pile of prosthetic hands in the gym bag.

"Don't touch any of that, all right?" Josh said. "We don't want your fingerprints on anything."

"They're probably already all over the gun, at least."

"But maybe they're not, so let's not put them there, okay?"

"Don't worry, I have no desire to touch any of this."

She looked like she meant it, so Josh headed outside. A red Buick Skylark sat in the driveway. Josh peered in the windows for a moment, shielding his eyes to see better, and saw nothing that concerned him . . . like a dead body in the backseat that he might have missed earlier, for example. He opened the passenger door, popped open the glove box, and removed a vinyl pouch in which he found the vehicle's registration.

Inside the house again, Josh was relieved to see that Caitlin had zipped the gym bag shut. She was still on the couch, her head tipped back, her eyes closed.

"Sleeping?" he asked.

"Thinking."

"Anything coming back to you?"

"Nope."

"Well, I have something that might help us narrow things down a bit."

She opened her eyes.

"Our plan was to go back to the first exit you remember on I-91. Well, I think we can do better than that."

"Yeah?" she said. "How?"

"With this."

He held up the Skylark's registration.

"That's from the car outside?" Caitlin asked.

He nodded. "It's registered to a Katherine Southard. She lives at 18 Jasmine Street, Number 1, Smithfield, Massachusetts. We'll start there. If I'm not mistaken, 91 South would take us right by there."

Josh expected her to be a little excited to have such a solid lead. Instead, she looked on the verge of tears.

"Caitlin . . . what's wrong?"

She spoke in a hollow voice. "I might have killed this woman. I might have killed her and taken her car."

"Now you're a carjacker?"

"How else do you explain my driving her car? It fits with the blood and the gun."

"Maybe you were friends with her. Maybe she loaned you the car."

"Maybe I followed her to her car, shot her in the back, and took her keys. Maybe that's why I, uh . . . woke up in a parking lot. Maybe I'd just shot her."

She seemed determined to be both judge and jury in her own case, and to find herself guilty.

Josh asked, "Do you remember seeing a body when you . . . when you woke up?"

She shook her head. "Doesn't mean it wasn't there. I wasn't exactly thinking clearly at first."

"You're getting ahead of yourself again, honey. How about this? We'll Google her. We have her name and address. Let's see if we get any hits."

He retrieved his tablet from the kitchen, where he'd spent a few hours last night surfing the web. When he returned, he sat at the opposite end of the sofa. He didn't want her looking over his shoulder in case bad news popped up on the screen. He didn't think Caitlin was capable of violence, even if she wasn't in her right mind, but in case his faith was misplaced, he didn't want her seeing a headline that screamed in bold type, *Local Woman Killed for Car Keys.*

He looked up at Caitlin and gave a small smile, which she returned, though hers was even smaller. It was practically microscopic, nothing more than a gesture for his benefit.

He called up a search engine and typed in the name Katherine Southard. There were several hits, including one for a former Miss North Carolina by that name, so he added "Massachusetts" to his search. No hits.

He looked up. Caitlin was watching him, biting her lower lip.

"Nothing, honey. Looks like you didn't murder Katherine Southard."

"Nothing about her being in critical care with a gunshot wound to the head? Or maybe just missing. Nothing like that?"

"Nothing. I didn't find a single mention of a Katherine Southard in Massachusetts on the web."

Caitlin exhaled softly with evident relief.

"Now," Josh said, "let's see if her car was reported stolen."

His fingers pecked away at his device's keyboard until he found a site for the local Smithfield police blotter. He checked it and found no recent mention of Katherine Southard or a stolen Buick Skylark.

"So what's next?" Caitlin asked.

"We try to call her. Tell her we found her car somewhere."

"What if I stole it from her at gunpoint and she was just too shaken up to have reported it yet?"

"If she was scared, she would have called the cops right away. But I'll call her and say that I found it abandoned."

She considered that, then nodded.

Josh used his cell phone to call directory assistance for Smithfield and asked for the number for Katherine Southard in that town. There was no listing.

"What does that mean?" Caitlin asked.

"Maybe her number's unlisted or it's in her husband's name. Or she just uses a cell phone."

"But if we can't call her," she said, "where does that leave us?"

He sighed. "It leaves us driving to 18 Jasmine Street in Smithfield and knocking on her door."

"Okay, so here's the big question . . . if she answers the door, assuming she's not dead, what then?"

"*When* she answers the door, because she's *not* dead, we'll tell her that we found her car, like I said. Then we'll try to figure out your connection to her. Maybe you'll remember her. Maybe she'll remember you."

"That's the plan?"

"Unless you can think of a better one."

She stared at the floor for a moment, then looked up at him. "Yeah, I've got nothing. When do we leave?"

"Right after we pack a few days' worth of things. Just a few days, then we come back here. We can't keep you a secret forever, Caitlin. The world needs to know you're alive, that you're back. And I really would like the cops to know sooner rather than later that I didn't murder you."

"I can see that. Apparently, our so-called friends need to hear that, too," she added.

"Yeah, them, too. And if we haven't gotten anywhere in a few days, we'll probably need to try a different tack anyway. Maybe hire a private investigator or something."

What he didn't say was that the longer they were in Smithfield, Massachusetts, the longer Caitlin could be in danger, whatever kind it might be . . . or the greater the chance that, if she *had* committed a crime, the police would find her and arrest her.

"Okay," Caitlin said almost cheerfully, "let's pack and hit the road."

He understood her sudden enthusiasm—she no doubt believed they were on their way to recovering her memory and solving this mystery—but he couldn't fully share it. Given all the circumstances, and especially considering the gun, the blood, and what were certainly stolen prosthetic hands, he hoped this wasn't a huge mistake for both of them.

CHAPTER SIX

DETECTIVE CHARLOTTE HUNNSAKER SURVEYED THE scene . . . what wasn't lost in the dark corners of the cavernous room, that is. There were skylights above—remarkably, most still even had their glass intact—but they were forty feet up and their exterior surfaces were covered with grime, so they did little to chase away the shadows below. Light fixtures hung suspended from the warehouse's high ceiling, but the owner of the abandoned building apparently had pulled the plug on the electricity long ago, so large areas around Hunnsaker were dark. The crime scene techs had set up battery-powered, high-intensity lights on tripods, but they lit only the small area at the back of the warehouse—a clearing among the shelves where forklifts might have been parked long ago. She couldn't see much beyond the first few rows of metal shelving that stretched off into the shadows. But at the moment, she was interested only in the corpse that was lying in the big pool of blood on the floor in the center of the illuminated space.

Her experienced eyes took in the position of the body, the gun near its hand—looking like it had belonged to the victim rather than the shooter—figured where the killer likely would have been standing, and imagined in which direction he would have fled when he was finished here. Hunnsaker knew she was being sexist by already thinking of the killer as a "he," especially considering that she had fought her own gender-bias battles over the years in the still predominantly male-dominated field of law enforcement—but statistics about violent crimes supported the bias, so the killer would continue to be a "he" in her mind until it turned out that he wasn't.

Hunnsaker looked at the long rows of shelving—six of them, each probably fifteen feet high and forty, maybe fifty yards long, empty but for some moldy boxes and a few dusty objects scattered here and there that looked like they might have been auto parts. She wondered down which aisle the killer had fled. Probably one of the outer ones, as that would have led most quickly to an exit—either the main entrance or the nearest back door—but they'd all have to be checked, one by one. It would take time to comb through the place. This was starting to look like a needle-in-a-haystack situation. But perhaps they'd get lucky this time. Maybe the perp had been kind enough to drop a little DNA someplace obvious before he left.

"This doesn't look professional to me," Hunnsaker said to her partner. "I'm guessing some sort of deal that went sideways."

Javier Padilla nodded. "That's how I read it, too. Victim got his .22 out but the other guy was faster." Hunnsaker glanced again at the gun near the victim's hand. The hands themselves had plastic bags over them, secured at the wrists. The medical examiner had already processed the hands and taken fingerprints. "Think he got off a shot?"

"ME said there was GSR on his hand," Hunnsaker said, "and gunshot residue rarely lies, so I'm hoping he hit his killer and we'll find his blood somewhere around here. Get ourselves some DNA to match to whoever we bring in for this."

She looked at the vic's pasty face, his empty eyes staring at nothing. Aside from the bullet hole in his cheek and his striking deadness, he looked like a million other guys.

"I don't recognize him," Hunnsaker said. "You?"

Padilla shook his head. "Anybody find anything interesting around here yet?"

"Not yet. Took a little while for the DA to get a warrant."

Despite what they showed in the movies and on TV, cops didn't always show up at a murder scene and just start digging around for evidence. Unless they were lucky enough to have a victim killed in his own house, it was generally prudent to make sure they had a warrant, which required getting the DA's office involved. No point in collecting evidence if it wouldn't be admissible later in court. So they'd done what they could to keep busy without disturbing anything until the warrant had come in a little while ago.

"The first officer on the scene said there weren't any cars in the lot," Hunnsaker said.

"So how did this guy get here?" Padilla asked. "One-way ticket in the killer's car?"

"Or there was more than one bad guy. Maybe they met here, and after they killed him, one guy drove off in the vic's car and left it somewhere. But why leave the body? Why not dump it with the car?"

"Didn't want to risk getting caught with a body in the trunk?"

Hunnsaker nodded. "Or maybe they left in a hurry. They may not have planned to ice the guy. Supports a deal-gone-wrong scenario. Things go all to shit, this guy takes a bullet, the perps panic and run. We should make a note to check into any abandoned cars that are called in or found by our guys on patrol. If one of them belongs to our vic here, it probably has bad-guy fingerprints and DNA inside."

Padilla nodded and scribbled something in a little notepad he'd pulled from his pocket. "What did the ME say?"

"That our unfortunate friend here was killed by a bullet to the face. For the record, that was pretty far up my list of guesses, too."

"That's why you get the big bucks, Charlotte," Padilla said.

He knew better than to call her Charlie. When Hunnsaker had first begun her career in law enforcement, back at the academy, everyone, it seemed—women as well as men—wanted to call her Charlie. But she never allowed it, not then and not now. It was true that she was a cop—a homicide detective for the past ten years, actually—but she was a woman, too . . . and one with a pretty nice figure for forty-one, in her opinion. Being a cop didn't make her any less of a woman, just as being a woman didn't make her less of a cop. She was good at both roles and proud of it. So she didn't care if her husband called her Charlie, and he often did. And hell, her brothers had done it since the day she was born. It was okay for her friends outside the force to do it, too. But most people she worked with called her Detective Hunnsaker. She might even answer to Charlotte for those she knew well enough. But never Charlie. No one on the force had called her that since the day she made a 230-pound slab of meat in a uniform, a fellow rookie at the time, sorry that he did.

Hunnsaker said, "ME's best estimate is a nine-millimeter."

"We get an approximate time of death?" Padilla asked.

That was another thing that wasn't quite the way Hollywood made it seem. On TV, the ME always gave a tidy little two-hour window, and anything that fell even five minutes outside of it completely exonerated a suspect. In the real world, such estimations were far from precise. There were a lot of variables that could affect an estimate—ambient temperature, the pre-death health of the victim, whether he had taken drugs shortly before he was killed, and a host of other considerations. But though timing a death was not an exact science, an experienced ME would use a combination of science, the available information, and educated guesswork to get pretty close most of the time.

"TOD is probably between nine p.m. and midnight last night," Hunnsaker said. "The ME's got an assistant somewhere around here finishing up the mundane stuff and waiting for us to be done with the body. He said we could ask her questions if we think of something that can't wait. Said she's pretty sharp."

For a few moments, Hunnsaker watched the crime scene techs go about their painstaking, methodical work, taking photographs, measuring distances, videotaping the scene, sketching it, setting little flags on stands beside things that could prove to be evidence. They obviously knew what they were doing, so Hunnsaker left them alone and went back to walking the scene in her flimsy little slip-on booties—required footwear at crime scenes to avoid site contamination. She hated wearing the things, which made her feel a little as though she were wearing clown shoes, but she'd be the first to drop a load of bricks on anyone she saw walking around without them. A minute later, she looked up to see a uniform walking quickly toward them, his body language screaming that he had found something.

"Got something you should probably see, Detectives," he said, his eyes dancing. Hunnsaker may have been on the wrong side of forty, but she still remembered being that young and enthusiastic.

"Lead the way," she said.

They followed the uniform and his flashlight down one of the outermost aisles, along the back of the building. They passed a few small offices, all of which would have to be searched thoroughly. Ahead, Hunnsaker saw a door on the rear wall, a strip of sunlight at the bottom.

"We going out the back?" she asked.

"No, ma'am," the uniform replied.

Just before he reached the door, he aimed the beam of his flashlight into a small opening in the wall, a few feet to the right of the exit. It had been a closet once, with double doors, but the doors were long gone. The closet wasn't empty, though. Several blankets were piled in one corner with a depression in the middle. It reminded Hunnsaker of a big bird's nest.

"May I?" she asked, taking the flashlight from the uniform. She shone the light into the closet. Crumpled fast-food wrappers. Cigarette butts. A skin magazine, its pages wrinkled and worn. A few empty beer bottles, one lying on its side.

"Think someone's been living here?" Padilla asked.

"Or just comes to get drunk now and then," Hunnsaker said. "Someplace he can be alone with the girls of his dreams. But whoever he is, it's not our victim. At least I don't think so. We'll dust in here for prints, but the vic looked too healthy to be living like this."

"So if it wasn't our vic using this hangout, it was somebody else," Padilla said. "And that somebody could be a witness, or even our shooter."

Hunnsaker knew that the squatter, if that's what he was, might not even have been at the warehouse when the killing took place. And if he was, he might have been dead drunk. Or sound asleep. Or busy focusing on Miss July's naughty parts. But then again, if they were lucky, maybe he was in the building and *did* see something . . . or someone.

She pointed the flashlight at the open bottle lying on its side. There was still some beer in it. A few inches away was an irregular shape in the grime on the floor that looked like a dried puddle of something in the dust and dirt around it. Hunnsaker stepped closer without entering the closet and squatted down.

"That look like spilled beer to you?" she asked Padilla. "From the bottle right there, before it rolled a few inches away?"

"Looks like it," Padilla said.

"A guy who hangs out here, drinking cheap beer, he's not the kind of guy to leave beer in a bottle, is he? I mean, even if he knocked over the bottle by accident, there's still beer inside. See that?"

Padilla picked up the thread. "So maybe he got startled by something and knocked it over, and was too distracted by whatever it was to pick it up and finish it off. Maybe he got up and shot our vic."

"Or maybe he heard the shots and realized he had to get the hell out of here fast. Either way, if he was here, we want to talk to this guy." She turned to the uniform and said, "Good job." The man nodded smartly and professionally in return, but Hunnsaker knew he'd be telling his wife or girlfriend tonight all about the big part he'd played in a murder investigation today. To Padilla, she said, "Let's hope we pull some good prints from in there, because I wouldn't be shocked to learn that the kind of guy who spends his time in that closet is in our system."

She turned toward the uniform, who stood waiting nearby, practically at attention. "You were one of the first on the scene, right?"

"Yes, ma'am," he said. "My partner and me."

"Did you interview the kids who found the body?"

The victim was found by two grade-schoolers who had planned to spend that morning exploring an abandoned warehouse instead of learning geometry. Surprisingly, rather than flee the scene and avoid exposing their morning of playing hooky, they actually called 911 on a cell phone that Hunnsaker thought the kids were probably too young to have. Then again, she wasn't a parent, so what did she know about it?

"I did, ma'am," the uniform replied, "but not too much. Just enough to make sure there were no threats that they were aware of. We left anything more to you guys, ma'am."

Hunnsaker and Padilla would be talking to the kids in a little while. "And they didn't mention seeing anyone other than the victim?" Hunnsaker asked. "Like our closet dweller, maybe?"

The uniform shook his head. "They said they didn't see anyone else."

"Did you believe them?"

"Seemed like they were telling the truth, but I couldn't swear to it."

Hunnsaker turned to Padilla. "If there's any chance they saw this guy, we need to know about it. Either way, somehow, we'll find him. And when we do, if we're lucky, we find our killer."

"And if he didn't pull the trigger himself . . ." Padilla added.

"Then maybe he saw who did," Hunnsaker finished for him.

CHAPTER SEVEN

CAITLIN INSISTED ON DRIVING. She knew that Josh hadn't slept a wink after she'd come home, while she'd stolen a few hours of admittedly fitful sleep. Sure, she'd tossed and turned and sweated her way through yet another nightmare encounter with the Bogeyman, but still, she'd slept a bit while Josh hadn't. Besides, she hoped that driving the same route she'd driven the night before—even though it was in reverse, and it was day now rather than night—might act as a mental Heimlich maneuver to make her mind cough up a little nugget of memory.

Caitlin had wanted to take separate cars on this trip. It made sense to her. She'd drive the Skylark she had—hopefully—borrowed from Katherine Southard, and Josh would follow in his Subaru. That way, they'd be able to drive his car home again after . . . well, after whatever they were going to do in Smithfield. But Josh had insisted on riding with her, saying they could rent a car when they were ready to return to New Hampshire. Caitlin almost stood her ground, arguing that it would be far more efficient to bring two vehicles, but then realized that Josh was probably nervous to let her out of his sight for long so soon after finally getting her back from her mysterious seven-month absence.

So Caitlin drove and Josh rode shotgun, using a GPS application on his tablet to guide them to Katherine Southard's address. Before they had left home, she thought about making a few calls to the people to whom she felt she owed them, those few she couldn't bear to keep in the dark any longer about the fact that she was alive and—at least physically—well. Then she realized, with no small amount of sadness, that other than Josh, there were no such people. Her wonderful parents, who had taken an orphan girl into their home and adopted her when she was five years old, had passed away years ago. Caitlin had no brothers, no sisters. Her father had been an only child himself, and it had been years since Caitlin had heard from Aunt Sophie, her mother's sister in San Antonio, despite the Christmas and birthday cards Caitlin sent her every year. And as for her friends, there didn't seem to be any left. She'd had some at the time she disappeared, some good ones, she'd thought, but they ceased being friends to her the moment they turned their backs on Josh after she went missing. So no, there was no one she needed to call.

Caitlin and Josh spent the first part of the drive just catching up, which was strange for her. Josh needed to bring her up to date on what he had been doing for seven months, but to her, it was as if no time had passed. She had no memory of what she had been doing all that time. The last thing she remembered apparently took place the day before she disappeared. Then she was in that warehouse parking lot. So it was a fairly lopsided conversation, with Josh filling her in on various things. At first, Caitlin wanted to keep things light, so she asked about movies that had come out in theaters while she was . . . away. And about which celebrities were dating each other now. She asked whether the president had become embroiled in any interesting scandals and whether any of the various dictators around the world had invaded one of his country's neighbors. So for a while, Josh caught her up on current events that weren't all that current several months after they'd taken place.

Finally, shortly after they crossed the border into Massachusetts, Caitlin asked Josh how he was, how he had fared while she was gone. He was silent for a few moments. Caitlin let her gaze drift from the road and stole a glance at him. His eyes were closed. He looked as though he were steeling himself for this part of the conversation. Finally, he looked over and said, "One day, everything was fine. We were happily living our happy life together. The next, you were just . . . gone. In a blink, everything changed. I didn't know that right away, but soon enough . . ."

He paused and took a deep breath.

"At first, of course," he said, "I thought it was because of our argument that night. That you needed some space. After a few hours, though, I tried calling your cell. You didn't pick up."

It was only then that Caitlin remembered that she no longer had a cell phone. She suddenly felt naked without it, like she'd left home without her pants. She made a mental note to buy a new phone when she got the chance.

"By three in the morning," Josh continued, "I figured you'd gone to stay at a friend's house. I called Lucy first, then Michelle."

"You woke them up?"

"I did. You weren't there. And you weren't at Bethany and Carl's place, either." He paused, then added, "I even tried Rick."

"Rick?" She looked over at him again. "You thought I went to stay at my old boyfriend's house?"

He shrugged sheepishly. "I didn't know how mad you were about . . . whatever we were fighting about."

Wow. She looked back through the windshield at the highway stretching up and over a rise in front of them. "I bet you were relieved I wasn't at Rick's," she added in a weak attempt to lighten the mood.

"Honey, I just wanted to know where you were. I didn't care where that was as long as you were safe."

She felt another pang of guilt for what she'd put him through, even though she hadn't meant to put him through it . . . or could even remember doing so.

"When six in the morning rolled around, I got really worried. I called the cops. They listened, but like on TV, they don't get too worked up about someone who's been missing for only eight hours. Especially when I admitted that you'd walked out after a fight. They said you'd probably come home after you cooled off. They didn't care that that behavior wasn't like you, that you'd never done anything like that before. They told me to call them back if you hadn't returned by dinnertime. Hell, dinnertime. Another *twelve hours*."

He fell quiet for a moment. She let him have his mental space and just focused on the road. Finally, he spoke again. "By the next day, everyone was looking for you. And everyone was looking *at* me. In the first few hours—*very* few hours—people were sympathetic. But the longer you were gone, the less innocent I began to seem, I guess. The police started asking me questions that anyone who has watched even a few hours of cop shows knows meant that I had become a suspect. They asked about our relationship, whether you might have been seeing anyone, whether that made me angry—"

"They thought I might have been cheating on you?"

"It was a theory."

"And then you found out and killed me?"

He shrugged. "Like I said, it was a theory. Or if you were still alive, maybe you ran off with the guy. That was a possibility, too."

"Well, none of that happened."

"I know that."

"Did they also consider the possibility that *you* cheated on *me*, or was I the only suspected adulterer?"

"Of course they did, Caitlin. Don't they always suspect the husband is having an affair when a wife disappears?"

"With anyone in particular?"

"First it was Eve, down the hall from me at work. When they got nowhere with that, they moved on to Gretchen, if you can believe it."

"Your boss's secretary? The trashy one who came on to you at the company picnic? How stupid would that have been?"

"That's the one, and she actually supports Mr. Rollins, my *boss's* boss, which would have been even stupider. Anyway, they poked and prodded and made everything I ever did—hell, everything *we both* ever did—seem suspicious. That was bad enough, but then the media started in on me. Again, at first I was the innocent husband, as much a victim in this as you were. Then when the police started eyeing me, the media began to circle. I swear to God, I could almost see their fins sticking out of the waves. I assume the cops leaked something about my being a suspect, because the reporters went into a frenzy like blood had hit the water. All of a sudden, I was a monster. I'd been having an affair, or I found out you'd been having an affair, so I killed you. For a while, I had drowned you. A few days later, they were saying I stabbed you to death. At some point there was talk of me stuffing you in a wood chipper."

"My God, Josh . . ."

"They scratched the word *murderer* on the hood of my car."

"Who did?"

"Neighborhood kids, I think. And they painted it on our garage door."

"No."

"After two months, they started throwing rocks through our windows. I had to replace nine of them. They smashed two mailboxes, too."

"Did you call the police?"

"Sure, but you might not be surprised to learn that they weren't terribly sympathetic. Said they'd send a patrol car by the house every now and then, but I never saw one. Hell, for all I knew, the cops were the ones throwing the rocks in the first place."

She kept one hand on the wheel while she reached out and took one of his with her other.

"For the first two months," Josh said, "the phone rang off the hook. Concerned friends, reporters, cops with more questions. Three different psychics called to say they'd heard from you."

"Psychics?"

He nodded. "Two of them offered to connect me to you for a small fee. The third one told me, free of charge, that you had run off to Barcelona with a Spaniard named Raul."

"I don't know where I was or what I did, but I know I didn't do that."

"Yeah, I wasn't buying that one. Anyway, I was getting calls like crazy for maybe two months. After another month or two, though, the cops called less, the media seemed to have lost interest, and only a few friends were left."

"Who?" Caitlin asked. "Who was left?"

"Bethany and Carl. Jessica. Andy and Karen."

"Good for them."

"A few weeks later, though, they seemed to have lost my number, too. Along with their access to voice mail."

She squeezed his hand. He squeezed back.

"God," he said. "Listen to me complain. I'm acting like I'm the only one in this car who went through an ordeal. I can't even imagine what you went through."

"Unfortunately," she said, "I can't, either. Anything else, Josh?"

After a brief hesitation, he shrugged, which she took to mean that there was something he wasn't saying. For the briefest of moments, she wondered if he'd met someone. She'd been gone for more than half a year. She had walked out of the house and simply hadn't come home. She'd never called. What was Josh supposed to think? Was it possible that after some time had passed, enough time for him to wonder if she had actually left him for good, he decided to try to move on with his life? Would it even have been wrong of him if he had? How long could she have expected him to wait in such circumstances?

Ridiculous, she knew. They were married. They were in love. He couldn't have gotten over her that fast, even if he *had* thought she had left him. Her disappearance had forced him to consider the possibility that something terrible had happened to her. He would have been devastated. He wasn't about to start hitting the singles bars. Still, there was something he wasn't telling her.

"Josh? What is it? What aren't you saying?"

He opened his mouth to speak, then stopped and shook his head, as if to himself.

"What?" she asked.

After a moment, he said, "I didn't want to worry you, not so soon after you got home, but . . . well, keeping the house has been a bit of a struggle on just my income. We have almost nothing left in the bank."

It wasn't good news, but given the universe of bad things he could have revealed, it could have been far worse. And she wasn't surprised. She had been gone a long time, and they had always needed both their earnings to save even a little every month after paying their bills.

"When we get home after all this," he added, "even once we're both working again, we're going to have to watch our spending for a while. At least until we build up a little cushion."

She nodded, though she wondered if she'd even be free to find employment after all this. Her next job might be serving runny mac and cheese to the other prisoners.

Then, in a case of exquisitely irritating timing, Caitlin heard the unmistakable *whoop* of a police siren behind them. Several thoughts elbowed one another for her attention. She was really, really glad they had left the gun back at their house. And the fake hands, too, which would have been tough to explain. Also, she had no idea how they were going to get around the fact that they were driving a car registered to a Katherine Southard. She prayed Josh was right that Ms. Southard had not reported the car stolen, or that she indeed had not been found somewhere with a bullet in her, both of which would have made things very difficult for them.

CHAPTER EIGHT

IN THE REARVIEW MIRROR, CAITLIN watched the silhouette of the state trooper behind the wheel of the cruiser parked on the shoulder of the highway not far behind them. Though he'd pulled them over a minute ago, he had yet to leave his vehicle.

"Why do you think he stopped us?" she asked Josh.

"I'm not sure. Were you speeding?"

"I don't know. Probably. Doesn't everyone? But I don't think I was *speeding* speeding."

"*Speeding* speeding?" Josh repeated. "Well, it certainly didn't seem like you were going too fast to me."

"You realize he's going to ask for my license and registration . . . the registration that's in Katherine Southard's name."

"Yeah, he will."

"And he's going to see that they don't match."

"Yeah," Josh said, "and we'll tell him that she's a friend of ours, that we borrowed her car. He's already checking to see if the car's been reported stolen. He'll find that it wasn't, so he'll have no reason to doubt our story."

That made sense. *If*, of course, the online police blotter Josh had checked was accurate, and *if* Katherine Southard hadn't reported the car stolen since they'd checked the web earlier or since the police blotter website had been updated. Then she thought of something else.

"You said my disappearance made local news. Even national news."

"For a while. Oh, I see where you're going."

"Yeah," she said. "What if he recognizes me? Suppose he wants to know where I've been and why the heck I haven't told anyone that I'm back?"

"You look pretty different, hon. Your hair's short and red instead of longer and blonde. *I* barely recognized you."

"Okay, but suppose when he sees my license, he remembers my name? Maybe then he'd recognize my face."

Josh squinted and pursed his lips. He often did that when he was concentrating. She hoped he came up with something good. "Well, I guess that would be it, then," he finally said.

"What?"

"I hate to say it, Caitlin, but that would be it. We can't deny who you are. We'd have to come clean about everything."

"But—"

"Hey, it's not like we knocked over a bank. We're not on the run here. I don't think there's a crime against being missing. Or failing to report in when you're no longer missing. Relax, we haven't done anything wrong."

"Maybe you haven't. Remember the gun and the blood?"

"I do, but you don't . . . at least not where it came from. If they find out about all that, be honest. You didn't do anything wrong. I know it in my heart. The truth will bear that out."

He was right. Not necessarily that she hadn't done anything wrong, but that there was nothing they could do about it if the trooper realized who she was.

Finally, in the mirror, she saw the trooper climb out of his vehicle.

"Here he comes," Caitlin said.

He was stocky and a little shorter than she expected. She tried to read his body language. Did he walk slowly, warily? Not particularly. Did he have his hand on his gun? Nope, but he had his thumb hooked in his belt very near his gun.

"I guess we're about to find out whether I stole this car," she said. "And whether he recognizes me."

She lowered her window. "Hi," she said and thought the little crack in her voice probably made her sound guilty of *something*.

"G'morning, ma'am. Can I see your license and registration, please?"

He was being polite, which Caitlin imagined was a good thing. Unless he just didn't want to tip her off that he was suspicious about the car, and about her, too, now that he'd seen her face. She couldn't read his eyes, though, because they were hidden behind dark sunglasses. For all she knew, he didn't even have any eyes. She glanced at the nameplate on his chest. Banuelos.

"Of course," Caitlin said. She lifted her purse from the floor of the car, fished her wallet from it, and slid out her license, which she gave to the trooper along with the vehicle's registration, which Josh handed to her.

Trooper Banuelos gave the documents a quick look before focusing on her again. He seemed to be checking out the car's interior, too, though it was hard to tell with those sunglasses.

"Do you know why I pulled you over?" he asked.

"I honestly don't," Caitlin said. "I'm sorry."

"You were speeding," he said. Caitlin had never been happier to hear a state trooper say those words. "I clocked you at seventy-three."

Relief washed over her. "Oh, I was speeding," she said almost giddily.

He frowned. That probably wasn't the reaction Trooper Banuelos usually witnessed after delivering such news. "Yes, ma'am, you were," he said.

"I'm sorry," Caitlin said. "I really am. It didn't feel like I was going that fast. If you have to ticket me, I understand. Really."

He seemed to be staring at her face for a moment, though his eyes could have been spinning wildly in their sockets for all she knew.

"I guess that won't be necessary," Banuelos said. "Promise me you'll slow it down a bit, though, okay?"

"I will," she said. "I promise. Thank you so much."

She watched in the mirror as the trooper swaggered back to his car. After he was behind the wheel again, he sat and waited for Caitlin to pull out. He would follow her for a mile or two, she knew, before turning around and finding someone else to pull over.

Caitlin slipped carefully back onto the highway and, as expected, the trooper pulled out right behind her. She nudged the car close to the speed limit. The cruiser was still behind them after a mile. Soon after that, though, she looked into the rearview mirror and it was nowhere in sight. Caitlin exhaled with relief.

"So, you weren't speeding, huh?" Josh said.

"I said I wasn't '*speeding* speeding.' And seeing as Trooper Banuelos didn't give me a ticket, he must have agreed with me."

"I wonder what the legal threshold is for *speeding* speeding," Josh said, smiling. "We dodged a bullet there. He barely looked at your license and the registration. Maybe it's getting near the end of his shift and he's tired."

"Maybe he didn't look at them at all. Maybe he *couldn't*. Did you see those black glasses? I expected him to have a seeing eye dog with him."

Josh smiled and Caitlin did, too, but her smile faded quickly. She wondered what lay ahead. Wondered whether she could live with what they would find. They were getting closer to Smithfield. Closer to where she had been when she'd awakened from her fog. And, for good or ill, closer to maybe finding some answers.

CHAPTER NINE

ONLY A FEW PEOPLE CALLED George Maggert by the name on his driver's license. Most called him Chops. He was fine with that. He understood where the name came from, how he'd earned it. And he *had* earned it. The first few times he'd heard it, he didn't like it and had made that fact plain to the person who'd said it. But he soon realized that whenever he heard the name, it was being spoken with either respect or fear, depending on the speaker and the circumstances, and that worked for him. He had not only come to like it, but he actually started thinking of himself as Chops. He even tried now, whenever the situation allowed, to do things to make sure that no one forgot that name.

He washed his hands at the sink, being very careful to clean under his fingernails. After he dried off, he slipped out of his coveralls and left his workroom, pulling the door shut behind him and locking it with a dead bolt. He walked through the outer room of this two-room workspace, where he kept a few tools, a computer, and some file cabinets—all of which made his contractor business seem completely legitimate. Anyone taking a casual look around this little office could believe that he derived all of his income from general contracting work, rather than a mere 25 percent.

Once outside, he walked across half an acre of green lawn—well, he noticed, it was brown in a few places . . . grubs, maybe . . . he'd have to do something about that—toward a contemporary house he shared with two of the handful of people in the world who didn't call him Chops. One called him George, and had since they'd first met six years ago, and the other called him Daddy, which she had done since she started talking two years ago.

Chops climbed the steps to the back door, noticing yet again that the second stair was starting to rot. It wouldn't do for someone who was supposed to be a contractor to let his own house fall into disrepair. He'd have to replace the board.

He entered the kitchen to find his daughter, Julia, sitting at the table in her pink booster chair, buttered toast cut into tiny little pieces spread out on the plate in front of her. He could see that it was the plate with the clown on it, her favorite. A matching sippy cup sat beside it.

Rachel turned from the stove with a sausage-and-cheese omelet on a plate.

"This okay?" she asked, looking up at him. She had no choice but to look up, even though at six feet she was the tallest woman Chops had ever dated, because he still had five inches on her. He sometimes thought her height was half the reason he'd married her. The other half was that he loved her. And she loved him. He could tell. He had no idea why. He wasn't a handsome man by any stretch of the imagination. Not even close. He was too tall. He wished his eyes were a little closer together. And for some reason he just couldn't hold a tan, even living in Southern California. But still, Rachel had fallen in love with him, which was a cause of endless wonder for him. It wasn't as though she was a head-turner or anything like that, but she was definitely the Beauty to his Beast. He didn't feel deserving of her love. And not merely because they weren't a good match in the looks department. No, it was because of other things about him . . . things his wife didn't know. He often wondered if she would still love him if she knew those things. He hoped he would never have to find out. But she did love him and he was grateful for that.

"Perfect," he said. "I was in the mood for an omelet."

She smiled. "You eating with us?"

"Wish I could, but I have paperwork to catch up on. I'll take this out back."

"You're out there early today. It's not even seven yet. The sun's barely up."

"I know, I got behind. But if the invoices don't go out, the money doesn't come in. Hopefully I'll get caught up today."

"Daddy eat," little Julia said.

"I will eat, pumpkin," Chops said. "I just can't sit with you today. Daddy has work to do while he eats."

He kissed the dark curls on the top of her head. She reached up with her chubby little hands and playfully laid down a drumbeat on his bald pate.

"That's enough, Ringo," he said, straightening up.

He grabbed two bottles of water from the fridge and took them, with his omelet, back to his office. He unlocked the door to his workroom, stepped inside, and locked the door again behind him with a separate dead bolt, one that couldn't be unlocked from the outside without a key. He turned to the man bound to a metal chair in the middle of the little room and said, "Give me a minute here. It's breakfast time."

The man didn't respond, maybe because he had nothing to say any longer, maybe because of the duct tape across his mouth, or maybe because he had no voice left after all the screaming he'd done lately.

Chops ate the first half of his omelet, then opened one of the bottles of water and drank half of it in four gulps. The man in the chair watched, his eyes wide and pleading.

"I guess you're thirsty, huh, Benny?" Chops said.

The man nodded weakly. Chops opened the second bottle of water.

"You've already learned how good the soundproofing is in here, right?"

Benny nodded again.

"So you won't be annoying me with any more screaming, right?"

Benny shook his head.

"Okay, then." Chops stepped over and yanked the tape from Benny's mouth. "Open wide," he said.

Benny opened his mouth, exposing bloody, toothless gums. Chops hadn't yet decided what to do with all the teeth in the jar on his workbench. He poured some water into the gaping mouth, gave the man time to gulp it down, then poured in the rest of the bottle.

When he finished swallowing, Benny said, "I told you everything." His voice was barely a croak, his words malformed, probably because of his lack of teeth. "I told you everything *two days ago*," he added.

"I know," Chops said as he stepped back into his coveralls.

"So why are you still doing this?"

"Well, the first two days was to get the information my employer wanted, to find who your boss was buying his shit from."

"But I didn't *know* who he got it from," Benny whined.

"Yeah, but I didn't know whether to believe you. I had to be sure. Now I am. I believe you. So that was the first two days. The last two have been to send a message. Well, several messages."

Chops had overnighted Benny's right hand to Benny's boss, Kenny Jacks, a small-time drug dealer who had arrived in town a few months ago. With the hand, Chops had included a note that read, *We found this in our cookie jar.* The hope was that Jacks would learn his place and understand that that place was some small street corner very far from the territory run by Bill McCracken, a much bigger dealer who had hired Chops to put the fear of God into Jacks. Chops wanted to go after Jacks himself, but McCracken wasn't sure yet whether he had connections about which McCracken should be concerned, so he paid Chops to make a statement without physically harming Jacks himself. Chops was good at his job. First he'd had Benny's hand delivered—though not hand-delivered—to Jacks. Then to spread the message, Chops had sent the fingers from Benny's remaining hand to the five guys who had been doing a little distribution for Jacks on the side, guys who used to work exclusively for McCracken. The hand alone should be enough to convince Jacks to pull up stakes and take his shit somewhere else, but just in case it wasn't, Benny's fingers should make it hard for Jacks to find anyone around here to work for him. And the longer that parts of Benny kept showing up around town, the less likely it was that some new dealer who tried to set up shop someday would be able to find anyone to work for him, either. But just in case . . .

Chops slapped another piece of tape over Benny's mouth. He picked up a pair of tin snips, which he'd used a lot over the last few days, and knelt in front of the man. He untied Benny's right boot and tugged it off. Benny grunted into the duct tape and whipped his head violently from side to side. He tried to kick out, but Chops grabbed his leg and gave it a quick, firm twist. Something snapped in the knee with the sound of a tree branch cracking, and something else tore with a popping noise, and Benny's muffled scream faded away as his head dropped forward to his chest.

"It's probably better for you this way, Benny," Chops said. He wasn't necessarily disappointed. It wasn't like he needed Benny to be awake during this so Chops could get his rocks off. No, this was business. As long as he took what he needed from Benny, something he could use to send another message, it didn't matter to Chops if Benny was asleep or awake when he took it. But before Chops could use the tin snips, his cell phone trilled in his pocket. He answered it.

"Hello?"

He listened to the caller for a few seconds.

"How do you know something happened to him? . . . Well, how long has it been? . . . Last night? That's not long enough to worry about. You know Mike. He's sleeping something off. Maybe he did too much of some kind of crap or another . . . No, just relax, I'm sure he's fine . . . No, I have work to do. If you don't hear from him by tonight, call me back."

He put his phone back in his pocket.

"Now where were we, Benny?"

He pulled off Benny's sock and counted in his head how many more people Benny had said were doing a little dealing on the side for Jacks . . . how many more people needed to receive a message.

CHAPTER TEN

THE EARLY AFTERNOON TRAFFIC HAD been light, allowing them to make good time. As they pulled off the highway, Josh began to pay closer attention to the GPS app on his tablet and the pleasant robotic female voice guiding them from the device's speaker. They were on the outskirts of Smithfield now, a city in western Massachusetts that Josh knew to be one of the largest in the state. It didn't appear as though Katherine Southard lived in the city proper, though, even though she had a Smithfield address, because according to the map on his device's screen, they'd be at their destination in four minutes, yet Smithfield's tallest buildings, which Josh could see up ahead, had to be at least ten driving minutes away. Instead, they were in a slightly more rural area on Smithfield's western edge, and the turns were coming more often now, more quickly as they neared their destination. Caitlin was driving slowly, just under the speed limit. Josh looked over at her behind the wheel, the way she watched the road with one eye while apparently scrutinizing every single thing they passed with the other. A bus stop there on the corner. A bagel shop on the other side of the street. A nail salon with a huge photograph of a woman's beautifully pedicured foot dominating its front window. A quaint but tired little movie theater that seemed to belong decades in the past. She slowed down even more to watch a sandwich shop drift past.

"Want me to drive so you can pay attention out the window?" Josh asked.

She shook her head.

"Anything look familiar?"

After a moment, she shook her head again.

"Not at all? Not even a little?"

She sighed. "Not even a little. Was I even here at all?"

"You tell me."

She shook her head again slowly. "I don't know. I was hoping that seeing this place would spark a memory, like I'd somehow recall grabbing a sandwich in that shop back there or something. Anything to break through this blank wall in my mind." She sighed. "We got off the same exit just now that I took to get on the highway last night. Shouldn't I recognize these things?"

"Well, it was the middle of the night when you came through here. The stores were all probably closed. Everything looks different in the dark. And I doubt you were thinking too clearly. You had just . . . woken up, or whatever you want to call it. I'm sure your head was still cloudy."

She nodded as though that made some sense to her.

"Also," he continued, "maybe you came at the highway from the other direction last night. Want to turn around and see if anything looks familiar that way?"

She mulled it over. "No, I think we should just go right to Katherine Southard's house, pray she's home, and ask if she knows me . . . and what the heck I did for the last seven months."

Josh nodded. From his tablet, Robot Girl told them to turn right onto Candace Street, which was a bucolic, tree-lined street that could have been torn from a calendar titled "Quaint Streets of the Northeast." Several turns later, they were on Pritchard Lane, which was still fairly quaint but would not have made the calendar's cut. Finally, after three more turns, they reached Jasmine Street, which was not quaint at all. Gone were the gingerbread Victorians and manicured lawns. Gone were the upper-middle-class cars in the driveways. Along Jasmine Street, the sidewalks buckled and the fences were chain-link rather than white picket. The houses were no longer single-family dwellings. Here, they were two-, even three-family residences. The newest car they passed was ten years old.

"Still not familiar?" Josh asked, actually hoping that it wouldn't be. He hated the thought of Caitlin spending any time in this part of town.

"Not at all."

Robot Girl announced that they had arrived at their destination. Caitlin pulled to the curb in front of a house with peeling mud-brown paint. Its two front doors—painted a yellow so faded it looked nearly colorless—told Josh that it was a two-family residence. According to her vehicle registration, Katherine Southard lived in number one.

Josh looked over at Caitlin. "Nothing?"

"Nothing."

"Okay, then. You wait here while I go knock on the door and ask for Katherine."

"Why should I wait here?"

"Because this isn't exactly Mayberry, and I'd feel better if you stayed in the car. Please?"

After a moment, she nodded. He opened his door, stepped out, and before he closed it, looked back at Caitlin and said, "Do me a favor and lock the doors until I get back, okay?"

He shut his door and was relieved to hear the locks engaging as he walked away. He looked up and down the block. Even in brilliant sunshine on a crisp, beautiful day in early October, this street was depressing. He looked over at the grizzled mutt chained to the next-door neighbor's porch railing. The dog, which had been lying down with its oversize head on its paws when he and Caitlin had pulled up, was now standing at the end of his chain, his body rigid. The dog looked to be half pit bull, half Kodiak bear. It didn't bark, but Josh figured that was because instinct told it that it didn't need to bark to be intimidating.

Josh reached the uneven risers leading to the porch; climbed them; and, without hesitation, knocked on the door to apartment number one, which appeared to be the downstairs unit. He heard nothing from inside. No dog barking, no baby wailing, no crystal meth cooking. Standing in that part of town, on that street, on that porch, Josh wished he were wearing denim jeans, preferably worn and a little torn, rather than the comfy tan khakis he was sporting. And he should have been wearing heavy boots of some kind, work boots, not hiking sneakers. And instead of a plaid flannel shirt, he should have . . . *Okay,* he thought, *the plaid flannel is all right;* he just wished it wasn't designed by Tommy Hilfiger. He rolled up his sleeves and knocked again. A moment later, Josh heard footsteps thudding inside. From the weight of their tread, it sounded like Katherine Southard wasn't answering the door herself, unless she was a very solid woman. No, that was a man's tread approaching. Those were man feet, wearing work boots. Of *course* they were wearing work boots. A lock disengaged with a solid clack and the door opened.

In the doorway stood a man roughly Josh's age. Maybe an inch taller, around the same weight, but with a little more of his weight distributed above his waist, up in his chest and arms, which weren't brawny but which Josh could see were well defined under a black T-shirt. By contrast, Josh wasn't overweight, but he wasn't as toned as he would like to be. The man standing before him either exercised more regularly and rigorously than Josh did, or he'd been born with far superior physical genes.

"Yeah?" the man said, eyeing Josh without curiosity but with thinly veiled suspicion. He gave a quick scratch to a cheek that was, not surprisingly, lightly stubbled. He wasn't bad-looking, Josh knew. Strong features, longish sandy hair. There were plenty of women who would approve of the guy's looks, which could best be described as—though Josh was loath to use the phrase, even in his own head—ruggedly handsome. As a man who didn't fit that description, Josh hated it every time he heard it.

"I'm looking for Katherine Southard," he said.

"Why?"

"Is she here?"

"Why?"

Josh tried to get a read on the guy. It didn't seem like he was trying to be hostile, but he definitely didn't seem the chatty type or the kind of guy who went out of his way to make others' lives any easier.

"I'm just wondering if she's here," Josh said. "If maybe . . . well, it's hard to explain . . ."

Josh heard a noise behind him. The man shifted his gaze over Josh's shoulder and smiled. "Finally," he said.

Josh turned and found, to his dismay, Caitlin standing just behind him. "I thought you were going to wait in the car," he said.

"Why would she do that?" the man asked.

Josh turned back to face the man. "Because I asked her to."

"And who the hell are you to her?"

Josh may have been far outside his comfort zone, but he was getting annoyed now. "I'm her husband," he said. "Now who the hell are you?"

The man stared at Josh for a moment before answering. "I'm her fiancé," he said, then he looked at Caitlin again. "Katie, I almost called the cops. You lose your phone? Where were you all night?"

CHAPTER ELEVEN

CAITLIN HAD HEARD THE MAN'S words, heard him say that he was her fiancé, but he might as well have been speaking an ancient, dead language. The words made no sense to her.

"You're her fiancé?" Josh said. "Bullshit."

"Heading down to the courthouse to say our vows on Friday," the man said. He turned to Caitlin. "Now would you tell me where the hell you went after closing last night? You had me out of my head. And then maybe you can tell me who this clown is and why he thinks he's looking for you."

Caitlin had no idea what was going on. Why would this man claim to be her fiancé?

"Look," Josh said, "maybe this kind of thing is funny to you, jerking around people who knock on your door, but we just want to speak with Katherine Southard. If she's here, we'd like to see her. If not, we can come back later."

The man laughed. "You want to see Katherine Southard, turn around, brother. For some reason I can't begin to imagine, you just told me you're married to her."

After a moment's hesitation, Josh turned toward Caitlin, his eyes confused. The man in the doorway was watching her, a slight smile playing at his lips. Caitlin said nothing. She just stood there.

And the longer she stood there, the more confused Josh looked. Slowly, the smile faded from the other man's face. He frowned.

"Katie?" he said.

"Caitlin?" Josh said.

"I think I need to sit down," Caitlin said.

———

Unfortunately, the approximately one hundred million people whose fingerprints were in the FBI's integrated automated fingerprint system did not include the victim from the warehouse. That meant he most likely had never been arrested, served in the military, been employed with the state or federal government, or received a gun permit in states requiring fingerprinting of applicants. There were still other scenarios in which a subject's fingerprints could find their way into the Feds' database, but none apparently applied to Hunnsaker's victim. John Doe remained a John Doe for the time being.

Hunnsaker hated John Does. A murder victim can be an invaluable investigative tool—not just his corpse but his life prior to his becoming a corpse. Did he take or deal drugs? Was he married? Cheating on a spouse? Who were his friends? His enemies? More often than not, a victim's activities in life hinted at or even pointed directly to the reason for his death, and just as often, a list of his acquaintances included the name of his killer.

That was why Hunnsaker hated John Does. In fact, she refused to refer to the victims in her cases as such.

In this case, Vic Warehouse—as Hunnsaker had come to know him—was not going to be identified by his fingerprints. And his description didn't match that of any recently missing persons, at least not that she could find. Nor did he conveniently carry ID in his pocket, which would have made Hunnsaker's job a lot easier.

She wished they could just put his face on TV with a caption reading, "Do you know this man?" but in the only photos they had of him, he was very dead with a bullet hole in his cheek, and the department's public relations people didn't want the police to come across as ghoulish. So Vic was still a mystery man.

Damn John Does.

Hunnsaker turned from her computer screen and decided she needed coffee. She loved the coffee in the squad's break room. Most detectives complained about it as though there were some departmental regulation requiring them to do so. But it tasted good to Hunnsaker. She had never liked coffeehouse java, and not just because it cost four times what it should. She just didn't care for the taste. But give her a cup from the eight-year-old Mr. Coffee in the break room and she was happy. She'd even bought the same model on eBay, though had never quite been able to replicate the flavor at home.

She was adding sugar to her mug when her cell phone rang. Caller ID told her it was Padilla calling.

"Hey, Javy."

"I might have a line on our potential witness," Padilla said.

Though Vic Warehouse's fingerprints hadn't been in the system, the prints of at least one person who had spent time in the closet at the back of the warehouse had been, and his prints were all over the place—on the beer bottles, the glossy-paged girlie magazine, the wall, the floor. Twenty-four minutes after those fingerprints had been entered into the national database, Dominick Bruno's brief stint in the military caused his name to pop out. They ran the name through their own systems and learned a little about Mr. Bruno. Currently thirty-four years old. Divorced. No discernible source of income. Two misdemeanor arrests for possession. So far in his life, Bruno had been able to avoid jail time. According to Padilla, he no longer resided at 481 Fieldstone Drive, Apartment C, which was his last known address. Padilla had interviewed the elderly man now living there, who claimed that he'd never heard of Dominick Bruno. The building super reportedly remembered Bruno, though, telling Padilla that "that scumbag" hadn't lived in the building for more than a year, having just disappeared one day, along with the formerly built-in microwave that belonged above the stove.

"So where is he?" Hunnsaker asked, stirring the sugar into her coffee.

"Not sure yet," Padilla said, "but the guy in the apartment next to Bruno's old one remembered him and said he used to hang out with someone Bruno called Stick Man. The neighbor says they seemed real tight. The guy used to crash at Bruno's place all the time."

"Stick Man? What, was he just a giant pencil sketch?"

"No," Padilla said, "but he was apparently very skinny."

"That was going to be my second guess," Hunnsaker said. "I assume you ran Stick Man through our system."

"Yup. Real name is . . . man, I can't even pronounce it. First name Kenneth."

"That's not so bad."

"Last name is . . ." He paused, then spoke slowly, evidently sounding out the name as he read it. "Kahana . . . hanu . . . kahale . . . nahuli . . . or something like that. Probably Hawaiian."

"No wonder he goes by Stick Man," Hunnsaker said as she added a small splash of creamer to her coffee. "You talk to him yet?"

"Heading to see him now."

"Want me to come along?"

"No, I got it, Charlotte."

"Okay. Let's hope he's still at his last known address."

"He'll be there," Padilla said.

"Why so sure?"

"Because he's got another two years left on his sentence. Mugged a little old lady."

"Ah. Where is he?"

"Hampshire House," Padilla said, which was his and Hunnsaker's shorthand for the Hampshire County Jail and House of Correction. "I'll be there in twenty," Padilla added.

Hunnsaker loved it when someone they needed to interview happened to be a guest of a nearby correctional facility. "Let me know what you find out," she said.

She pocketed her phone, stirred her coffee, then took a sip. It had cooled a little but was otherwise just the way she liked it. Why the hell couldn't she get her Mr. Coffee at home to brew something like this? Same coffeemaker, same coffee brand, same sugar, same everything. Why couldn't she figure it out? Some detective she was.

She headed back to her desk with slightly more bounce in her step. She may have struck out so far trying to ID Vic Warehouse, but at least she had a mug of good coffee in her hand and a partner who might be on his way to finding them a real live witness to a murder—that is, unless they got really lucky and the guy had pulled the trigger himself.

Hunnsaker sat back down at her desk. She pushed the toxicology report to one side—the guy's blood was clean—and pulled the crime scene photos toward her. The top photograph was a close-up of the victim's face.

"Who did you piss off enough to kill you, Vic?"

—•—

Caitlin was sitting on the sofa of the man who claimed to be her fiancé, a glass of water in her hand. She wasn't yet ready to look at her husband or . . . well, the other guy, so she looked around the apartment. It was small and a bit cluttered, but it was clean and smelled surprisingly fresh. It had a darkly colored, masculine feel to it, though there were tasteful touches here and there that suggested a gentle, feminine hand. She knew she was being slightly sexist, but the overall impression she got from the apartment was that it belonged to a man but a woman had exerted some influence here. She looked over at Josh, who sat in an armchair facing the couch. The other man had brought a wooden chair into the living room from the kitchen and straddled it backward, his arms resting on top of the chair's back. They were both watching her drink her water.

Finally, the man said, "Katie, what's going on here? Who is this guy?"

"Her name is Caitlin," Josh said. "No one calls her Katie."

"Well, I do, pal," the man said, "and I'm not the only one. And her name is Katie, short for Katherine, not Caitlin."

"No, *pal*, her name is Caitlin."

They turned their heads as one toward Caitlin. She blew out a nervous breath. She didn't want to admit it, even to herself, but she knew what must have been the truth.

"Josh," she said, "you see what's going on here, right?"

"Yeah?" the man said. "Well, someone needs to explain it to me, and pretty damn quick."

"Josh?" Caitlin said.

The muscles of his jaw bunched. Finally, he nodded. He obviously didn't like it any more than she did, but at least he seemed to understand what was happening.

"Katie," the other man said, softly this time, "who is this guy really?"

She turned to him and took a deep breath. "My name is Caitlin. And this is my husband, Josh."

The man said nothing for a moment. He scratched at the stubble on his chin. Then he nodded, almost to himself, as though this had confirmed something in his mind. "Is he the one you were running from?"

"The one I was . . . what?" Caitlin said.

"Look, I'm no fool. I meet a pretty girl in a bar, she comes home with me, dyes her hair the next day, doesn't want to answer personal questions, chooses not to leave . . . it was obvious you were trying to get away from someone. I figured that part out. And I didn't care who you were running from. I was just glad you ran to me," he added sincerely.

"She wasn't running from me," Josh said. He was still grinding away at his teeth, the knots of muscle at the top of his jaw bubbling under his skin. Caitlin knew this had to be terribly difficult for him to hear. Heck, it wasn't easy for her to hear. If this man was to be believed, she'd lived with him for months. That meant they had no doubt been intimate. The thought made Caitlin's cheeks feel warm. She hoped the men didn't notice her blushing.

"I guess it was his rings you sold?" the guy said.

"I what?" she asked. "I sold them?"

"Of course you did," he said. "Don't tell me you don't remember?"

"It's hard to explain, but no, I don't."

If he thought that was odd, he didn't say so. Instead, he said, "I figured you had an ex-husband somewhere. It honestly didn't occur to me that he wasn't exactly an ex. It probably should have."

"That's what happened to your rings?" Josh asked. "You sold them?"

The man answered for her. "Sorry to break the news. She got almost a thousand bucks for them, though. Tell him, Katie."

"A thousand? Seriously?" Josh said. "They cost ten times that."

"I'm sorry," Caitlin said. "I don't remember doing it." She felt terrible. She loved those rings.

Josh sighed. "I know. Sorry. It's just . . . Don't worry about it. When we can afford it, we'll get you new ones."

Caitlin nodded, absentmindedly rubbing her empty ring finger, which felt utterly naked. She let her eyes wander around the apartment again.

"I lived here?" she asked.

"You *live* here," he said. "And why are you asking me? You know as well as I do. And how can you not remember selling those rings? It was just a few months ago. And why the hell is this guy saying that he'll get you new rings? What's going on here?"

"For how long?" she asked.

"What?" the man said.

"How long did I live here?"

He squinted at her. "Just what the hell is this? I don't get what you're up to here, Katie. Is this some kind of scam you and this guy are pulling? Is that what this is? Some kind of weird setup? Because I just don't see the angle."

Caitlin thought he looked hurt but was too manly to let it show.

"How long did she live here?" Josh asked.

"None of your business, brother," the man said.

"The hell it's not, *brother*," Josh said. "So answer the damn question."

The man gave Josh a hard glare that reminded Caitlin of a sharp-edged weapon.

"Listen," she said, jumping in, "would you please humor me? I'll explain everything. I promise. Okay?"

The man shifted his gaze over to Caitlin, and the edge on it dulled a bit. He shrugged.

"Okay," Caitlin said. "First of all, what's your name?"

"You gotta be shitting me," the guy said.

"Please, just tell me your name. I promise we'll explain everything."

The man let loose a soft chuckle that was clearly meant to say, *This is bullshit, but I'll go along for now.* "Bixby. Desmond Bixby. Parents call me Dez, nearly everyone else calls me Bix. But you usually call me baby."

She wasn't about to call him baby. "Mr. Bixby . . . Bix . . . this is going to sound crazy, but I don't remember you."

The man, Bix, blinked once, then again. "Bullshit," he said.

"No, it's true," Caitlin said. "It sounds strange, I know, but I can't remember anything about the last seven months."

Bix looked from her to Josh, then back to her. "What the hell are you two up to? What are you trying to tell me?"

"The truth," Josh said.

"The truth," Bix repeated. "She can't remember anything?"

"Not about the past seven months."

"What are we talking about here?" Bix asked. "Amnesia? Like in the movies?"

"I know it sounds crazy, but . . . yes," Caitlin said. "We came here today to try to figure out what happened to me. How I ended up here. Why I . . ." She trailed off. She had almost said, *Why I woke up with a gun and a bag of fake hands, covered with blood.* "What I did here," she added.

Bix squinted his gray eyes at her again. Then a little light twinkled in them. "Are you messing with me, Katie? Is this some kind of weird joke?" He smiled as if acknowledging that she'd almost had him.

She shook her head sadly. "I really wish it were." Bix's smile disappeared. "But you have to believe me when I tell you that I don't remember you at all. I'm truly sorry if that hurts your feelings," and at that she saw him smile, as though such a thing couldn't hurt him, though she thought she could see that it did. "But it's true, and there's nothing I can do about it. I don't remember you. Or this house. Or this town. The last thing I remember, before essentially waking up across town last night, happened seven months ago."

Bix looked at her . . . no, not at her, but into her eyes, and he held his gaze there.

"I'm lost here, Bix," she added. "I'm lost, and you might be the only person who can save me."

Caitlin couldn't stop herself from stealing a glance at Josh, who was looking down now. She knew that probably hurt him, but she had spoken the truth. Bix might be able to tell her almost everything she'd done over the past seven months, everything she needed to know to patch the gaping hole in her mind.

"Seriously, Katie?" Bix said. "No bullshit?"

Caitlin shook her head. "No bullshit."

CHAPTER TWELVE

BIX BELIEVED KATIE . . . THAT IS, Caitlin, as she was calling herself now. So much about her had changed. She looked the same as she had when she'd left the house yesterday, but her manner was different. She spoke in a softer voice than his Katie did. She seemed a little less sure of herself. She didn't maintain eye contact for as long, while the Katie he knew grabbed your eyes with hers and wouldn't let go. Tractor beams, he'd thought of them the first time they had locked onto his own eyes over a pool table in the back of a pub seven months ago.

Even though he believed that Katie—uh, Caitlin—wasn't who he thought she was, that she didn't remember him, he found it hard to believe . . . no, hard to *accept* . . . that their life together was over. But it had to be, right? If she were telling the truth, then the woman he had planned to spend the rest of his life with was as gone to him as if she'd never shown up at his door, either today or seven months ago. One minute he was waiting for her to come home, hoping she had maybe flopped at her friend Janie's house after work last night rather than having run off on him—like he figured she must have run off on somebody before him. Then the next minute, she was standing on the porch with a new name and an old husband. And just like that, Bix had lost the only thing he loved about his life.

And it wasn't even like Bix could ask her to choose between him and her husband, because how could she choose Bix if she didn't even remember him? How could she choose a life she couldn't recall?

He had to try to accept that she no longer loved him, if she ever truly had. The problem was, he couldn't just forget her the way she had forgotten him. Their life may not have been real to her, but it had been to him. And while she might never remember the past seven months, he'd always think of them as the best of his life. With sadness, he realized that he still loved her. So if she needed something from him before she disappeared forever with some other guy, if she needed answers, he'd give her what he could.

"Okay, then," Bix said to Katie—no, Caitlin. "Guess we need to talk. First, though, I know it's early, but I could use a beer." He went into the kitchen, grabbed three Buds from the fridge, and returned to the living room. "I didn't have any Perrier," he said to Josh, handing him a beer.

"This is just fine, thanks," Josh said with what Bix considered the appropriate level of attitude.

Next, Bix handed a beer to Caitlin.

"She doesn't like beer," Josh said.

"Since when?" Bix asked.

Caitlin looked at the beer in her hand.

"She's never liked the taste," Josh added.

"Sure she does," Bix replied.

"I'm telling you, she's not a beer girl. She's more of a red-wine woman."

"Well, she sure did a damn fine impression of a beer girl with me," Bix said, smiling. "Never saw her drink wine, though."

He looked over at Caitlin. She lifted the mouth of the bottle to her nose, took a sniff, then followed that with a small sip. Josh watched with a frown. Bix watched, smiling. Caitlin took another sip, a longer one, and swallowed.

"Looks like a beer girl to me," Bix said. "Guess you don't know her as well as you think you do, pal," he said to Josh.

"It's not that I never liked the taste," she explained, turning to Josh. "I drank it when I first went to college. It's just that you always prefer wine, and I like wine just fine, so that's what we've always had together. I never really missed beer, but I never disliked it. And I have to admit, this tastes pretty good."

Josh nodded and said nothing.

"Well, I'm glad we cleared that up," Bix said. "What else do you need to know?"

"Well," Caitlin began, "I guess . . . uh . . . everything."

———

Bix talked and Caitlin listened. She also watched his mouth when he spoke, the way his lips formed words. She couldn't help but think about the fact that she and Bix had lived together, right in this very apartment. According to him, they were even planning to get married in a few days. She wondered if they had talked about saving for a house of their own somewhere with its own yard and without a scary guard dog next door. She watched him speak, knowing that those lips must have kissed hers. How many times? Hundreds? A thousand? What else had they done to her? And his hands. She looked at them resting on the chair back in front of him. Big, strong hands. Her face felt warm. Was she blushing again? Was he looking at her lips now, thinking about them kissing his? About other things she had done with them? That, and her—

She tilted her bottle up, downed the last of her beer, and felt some go down the wrong way. She coughed.

"You okay?" Josh asked.

She coughed again, then nodded. "I'm fine. Sorry."

"Where was I?" Bix asked.

"The bar," Josh offered in a tone that left no doubt that he wanted Bix to spit out his story already so Josh could get Caitlin the hell away from there.

"Right. So she comes in. I'd never seen her there before—and this is one of my regular hangouts, understand—and she struts in like she owns the place."

"Really?" Caitlin said. She didn't think that sounded anything like her.

"Hell, yeah," Bix said. "And I loved it. When I saw you walk in, it was like the air had been sucked from the room. It was like something very cool . . . something *special* . . . had happened, and everyone could feel it, only nobody else knew what it was yet. But I knew right away what it was. It was you."

Caitlin heard Josh make some sort of derisive little sound, a species of snort. Caitlin, though, was surprised at the way Bix expressed his feelings.

"Soon enough, though," Bix continued, "others noticed you. I had to elbow my way past a few local meatheads to buy you your first beer, but I made sure nobody but me bought you a drink that night."

"That's beautiful," Josh said. "I'm getting teary."

Keeping his eyes on Caitlin, Bix said, "You want to hear this or not, buddy?"

"No, *buddy*, I don't. But Caitlin does, so lead on, MacDuff."

"I don't even give a shit what that's supposed to mean," Bix said. "So there you were, Katie"—not wanting to stop the flow of the story, Caitlin didn't correct him—"wearing an attitude that didn't match your conservative clothes. I bought you that beer, which you drained in three sips, by the way," he added with a smile. "You told me your name was Katherine, and when I asked if you went by Katie, you said, 'Sure.' We hit it off, I bought you another beer, and before I could buy you a third, we left together. Came back here."

Caitlin had a pretty good idea what happened next, at least if the story so far was true. "Bix, would you mind if we skipped ahead a little?"

"What's that?" Then he smiled. "Yeah, sure. I just have to say, though . . . you may not remember that night, but that doesn't mean it wasn't memorable."

"Jesus, Caitlin," Josh said. "Do you really want to hear this?"

"No," she said, looking pointedly at Bix, "but there are things I do want to hear. That I need to hear. Bix, would you *please* not do that?"

He shrugged.

"How about just skipping to the parts we actually need to hear?" Josh said.

Bix thought for a moment. "Okay, but before I go on, I think we need to get something on the record. I hate to break it to you two, but Katie and I lived together for more than half a year. You think we never made it past first base?" He looked directly at Josh. "So do what you have to do to come to grips with that, or we're gonna keep getting sidetracked."

Caitlin gave Josh a sympathetic look. At first he scowled, then he shook his head and nodded, resigned.

"We all okay here, kids?" Bix asked.

"Let's just move on," Josh said.

"Okay," Bix said. "So I start asking a few questions . . . you know, where are you from, what do you do for fun, your last name, things like that."

"And I said my last name was Southard?" Caitlin asked.

He nodded. "I'm guessing it's not."

"No, it's not. It's Sommers."

"Katherine Southard," Josh said, looking at her, very deliberately avoiding looking Bix's way. "Why would you use that name? Does it mean anything to you, hon?"

She thought about it. She ran through all the Katherines she could remember in her life. A few in grade school, two in high school, three in college, one to whom she sold a house last year. None of them had Southard for a surname. And Josh had already Googled the name on the Internet. It wasn't somebody famous. Maybe she'd heard the name one time, possibly right before she disappeared, and adopted it as her own. Or maybe she'd simply made it up.

"It doesn't mean anything to me," she said.

"It sounds a lot like Caitlin Sommers, doesn't it?" Josh asked. "You obviously weren't in your right mind for whatever reason. Maybe you just scrambled your name a bit and it came out sounding like Katherine Southard."

"Maybe," Caitlin said.

"Anyway," Bix said, "you weren't really answering my questions that night. I told you everything you wanted to know about me, but it didn't take me long to realize that you just didn't want to talk about your past. And that was okay with me. A lot of women I meet in bars—hell, men, too—are living different lives than they're letting on. Even after a day or two, when you hadn't left my apartment yet and didn't seem inclined to do so anytime soon, you weren't exactly overly sharing. After three days, we both knew you weren't going anywhere. We never talked about it, never agreed to it. You just didn't leave and I didn't want you to."

"And the fact that I didn't seem to want to tell you anything about myself didn't bother you?" Caitlin asked.

He shrugged, swallowed the last of his beer, and stood. As he headed for the kitchen, he said, "Like I said, I figured you were . . . well, maybe not running from something, but you were trying to move on from something that you didn't want to talk about. Maybe an abusive relationship. Maybe trouble with the law. Whatever it was, I didn't care."

He returned with a beer for himself and handed a second to Caitlin. He didn't have a third for Josh. He straddled the chair again and took a swig of his beer. "No, I didn't care about whatever past you might have had. By that time, I was hooked." He smiled.

Caitlin took a sip and realized that both men were watching her . . . Bix amused, Josh far less so as he eyed her beer.

"What?" Caitlin said to her husband. "It's good." She held her bottle out toward him. "Want to share mine?"

"Thanks, no," Josh said. "So then what?" he said to Bix like a federal agent interrogating a suspected terrorist.

"Then," Bix said, looking at Caitlin, "you needed to start a life outside of this apartment. A life here in Smithfield. I didn't know where you were from, but if you were going to stay here—which we both wanted—you needed a few things. There were steps we had to take."

"Like what?" Caitlin asked.

"Well, you wanted to trade in your car, we had to find you a job, get you a driver's license, buy you—"

"I didn't have a driver's license?" Caitlin asked.

"If you did, you didn't show it to me."

"If you had one," Josh said, "it would have had your real name on it."

Caitlin lifted her purse from the floor where she'd set it and zipped it open. She slid her driver's license out of her wallet and looked it over. Instead of her New Hampshire license, this one was issued by Massachusetts. It had her picture on it, showing her with her new short red hair. It also had Bix's address. And the name Katherine Southard. She told Josh what she was looking at. "How easy is it to get a new driver's license with someone else's name on it?" she asked Bix.

Bix smiled. "Easy enough if you know the right people. One of my friends does IDs. Good ones, too. Licenses, real Social Security numbers, even credit cards if you need them. Passports are hard. He'll make you one and it will look good, but I wouldn't use it to try to leave the country . . . or worse, to get back in. But his stuff will fool most people, including a lot of cops."

"You have a friend who makes false IDs?" Josh asked.

Bix nodded.

"Why am I not surprised?"

Bix shrugged. "Anyway, he does nice work, like I said." He kept his attention on Caitlin. "So we set you up with an identity as Katherine Southard, which I'd sort of suspected might not be your real name, but I didn't give a damn about that."

"This explains why the trooper didn't have a problem with my license or the car registration," she said to Josh, looking at the license in her hands. She realized that she'd never looked at it when she handed it over a couple of hours ago. "Because they match. They both have Katherine Southard's name, along with this address." She looked at her picture on the license. "And I'd already cut my hair and dyed it red by the time this picture was taken, so what the trooper saw when he looked at me matched my photo."

"Yeah," Bix said, "you changed your hair the first day you were here, after the night we met. You said you felt like a change. Was it just a coincidence that it also would make it harder for someone to recognize you? Again, I didn't care."

"Why would you?" Josh asked. "You pal around with criminals. That's probably how all the women you meet behave."

Bix ignored him. "I liked you as a blonde," Bix said, "but I was A-OK with red, too. Besides, you said it was . . . what was the word you used?" He thought for a moment. "You said it was *right*. That you were *supposed* to be a redhead."

"What does that mean?" Josh asked.

"I have no idea," Caitlin said. "Maybe I always secretly wanted to be a redhead."

"Wait," Josh said to Bix. "You said you had to trade in her car. She had a car?"

"That's the way trades work."

"Caitlin . . ." Josh began.

"Yes?"

"Well, your car . . . the day after you disappeared, it was found abandoned in the parking lot of a strip mall across town. It was one of the main reasons people thought you were . . . that something had happened to you."

"Really?" she said. "So whose car did I drive here to Smithfield? And how did I get it?"

CHAPTER THIRTEEN

"THE NIGHT WE MET," Bix said, "you followed me home from the bar in a crappy old Dodge Charger."

Somehow, between the time Caitlin walked out of her house in Bristol, New Hampshire, and the time she arrived in Smithfield, Massachusetts, she had acquired a car, albeit a junky one, according to Bix. Caitlin didn't remember it at all.

"When we realized you'd be sticking with me," Bix continued, "we knew we had to get rid of it. You never said so, but I knew it wasn't yours. So I tossed the registration, dumped a few things from the car into a box in case Katie might want them, and took the car to a friend of mine."

"Another friend?" Josh asked. "Let me guess . . . he traffics in stolen cars."

"But he'll give you a fair deal. We came home with that Skylark out there, which was a lot nicer than that piece-of-shit Dodge. And seeing as he and I are friends, I got a steal."

"Literally, I'm sure," Josh said. "You know a lot of shady characters, Bix. Are you some kind of criminal?"

"No," Bix said, shaking his head, "but a lot of my friends are."

"What is it you do, then?"

"Whatever I have to."

Josh shook his head and Caitlin stepped in. "Do you remember the name on the registration you took from the Charger?"

He shook his head. "Didn't seem important at the time. He wasn't getting the car back, whoever he was. I didn't need to know his name."

Caitlin frowned. Bix had thrown out what could have been an important clue. Damn. An opportunity lost. Still, there was a lot Bix could tell them.

"Please go on," Caitlin said.

"What else do you want to know?" Bix asked.

"Everything. What I used to do. What I liked. Any friends I made. Everything you can think of about me . . . about us."

Bix nodded. He seemed to be thinking.

She added, "Anything you say might spark a memory, Bix. Even a small memory, something minor, might get the dominoes to start falling."

"You want to hear about us?"

"Among other things."

"If you want me to talk about us," Bix said, keeping his eyes locked on Caitlin's but pointing at Josh, "then *he* either keeps his mouth shut or he goes outside and sits on the porch."

"He'll be good," Caitlin promised for Josh. She looked at her husband, who shook his head in resignation.

Over the next several minutes, without Josh's occasional interruptions—for which Caitlin couldn't really blame him—the information flowed faster and more freely. Caitlin learned a lot, but nothing she heard created a spark to ignite a memory. According to Bix, after Caitlin was equipped with a new appearance, a new used car, a new identity, and some new clothes that Bix had paid for, it was time for her to get a job. Bix had another friend—at this, Josh chuckled under his breath—whose cousin was willing to hire her to wait tables and pay her off the books, which they thought was a good idea given her phony identity documents. So Caitlin worked her hours, Bix did whatever Bix did to make money—he was not terribly forthcoming about that—and, if he was to be believed, they fell in love.

At that, Josh was unable to contain a scoff, and Bix turned to him. Instead of being angry, he smiled.

"You don't believe me?" he asked.

"That she was in love with you?" Josh said. "No, I don't. It may have seemed that way to you. Maybe she even enjoyed your company, for some reason I couldn't possibly imagine. But she couldn't have been in love with you. Not really."

"Yeah," Bix said as he rose from his chair. "You're probably right." He grabbed a couple of the empty beer bottles and headed to the kitchen. A moment later he left the kitchen, but instead of returning to the living room, he headed down what appeared to be a hallway.

"You think I hurt his feelings?" Josh asked without seeming the least bit concerned that he might have done so.

"You are being a bit rude," Caitlin said. "He's trying to help us. Besides, think about it from his point of view. Up until a little while ago, he and I were in love." The look on Josh's face made her rephrase that. "I mean, he *thought* the two of us were in love. One minute, we're a happy couple in his mind, the next he finds out I'm married to another man and I don't even remember him. That's got to be hard, right?"

Josh mumbled something Caitlin couldn't make out.

"I'm sorry, Josh," she said. "I know this can't be easy for you. It's not easy for me, either. Bix knows . . . things about me. He has intimate memories of the two of us that I don't have. It's almost like I was roofied or something," she said, referring to Rohypnol, the infamous date rape drug, "but the effects of the drug lasted half a year."

After a moment, Josh sighed. "I'm sorry, honey," he said. "Yeah, it sucks to hear that guy talk about . . . the time he spent with you, but I keep forgetting how terrible it must be to have no memory of a significant chunk of your life."

"Are you mad at me?" she asked.

"For what?"

"For . . . whatever I did with him. For everything he and I . . . for all of this," she said, taking in the room with a sweep of her hand.

He dropped his eyes and said nothing for a moment. When he looked up again, his eyes were sad. "Caitlin, I'm sorry. I'm sorry I made you ask that question. Of course I'm not mad. None of this is your fault. You didn't mean to lose your memory. You didn't choose to come here. To take up with that guy. No, I'm not mad. I'm not real happy about the way this is playing out," he added, "but I'm definitely not mad at you."

She smiled at him gratefully.

"What's that they say about pictures?" Bix asked, walking into the room. He had a large picture frame in each hand, maybe twenty inches by twenty. He'd obviously taken them down off a wall somewhere. Caitlin could see that each was a collage comprised of several photographs. "Something about them being worth a thousand words?" he added, dropping one frame onto Josh's lap and handing the other to Caitlin.

Part of Caitlin was afraid to look down at the frame, afraid to see the pictures. But that part of her had no chance against the part that needed to see them. She looked down. The first photo she saw was of Bix standing at the edge of a lake with Caitlin on his back, piggyback style, her arms around his neck. Bix was smiling. Caitlin thought she looked—she had to admit it—happy. In the next photo, Bix stood behind Caitlin, his arms wrapped around her this time. She was laughing hard, her head tipped back against his chest. In the third picture, Caitlin sat beside Bix surrounded by a crowd. Maybe they were at some sort of sporting event. She had her head resting on his shoulder, her mouth set in a sweet smile.

They were all like that, all nine pictures in the frame. In each, the happiness displayed on her face was genuine. In a few, she was positively beaming. She was also more heavily made up than she had been for most of her life—the part of her life she could remember, that is. But what was most evident from the array of photos was that Caitlin looked as though she had been truly happy with Bix. She glanced up and saw Josh staring down at the picture frame in his hands. He looked up, and she knew he had seen the same thing she had. She dropped her eyes to the photos again and focused on the images of Bix. There was no mistaking it—the man in the pictures was a man in love. She raised her eyes and saw him watching her. He threw her a quick wink and smiled, but Caitlin imagined she saw an underlying sadness in it.

Caitlin could doubt it no longer. She and Bix had been in love. Somehow, although she already loved Josh, she had fallen in love with another man . . . and she couldn't remember a second of it.

———

"And this is where the magic happens," Bix said, pushing open a door to reveal a bedroom. When Josh saw the double bed and rumpled sheets, he wanted—for the tenth time in the last hour—to punch Bix in the face.

"Come on, Bix," Caitlin said. "Is that necessary?"

Josh tried to keep his eyes off the bed. It was bad enough for him to see the pictures of Caitlin—his wife, for God's sake—captured forever in moments of domestic bliss with another man, moments that she should have shared with no one but Josh. He noticed two picture hooks on the otherwise empty walls.

He felt so, so sad. And terrible. He wished to God he had followed her out of the house that night, convinced her to come back inside and talk things out. Still, a small voice in his head, one he wasn't proud of, wondered—even if she had been angry with him when she left—how much she could have ever truly loved him if she could run off and fall in love with another man in literally a matter of days. But he told that voice to shut up, reminded it that none of this was Caitlin's fault. If anything, it was his fault for giving her a reason to leave that night, thereby setting everything in motion. Besides, she hadn't been in her right mind for the past seven months. In a sense, it was almost as though it wasn't really Caitlin at all who had taken up with Bix . . . though it sure as hell looked like her in the pictures. No . . . he refused to blame her. He knew she loved him, even if she might have forgotten it for a while. And, despite all that had happened, he would never stop loving her back and trying to be worthy of her love.

Caitlin stepped past Bix into the bedroom and Josh followed, still keeping his eyes off the bed. He watched Caitlin study the room. She turned to a set of sliding closet doors.

"May I?" she asked.

"Go ahead," Bix said. "It's your closet."

"It *was* her closet," Josh said.

Caitlin slid a door open and saw men's clothes. Then she slid the doors to the other side, revealing a good deal of women's clothing. For a moment, she just looked at it all.

"Anything familiar?" Josh asked.

Caitlin shook her head. She poked through women's tops, a few blouses, some sweaters. From where Josh stood, they didn't look like the kinds of things Caitlin would wear. The clothes in her closet at home were quite a bit more conservative. To his admittedly untrained eye, these clothes seemed to be stylish enough but a bit showier than she was used to. Caitlin may have been thinking the same thing because she turned to Bix and asked, "These are really mine?"

"Sure are," he said. He leaned forward and touched the sleeve of a low-cut V-neck shirt. "You're wearing this one in that shot," he said, pointing to a single photo in a frame on the nightstand. Josh looked over and saw that, indeed, Caitlin was wearing the same shirt, which was indeed cut low, revealing the tops of her shapely breasts. Thankfully, Bix wasn't in the photo with her this time, though the way she was grinning, the way her eyes seemed to be sparkling as she looked right into the lens, Josh had to wonder if Bix had been the one behind the camera.

God, this is hard, Josh thought. He wanted it to be over. He wanted to forget all about this guy, and he wanted Caitlin to do the same. He wanted her to learn enough to move on with her life, but nothing that would change the way she felt about him and the life they once shared together.

"I don't remember any of this," she said.

They had now completed the tour of the entire apartment, which hadn't taken long—just the living room, eat-in kitchen, two bathrooms, a spare room—which Bix had announced belonged to Pedro, a seven-year-old boy Caitlin and he had adopted last month, before admitting that he was only joking—and finally, the bedroom. Caitlin said she couldn't recall any of it. Yet Bix had shown them Caitlin's things—her pajamas, makeup, the books she was reading, which, from their titles, didn't seem to be the kinds of things Bix would read. He'd shown them notes she had jotted on various pads of paper—a grocery list in a kitchen drawer, a message by the telephone in the living room . . . even a note pinned to the door of the fridge with a magnet in the shape of a pineapple, which read simply, *Love you lots*. That one was a kick in the gut for Josh.

Each of the notes was written in handwriting Josh recognized at once as Caitlin's. Finally, there were the photos, the existence of which Josh couldn't deny, despite his overwhelming desire to not only deny their existence but to shred them all and wipe the memory of them forever from his mind. He'd have paid good money for just a small touch of Caitlin's amnesia just then. If it hadn't been for the pictures and maybe the handwriting, Josh might have thought that Bix had cooked up some sort of scam, that *he* was the one who had somehow slipped Caitlin the hypothetical industrial-strength roofie. But the photos did exist, as did the notes Caitlin clearly had written in her own hand, including the one saying that she loved Bix "lots." Josh couldn't deny those things, so he could no longer deny that Caitlin had lived here with Bix . . . and that she had perhaps loved him to some degree.

Caitlin's eyes met his, and he knew that she had come to the same conclusion. She turned toward Bix and said, "I think we need your help. You know things we probably can't learn anywhere else."

Bix said nothing.

"You can't imagine how hard it is not to remember anything from the past seven months," Caitlin added. "I just want to know what I was doing, what I did. I want . . . no, I *need* to *remember.*"

Josh truly wondered what Bix would say. Would he just tell them to leave? He'd had the plug pulled on his life with Caitlin. Who could blame him, now that he had answered so many of her questions, if he just wanted them gone? And as much as they needed to know whatever he knew, a big part of Josh hoped he would tell them both to go to hell. Josh watched Bix's eyes move slowly around the room, then come to rest on the picture of Caitlin, the one by the bed, in which she was alone, smiling at the lens. He looked back at her and said, "What can I do?"

CHAPTER FOURTEEN

THEY DECIDED THAT IT MIGHT jog Caitlin's memory to visit specific places around the city, places with which Caitlin was familiar . . . well, with which she had been familiar when she was Katie. At almost six in the evening, it was close to dinnertime, so they drove from Bix's neighborhood into the city proper, their general destination being an area known locally, though not officially, as the West End, where a higher concentration of restaurants could be found than in other parts of Smithfield. The first stop on the Caitlin memory tour was the Fish Place, which, according to Bix, was the pub where they had first met, and also happened to be her favorite place to eat. Also according to Bix, the place didn't serve any fish but rather was named after Ted Fisher, the owner. At the Fish Place, you ordered steak or chicken that came with sides of potatoes. In addition to no fish, there was also a complete lack of pasta on the menu. There was salad for those who insisted on it, but the servers were reluctant to give you one unless you also ordered something that had at least a decent chance of clogging an artery somewhere down the line.

Stepping into the restaurant, Caitlin was disappointed to find that the Fish Place wasn't the least bit familiar to her. It smelled great, though, despite giving her the feeling that she was putting on weight merely by breathing the air in here. But though she remembered reading one time that smells were possibly the most powerful memory triggers—and the aromas here were certainly powerful—it felt as though she were visiting this restaurant for the first time. Rough wood floor, a bar along one wall, booths along the other, tables in between, and two pool tables in back where Bix said he had first laid eyes on Caitlin. There were light fixtures hanging from the ceiling and a long string of Christmas lights running around the perimeter of the place, even though it was October. They probably stayed up year-round. She recalled none of it.

A smiling young woman walked toward them, menus in hand. She wore a pale blue T-shirt with a white graphic of a smiling fish head on it. "Hey, you two," she said with what seemed to Caitlin like familiarity. "Got a friend with you for dinner tonight, I see."

"If you say so, Candace," Bix replied.

The woman laughed in the way that people do when they're pretending they understand a joke that they weren't actually in on. "This way," she bubbled, heading toward an empty table, of which there were several, given that it was still a bit early for most folks outside of Florida to be eating dinner.

On the way there, the bartender called out to them, "What do you say, Bix? What's up, Katie?" Bix responded and urged Caitlin to wave, which she did, and to smile, which she tried her best to do.

They arrived at their table and Candace said, "Here you go," as she placed menus in front of three chairs. She leaned toward Caitlin and, tipping her head theatrically in Josh's direction, said in a faux stage whisper plenty loud enough for all to hear, "So who's the cute guy, Katie?"

They had decided that Caitlin should pretend to know everyone she would be expected to know, so as not to attract unwanted attention, but she had no idea how to answer the hostess's question. She knew she couldn't say, "He's my husband," though that's how

Josh would want her to answer, because this woman thought Caitlin and Bix were a couple. So instead, she just laughed and sat down. Candace seemed to understand pretty quickly that she wouldn't be receiving a response to her question, and if she were disappointed, she didn't show it. She said, "Tim will be serving you guys again tonight. He'll be right over to take your drink orders."

Candace left their table and Bix said, "I think she likes you, Josh. Hey, Katie, why don't you put in a good word for Josh with Candace?"

"She knew my name," Caitlin said, ignoring him.

"Not *your* name, Caitlin," Josh said. "The name you were using for a while, remember?"

"That's right," Caitlin said. "That's what I meant."

"No shit, she did," Bix said. "I told you we're regulars here. Your favorite is the steak tips on toast, by the way."

"They're good here?"

Josh let slip an exasperated sound.

"Sorry," Caitlin said, "but I'm hungry." She generally wasn't much of a carnivore, eating red meat infrequently, but it sounded good tonight.

Out of the corner of her eye, she saw Bix smiling. Out of the corner of her other eye, she saw Josh frowning. No, scowling. She reached over under the table and found his knee. A moment later, his hand found hers and held it.

A skinny, redheaded college-age kid in another smiling-fish-head shirt walked up to the table and said, "Hey, guys," in that same familiar tone Candace had used. His name tag read Tim. "Are we starting with drinks?"

"Sure," Bix said.

"The usual for you two?" he asked, looking first at Caitlin, then at Bix.

"Sounds good to me," Bix said. "Katie?"

Caitlin started to order a glass of wine, which Josh no doubt was expecting her to do, but instead she decided to see what her "usual" was. "The usual for me, too."

Josh ordered whatever they had on tap even though he rarely drank beer and almost never did so with dinner.

While they waited for their drinks, Josh looked at the menu. Caitlin didn't bother—the steak tips sounded good, and Bix said she loved them—so she was free to let her eyes roam around the restaurant. It still didn't look familiar, so she started scanning the faces of the two dozen or so people in the place. No little bells sounded in her head.

"Do I know anyone here?" she asked Bix.

Bix's menu remained closed on the table in front of him. Apparently he had a favorite, too. "Well, Tim serves us pretty often. Recognize him?"

She shook her head. Bix looked around for a few seconds, then tipped his head toward a very old man sitting alone in a booth.

"How about Phil over there? Widower. Eats here every night. Every once in a while you invite him to join us. He insists on paying every time you do. He calls you his little cutie when he sees you. 'Hey, there's my little cutie,' he always says. Anything?"

Caitlin watched the old man raise a quivering forkful of pie to his mouth. It was like she was seeing him for the first time in her life. She shook her head.

"And you don't remember the bartender, I assume?"

"Nope."

He looked around. "That's it for now. Sorry."

So was she.

Tim brought over their drinks. A glass of some kind of beer for Josh, a bottle of Harpoon IPA for Bix, and a Corona Light with a slice of lime for Caitlin. Josh glanced away from her beer and took a sip of his own. She gave his hand a little squeeze under the table and was pleased to feel him squeeze back. He wasn't enjoying any of this, but he was handling it as well as could be expected given the circumstances.

Tim took their orders—steak tips for Caitlin, steak sandwich for Bix, and a chicken club for Josh. Soon enough, Tim was back with their food. Bix was right; Caitlin liked the steak tips.

They talked during dinner, Caitlin and Bix playing "What Else Doesn't Caitlin Remember?" throughout. Josh spent most of the meal on his tablet, which he'd brought into the restaurant. He said he was doing research. Every now and then he muttered something like "hmm" or "ah." After they finished their meals, they ordered another round of beers.

"Pool table's free," Bix said. "Want to shoot a game?"

"Not really," Josh replied civilly, "but thanks."

"No offense, Josh—I mean it—but I wasn't asking you. Sorry, brother."

"Caitlin doesn't play pool."

"Oh," Bix said, nodding and smiling good-naturedly. "How about you, then?"

"There are some things I want to talk to Caitlin about." He turned to her. "Listen, I found some interesting stuff online. I think I might have—"

"You don't play pool, either, I guess," Bix said, shrugging in a way that made it clear that the information didn't surprise him.

Josh seemed to consider it for a moment, then stood. "I guess we can talk about it after a game or two."

"Now you're talking, pal," Bix said, clapping him on the shoulder. "Bring your beer. Come on, Katie . . . I mean, Caitlin."

———

Hunnsaker took a bite of her veggie wrap and stared at the photographs taped to a whiteboard. She and Padilla had commandeered an interview room, rolled in a whiteboard, and started filling it with information. Some detectives could work by flipping through files and stacks of paper and photos, but Hunnsaker liked to see everything at once, all laid out in front of her. So she taped photos of Vic Warehouse taken at the crime scene in the center of the whiteboard—a close-up of his face, complete with bullet hole, and shots of his body from four different angles. To the right of those pictures, she had taped mug shots of Dominick Bruno, their potential squatter, and Kenneth "Stick Man" Kahanahanukahalenahuli, a known associate of Bruno's. On the far right side of the big board, Hunnsaker had put photos of the scene itself—pictures of the warehouse's exterior, shots from various angles inside, a photo of the closet in the back, along with close-ups of each of the items found inside it. Each photo had a small typed description taped beside it.

Hunnsaker had begun a timeline on the left side of the board. She liked to use index cards for that so she wouldn't have to erase anything if they needed to slot some fact between two they had already written. At the moment, there were three cards. The first read, *Vic shot between 9 p.m. and 12 a.m.?, Oct. 3–4*. On the second, she had written, *Kids find vic approx. 8 a.m.; call 911 at 8:14 a.m., Oct. 4*. The last card read, *Cops on scene at 10:36 a.m., Oct. 4*. All alone in the lower left corner of the board was an index card noting that the gun found by the victim's body had been identified by its serial number as one that had been stolen during a residential break-in fourteen months ago in Philadelphia. That fact led to a communication with the Philly police. The gun was discussed along with the circumstances in which it was found here in Massachusetts. Also discussed was the warehouse victim, whose photograph and fingerprints were sent by e-mail. His fingerprints may not have been in the national database or in the local database here in Smithfield, but maybe Hunnsaker would get lucky and they'd be on some computer server in Philadelphia. It was possible, too, that they'd get a hit on the photo. Maybe the victim matched the description of someone that somebody was looking for—be it friend, family, or the police themselves. So far, nothing helpful from Philly, but it was still fairly early in the game.

Hunnsaker surveyed the board. Despite all the photos and notes, there was still a depressing amount of blank whiteness glaring back at her. And the various reports scattered on the table beside her didn't yet add a whole lot. There was far too much they still didn't know. She took another bite of her veggie wrap, which wasn't bad, but which also wasn't the pan-seared Moroccan salmon her husband had planned to make for dinner tonight. It was his turn to cook, and he was far better at it than she was, though she never admitted that to him.

Hunnsaker had called Thomas earlier with the bad news that she'd be working late again, which didn't seem to bother him because he understood her. He totally got the fact that she was never quite able to rest in the early days of an investigation. Those days were the most critical and she hated taking time even to sleep. Besides, Hunnsaker had been a bit more accessible recently, so they'd been able to spend a little more time together lately. Her remaining caseload kept her plenty busy, but she'd been able to clear a little excess by closing a couple of old cases in the last two weeks. Plus, remarkably, this was the first new murder to cross her desk in almost two months, which shattered her personal record of five weeks, and it was the first murder reported in the entire Smithfield/North Smithfield area in more than a month, which was unusual, as Smithfield alone—one of the largest cities in the state—averaged a murder every two-and-a-half weeks. Technically, the murder had occurred in North Smithfield, but that city didn't have its own homicide division and relied on the Smithfield PD to work its homicides. So with fewer people killing other people lately, Hunnsaker and Thomas had been able to go out to dinner twice last week alone and had found the time to catch up on several movies on cable that they'd missed in the theaters. Her recent nine-hour workdays had almost been like a mini vacation. But it was time to hit it hard again, and she was more than ready. So the Moroccan salmon would have to wait a day or two—though she figured Thomas was preparing it anyway and she'd find a gourmet meal waiting for her in the fridge whenever it was that she dragged herself home. That man was a keeper.

"Any word on Bruno?" Hunnsaker asked.

Padilla held up one finger. "Give me a second," he said around an extra-large mouthful of tuna-salad sandwich.

"I thought you were juicing," Hunnsaker said.

Padilla chewed a bit more, then finally swallowed. "Steroids make your nuts shrink. I wouldn't touch the stuff."

"Yeah, I imagine you can't afford to shrink even a tiny bit in that area, Javy. But what I meant was, isn't Elaine making you do some sort of disgusting diet with her? Smoothies made of seaweed or kale or something like that? Did she give it up?"

"Nope."

"Oh," Hunnsaker said, "she just let you off the hook."

"Not quite."

Then Hunnsaker understood. "Ah, so she thinks you're being a good boy and drinking that crap at work, and you don't disabuse her of that idea."

"I'm invoking my Fifth Amendment right not to incriminate myself. Besides, I'm a grown man. What I do at work is my business." After another bite of tuna salad, he said, "Don't tell Elaine, okay?"

"We're all brothers and sisters in blue here, Javy," Hunnsaker said. "I wouldn't do that. Besides, I don't give a damn. So, back to Bruno."

Apparently, Dominick Bruno and Stick Man Whatever-the-Hell-His-Real-Name-Was weren't as tight as Bruno's old neighbor thought they were, because when Padilla visited Stick Man in prison, it didn't take much to get him to volunteer Bruno's favorite place to be when he wasn't catching a buzz and jerking off in a warehouse closet. At first, Stick Man tried to negotiate for a reduced sentence. After realizing a mere few seconds later that he was overreaching, he tried for a television in his cell. When that didn't work, he asked for extra dessert for a week. Eventually, he answered Padilla's questions without any incentive, probably for no other reason than that it would allow him a few more precious minutes away from his cell, away from other inmates, doing something—anything—to break the monotony of his daily routine.

"It turns out he shows up most nights at a dive on Preston Street called the Pit Stop," Padilla said.

Hunnsaker had heard of the place. Everyone called it the Piss Stop, but that didn't seem to keep people from going there.

"Got an officer watching the place right now," Padilla said. "I gave him your number. He'll bring Bruno in when he shows, which will be sooner rather than later, according to Stick Man."

Hunnsaker finished her veggie wrap and said, "You don't have to stay, Javy. It's getting late. I can talk to Bruno myself when they bring him in. We can follow up on anything in the morning. Besides, Elaine probably wants you home so she can pump another spinach smoothie into you."

"Why do you think I'm still here with you?"

Hunnsaker smiled. "Tell you what—if Bruno doesn't show by midnight, we both go home and get some sleep, then start fresh in the morning."

Padilla nodded.

Hunnsaker sipped her delicious squad-room coffee and took a long look at the close-up photo of the victim's face. "I really want to figure out who this guy is," she said. "Somebody out there knows, goddamn it."

———

As Josh lined up a bank shot on the eight ball that would close out the game, he had to admit to himself that Bix was the better pool player. Bix won the first game handily, then Josh won the second on a miracle shot that seemed to impress Bix, but which Josh knew he'd miss nine times out of ten. Josh dropped the next three games and, though they were fairly competitive, found himself playing from behind in every one and never really felt like he was going to catch up. Then Bix lost the sixth game by just barely scratching after successfully banking the eight ball into a corner pocket. At the moment of that victory, Josh still had three balls on the table. But now he was sighting down his cue with a bead on his third win. He sent the eight smoothly into a side pocket. Four games to three, though Josh knew it easily could have been six games to one.

"Your turn to rack," Josh said, knowing full well that Caitlin was bored silly watching them play. Her body language had been an open book since they'd started. Patient through two games, less so through the next three, and downright unhappy during the last two. Josh would feel better if he could just tie up the match, though. He was being an idiot, he knew, but he really wanted to even the score.

"You sure you want to play again?" Bix asked, smiling. Then, in the same stage whisper Candace had used when asking about Josh's availability, he added, "I've been taking it easy on you because Caitlin's watching."

Josh smiled back again in as close an approximation of a genuine smile as he could muster, and said, "Sounds to me like you're afraid I'm hitting my stride. I won the last two games."

"A couple of lucky shots in there, though, you gotta admit."

"Me? How about that combination you hit in the third game—"

"Seriously, guys?" Caitlin said, her voice dripping with exasperation. She set down her third beer of the evening—fifth of the day if you counted the two at Bix's place, which Josh did—and stood up. "Look down at the table, boys," she said.

Josh and Bix looked down at the few balls scattered across the green felt.

"Know what I see?" Caitlin asked.

The men shrugged.

"I see that your balls are exactly the same size."

Bix chuckled. Josh looked up at him. His eyes seemed to be saying, *Well, buddy, she'd know, wouldn't she?* Then again, Josh may have been imagining that.

"So we can end this, right, fellas?" Caitlin added.

After a hesitation, Josh nodded. Bix stepped over and took the pool cue from his hands. "Here, I'll take that for you," he said, then added quietly, "Looks like my stick's longer than yours."

"What is this, high school?" Josh responded, though sure enough, now that Bix held them together with their butts on the floor, Josh saw that his cue was at least an inch shorter than Bix's.

Bix smiled and turned to Caitlin. "Come on, Katie . . . you and me. Just one game."

Josh sighed loudly. "Caitlin, would you tell this guy that you don't play?" He looked at Bix. "I've seen her try a few times. She's just not good." He laughed and said, "No offense, hon. Remember the seventies party Ed and Tammy threw last year?"

Caitlin smiled. "I was awful, wasn't I?"

"Your words, not mine," Josh said, still smiling. She was right, though. Another couple had challenged Caitlin and him to a game of doubles. And Caitlin had been spectacularly terrible. It became a source of great humor for everyone at the party, and then for months afterward between Josh and Caitlin. She had handled it beautifully, of course, because she obviously could not have cared less that she wasn't any good.

"Just give it a try," Bix said. "One game."

Give it a rest, Josh thought, though there was something unsettling in the way Bix kept asking.

Caitlin shrugged. "Okay, if it will shut you up."

Bix racked the balls and rolled the cue ball to Caitlin.

"I'm breaking?" she asked.

"If you're going to flame out, flame out big," Bix said.

Caitlin shrugged and bent down to line up her shot. She was about to hit when Bix spoke softly. "Close your eyes," he said.

Caitlin looked up. "What?"

"Close your eyes, Katie."

"I won't be able to see the balls."

"Just for a second. Before you shoot."

"What's that?" Josh asked. "Some sort of Jedi mind trick?"

Bix ignored him. "Close your eyes for a second, and don't even think about the shot. Don't think about anything. Just feel the stick in your hands."

Caitlin closed her eyes. For some reason, despite her almost infamous billiards history, Josh had a bad feeling about this. "Come on, Yoda," he said, "don't embarrass her."

To Josh's irritation, Bix kept ignoring him.

"Now give it a try, Katie," Bix said quietly. "Let your hands take control."

Caitlin opened her eyes, drew back the stick, and let fly with a solid break, the clack of the initial impact loud enough to make several patrons look up from their meat loaf. The balls scattered nicely and one even trickled into a corner pocket. Josh had never seen her hit a shot like that. She'd never even made solid contact before. Bix smiled. Caitlin did, too. Josh didn't. At least not at first. He recovered quickly, though, and said, smiling, "Hey, great shot."

Caitlin threw a small smile his way as she moved around the table. She closed her eyes again, briefly, then sunk a striped ball into a side pocket. Then she dropped another into a corner, yet another in the side, before finally missing—just barely—on a shot three-quarters the length of the table. She wasn't even closing her eyes before each shot any longer.

"You taught me to play pool?" she asked Bix.

"I told you, we're regulars here. We play all the time. I taught you a few other things, too."

Just in case Bix was about to make some suggestive crack that would have made Josh split Jedi Bix's skull with a pool cue, Josh quickly turned to Caitlin to tell her how impressed he was with her newly discovered billiards prowess. But she was looking over his shoulder, her eyes wide, her mouth open.

"Caitlin?" he said. He turned to the flat-screen television mounted high on the wall behind him. A stone-faced reporter with a microphone was standing in front of a warehouse, but Josh couldn't hear what she was saying because the TV was muted. All he heard was an old Greg Allman Band tune called "I'm No Angel" playing over the restaurant's sound system. Beneath the reporter's face, a bold caption read, *Unidentified man found shot to death in local warehouse.*

Josh turned back to Caitlin. She said, very quietly, too soft for Bix to hear from where he stood on the other side of the table, "Did I do that?"

CHAPTER FIFTEEN

CAITLIN SAT ON A HIGH stool near the pool table, staring into the empty beer glass she was holding in her lap with both hands. She'd said nothing since Josh had guided her there a few minutes ago. She didn't want to speak. She didn't even want to think, either . . . but she couldn't stop herself. *The gun . . . the blood . . . the warehouse . . .*

"What's wrong, Katie?" Bix asked.

"It's Caitlin," Josh snapped, "and can you give us a little space?"

Josh put a gentle hand on Caitlin's shoulder. She thought about shrugging it off, but it actually felt nice. It almost made her feel like she wasn't alone in this, though she had begun to realize just how alone she was . . . or should be, at least. She knew now that she shouldn't have dragged anyone else into this, not even her husband. And not Bix, her . . . whatever he was.

Finally, she said quietly, "I think I . . . killed someone."

After a brief silence, Bix said, "I definitely didn't see that coming. What the hell are you talking about, Katie?"

Josh ignored him. "Don't be ridiculous, honey. I keep telling you, you couldn't kill anyone."

Caitlin wasn't so sure about that. There was the blood on her clothes when she returned home last night. And a gun in a bag. And fake hands, though she couldn't begin to imagine what those were all about. And she had regained her senses outside a warehouse, the same warehouse she'd just seen on TV, the one where a man had been found shot to death.

She was tired suddenly. Very tired. She had slept only a few restless hours last night. And she'd grappled all morning with the uncertainty of her life over the past seven months, then spent the hours since then riding an emotionally exhausting mental Tilt-A-Whirl, with every new revelation about her life in Smithfield, with Bix, sending her mind spinning faster and faster. It was all catching up with her. She just wanted to go home, go to sleep, and not think about any of this. But she couldn't do that. Home was in New Hampshire, and the answers she sought were here in Smithfield. Still, she was tired. She really needed to close her eyes.

"Look at you, hon," Josh said. "You need some rest. Let's get out of here."

"But what about—"

"We'll go there tomorrow," Josh said.

Caitlin nodded. Their next planned stop was the pub where Caitlin had worked. But the mere thought of going there now and coming face-to-face with all new people she'd see and meet, people who would all know her and whom she'd have to pretend to recognize, was exhausting. She knew she wouldn't be able to pull it off tonight, so she nodded and stood. As they headed across the restaurant, the bartender called, "See you tomorrow, guys." Then they passed Candace, who said brightly, "Good night, guys." When they were halfway to the door, the little old man from the booth in the back wobbled up to them slowly, a fedora that had been brand-new back in the 1950s in his hands. Caitlin thought he looked close to ninety years old.

"Hey, little cutie," he said in a paper-thin voice.

Caitlin mustered a smile, which wasn't easy for her just then. "Hi, there," she said.

"I thought you were going to sneak off without saying hello to me."

"I wouldn't do that."

The man smiled, exposing dentures too big for his mouth. "I didn't think so." A second later, his smile faltered.

"Are you okay, cutie?" he asked as the creases multiplied on his already wrinkled brow.

She smiled again. "I'm fine. Just tired, is all. Thanks for asking . . ."

A brief but uncomfortable pause followed before Bix jumped in. "Sam, we've got to get home. Katie's being a tough guy here, but the truth is, she's not feeling great. One beer too many, maybe."

Sam nodded. "Well, wouldn't be the first time," he said, winking at her. "Guess I've seen her a few times after a beer too many in her, right?"

He smiled, exposing those big teeth again. Bix returned the smile and Caitlin did her best, too. Josh didn't smile at all.

"Well, good night, then," Sam said, nodding to the men. "Feel better, cutie pie," he said to Caitlin, then slowly toddled off and out the door. Before the door even closed, a couple of guys came in with pool cue cases in their hands.

"Hey, Bix, Katie," one of them said as they passed.

Caitlin no more recognized them than she had anyone else she'd seen or met in this town. She walked out the door with Josh and Bix right behind her.

———

Chops stepped out of his coveralls, balled them up, and stuffed them into a plastic bag to dispose of later, along with the long, plastic-wrapped bundle lying on his workroom floor. The bundle was exactly two feet shorter than Benny had been when Chops had brought him here four days ago—not two feet as in twenty-four inches, but two feet as in the kind that usually had toes attached to them, unless someone removed those toes.

Chops turned to his workbench. Wearing latex gloves, he used plastic sandwich bags for the smaller pieces and gallon-size plastic Ziploc bags for the larger ones. These he placed inside various-size boxes. When he was finished, he had eleven packages sealed tightly with packing tape to put in the mail today. Given the six other packages he'd mailed just yesterday, he'd gotten a lot of use lately from the postal meter and scale he kept in his office. This way, he could just drop the boxes into a mailbox and never let a postal worker see his face.

He had just started washing his hands when his cell phone rang. He dried off quickly and answered.

"Yeah?"

He listened for a moment, then said, "I told you to wait till dinnertime to call me back if you haven't heard from him by then . . . Well, I meant dinner where I am, not where you are. It's barely even dark out here . . . Okay, whatever. Look, I'll call him again. If I don't reach him, I'll leave a message. He doesn't call me back tonight, I'll fly out there in the morning. Good enough? . . . Well, it'll have to be. I can't go tonight . . . Look, relax, like I said, he's probably just sleeping off a bender. Wouldn't be the first time. I'll let you know if I hear from him."

Chops ended the call, gathered up his packages, and left his workroom, locking the door behind him as always.

In the kitchen of their house, Rachel was sitting at the table eating an apple while little Julia ate cantaloupe cut into tiny cubes. Chops stacked the packages on the table, then grabbed a bottle of Gatorade from the fridge.

"What's all that?" Rachel asked.

"I sold a few small tools on eBay," Chops said, "ones I've replaced or just don't use anymore. I want to get them into a mailbox so they go out first thing in the morning. You need anything while I'm out?"

"You won't be gone long, right? Everyone's coming in two hours."

"No problem."

Rachel had invited two couples over for dinner followed by after-dinner board games—Pictionary, maybe. Chops didn't mind these people. They were among the small number who thought of him as George, who didn't truly know him, though they probably considered him a close friend. Chops needed people like that in his life, both to keep up appearances and to help him remember that there were people in the world, in addition to his wife and daughter, who didn't need to be intimidated, hurt, or killed, or who didn't want to hire him for his particular set of skills. People like the Braddocks and the Haydens were just decent folks.

"Okay, as long as you're back before they get here," Rachel said. "Your daughter has maybe two diapers left, so we could use a box."

"Pampers, right? The ones with the contoured fit?"

Rachel nodded, impressed. "Well done. And can you pick up two bottles of pinot grigio for tonight?"

"Will do. They probably don't have that at Babies 'R' Us, do they?"

Rachel smiled. She had a great smile. Chops bent down, kissed the top of his daughter's head, and snatched a little cube of cantaloupe from her plate.

"Daddy!" Julia said.

"Sorry, pumpkin," Chops said. Then he stole another cube and grinned at her.

"Shouldn't eat with dirty hands, Daddy," Julia scolded.

Chops looked down and saw flecks of dried blood on the knuckles of his right hand. "You're right, Jules," he said, stepping over to the sink. After washing his hands thoroughly, he scooped up the packages from the table. He wished he also had the time to dump the big bundle still in his workroom, but he couldn't do it before their company arrived in two hours. It would have to wait until morning, because he knew the evening would go late and he'd be drinking, and the last thing Chops needed was to get pulled over for weaving and have a cop decide to search his truck and find what was left of Benny in the false bottom of the big tool chest that spanned the width of the truck's bed.

Chops stooped a little and kissed his wife on the cheek, then headed for the garage. On the road a few minutes later, the packages stacked on the passenger seat and floor of his Dodge pickup, Chops pulled out his cell phone and dialed. When voice mail eventually answered, Chops began to leave his message. "Where the hell are you, Mike? Call me back as soon as you get this, because if I don't hear from you by morning, I have to fly out there. Don't make me do that. I'll be pissed off about it and I'll want to take it out on someone. And you know how I can be when I'm pissed off. So call me back."

He hung up and hoped he didn't have to fly to Massachusetts in the morning. If he did, he'd probably miss the circus tomorrow night. It was only in town for a week, and they had center-ring, front-row seats. He and Rachel doubted that Julia was old enough to appreciate the skill, the humor, or the acrobatic athleticism of the performers, but they knew she'd get a big kick out of the animals and all the bright colors, and Chops wanted to be there to see her face. Plus, Rachel would be upset if she had to go without him. So the sonofabitch better call back before morning.

———

Bix was behind the wheel of his Ford Explorer. Josh sat in back with Caitlin, where he had directed her when they left the restaurant. Bix felt like a chauffeur, though this was better than the drive to dinner a few hours ago, when Caitlin was in the passenger seat and Josh was in the backseat but spent the entire ride leaning forward with his head almost right between Bix's and Caitlin's.

After a few minutes of driving in silence, Bix said, "So what's this about Katie killing someone?"

"She didn't kill anyone," Josh said. "Don't worry about it."

"Well, seeing as I'd be aiding and abetting if you're wrong and Katie's right, it seems like I have a right to know what the hell she's talking about."

"Your friends are all crooks and suddenly a little crime makes you nervous?"

"Murder isn't a 'little crime,'" Bix said. "And for the record, I don't think she could do anything like that, either. But I have a right to know."

"Listen, just take us back to our car and we'll get out of your life forever."

Caitlin spoke up. "He's right, Josh. I wish it weren't the case, but we brought him into this. I'm sorry we got you involved, Bix, but Josh is right. Maybe we should just get out of your hair. I don't want to get you in any trouble."

"Look," Bix said, "like it or not, you got me involved seven months ago. You may not remember me, but up until a few hours ago, we were planning on heading to the altar in a couple of days. So if there's something going on here, like I said, I have the right to know."

After a moment, Caitlin said, "He's right again, Josh."

Josh grunted. "Hon, we don't know if this guy—"

"We have to fill him in."

Josh grunted again, then Caitlin recounted for Bix how she'd woken up—if it could be called that—at a warehouse last night, with blood on her clothes and a bag with a gun and half a dozen fake hands inside.

"Fake hands?"

Caitlin shrugged.

Bix seemed to consider that a moment. "And you don't remember anything before that?"

"Only . . . my life before Smithfield, including almost everything that happened in the days before I . . . disappeared, I guess."

Bix already knew that she didn't remember any of her life with him, but hearing it again stung nonetheless. "Nothing of the warehouse, though?" he asked. "Or how you got the gun? Or where the blood came from, or . . . the fake hands?"

She shook her head. "So what do you think?"

"Kind of sounds like you shot somebody."

"Sounds that way to me, too," Caitlin said in a quiet voice. Bix looked into the rearview mirror. Caitlin was gazing blankly out the side window at the passing storefronts, all of them dark at this late hour.

"But hey," Bix said, "if you did shoot someone, I'm sure you had a good reason. Self-defense or something like that."

Caitlin met his eyes in the mirror. "So you think I should turn myself in? Let the police investigate?"

"What?" he said. "God, no. Why the hell would you do that?"

"If I'm innocent," she said, "or if what I did was at least justified, they'd figure that out, right?"

"Katie, despite what Josh here probably thinks, I don't have anything against cops personally. I'm sure most of them do damn fine work. But on the off chance your case landed on the desk of one of the less dedicated or even less trustworthy officers of the law, the kind more interested in closing cases than in getting the right bad guy, I'd rather you not waltz into a police station and tell them you probably shot that guy in the warehouse but, gosh darn it, you just can't remember doing it."

"But—"

Bix shook his head. "This case would be a dream for them. They'd have a suspect, and physical evidence, and you'd give them the murder weapon, I'm sure. And not only don't you have an alibi, but you think you actually might have pulled the trigger. So how hard do you think they'd work to prove that it was self-defense? And with you not remembering anything and the dead guy dead, who's gonna tell the cops it wasn't your fault?"

After a moment, Caitlin said, "So what do we do?"

Bix looked into the mirror again. Caitlin was looking back at him. She looked so tired. Tired and scared. But mostly tired.

"For now, we go back to my place," he said. "You get some sleep. In the morning, we'll decide what to do next."

"Thanks, but we can find a motel," Josh said.

Bix nodded. "Sure you can. Is that what you want to do, Katie?"

After a moment, she said, "It's late. If Bix will let us stay there, I think we should. Besides, spending the night where I lived for seven months, surrounded by things that were once familiar to me . . . well, who knows? Maybe it will help me remember something."

Bix thought he could hear Josh's teeth grinding.

———

Bix dropped a blanket, two pillows, and a set of sheets on the sleep sofa in the second bedroom. "You sure you don't want to sleep in your own bed, Katie?" he asked, smiling. "More comfortable than this pullout."

Caitlin thought for sure that Josh would rise up and take the bait, but he let her answer, and his restraint surprised and impressed her. "No thanks, Bix," she said. To make Josh feel better—which Caitlin thought he deserved, given how hard this all must have been for him—she added, "Josh and I will be fine here."

"Well, I'm right across the hall if you need me for anything during the night," he added, looking at Caitlin with what was probably his most devilish smile.

"Thanks," Josh said with a smile of his own. "I'll be sure to let you know if I need anything."

Bix chuckled and closed the door behind him as he left.

"He's a dick," Josh said as he removed the cushions from the sofa and pulled out the bed. The mattress was thin, and the top and bottom rose a few inches from the frame as it tried to relax after God knew how long folded and crammed into the sofa.

"He's probably hurting a little," Caitlin said. "Or maybe he just feels like a fool. He may act like a tough guy, but this can't be any fun for him, either." She began putting the fitted sheet on the mattress. "And even though this is a lousy situation for him, he's helping us." She spread the top sheet over the fitted sheet, smoothed it out, and tucked it in at the bottom.

"He's helping you, not me," Josh said. "And he's still a dick."

Caitlin didn't have any other counterarguments, so she let it go. Josh took the other side of the blanket, and together they laid it on top of their bed. They each stuffed a pillow into a pillowcase, then finished getting ready for bed before sliding under the covers. Josh reached over to a wall switch and turned off the overhead light. Caitlin could see him in the dim moonlight leaking into the room between the slats of a venetian blind. He was lying on his back, his arms behind his head, staring at the ceiling.

"You okay?" she asked softly. She was on her side, facing him.

He turned his head toward her and frowned. "Stop worrying about me, okay? You shouldn't have to worry about anyone but yourself right now."

"Hey," she said, "this is affecting you, too."

"I know, but I don't want you worrying about me." After a moment, he added, "It's just that guy . . ."

"I know," she said.

"But I'm okay, hon," he said. "Really." He took his arm from behind his head, reached over, and rested his hand on her upper thigh. She liked the contact, so she scooted closer to him and laid her hand on his stomach. She heard a small intake of breath from him and realized that, while it seemed to her like just two days ago that they had slept in the same bed, shared this kind of physical intimacy, for Josh it was more than seven months. She considered sliding her hand lower on his belly, and lower still—he probably wanted her to, and she wouldn't blame him—but she was so very tired. Still, she loved him. She tried to imagine him spending all those nights alone in their bed. She looked into his eyes and moved her hand down past his belly button.

He kept one hand on her leg but reached down with his other and placed it over Caitlin's hand, stopping its movement. He held it tight.

"It's okay, honey," he said, smiling. "You get an A-plus for effort, but you're exhausted and we have the rest of our lives."

She smiled tiredly back at him, then slid even closer to him and closed her eyes. It had been a long day.

CHAPTER SIXTEEN

HUNNSAKER'S CELL PHONE WOKE HER. She pulled it from her pocket, groggily checked the time on its screen—2:23 a.m.—and answered the call. Someone apologized for calling her at that hour, then told her that he'd been informed that she wanted to be called immediately when a person of interest named Dominick Bruno had been located. Hunnsaker confirmed that she had indeed wanted to be so informed. The cop on the phone said he'd be arriving at the station with Bruno in about fifteen minutes. He asked whether Hunnsaker planned to come down to the station to interview him tonight or whether they should hold him until morning.

"I'll be there," Hunnsaker said.

She disconnected the call and stood up from the two chairs she had positioned opposite each other so she could sit in the first one and stretch her legs across to the second. With her head tipped back, she'd managed to catch almost two hours of sleep after Padilla finally went home for the night. She looked around the interview room, at the photos and reports, and realized she'd need another room in which to interview Bruno.

Less than half an hour later, Hunnsaker sat across an empty table from Dominick Bruno. In front of her was a small tape recorder, which she switched on.

Bruno wasn't handcuffed. He hadn't been Mirandized or even arrested. He was there voluntarily . . . or at least Hunnsaker wanted him to feel that way, and she made the voluntary nature of his visit to the station that night clear on the tape.

Bruno looked exactly like the kind of guy who spent his time sleeping while the sun was up, and drinking and wanking when the world grew dark. Midthirties, doughy physique, pasty-gray complexion. Even though the uniform watching the Pit Stop had spotted Bruno on his way into the place, it was evident to Hunnsaker, based on Bruno's smell and demeanor, that he'd already had a few beers somewhere that night.

She reminded him that he wasn't under arrest, that she just wanted to talk to him, that his cooperation would be appreciated, and all the other things she had to say to get him talking. The truth was, she didn't think he had killed Vic Warehouse, though she had to admit she wouldn't have been surprised to learn that he did. But her gut told her otherwise.

With the preliminaries out of the way, she explained why he had been invited by the police to come in for a nice, friendly chat.

"We found your fingerprints in the warehouse out on Demerest Road."

"They aren't mine," Bruno said as he sat slumped in his chair.

"They are, Dominick," Hunnsaker said. "All yours. We pulled them from several beer bottles and from some . . . reading material."

Bruno picked at a hangnail.

"So we know you've been there," Hunnsaker said. "That you spend time there."

He looked up. "Is that a crime? I guess it is, right? Trespassing, probably. That wouldn't get me jail time, though, right? So what's the big deal, then? I won't go back there. I swear."

"Relax, Dominick. I just want to talk about last night."

Bruno looked down quickly and went back to work on his hangnail.

"We know you were there last night," Hunnsaker bluffed.

"I didn't do anything wrong," he said quickly.

Hunnsaker almost smiled. He'd been there, all right. The question now was whether he'd seen or heard anything.

"Well, maybe and maybe not," she said. "You saw a crime and didn't report it. That's a crime in itself."

Also a bluff, at least with respect to Massachusetts law, but Hunnsaker was pretty sure Bruno wouldn't know that.

"You see a crime in this city," she continued, "you have an obligation to report it. Penalty for failure to do so is up to three years in jail."

Bruno was gnawing agitatedly at his hangnail now.

"Dominick?" Hunnsaker said. "Do I have to read you your rights?"

The last thing she wanted to do was read him his rights, reminding him that he could remain silent if he chose to do so and have an attorney present if he wanted one. Besides, she was lying about his having committed a crime, anyway. But her bluffs had paid off so far.

"I didn't see a crime," he said.

"But we know you saw something last night . . ."

He shook his head. She could see him wrestling with something, and she let him fight it out with himself for a minute. Finally, she lifted a pair of handcuffs into view and said, "Okay, put your hands on the table, please."

"Wait," Bruno said. "Hold on now. I said I didn't see a crime. I didn't say that I didn't see . . . something."

Again, Hunnsaker had to suppress a smile.

The Bogeyman was back. He loomed over Caitlin, staring down at her from twice her height, his dark little eyes glinting faintly in the moonlight. Caitlin screamed and tried to run, but the Bogeyman loped after her on legs almost as long as she was tall, and he caught her with ease. His clammy fingers crawled over her bare arms as he pulled her close and wrapped his own arms around her. The rotting garbage odor that clung to him filled her nostrils. She tried to fight, but his bear hug was too strong. His breath was hot on the back of her neck as he said, "You think I'm a monster?"

He had chased Caitlin through her nightmares for twenty years, speaking to her on some nights, pursuing her in terrifying silence on others, but he had never said those exact words before.

The Bogeyman tucked her under one arm and carried her toward a dark, yawning hole in the ground, a troll's lair or goblin's tunnel by the look of it. As she passed into its darkness, Caitlin knew if she went in too far she would never leave, never see the moon above ever again, or the stars, or the sun and sky. She had to get out now before she was too deep in the ground. She bit down hard on the Bogeyman's arm, feeling a greasy film between her lips, tasting salty sweat. The Bogeyman threw her to the floor in anger and she sprang to her feet and ran as fast as her feet would fly.

But which way to run? The mouth of the tunnel was nowhere in sight now. Nearly total darkness was everywhere. She ran, almost blind among the shadows, ran simply to get away. She passed empty shelves. She passed doors, not daring to slow down long enough to see what was on the other side of them. She ran and the footsteps followed fast behind her.

"Where's my pretty one?" he called as the distance shrank between them.

She reached a clearing among the shelves, an open space. She couldn't see beyond a dim circle around her. The footsteps were almost upon her. She whirled to face the Bogeyman and, as she did, felt a weight in her hand. She looked down and saw that she was holding a handgun. As the monster thundered toward her, arms outstretched, she raised the gun and fired, and the Bogeyman dropped to the cement floor.

For a long moment, Caitlin watched him lying on his back, waited for him to stir. When he didn't, she stepped closer, and closer still, then looked down at him. To her horror, she hadn't killed the Bogeyman. This man was young and fair-haired and completely average-looking—but for the bullet hole in his cheek, even though Caitlin thought she'd fired at his stomach. She dropped the gun.

The Bogeyman's voice came from right behind her. "You think I'm a monster?" It sounded to Caitlin as though he had emphasized the word *I'm*, implying that *she* was the true monster here. The Bogeyman spun her around and lifted her up into a strong embrace. They were chest-to-chest, face-to-face, Caitlin crushed against him, him staring into her eyes. He smiled and opened his mouth and something squirmed inside it and—

Caitlin opened her eyes and barely managed to stifle a scream. She was still in bed, on her side, facing Josh from just inches away. He was on his side, too. His eyes were closed and his mouth was slightly open, allowing a gentle snore to slip from his lips. One of his arms was draped across her hip. She slid gently from beneath it, rolled onto her back, and took a few calming breaths. She was relieved that she'd been able to keep from screaming herself awake. This wouldn't have been the first time she'd thrashed herself out of a nightmare, startling Josh from his own pleasant, Bogeyman-free slumber, but this had been the most detailed, most terrifying dream yet.

She stared at the ceiling, not bothering to close her eyes. There wasn't much chance of her falling back to sleep anytime soon, and she wasn't even certain she wanted to.

Bix stared at the dark ceiling of his room. Even though Katie—that is, Caitlin—wasn't beside him, he stayed on his own side of the bed, leaving her side, the one she'd occupied for seven months of his life, empty. Over the past couple of hours, as he tried to fall asleep, he'd find that his arm had reached out to her side on its own, seeking contact with her. Every time, it was disappointed, as was he.

Everything had changed in a matter of hours. For the second time in a year, his life turned upside down. Earlier this year, he was a man who had never had a serious relationship in his thirty-two years of life. He hadn't been avoiding that; the right woman had just never come along. And he hadn't expected her to. He was fine with that. Then seven months ago, Katie walked into a pub as if her name were on the deed to the place, even though she'd never set foot in there, and Bix's days of waiting for someone he hadn't realized he was waiting for were over.

And though it took him a few days to admit to himself where things were going, once he realized it, he jumped onboard and hung on tight. He didn't care that she was hiding something. He didn't care that she might have had a past that left her holding some heavy baggage. He was willing to let her reinvent herself, to tell him as much or as little as she wanted to share, because he knew she wasn't holding back her feelings for him. He'd let her lie about everything else if she wanted, but he could tell she wasn't lying when she said she loved him. She wasn't faking the smiles, the laughter, the intimacy. Whatever else was false about her, their feelings for each other were genuine, and that was enough for him.

Until this morning, when she showed up at the door with her husband and no memory of Bix or their life together. Now he had to just lie there and think about the fact that his fiancée was in the room across the hall with her husband, and about how, as soon as Bix helped Caitlin with whatever she needed—and he had to help her, he knew that—she would be gone from his life forever.

Getting back to sleep at the moment seemed unlikely, so he rolled out of bed, slipped into a pair of sweatpants so that neither of his housemates would see him strolling to the kitchen naked if they decided to take a leak in the next few minutes, and opened the door to his room. As he reached the kitchen, he caught movement out of the corner of his eye. He turned quickly and saw a silhouette sitting on the sofa in the dark living room.

"Katie?" he said softly.

"It's me," she whispered.

He took a few steps toward her. "You all right?"

"Just a nightmare," she said. "I'm okay."

He walked over and sat at the far end of the sofa so that she wouldn't mistake his intentions. "The Bogeyman again?"

Her face was in shadow, but he could tell she was looking at him.

"You know about him?" she asked.

"You woke up from more than a few of those in our bed."

She nodded. "I guess it really is true, then. I lived here. With you. All that time."

"You didn't believe me?"

"No, I did. It's just . . . strange, you know? All of that happened and I don't remember any of it."

There it was again. The sting Bix felt from another reminder of that fact. Another dagger in the heart. "You really don't remember *anything*, Katie?" he asked. "Not a single thing?"

"No. I'm sorry."

"Me, too."

It was so hard to believe. It was the stuff of fiction, of soap operas and movies. Maybe you came across a story about it now and then and you thought, *Wow, that really happens?* But if it did happen, it never happened to you or anyone you knew. Until it did.

"I see the pictures," she said, "of us together. We look . . . happy."

"We are," Bix said. "I mean, we were."

"We look . . . in love."

"We . . . were. Totally."

"How does someone forget that?"

Bix was wondering the same thing.

"Can I ask you a favor?" he said. "It's a big one and I'll completely understand if you say no."

After a slight hesitation, she said, "Sure."

"Can I kiss you?" She said nothing, so he added, "I'm not trying to make a move on you. I swear to God. I know you wouldn't be interested. And I know your husband's right in the next room. I just . . . I'm wondering if maybe you'll remember something if we kiss. Probably not, but . . ."

"Like in a fairy tale?" Caitlin asked.

"Hold on a sec. Wouldn't one of us be a frog or something in that fairy tale?"

"That would be you."

"I'm offended. But I promise not to hold it against you if you kiss me."

"Bix . . ."

"One kiss. Maybe it will spark something . . . a memory, I mean," he added quickly.

It was true. He thought there was at least a chance she'd remember something, that an act of physical intimacy might do what mere words hadn't been able to. And he had promised to help her, after all. If she remembered everything, she would presumably find closure. Of course, once she did remember everything, she'd go back to her old life, with her old husband, and she'd be gone forever—assuming she wasn't imprisoned for murder. But maybe, just *maybe*, once her memory returned completely, she'd remember how good things were with Bix and she'd consider sticking around and giving life with him a try. It was a long shot, he knew, but you can't win if you don't play. Also, he had to admit, if Caitlin did leave with Josh forever, then Bix wanted one more kiss.

"It doesn't have to be an epic kiss, Katie, something out of a romantic movie or anything like that. Just a little kiss. Who knows? It might help. And if it doesn't . . . well, what can it hurt?"

"I'm married."

"I know. You're also engaged. You and I had been . . . with each other for seven months. Would one kiss make that big a difference? Up until this morning, I was your fiancé. Don't I deserve at least a kiss good-bye?"

Bix couldn't see her face, couldn't tell if he had gotten through to her. Then she moved closer to him on the couch. He met her halfway and reached up and touched her hair. She put her hand on his face. It was warm and soft on his cheek. He leaned forward and she did, too, and their lips touched softly. As deeply as they had been in love—and there wasn't a shred of doubt in him that they *had* been in love—this kiss was the most tender they had ever shared. Her lips were soft and welcoming and he didn't want this to end. Too soon, she sat back, though she kept her hand on his cheek for a few moments longer. Her head had turned a little, or the moon had moved in the sky, and he could see her eyes now in its dim light. They looked a little sad. His probably did, too.

He didn't bother to ask if she remembered anything. He figured he'd have been able to tell by her kiss whether she did. She stood, touched his shoulder gently, and said, "I'm sorry."

She walked back to her room. Bix sat in the darkness for a while longer.

CHAPTER SEVENTEEN

CHARLOTTE HUNNSAKER TOOK A SIP of coffee, already her second cup of the morning and it wasn't yet nine a.m. Then she lifted a sheet of paper from the table and taped it to the whiteboard, right next to the photo of Vic Warehouse with his dead, vacant eyes and the bullet hole in his face.

"There's our victim, looking less dead," she said, indicating the second sheet of paper. On it was a richly detailed, computer-generated rendering of Vic's face the way it no doubt would have looked before it had acquired a bullet hole. The image had been created by someone in the department—a technician far more skilled at such things than Hunnsaker—using FaceFirst, the latest and greatest facial-composite computer software available to law-enforcement personnel. The program's database contained nearly five thousand facial features and, when employed by someone skilled in its use, could create incredibly accurate portraits of people of either gender and any race.

Hunnsaker's sketch of a still-living Vic—even though it had been created on a computer rather than drawn by hand, she couldn't help but think of the image as a "sketch"—had captured his face as it had almost certainly looked when he was still breathing. The bullet hole was gone, of course, and his eyes were full of life. The computer artist had given him an expression that might have been saying any number of things, but which mostly said, *I'm not dead. I look very much alive. So if you recognize me, please tell the cops who I am.* Hunnsaker planned to have the news media get this photo out and see what the police got in return.

"That's a great job," Padilla said. "Looks so lifelike, like he might open up his mouth and start talking."

Hunnsaker said, "That would be really helpful. If he does, ask him his name. And who shot him."

She picked up another sheet of paper and taped it next to the sketch of the victim. It was a second computer-generated sketch by the same technician, though far less detailed than the first. That was to be expected. For the sketch of Vic, the tech had been able to work from photographs. For this one, he'd had to rely on the drunken recollection of a homeless man.

"That's her, huh?" Padilla said.

Hunnsaker nodded. Dominick Bruno had tried his best to describe the girl or woman he'd seen hurrying past his closet two nights ago, but he was admittedly very drunk when he saw her. According to Bruno, he'd been drinking heavily—but *not* masturbating—that night. He might even have passed out at some point. Either way, he was drifting in and out much of the night, and it was hard to keep track of things. It was all sort of jumbled for him, he said. All he knew was that he heard voices and something loud that could have been a gunshot, but he didn't know which had come first or how many voices he heard or even how many gunshots there were. He knew he should have gotten the hell out of there, but he was "piss-ass drunk" and didn't think he'd be able to stand up, much less walk. So he'd pulled the blanket up above his nose and tried to keep his eyes open. And that was when he saw her. She was only a shadow at first in the dark warehouse, moving quickly toward him, feeling along the wall as though searching for an exit. When she came to the door near the closet, she opened it, and when the thin moonlight spilled in from outside, Bruno got a quick look at her. Average height, cute, with short red hair. Then she was gone, and Bruno covered his head and tried to look like a pile of blankets until he could sleep this off. When he awakened early the next morning, he left. He said he didn't search the warehouse or see the body. He just got out of there as soon as he could, leaving by the same door the woman had used the night before.

"Not a bad sketch," Padilla said. "A little more detail would be helpful, but it's good."

"Bruno said it looks a lot like her, only—and these are his words, not mine—you can't see her rack in the drawing, which is too bad because he thought it was nice. Not too big, but just right, in his opinion."

"You sure he wasn't describing a girl from one of his skin magazines?"

"I know you're joking, but I actually looked at those magazines he left behind to see if any of the women in them matched his description of the girl he saw, just in case he got confused."

"You should have asked for my help with that," Padilla said.

"You can have them when the case is over."

"Fair enough. And what did you learn from looking at the girlie mags?"

"That I need to go on a diet," Hunnsaker said. "Also, that none of the women had short red hair. So assuming his description is accurate, it narrows things down a bit for us."

"Did you get these sketches to the papers in time for the morning editions?"

"I did. Just barely. And the local news stations will show them periodically throughout the day."

"Well," Padilla said, "we'll see if Bruno's description does us any good. Hopefully someone who isn't a crackpot calls in."

"Bruno already did us good. We know this woman exists now. She was there. Maybe she's a witness, maybe the shooter. Either way, I bet you dinner at DeSouza's," she said, naming the current trendiest and most expensive restaurant in town, "when we find her, we close this case."

———

Caitlin was quiet at breakfast. Josh thought she still looked tired, though she should have gotten a good seven hours of sleep. Thankfully, she didn't seem to have suffered one of her nightmares, at least not that he felt in the night. Still, she was picking at her scrambled eggs without enthusiasm. Bix had made them, and Josh had to admit that they were pretty good. It was the Tabasco sauce, Bix said. Josh didn't care. There was no way he'd ever make eggs that way for Caitlin, so he didn't give a damn how they were prepared. He couldn't help but remember yesterday morning, when he had made a terrible omelet for Caitlin. Despite his feelings about Bix and his eggs, he ate . . . though he tried not to enjoy the food despite how good it was.

The three of them sat at Bix's kitchen table, each eating while apparently lost in his or her own thoughts. Josh saw Bix sneak a glance at Caitlin, but she didn't look up from her plate. Finally, Josh spoke. "There's something I wanted to talk about last night, but you were too tired, Caitlin."

Caitlin and Bix looked at him.

"At dinner, while you guys were trying to see if Caitlin remembered anything or anyone in the restaurant, I was looking around the web some more."

"Yeah?" Bix said with his mouth full of Tabasco-covered egg. "What'd you learn?"

"I think I know what Caitlin experienced."

"I thought it was amnesia," Bix said.

"It is," Josh said. "It was, I mean. Sort of. It's more than that, though."

"Was?" Caitlin said. "I can't remember anything, so aren't I still suffering from amnesia?"

With his tablet on the table next to his plate in case he needed it for reference, Josh said, "I'm pretty sure you experienced something called a fugue state, or at least that's one name for it. Or *was*, anyway. It's also called a dissociative fugue. The terminology seems to change now and then. Actually, I think the current proper technical terminology is 'dissociative state with dissociative fugue.'"

"Damn, Josh, who cares what it's called?" Bix asked. "Just tell us what it is." He shoveled another load of eggs into his mouth.

"According to what I found, it seems that Caitlin suffered from generalized amnesia—"

"Generalized?" Caitlin asked.

"That means it was amnesia relating to identity or life history," Josh said, "not for specific events, which would be considered localized or selective amnesia."

"Okay," Bix said. "She suffered from amnesia. I think we knew that."

"There's more," Josh said. "With this specific thing, this dissociative fugue, the person not only loses her memory and her knowledge of herself, but she might travel to a new place and set up an entirely new identity somewhere."

"Sounds familiar," Bix said.

"That's a real thing?" Caitlin asked, and Josh thought he almost heard relief in her voice, as if despite suffering through such an unusual and frustrating experience, she was happy to know that she wasn't just plain crazy.

"It is," Josh replied. "In fact, what differentiates a diagnosis of a fugue state or dissociative fugue or whatever from more common amnesia is the fact that the person traveled or wandered off. Now, this isn't a common occurrence by any stretch, and verified cases of it are rare, but it has definitely happened. It can last as short as a few hours, where people just pick up without warning and wander off for part of a day, but it can also last for days, months, or in the rarest cases, it could be years before they somehow remember who they used to be."

"So they suddenly just walk out of their lives," Caitlin began, "move somewhere new, and then . . . reinvent themselves there?"

He nodded. "And while they are in their new identities, they are fully functioning. They establish new relationships"—Josh couldn't help but steal a glance at Bix—"make new friends, get jobs, whatever."

"Then they just . . . wake up?"

"I'm not sure. No one seems to know exactly what makes them come out of a fugue state. It could be . . ."

"What?" Caitlin asked.

"Well, like I said, no one knows for sure, but there are theories. It could be seeing something small, something that reminds them enough of their former life. Or . . . well, some experts think that a traumatic event of some kind could snap a person out of a dissociative fugue, especially if it somehow relates to whatever put them in that state in the first place."

"Like what?"

Josh shrugged. "I don't know. Something pretty big, I'd guess."

"And that's what causes a fugue state?" she asked. "A traumatic event?"

"Well, remember, the condition is rare, so there aren't a lot of cases to go by. But that seems to be one of the main causes."

Caitlin chewed on that for a moment. Josh waited. Finally, she said, "I don't remember anything traumatic happening to me before I . . . went away. You said we had an argument and then . . . you said

I left the house, right? You didn't know where I was, so you called our friends."

"That's right, hon," Josh said.

"So maybe something happened to me after I left. Something traumatic."

"Maybe," he said. *That* has *to be the case,* he thought. She'd been completely lucid when she walked out after their argument, so it *had* to be something that happened to her after she left.

"I sure as heck don't remember anything like that," Caitlin said.

"From what I read, you might never remember it, if that's what happened. Or it could come back to you one day, either all at once or a little at a time."

"So I might remember? Heck, if it was bad enough to screw with my head like it did, do I even want to remember that part? I'd like to remember what happened after that, though. Will I?"

Josh could understand Caitlin wanting to fill in the huge gap in her memory—anyone would want that—but he had to admit that, selfishly, he wouldn't mind if her time with Bix was lost to her forever. And it probably would be, to be honest.

"From what I read, hon," Josh said, "you're unlikely to remember that. You should remember almost everything about your life before your fugue state, except maybe whatever triggered it—though that could come back to you, too—but what happened over the past seven months . . . it will probably be like those days never happened for you."

"They happened," Bix said firmly.

"I'm not saying they didn't," Josh said. "I'm just saying that it's like the memories of those days are in a box she might never unlock. At least that's how a psychologist described it in one of the articles I read."

"But she remembered how to play pool," Bix replied. "You said she didn't know how before. But I taught her and she remembered."

Caitlin suddenly looked hopeful.

Josh shrugged. "Muscle memory, maybe. All I know is what I've read, what the experts say, what has been the experience in the reported cases so far. And everything I've read indicates that she's probably not going to remember anything about this place."

Bix looked over at Caitlin, who was looking down at the table now. He nodded, stood, and took his plate to the sink. Then he busied himself with clearing the table, scraping food scraps into the trash, and washing their dishes. While he did that, Josh looked at Caitlin. She was staring out a window at the next-door neighbor's weed-choked backyard.

"Okay," she said quietly. "Maybe I won't remember anything or . . . anyone here. But I still need to know what I did. Even if I don't remember things, they still happened. There's a man who's dead and I might have killed him. If so, I need to know why. And even if I didn't do that, I still want to know what I did here, what I was doing all that time, what I did when I wasn't around Bix . . . even if I'll never remember it, I want to know. I want to fill in the blanks. No, I *need* to."

"And I'll do everything I can to help you do that, hon," Josh said.

Bix turned off the water, finished drying a plate, and said, "I will, too."

"Really?" Caitlin said, turning his way. "I thought maybe . . ."

"You need my help," Bix said. "You have no idea where to go or who to talk to in this town. You don't know where you've been or anything you've done. I don't know everything you did, either, but I know some of it. And I'll help you as much as I can."

Josh actually found himself grateful to hear that. He loved Caitlin and wanted her whole again, and if Bix could help with that, Josh wouldn't stand in the way. Besides, he had to admit that he felt just a tiny bit sorry for Bix. Sure, the guy had taken up with

Caitlin, but he hadn't known that she was someone else's wife, not for certain, anyway. And the poor bastard was obviously in love with her. One day they were headed to the altar, the next she was married to another man. Josh couldn't help but pity the guy a little.

Then Bix said, "Hell, Katie, maybe spending more time with me will make you realize how terrific I am and you'll change your mind about heading back to New Hampshire with good old Josh here when this is all over."

Then the sonofabitch smiled and threw Josh a wink, and Josh no longer felt sorry for him.

CHAPTER EIGHTEEN

CHOPS POURED THE PANCAKE BATTER into the shape of a big letter *J*, which he knew his daughter would recognize. She loved when he made Juliacakes for her. Chops wasn't a cook by any stretch of the imagination, but he also wasn't an idiot, so he was more than capable of mixing together ingredients in a just-add-water pancake mix. He watched tiny bubbles form and pop on the surface of the pancake and knew when to flip it over. A minute later he slid the J-cake onto a plate, poured a little syrup beside it, and slid the plate in front of his daughter. She clapped her hands and said the letter *J* with delight in her voice, then picked up the pancake, dipped it in the syrup, and started eating.

"Really good, Daddy," she said.

Chops figured she mostly tasted the syrup, but he acknowledged her compliment by ruffling her hair. He poured apple juice into a sippy cup and put it beside her plate. Then his cell phone rang, as he'd known it would soon.

"It's six thirty in the morning here in California," he said by way of a greeting. He listened for a moment. "I know. He didn't call me back, either . . . Yeah, I hear you . . . I'll fly out there like I promised. And when I find him shacking up with some girl or coming down off of some shit, I'll kick his ass."

"Bad words, Daddy," Julia said.

"Sorry, pumpkin," he said to her.

Chops heard footsteps upstairs and poured batter onto the griddle for two more pancakes, this time opting for the traditional circular shape.

Into the phone, he said, "Listen, I gotta go. Just relax, will you? This isn't the first time he hasn't called you for a day, is it? . . . Oh, well, I'm sure he's fine. I'll come back there and track him down."

He dropped two slices of bread into the toaster—he knew how to make toast, too—and poured a glass of orange juice for Rachel.

"Relax, I'll be there when I can. There's something I have to do this morning, then I'll get on a plane . . . No, it can't wait. I'll call you when I find him."

He disconnected the call and stuffed his phone into his pocket as his wife shuffled into the kitchen in her pajamas and slippers.

"I knew I smelled pancakes," she said.

"They're Juliacakes," Julia said with her mouth full of pancake.

"I stand corrected," Rachel said. "You're up early again today," she said to Chops.

"Something came up."

"Oh?"

He slid the pancakes onto her plate, added the toast from the toaster, and set the meal down in front of Rachel. He sat across from her.

"You're gonna kill me," he said. "I really hate to miss the circus tonight, but I have to fly back to Massachusetts today. There's something I have to take care of, and it can't wait."

———

Caitlin stood in front of the mirror in Bix's bathroom, her hair wet, a towel wrapped around her, tucked into itself above her chest so it wouldn't fall. She still wasn't used to seeing that slightly thinner face framed by short red hair staring back at her. She scrutinized her reflection. She smiled, just to test it out. It wasn't a bad look on her, actually. Not the appearance she was used to, the one she'd had for the first twenty-seven years of her life, but she had to admit that she was pulling it off pretty well.

Without thinking, she opened the left-hand drawer of the vanity and found a big comb and a hairbrush, along with various cosmetics. She paused. There were four drawers in the vanity, two on either side, and she'd found the one she was looking for on the first try. Could she have somehow remembered it? More likely, it was a lucky guess. The upper left-hand drawer was the same one in which she kept her hairbrush at home, so that was probably why she instinctively tried it first. It may have even been the reason she had chosen to keep her things in the same drawer here at Bix's place. She probably remembered it subconsciously. Still . . . maybe she had actually *remembered* it, despite Josh saying that she might never recover her memories from the last seven months. How had he said it at breakfast? It's like that period of time is in a box she might never unlock.

Something struck her, a flash of . . . well, something, but she couldn't immediately put her finger on what it was. She frowned as she took her hairbrush from the drawer and started dragging it through her wet hair. Something had flitted through her mind but disappeared before she got a good look at it. What was it she had almost seen?

Then she had it. Josh had said her time here in Smithfield was like a box she might never unlock.

A box.

She left the bathroom and walked into Bix's room without knocking, pushing open the door that had been ajar. Bix was bare-chested and buttoning a pair of faded jeans. Caitlin couldn't help but notice a bit of chiseling of the muscles of his chest, abdomen, and arms. He wasn't buffed or ripped—terms Josh's friends used. Nor would Caitlin describe his physique the way romance authors did in their novels—which Caitlin didn't read often but which she had to admit she skimmed from time to time—using phrases like "steely contours," "titillatingly muscled," or "smoothly rippled." No, Caitlin simply thought it was precisely the kind of body she'd want if she were a man—not ostentatiously muscular but lean and solid and, yes, chiseled in the right places.

He smiled at her. After a moment, she blurted, "Sorry. Should have knocked."

"Don't worry about it," Bix said. "Want me to hold your towel for you?"

She laughed in spite of herself. "Thanks, but I've got it."

"Caitlin?" It was Josh's voice, coming from behind her. He must have heard her leave the bathroom.

"Hey, there," she said, turning.

"Am I interrupting?" Josh asked.

"Well, if you must know . . ." Bix said.

"Of course not," Caitlin said quickly.

Josh looked over at Bix. "You out of clean shirts? Need to borrow one?"

"Not sure yours would fit, Josh, but thanks."

"Would you please put a shirt on, Bix?" Caitlin asked.

"Says the girl wearing nothing but a towel," Bix said, smiling, as he lifted a folded T-shirt from the bed and slipped into it. "Now, does everyone feel—"

"Caitlin, what the hell is that?" Josh said suddenly.

"What?"

"On your hip."

She followed his gaze down to where the towel she had wrapped around herself had opened an inch or two. She turned away from

Bix and parted the towel a little more. Josh, who could still see what he had been looking at a moment ago, asked, "Is that a tattoo?"

"Sure looks like one," Caitlin said, recognizing the image at once. "It's a Wild Thing."

"A Wild Thing?"

"From *Where the Wild Things Are*."

"Exactly," Bix said, though he wouldn't have been able to see the tattoo from where he was standing. "You said it was your favorite book as a little girl."

And it was. Written decades ago by Maurice Sendak, it both frightened and delighted her in equal measures as a child. In it, a boy named Max wreaks havoc in his home and talks back to his mother and so is sent to his bedroom, which mysteriously transforms into a forest, and which somehow contains an ocean on which Max sails to an island inhabited by strange beasts he calls "Wild Things." He becomes their king but grows bored and misses his home, so he leaves the island, to the dismay of the Wild Things. When he sails home again to his own room, he finds a warm supper waiting for him.

As much as Caitlin loved the story, it was the creatures that kept her entranced. There were several Wild Things, and they all looked like monsters of one kind or another. The one adorning Caitlin's hip had a broad, semi-smiling mouth with a row of short fangs running from one side to the other, yellow eyes, light-colored fur, and claw-toed bird feet. Caitlin's eyes were particularly drawn to the creature's wavy hair, which looked to be the same shade of red as her own. She had to admit that she kind of liked the tattoo.

"Seriously?" Josh said. "You got a tattoo?"

"Sure she did," Bix said. "We both did."

He pulled up his shirt and turned so they could see the tattoo on the back of his shoulder. Bix's Wild Thing looked a lot like a Minotaur from Greek mythology, which was depicted with the head of a bull and the body of a man. Sendak's Wild Thing version was a bit different, though. It had a bull's head and stood erect like a man, but its entire body was covered in blue-gray fur—except for its big, naked human feet.

"Nice work, huh?" Bix said as he tugged down his shirt. "My little Wild Thing," he added, smiling at Caitlin.

"Not anymore, Bix," Josh said. "So what's going on in here?"

Caitlin took a last look at her own tattoo, then turned back to the men. She'd forgotten for a moment the reason she'd barged in on Bix.

"You said that before we sold the car I came here in, you dumped everything from it in a box."

"Yeah, it's in the closet," Bix said as he stepped over to the closet and slid open one of the doors. He reached up and took a cardboard box down from the shelf. It was a little bigger than a shoebox. He put it on the bed.

"There could be answers inside," she said as she sat down next to it.

"Whoa, there," Josh said.

Caitlin glanced up, then followed Josh's gaze to her thighs, where her towel had ridden up, exposing most of her legs and, she feared, a little too much beyond that. She quickly adjusted the towel before Bix could see anything private, though she realized a moment later that it hardly mattered. Still . . .

"Could you guys give me a minute or two here?" she asked.

"Sure," Bix said.

They closed the door behind them as they left. Caitlin removed the lid of the box and peered inside.

———

Bix sat in the armchair in his living room with his head tipped back, his legs sticking out in front of him, crossed at the ankles. He had his eyes closed so he wouldn't have to make eye contact with Josh, who was sitting on the couch doing something on his tablet. Even though Bix had been sleeping with the guy's wife, he resented the hell out of Josh. It didn't matter to him that Josh had been with Katie for years before Bix ever met her. Bix loved her. And even though she didn't remember being in love with Bix, the fact was, she *had* loved him. There was no doubt about it. And deep inside, he believed she'd remember that one day—maybe not in time for her to decide to stay with him, but she'd remember.

Bix's thoughts wandered to the film *Cast Away*, in which Tom Hanks gets stuck on a deserted island for four years. The only thing that sustains him during that time, that gives him the strength and will to survive and ultimately risk his life to be saved, is a photograph of his girlfriend and the thought of reuniting with her one day. And miraculously, years later he makes it back to her, only to find that he's been presumed dead by everyone and his girl is married to another man. For four years he thought of nothing but her, but she had moved on, started a whole new life. She's happy again. So Tom has to let her go.

Bix and Katie had rented the movie a few months ago, and he remembered being pissed off for Tom. She was with *him* first. He was the goddamn star of the movie. When he came home, she should have left the second guy. It occurred to Bix now that Josh was a little like good old Tom in the movie, having lost his wife for a long time before getting her back. It was Bix who was the second man. Josh reuniting with Katie was like the happy Hollywood ending Bix had wanted for Tom Hanks. It didn't seem so happy, though, when Bix was on the losing end.

He heard his bedroom door open and Katie came down the hall, the cardboard box in her hands.

"What are you wearing?" Josh asked.

"Oh," she said, looking down at herself. "I was in Bix's room in nothing but my towel, so I threw on some of my old clothes. I mean . . . the clothes I wore when I was . . ." She trailed off.

"You look good, honey," Josh said.

It was probably the first thing Josh had said with which Bix agreed. Katie looked amazing. Gone were the shapeless sweatshirt and department-store blue jeans. As she stood in the middle of the room, the morning sunlight seemed drawn to her as if according to some previously unknown law of nature. She absolutely glowed. Her hair was still sexy damp. She wore a pair of stylish jeans that fit her in a way that would make store mannequins jealous, topped off by a thin belt with cool, feminine little silver studs. Above that, a tiny sliver of her belly showed below a tight blouse that was short in the waist and the sleeves, coming down only just below her elbows, and was cut so that it was open enough in the neck to show a perfect amount of cleavage—not enough to make her look like a hooker, but enough to draw your eyes and hold them for longer than was polite.

"There's the Katie I know," Bix said, grinning. For the first time since she had appeared on his porch and announced that she was actually married to another man, Caitlin looked like Katie again. She looked fantastic. But as much as Bix enjoyed seeing her like this, it felt bittersweet. He was reminded yet again about all he was losing.

"Seriously, Caitlin," Josh said, "you look great."

"That always was my favorite shirt on you," Bix said.

"Of course it was," Josh said.

"Okay, guys, thanks," she said, suddenly seeming uncomfortable under their scrutiny. "But let's forget about my clothes for a second."

She crossed to the couch and sat beside Josh with the box in her lap. She removed the lid and pulled out a wrinkled piece of light-blue paper.

"What's that?" Josh asked.

"I think," Caitlin said, "that this is the reason I came to Smithfield."

"It looks like a takeout menu," Josh said.

"It is. For the Fish Place."

"I know you said the steak tips were good there," Josh said, "but you think you started a new life just to try them?"

"Do you remember where in the car you found this, Bix?" Caitlin asked.

He thought for a moment. "I think it was right on the seat, along with some garbage. To be honest, I thought you were a bit of a pig, Katie. That menu was there, along with some empty water bottles and old food wrappers."

"You mean these?" Caitlin asked as she removed three plastic water bottles, empty and hand-crushed, and a crumpled ball of fast-food wrapper.

"Yeah, that's it."

"You didn't throw the garbage away?" Josh asked.

"Like I said, before we traded in her car, I dumped everything I could find into a box and set it aside. When we got home, I just stuck it in the closet and forgot about it."

"Why do you think that menu is the reason you came to Smithfield?" Josh asked.

"I figured it might have been right there on the seat when I got in the car," Caitlin said, "and Bix just confirmed that. I probably saw it, saw the address, and drove straight there . . . which makes sense, because Bix says it's where we met."

"Okay," Josh said, "but how did you find the place? If you had just entered a fugue state, I doubt you were thinking very clearly."

"The car had a plug-in GPS mounted on the dash," Bix offered.

"But is it possible I could have programmed in the address in whatever frame of mind I was in?" Caitlin asked.

Josh considered that. "My first thought was that it might have been tough for you, but they say you can be fully functioning in a fugue state, so I guess you could. Anything else in there?"

Caitlin took items out of the box one by one as she listed them. "A couple of CDs—Iron Maiden and Anthrax—a roll of duct tape, a small pouch of tools . . . looks like a pair of pliers and a couple of screwdrivers . . . a cigarette lighter and half a pack of cigarettes."

"I forgot about the cigarettes," Bix said. "You don't smoke, Katie."

"I think we've established that this wasn't Katie's car, Bix," Josh said. "These are obviously the real owner's things."

Bix looked at the collection of items on the couch beside Caitlin. He hadn't given much thought to them when he'd boxed them up, but now that he knew the car hadn't been Caitlin's, that the vehicle and the items inside had belonged to someone else, they started to look a little different to him, taking on new meaning. Duct tape, food wrappers, empty water bottles, cigarettes . . . They looked like things someone might bring on a stakeout. And the presence of the duct tape gave that stakeout a sinister feel.

Caitlin took another item from the box. It was a small notepad, the kind that could fit in the palm of a hand.

"Was that in the box?" he asked.

Caitlin nodded. "Sure."

Bix frowned. "I know it's been a while since I put that stuff in there, and I know I forgot about the cigarettes, but I definitely don't remember that notepad."

Caitlin flipped open the cover. From where he sat, Bix could see handwriting on the top page.

"What's it say?" he asked.

"It's a list," Caitlin said.

"That looks like your handwriting," Josh pointed out.

"It is."

"What's on the list?" Bix asked.

"Names," Caitlin said. "Well, sort of, I guess." She stared down at the notepad in silence for a moment, then said, "The first one is Bogeyman."

"Bogeyman?" Josh said. "Seriously? Is that the Bogeyman from your nightmares, do you think?"

"No, Josh," Bix said. "It's the real Bogeyman."

Josh ignored that. "Caitlin?"

Caitlin shook her head. "I have no idea. I still have nightmares about him all the time, but I have no idea why I would write a list with him on it."

"What are the other names?" Bix asked.

Caitlin read, "One-Eyed Jack and Bob."

"Bob?" Bix said. "Doesn't really seem to fit with Bogeyman and One-Eyed Jack, does it?"

"There's also something that looks like an address," Caitlin said. "1108 Greendale Boulevard. Next to it, in parentheses, it says, 'Ten to four.'"

"Sounds like a business address, maybe," Josh said. "And those are the hours it's open. You know where that is, Bix?"

Bix thought for a moment. "I know the general area. It's near the brewery on the other side of the city. Not a great part of town. No idea what business might be at that address, though."

"It's something we need to check out," Caitlin said. "And last but not least, there's this," she said as she took a stack of paper money from the box.

"Whoa," Bix said. "That definitely wasn't there when I put that box in the closet. How much is it?"

"Twelve hundred dollars."

Bix frowned. "Why were you hiding that from me?"

"Guess you don't know her as well as you think," Josh said, taking evident pleasure from that fact.

Without taking his eyes off Caitlin and the money, Bix gave Josh the finger.

"This is weird," Caitlin said, looking down at the things she had removed from the box. "Bix says he put this box in the closet seven months ago and this notepad and the money weren't in it. That means that sometime since then, I wrote this list and hid it in the box, along with twelve hundred bucks. Why would I do that?"

Bix couldn't help but feel that she had hidden the list specifically from him. And the money, too.

"Well, we have a few clues now," Josh said, "for whatever they're worth. Make sure you bring that notepad with us today."

"And the money," Bix said. "We may need it for . . . whatever." As Caitlin stuffed the bills into a front pocket, he added, "Let's get going."

The restaurant where Caitlin worked was still their first stop. Hopefully, someone there would tell them something helpful. Bix wasn't optimistic. In his experience, nobody really helped anybody with anything if they could avoid it, especially when doing so required the sharing of information. And sadly, it looked like the three of them were going to need a lot of help.

CHAPTER NINETEEN

HUNNSAKER WAS HUNCHED OVER HER desk with the *Boston Globe* and the *Smithfield Beacon* in front of her, both newspapers open to stories about the warehouse shooting. Apparently, the murder was already old news to the editors of both papers, having occurred as long ago as yesterday morning, because neither of the articles was featured prominently, meriting only a few inches of column space toward the back of the local news sections. But they did print the sketches of both the victim and the redheaded "person of interest," as Hunnsaker had requested she be labeled, along with more detailed physical descriptions. Now it was time to see how many calls from nutjobs and cranks they would have to sift through to find out if anyone out there actually had useful information. Someone must have seen the victim. Someone must know the redhead. The question was, would they see the sketches? And even if they did, would they call the cops?

———

Martin Donnello sat at the counter and picked at his omelet. It was a little late for breakfast but still a bit early for lunch, and he wasn't all that hungry anyway. But he knew he should eat something. He hadn't slept much since everything went wrong at the warehouse the night before last. Guns came out, Donnello's partner seemed to have gotten himself shot, and then that damn redhead led them on a chase before somehow getting away. Donnello had spent most of his time since then looking for her. He wished he'd gotten a better look at her. He wasn't even sure he'd know her if he saw her again.

His eggs had grown cold, so he dropped his fork and picked up a piece of sausage and took a bite. He was so lost in thought about the shit that went down the other night that he almost didn't hear the old guys talking behind him. He wasn't sure what it was that had snagged his attention, but when he tuned in to the old guys' conversation, he grew interested.

"'Person of interest,' they call her," one of the old men said.

"I could get interested in her person," the other said, causing them both to chuckle.

"What the hell was she doing in an abandoned warehouse in the middle of the night?"

"Probably a hooker."

"I'd pay for some of that."

"You'd *have* to pay. Nobody's gonna give a dried-up old sonofabitch like you anything for free."

Donnello turned to his left to look behind him. He always turned to his left. No point turning to his right, seeing as he'd lost that eye in a fight a few years ago. Who was he kidding? It's hard to call anything a fight that consists of four guys holding you down while a fifth pops your eye out with a spoon like a chef with a melon baller. He'd grown accustomed to turning to the left all the time, just like he'd gotten used to his eye patch. When he turned, he saw two old men sitting across from each other in a booth, both of them looking over Donnello's shoulder. He turned back around and saw the bulky sixteen-inch television on a corner shelf above the cash register. The news was on and coverage of a story was under way. On the screen was what appeared to be a police sketch of a young woman. Evidently, it had been there for a little while already, because Donnello saw it for only three or four seconds before the sketch disappeared and the program cut to a reporter standing in front of a warehouse.

Donnello knew the warehouse, of course.

And he'd seen the young woman before . . . at the warehouse two nights ago. He hadn't gotten a good look at her then. Things got confusing when the bullets were flying. Plus, the warehouse was dark. When she started running, it was hard to keep up. They had searched for a while but they'd ultimately lost her. Donnello had been searching ever since. And now maybe he'd finally find her. Because he recognized her, and not just from the warehouse. No, he'd seen her before. He wasn't yet sure where, but he definitely had.

He would remember eventually, he was certain of it. And then he'd track her down. And when he did, he'd do what he had to do.

———

Caitlin sat in the front seat, her eyes scanning the sights as they drove through the city. They had passed through the West End, where they'd had dinner last night, and were heading through the heart of Smithfield on Barstow Boulevard, one of the city's main drags. From the driver's seat, Bix pointed out various landmarks and gave points of reference for them while Caitlin struggled to call forth a single memory.

"That corner is where you gave that homeless guy with the dog half your bagel, then went back and bought another one for him to split with his mutt."

Caitlin didn't remember that.

"And in front of that 7-Eleven is where we saw that idiot kid try to jump his skateboard onto the railing there. Spectacular wipeout.

But he didn't break any bones so we were free to laugh our asses off." Bix chuckled.

"I have no memory of that."

"Okay, see that frozen-yogurt shop?"

"Yeah."

"Right there some guy tried to snatch your purse. You hung on, and when he tried to yank you down, you yanked back and he fell."

"Wow," Josh said from the backseat. "What happened?"

"I kicked him in the ass as he ran away . . . without Katie's purse."

"It's Caitlin," Josh reminded him.

"Give me a break, will you?" Bix said. "She was Katie to me for seven months. She's only been Caitlin for two days. So cut me some slack if I slip up."

Caitlin watched the sights continue to drift past the car. Every so often, Bix pointed out something and tried to remind her of the memory attached to it. It was as if she were seeing everything for the first time. Fifteen minutes later, she realized that Bix had been pointing out fewer and fewer sites. In fact, he hadn't mentioned one in several minutes. The part of town they were now in was seedier, she noticed, far more run-down than where they'd been just minutes before. Graffiti. Broken windows. The occasional homeless person in a doorway huddled under a ragged blanket. People leaned against buildings or stood on street corners with bad intentions almost visibly rolling off them in waves. Because the pub where Caitlin used to work didn't open until lunchtime, they had decided to visit the address on the list Caitlin had found in the box in her closet, the list she had kept hidden away. According to what she had written, the place would be open from ten to four. Looking around now, she questioned the wisdom of coming here.

"I don't expect you to recognize anything around here," Bix said. Caitlin didn't, and she was glad about that for a change. "I can't imagine you spent much time in this part of town," he added. Caitlin sure hoped she hadn't.

"There it is," Bix said. "Across the street."

She looked at the plain, single-story brick building. There were bars on the windows, but she had seen bars on a lot of the windows on this street.

"Are you sure this is the right place?" Josh asked.

"It's the address on Katie's mysterious list."

"What kind of place is it?" Caitlin asked.

"I can just make out the sign next to the door," Josh said. "It says . . . the King of Pawns. I think it's a pawnshop."

"It doesn't look open."

"What time is it?" Bix asked.

"Ten twenty," Josh said.

"Should be open. On Katie's list it said ten to four, right?"

"No," Caitlin said. "I mean, it doesn't even look like it's in business any longer. Nothing in the windows."

"Yeah, it does look closed for good," Bix agreed. "Only one way to find out." He opened the door and stepped out of the car. He leaned down, poked his head back in, and said, "As you can see, this isn't the best part of town. You might be safer if you stayed in the car."

"I'll be fine," Caitlin said.

"I was talking to Josh."

"You're an asshole, Bix," Josh said as he opened his door and stepped onto the sidewalk. Caitlin followed.

Something was different about this area. Caitlin knew it had to be her imagination, but she sensed a palpable tension in the air, like something bad was just waiting—and even hoping—to happen. As she and Josh followed Bix across the street, she became aware of eyes marking their progress. The guys in muscle shirts on the corner down the block. Someone in a window next door to the pawnshop. A couple of rangy teens with cigarettes in their mouths and tattoos covering their arms sitting on the hood of a car across the street. Caitlin wondered if they had some sort of sixth sense that would alert them to the fact that she had twelve hundred dollars in her pocket.

As soon as they reached the King of Pawns, which Caitlin had to admit was a little clever, they confirmed that the shop was out of business. Through the bars, they saw empty shelves and display cases displaying nothing but broken glass. A length of rusty chain wove through the handles of the glass doors, secured in place with a bulky padlock.

"Well," Bix said, "that answers that." He frowned. "I can't imagine why this address would be on your list, Katie, and why you bothered to write down its hours. The place has obviously been closed for years."

"I don't know what to think," Caitlin said. "Wait. Yes, I do. I think we should get the heck out of here now."

Bix nodded. "Not a bad idea."

They walked together back to Bix's SUV to find that the tattooed teens had left the hood of whoever's car they had been sitting on and were now leaning against the car immediately behind Bix's. Bix walked past them as if he owned the street, and Josh followed right behind, doing a credible job of appearing unconcerned about anything at the moment. Josh opened Caitlin's door for her and she slipped inside, and Josh slid into the backseat while Bix cranked the engine. For a terrible moment, Caitlin feared that the Explorer wouldn't start . . . that the teens had somehow disabled it in the few seconds she and the guys had been across the street, and that, like cats playing with cornered mice, they'd allowed them to reach what they considered the safety of the car only to find that they could go nowhere. But the engine turned right over and Bix hit the gas, and soon they were down the street, then around the corner and thankfully on their way back to parts of the city where the citizens didn't need iron bars to protect them.

———

The hole was almost big enough for Benny now . . . or, rather, what was left of him. Chops figured another ten minutes of digging and he'd be finished. Good thing, too, because he had a 10:40 flight out of LAX that morning. Traffic was always a bitch around Los Angeles, but any time near rush hour was particularly horrible and enough to drive almost anyone to violence. If Chops wanted to be at the airport at least an hour before his flight, he'd have to get back on the road soon.

The *thunk* of Chops's shovel sinking into the earth almost masked the approaching footsteps. Standing nearly knee-deep in a six-foot-long hole in the forest floor, Chops turned and saw a young man walking toward him. He wore a T-shirt, cargo shorts, hiking boots, and a goofy smile. Over his shoulder he carried a curved metal pole with attachments at one end and a circular contraption at the other.

"Hey, looks like you found something," the man said.

Chops saw now that the device the man carried was a metal detector.

"It does?" Chops said, stepping out of the hole. He kept the shovel in his hands.

"Good for you," the man said. He stopped a few feet from Chops. The smile hadn't left the idiot's face.

"Thanks," Chops said, because he had no idea what else to say.

"I think we might be the first ones out here," the man said.

"I guess."

He stood there, shovel in hand. The other guy stood nearby, leaning a little to the side now, trying to peer around Chops into the hole.

"You get a good read?" the man asked.

Chops said nothing, because he didn't have a clue what the guy was talking about.

"A good hit?" the man added, which didn't clear things up at all, so Chops remained silent. "Come on," the guy said. "Just between you and me . . . you find something big?"

Chops had no idea what to say. He couldn't get a read on the situation.

"Listen," the man said, "it's just the three of us out here so far . . . well, four, including you . . . at least as far as I can tell. But more could be coming soon. We want to work fast, right? I'm assuming you don't own this land any more than I do, am I right?"

He was right. They were in the hills of Angeles National Forest, which was probably owned by the state or the county or something. Where they were was remote and, to the best of Chops's knowledge, the six bodies he had buried around here over the past few years hadn't yet been discovered.

"There are three of you?" Chops asked, thinking about how big a complication that could be. He looked at his watch. He had a plane to catch.

"Yeah, my brother and his buddy," the man said. "I'm Doug, by the way."

Doug wouldn't stop smiling and Chops was getting frustrated enough to use his shovel to wipe that stupid, friendly grin off the guy's face.

"What's in the big Hefty bag?" Doug asked.

Chops knew the guy would finally stop smiling if he heard the truth, but instead Chops replied, "More digging tools."

"Where's your metal detector?" Doug asked. "What kind do you have? I've got a Treasure Pro. Latest model. Set me back eight bills, but it'll be worth it if we find what we're looking for up here, right?"

"Sure," Chops said, nodding. "There are two others with you, huh?"

"Yeah. Usually it would just be my brother and me on something like this, but his buddy was over last night and we were watching TV together when that show came on, and Ron and me—Ron's my brother—we figured, what the heck? Let's let Chuck come on this one. To be honest, we thought we'd be the first ones up here this morning, but then we saw your truck off the road near the trailhead. Looks like you might have been trying to park it inconspicuously"—and here he winked at Chops—"but we had our eyes open for other people, so we saw it."

Chops had indeed been trying to park inconspicuously. It was the smart thing to do when you had to leave your truck somewhere while you lugged a dead body deep into the woods to bury it.

"Here's the deal," Doug said. "You don't have any more right to be here than we do, right? You don't own this land and neither do we. But there could be a fortune around here . . . heck, maybe right where you're digging, am I right? Seems to me there'll be plenty to share. So why don't I get Ron and Chuck over here and we all dig together and split whatever we find?" When Chops didn't respond right away, Doug quickly added, "Look, you were here first. You found this spot. You can keep half and we'll split the other half among the three of us. That's fair, right?"

Chops tried his best to process what the hell Doug was talking about. Whatever it was, Chops knew he had to meet Ron and Chuck, too. "Listen, Doug," he said, "you obviously caught me in the middle of something here. Before we can make a deal, I want to be sure exactly what we're talking about. So why don't you tell me about the TV show you guys saw that brought you up here, okay?"

"Come on," Doug said, "you must have seen the same show. Why else would you be up here?"

"Humor me," Chops said. "If we're gonna make a deal, I need to know we're on the same page. Tell me about the show."

Doug shook his head, smiling. "I'm talking about *60 Minutes* last night. The story about that professor's new theory about a few of Cortez's men going AWOL or whatever with a bunch of Aztec gold and running north with it, out of Mexico. This guy's supposedly an expert, and he thinks they ended up burying it in this area before they were tracked down and killed. He had a bunch of evidence supporting his theory—maps and old diaries and stuff. All of it came to light when it was found in some archive in some library somewhere."

"And you're what?" Chops asked. "A treasure hunter?"

"Same as you," Doug said, somewhat defensively.

"Ever find any?" Chops asked, genuinely curious.

"Found some silver coins once. Thought they were pirate coins but they weren't. Got five hundred bucks for them anyway, though."

Chops found himself disappointed. It would have been a better story if Doug had found pirate treasure, even if only a few coins' worth.

"How about you?" Doug asked. "Ever find anything good?"

"Not yet," Chops said.

"Well, today could be your lucky day," Doug said, grinning again. "A very lucky one."

Chops doubted it. He'd already been terribly unlucky this morning. All the times he'd been up here, he'd never run into a single soul. Yet there he was now, trying to lay Benny to rest on a tight schedule, having to deal with Doug the treasure hunter.

"So what's the story?" Doug asked. "You get a strong reading right there? Get a gold signature? Silver, maybe?"

Chops looked at his watch again.

"Listen, man," Doug said, "I've gotta get back to the guys. Even if you don't want to work together, we're gonna come over here and start digging, too. It's a free country, and we can't let you have all the fun. So we might as well dig together, right? What do you say? Half for you, half for the three of us? Do we have a deal?"

Chops didn't know anything about gold or silver signatures, but he figured they had to do with the way metal detectors worked. And he didn't know about Cortez or *60 Minutes*. What he did know, though, was that he needed to meet Ron and Chuck.

"What the hell?" he said. "You go get the guys and I'll keep working the shovel."

Doug grinned even wider and hurried off.

Chops was glad he'd soon have help digging. He still had a plane to catch, and this hole needed to be a lot bigger now.

CHAPTER TWENTY

AS BIX DROVE, CAITLIN KEPT her eyes open for anything that might be familiar to her, but she was getting close to quitting that game. It seemed less and less likely she was going to remember anything around here. Then something flashed in her mind like an image projected for an instant on a screen, an image of . . . an overcooked chicken. But Caitlin sensed that it wasn't from her time in Smithfield.

"Josh," she said, "I'm remembering burned chicken . . . and Chinese food."

After a moment, Josh said, "Wow, honey, I can't believe you remember that."

"What is it?"

"The night you disappeared, you and I were chatting and you lost track of time and completely burned the chicken you were baking for dinner. We had to order from Happy Garden."

Happy Garden was their favorite Chinese restaurant back home. Caitlin felt a sense of accomplishment for having remembered something else from that night seven months ago. If only she could remember what happened since then.

"We're here," Bix said as he slowed down the car.

"I saw an open parking spot two blocks back," Josh said.

"It's okay, I found one," Bix said.

He pulled the Explorer into a handicapped spot near the street corner, then pulled a blue plastic handicapped-parking tag from a pocket on his door and hung it from the rearview mirror. Caitlin heard Josh sigh as they all climbed out of the car.

"Now, come on, Katie," Bix said. "You must remember this place."

They were standing on the sidewalk looking at a brick-faced pub with neon beer signs in the windows. All of the signs were turned off at the moment. A sign over the door read *Commando's*.

Caitlin sighed. Sadly, she wasn't surprised to find that she didn't recognize it. "I worked here, huh?"

"Since the week after you came to town," Bix said.

She shook her head.

"Okay," Bix said, "shake it off. Let's go inside and talk to a few folks. Maybe someone can tell us something useful. Other than me, these are the people you spent more time with than anyone else around here. Maybe you told someone about where you were going the other night, and why you would have ended up in that warehouse."

"I don't think they're open yet," Caitlin said.

"You work here, Katie," Bix said. "They'll open the door for you. Hell, for all we know, you're on the schedule for the lunch shift today."

Caitlin nodded but didn't move. Josh put a gentle hand on her lower back and guided her toward the door. He pulled on the big, worn brass handle but the door was locked. He knocked. When no one answered, he knocked again, louder. A face appeared in one of the windows, and a moment later, a lock inside disengaged with a sharp clack and the door opened. A short, middle-aged woman with dry hair, bad skin, and more than a few extra pounds stood in the doorway. She wore a waitress's apron. Not surprisingly, Caitlin didn't recognize her.

"It's you," the woman said.

Without a clue as to the proper response, Caitlin said, "It sure is." She smiled, though for all Caitlin knew, she and this woman hated each other. Or maybe they'd been fast friends. Caitlin had no idea.

"What do you want?" the woman asked. So much for them being buddies.

Caitlin dropped her eyes quickly to the woman's plastic nametag and said, "Hi, uh, Martha. Can we come in?"

"Why? We're busy, as you should know. We open in half an hour."

"Yeah . . . of course I know. I just . . . uh . . . am I on today? I forgot to check the schedule."

Martha stared at her blankly for a moment. "You stop coming to work two weeks ago, you don't answer my phone calls, and now you wonder if maybe you're on the schedule today?"

"I . . . what? I stopped coming to work two weeks ago?"

After a pause, Martha said, "Are you freaking kidding me?" Then she closed the door.

Bix looked at Caitlin. "You stopped going to work two weeks ago?"

"I . . . I guess."

"So where the hell were you going when you left the house every night lately, when you were supposed to be working the late shift?"

She shook her head. "I have no idea."

"You really didn't know her as well as you thought, did you, Bix?" Josh asked.

"We already covered that, Josh. Neither of us does, remember?"

"Make that all three of us," Caitlin added.

Josh knocked on the door again. When no one answered, he knocked loud and long until the door opened again, quickly this time, having been unlocked and yanked open with attitude. Stout little Martha was nowhere in sight. In the doorway stood a man with a thick gut, thick arms, a scowl on his face, and a toothpick stuck between his teeth.

"What the hell is this, Katie?" the man said. "You stop showing up for work and don't answer calls, that's quitting. So I can't imagine what the hell you're doin' here now." He pointed at Bix with a finger that looked like a fat cigar and said, "This is what I get for helping out your friend and paying this one under the table."

Bix shrugged. "Hey, he's my friend but he's your cousin."

The man looked back at Caitlin. "You can't be here for money, because I paid you the last night you worked, like I did every night. So why are you here?"

Caitlin had no idea what to say. Fortunately, Josh did. "Look, I'm sorry if Caitlin . . . uh, if Katie's absence caused you any problems. The fact is, she had an accident. She sustained a head injury and now she's having problems with her memory."

The man narrowed his eyes. "This is a joke, right?"

"It's not," Josh replied.

"She looks fine."

"Well, she's not, not really. She has big gaps in her memory, and we're really hoping someone here can help her fill them in."

The man used his tongue to move the toothpick from one side of his mouth to the other. Finally, he said, "We're trying to get ready for lunch. Sorry."

"Oh, just let 'em in," Martha said as she appeared behind the man. "It's not like she's asking for her job back. Are you?" she asked, frowning.

"No," Caitlin said.

"So let 'em in, Joe."

Joe was quiet a moment, then said softly, "We don't need trouble, Martha."

"It can't be her," Martha replied just as softly. "Maybe it looks like her, but we know her, and it can't be her. So let 'em ask their questions or whatever. If it will help her, great. If not, it's not our problem."

"Maybe we shouldn't try to help," Joe said. "Maybe that makes it our problem."

"Oh, just let 'em in, will you?"

Caitlin had no idea what they were talking about. Finally, Joe grunted and stepped back so the three of them could enter the pub. Confused, Caitlin looked around the place, at the bar, the tables, the odds and ends affixed to the walls for decoration—an old wooden sled, an old catcher's mitt, an old wooden oar—but nothing looked familiar to her. She was getting used to that.

"I have to turn on the fryer," Joe said. "You deal with this, Martha. And don't be long."

With that, Joe disappeared through a door in the back wall. Martha walked over to the dark wood bar and stepped behind it. She picked up a towel and started drying wet glasses that were lined up on a towel spread out on the bar. Caitlin took a seat on a stool, and Josh and Bix did the same on either side of her.

"You heard the man," Martha said as she rubbed at a particularly troublesome smudge on a glass. "I need to be quick here." She looked up at Caitlin again, and her face softened for the briefest of moments. "Sorry about your head." Then her features hardened into what were apparently their natural states.

Caitlin began. "Uh, what was that you and . . . and Joe were saying? About trouble?"

"Nothing," Martha said in a tone that completely closed off that avenue of discussion. "Now ask your questions and get on out of here, okay? What do you need to know?"

Caitlin knew she should have had questions ready, seeing as their answers were the reason they had gone there, but she didn't. She thought for a moment. What did she need to know?

"I stopped coming to work two weeks ago?" she finally asked.

"I think we went over that," Martha said.

"Any idea why?"

"You're asking me?"

"Well, when I was last here, did I give any indication that I wouldn't be coming back to work?"

"Not to me," Martha said. She squinted her eyes at Caitlin. "You really hurt your head?"

Ignoring that, Caitlin said, "Had I started acting differently? You know, before I stopped coming to work. Did you notice anything like that?"

"I have nine servers working for me . . . well, eight since you flaked on me . . . plus four bartenders and two guys who rotate doing the cooking with Joe," Martha said. "I don't really pay attention to everybody's moods."

"Do you remember anyone telling you that I was acting differently or anything like that?"

Martha did something weird with her lips—pursed them, maybe—while she thought. "Look," she finally said, "I never heard anyone complain about you. They all liked you. Your coworkers, the customers. No one had anything bad to say about you. And no one ever said you were acting funny or anything. Okay?"

Caitlin nodded. What else could she ask? She had hoped that someone here would have some idea of what she had been doing lately, some sort of clue as to how she had ended up with a gun and fake hands and covered in blood. Why she would have been in that warehouse two nights ago. But seeing as Caitlin hadn't even been to work in weeks, she didn't see how anyone could give them insight into her recent behavior.

Rather than learning any answers here, all Caitlin had found were more questions.

"Listen," Martha said, "I really do have things to do before we open. Like I told you, Katie, you seemed fine, everyone seemed fine with you, so I don't know what else I can tell you. Did you talk to Janie? I asked her where you were, but she said she didn't know, which I had trouble believing."

"Janie?" Caitlin asked, looking over at Bix.

He nodded. "You two are friends."

Caitlin turned back to Martha, who was openly staring at her.

"It's true, huh?" Martha said. "You really don't remember much, do you?"

Caitlin shook her head. She looked at Bix again. "Do you think we have Janie's phone number?"

"It's probably in your phone," Bix said, "but you lost that, right?"

She nodded and turned to Martha. Martha sighed and shook her head resignedly, then reached under the bar and came back up with a spiral notebook. She opened it, flipped past a few pages, then turned the book around so Caitlin could read the number to which she was pointing. Caitlin leaned forward and felt the men beside her do the same. She looked at the page. At the top, the word *Employees* was written in blue ink. It was underlined. Below that were more than a dozen names and phone numbers. One name had a line through it. It was Caitlin's . . . or, rather, Katie's. Martha was pointing to a phone number beside the name Jane Stillwood. It didn't ring even the tiniest bell for Caitlin.

"Do you have a pen and a piece of paper so I can write this down?" Caitlin asked.

"No need," Josh said quickly. He pulled his cell phone from his pocket, touched the screen, then snapped a flash photo of the page. He took a quick look at the screen to confirm that he had captured a good image, then smiled and said, "Who needs to write things down these days?"

Caitlin quickly scanned the other names on the list with the faint hope that one of them would sound familiar. Her eyes fell again on her own crossed-out name . . . that is, Katie's name. And that's when she realized why Josh had taken the snapshot.

"Well, that's all I can tell you," Martha said. She looked at Caitlin and her face showed a glimpse of her softer features again. "Like I said, sorry about your head. Hope you get it all figured out."

"Thank you," Caitlin said. "I appreciate that. And I'm really sorry about . . . well, about not showing up at work and everything."

She stood, squeezed out between Josh and Bix, and started for the door. Josh followed. At the door, she turned and saw Bix still seated at the bar.

"Bix?" she said.

"In a minute," he called over his shoulder.

Caitlin walked back to him.

"You need me to show you to the door?" Martha asked.

Bix reached for a bowl of mixed nuts on the bar and pulled it toward him. As Caitlin watched him dig a small handful of nuts from the bowl and toss them into his mouth one by one, she couldn't help but wonder whether they were fresh from a can this morning or left over from last night. "Just wondering, Martha," Bix said, "what was that you and Cookie were saying before about not wanting trouble?"

"You mean Joe?" Martha asked.

"Sure."

"Nothing."

"Bullshit," Bix said. "What were you talking about?"

"It's nothing," Martha repeated. "I'm telling you."

"Well, it seemed like you were worried about trouble, and you thought Katie being here could cause it. So how about we just sit here until you open up? In fact, as your customers start filing in, Katie will be sure to greet them one by one, reminding them how fantastically helpful you've been to her today, letting us hang out here, giving us phone numbers, stuff like that."

Martha glared at Bix.

"Or is there some reason you'd rather people not know she was here today? That you gave us a hand?"

"You sonofabitch," Martha said. "We opened our door to you . . . to her . . . tried to help her a bit . . . and this is how you thank us?"

She's right, Caitlin thought. They did open their door to her. They did try to help out. She didn't like the way this was going all of a sudden.

"Bix . . ." she said.

He ignored her and watched Martha. Martha scowled back. Caitlin couldn't remember Martha from before this morning, but she'd have been willing to bet that plenty of people withered under that scowl. But Bix stared back impassively as he munched another mouthful of nuts. Finally, Martha said, "Hell, I don't know why it matters. Take it and go," she said as she grabbed a newspaper from beside the cash register and shoved it across the bar at Bix.

Instead of leaving, Bix opened the paper, turning pages until he found it. Caitlin leaned over his shoulder and looked. A headline on page six—*Woman Sought in Warehouse Slaying*. Beside the article were two police sketches, one of a man and the other of a woman. Caitlin's eyes focused for a moment on the sketch of the woman, which wasn't terribly detailed, but which nonetheless looked—Caitlin had to admit—remarkably like her. After looking briefly at what could only be a sketch of her own face, she slid her eyes over to the image of the man, which was far more detailed than the sketch of her. She sucked in a sharp breath.

"Caitlin?" Josh said.

She recognized him. He had been in her dream last night. She couldn't remember seeing him before in her life—that is, her real life—but he had been there in her nightmare. For what felt like the millionth time, she'd been running from the Bogeyman last night. This time, though, she'd had a gun in her hand. She'd turned and fired and hit the Bogeyman dead center, yet when he fell to the floor, he was . . . well, somehow he was the man in the sketch. Caitlin studied the drawing. No doubt about it. Add a bullet hole to the left cheek and he was a dead ringer—pun accidental but far too apt—for the man in her nightmare. The man Caitlin had shot. She hadn't meant to. She had meant to shoot the Bogeyman. In fact, that's exactly what she'd done. She remembered that part of the dream clearly. The Bogeyman had been rushing at her, loping with his long legs, and she'd fired the gun. She thought she'd hit him in the stomach, but when she had stood over the body and looked down, she saw the man from the police sketch lying on his back, a hole in his cheek, his eyes dead and staring. It was him. Caitlin knew it for certain. Which meant that . . .

"I killed that man," she said softly.

"Jesus, Caitlin," Josh said.

"Whoa, Katie, let's watch what we say," Bix said quickly.

Martha watched them and said nothing.

"I . . . I don't remember doing it," Caitlin said. "Not really. But I dreamed that I did it."

"Honey," Josh said in a calm, reassuring tone, "just because you dreamed it doesn't mean you did it."

"How else would I know that face?" Caitlin asked, looking first from Josh, then to Bix, then to Josh again. "I don't remember ever seeing it before, yet I remember seeing it in my dream, first without the bullet hole, then I shot him . . . well, I shot the Bogeyman, but then the Bogeyman was him. He was dead and I shot him."

Martha was clearly listening to every word they said. Her eyebrows were high on her blotchy forehead.

"She doesn't know what she's saying," Josh said to Martha. "I mean, you hear her, right? Bogeyman? Dreams? This is obviously a result of her head injury."

Martha nodded but Caitlin knew she wasn't convinced. But Caitlin was. Whoever that guy in the picture was, whatever her reason could have been, Caitlin had shot him in the warehouse the other night. She didn't remember it, but her subconscious mind did, and it had replayed the scene for her last night while she slept. Sure, it twisted the facts a little, as nightmares are known to do, but the important facts were there and in plain sight.

"I killed him," she said.

"Katie," Bix said, "I think you should probably stop saying that."

"Let's go, hon," Josh said, tugging her elbow gently as he turned toward the door. "Can we keep this?" Josh said as he grabbed the newspaper.

"Be my guest," Martha said.

Halfway to the door, Bix stopped and turned. "Any chance you aren't going to call the cops the second we walk out the door?"

"You think I need that kind of publicity?" Martha said.

"Some people say there's no such thing as bad publicity."

"Not sure I agree. I wouldn't brag about it if Osama bin Laden tended bar here before he took down the towers."

Bix nodded. "Yeah, but Katie's not bin Laden."

"No, she's not," Martha said. "I'm not good at showing it, but I always liked you, Katie. So if that's you in the paper, if you had anything to do with that business in the warehouse . . . well, I figure you probably had your reasons, even if you can't remember 'em any longer. So I'll keep my mouth shut. Joe will, too. I can't speak for anyone else around here. Maybe one of your coworkers will recognize you in that drawing, or one of the customers will, but as far as Joe and me, we won't say anything."

Caitlin managed a smile, which she achieved only through an act of sheer willpower, then she walked out of the pub with Josh and Bix behind her. They got back into Bix's Explorer and no one spoke for a moment. Then Caitlin said, "I think it's time to go to the cops."

"The hell it is," Bix said. "I already told you, you can't trust them. As soon as they have you in custody, they'll stop looking for the real killer."

"*I'm* the real killer," Caitlin said.

"No, you're *not*," Bix said.

"And why do you think that, Bix?" Caitlin asked, her voice suddenly dripping with scorn that she regretted but couldn't tone down. "Because you know me so well? Hell, the Katie you knew isn't even real. She didn't exist before she met you. And she's been lying to you and keeping secrets for the past two weeks at least. So who are you to say that I didn't kill anyone?"

"Hon," Josh said, "for once, I agree with him. You couldn't kill anyone."

"Oh, and you think *you* know me?" Caitlin said, turning to glare at Josh in the backseat. "And did you know that somewhere inside the Caitlin you knew all those years, the Caitlin you married, lurked this pool-playing, beer-guzzling woman who could run off and shack up with a guy she met in a bar? Did you know that about me, Josh?"

She was being horrible, saying terrible, hurtful things to people who cared about her, the only two people who knew her at all—though neither of them knew her nearly well enough. She fell silent and sat there, feeling ashamed. She didn't deserve to have either of these men standing by her side, much less both of them.

"Guys . . ." she began.

"You're right, Caitlin," Josh said. "It's obvious that I didn't know you as well as I thought I did. But still, I think I know you well enough to know that you wouldn't kill anyone unless you had no other option. I have no idea if you shot that man, but if you did, I know . . . I *know* . . . you must have had a good reason. I'd bet my life on it."

And he was doing just that, Caitlin knew. If not his life, then at least his freedom. He was aiding and abetting someone they all were pretty certain had shot a man to death.

"Must be a full moon coming on or something," Bix said, "because I find myself agreeing with Josh again." He smiled briefly. "Katie, there's no way you're capable of cold-blooded murder. I don't know what you got yourself mixed up in or how you ended up at that warehouse the other night, but if you pulled that trigger, I'm sure you had no choice. And I'd be willing to bet Josh's life on it, too."

Josh grunted, but Caitlin couldn't help but smile a little.

"Okay," Caitlin said, "let's assume I had a good reason to shoot that man. Like I said yesterday, shouldn't I still go to the cops and let them investigate the case? Won't they find out the truth, and if it sets me free, fantastic, and if it doesn't, don't I deserve whatever I get?"

Bix shook his head. "You're assuming that once they lock you up, they'll work the case as hard as they did before they caught you. Human nature, Katie. They'd have you admitting that you think you killed that guy. You'll probably offer up your bloody clothes and the gun. Why should they even bother trying to look harder into it? They'd have everything they need, gift wrapped and tied with a red ribbon."

"He's right," Josh said. "I have nothing against the police, but it just seems like once they had all of that, they wouldn't really have a lot of incentive to dig deeper. They may not find a motive, but how badly would they need one if, like Bix says, they have the weapon, the victim's blood on your clothes, and the next best thing to a confession?"

Caitlin closed her eyes and let her head fall back against the seat. "So what are you guys saying? Do I go on the run? Get fake IDs from Bix's friend and set up yet another new identity somewhere? I don't want to live like that."

"I'm not saying that," Josh said.

"I am," Bix chimed in. "And if Goody Two-shoes here won't go on the run with you, I sure as hell will."

"I'm not saying I wouldn't go on the run with her—"

Caitlin opened her eyes. "Guys?"

"Well, are you saying you would?" Bix challenged Josh. "Because that's not what I'm hearing. But that's exactly what I'm willing—"

"Whoa," Josh said. "I never said I would or I wouldn't—"

"*Guys*," Caitlin said again, much louder this time, silencing them both. "I'm not going on the run. As I've said, I have no desire to live like that, always looking over my shoulder. And I couldn't drag either one of you into a life like that with me."

"Either one of us?" Josh asked. "Like there's a choice? I'm your husband."

Caitlin sighed. "I know that, Josh. I didn't mean . . . Look, forget about going on the run. That's just not happening."

"Please tell me you're not going to turn yourself in to the cops?" Bix said.

"I'm not," she said. "At least not yet."

"So what *do* you want to do?" Josh asked.

Caitlin took a breath, then another. "Despite the evidence—that is, the gun I had and the blood all over my clothes, and the fact that I woke up near that warehouse, and I saw the murder victim's face in my dream . . . heck, I even shot him in my dream, sort of—well, despite all of that very compelling evidence, you guys seem certain that I couldn't kill anyone, at least not in cold blood." The men were nodding along now. "So I'm selfishly willing to give you both the benefit of the doubt for the moment. But we all have to admit that the evidence seems to indicate that I shot that guy for some reason, right?" The men nodded again, but with less enthusiasm this time. "Okay," Caitlin continued, "so for now we'll proceed under the assumption that I was justified in shooting that guy—"

"If you truly did," Josh interjected.

"If I did," Caitlin agreed, nodding. "So what we need to do is try to figure out why I might have shot him. If we can figure that out, we can decide the right time to go to the cops."

"Never," Bix said. "I don't care why you did it."

"Well, I do," Caitlin said. "If it was cold-blooded murder, I'm turning myself in and you guys won't be able to stop me."

"And if it wasn't?" Josh asked.

"If it wasn't, if I was somehow justified in killing him, then we'll take what we know to the cops. They won't ignore evidence that proves I had no choice but to shoot that man. They can't."

"So either way, you're going to the cops?" Bix said.

Caitlin nodded. "I am. But I'd much rather do it with an armful of evidence showing that I acted in self-defense or something like that. But if we can't find anything like that, or if we find out that I'm nothing but a murderer, plain and simple, well . . . I'm still walking into that station."

"I think that's a really bad idea, Katie," Bix said.

Caitlin turned to look at Josh again. He had a sad smile on his face. She knew why. He may not have known her quite as well as he thought he did, that she had this other person hiding inside her all these years, but he still knew her pretty well. He knew this was what she ultimately would decide to do. And he knew he couldn't stop her.

"How long will you give it?" he asked. "How long until you turn yourself in?"

"Hey, don't get me wrong," she said. "I'm not in any rush. Let's work our asses off to get to the bottom of whatever I did, whatever I was doing that led up to whatever I did. I'd much rather find those answers than give myself up empty-handed."

"And let's not forget," Bix said, "the decision whether to turn yourself in might not end up being yours, anyway, Katie. After all, the cops are looking for you. And now that your face is in the papers, how long will it be before someone recognizes you and drops a dime on you?"

That was a good question.

"So what do we do next?" Bix asked. "We can take another look at the list you kept hidden in the box in your closet. Try to figure out how the things you wrote factor in here. We think we know who the Bogeyman is, though not why the monster from your dreams would be on the list. But maybe if we ask around a little, we can figure out who this One-Eyed Jack is. And when we find him, maybe he'll tell us who the other guy on the list is. What was the name? Bob?"

"Bob, yeah," Josh said.

"But the address won't help us, right?" Caitlin said. "That was a dead end. So who's to say the whole list isn't a wild goose chase?"

Bix said, "Well, I say we go with it. It's all we have."

"I agree we should go with it," Josh said. "But it's not all we have. We also have your friend, hon. Janie Whatever-Her-Name-Is.

You should call her. See if she can tell us anything. If you two were close, maybe you confided in her, told her something about whatever was going on."

Caitlin nodded. "Right. And we also have—"

"Martha's list of employees," Josh finished for her.

"I *knew* you saw it, too. That's why you took a picture of it instead of letting me write down Janie's number. I didn't see it at first," she admitted, "but after you took the picture, I read the rest of the names to see if any of them rang a bell, and that's when I saw it."

Josh slid his tablet from under Caitlin's seat in front of him, where he'd stashed it when they'd gone into the pub, then set it on his lap and started typing.

"What did you see?" Bix asked.

"My name," Caitlin said.

"What about it?"

"Just give me a minute, guys," Josh said, his fingers tapping away at the tablet's screen. "This shouldn't take long. Maybe it's nothing," he added, almost to himself, "but maybe it's not. Maybe it's . . . something."

CHAPTER TWENTY-ONE

AS DETECTIVE CHARLOTTE HUNNSAKER SAT at her desk scanning a report, she thought for the twentieth time in the last hour how much she hated reviewing tips called in to the department's tip line. The computer sketches of Vic Warehouse and the mystery redhead had been shown on that morning's early local TV news, and they had made it into the morning editions of both the *Globe* and the *Smithfield Beacon*. Television viewers and newspaper readers were asked to call the tip line if they had any information about the person in either sketch. Then the fun began, as it always did. As usual, some people called just to talk about the ongoing case, as if the act of dialing the phone number earned them a backstage pass into a police investigation. Other callers, possibly well intentioned but totally off their rockers, called to report valuable information such as the fact that the people in the sketches had been invading their dreams, or they looked like people with whom they attended kindergarten three decades ago. A few folks called to try to convince the police that the people in the sketches looked like their ex–spouses or ex–significant others in the pathetically transparent hope that the police would hassle a former paramour with whom they'd had a falling out. Of course, there were always the high school pranksters who called because their idiot friends thought they were funny. It went the way it always did—calls came in, information got recorded, and reports were generated.

Hunnsaker requested that the reports on this case be sent to her every two hours. Then she would begin the work of separating the cranks from the nutjobs from the callers with marginally promising leads. Armed with a variety of different colored highlighters, she was halfway through the first list of the day. Pink for the pranksters and the crazies, blue for the tips that might be worth checking out, and yellow for the most promising leads. So far, after forty-one calls, she had highlighted twenty-four in pink, nine in blue, and eight in yellow. Two desks away from hers, Javy Padilla was slogging through the same report, using the same color-coding scheme.

Hunnsaker looked over at him and called, "You finished yet?"

Padilla looked up, and for a moment Hunnsaker thought he was having a heart attack. His eyes were squinted shut and his lips were pulled back from his teeth in an agonized grimace. Before Hunnsaker could leap to her feet, Padilla's face began to relax. "Oh my God," he said, "I hate this shit."

Only then did Hunnsaker notice on Padilla's desk the big, clear, plastic travel cup three-quarters full of a thick spinach-green liquid. On the inside of one side of the cup, the sludgy concoction was slowly receding from the rim, from where Padilla had clearly just sipped.

"I thought you only drank that stuff at home," Hunnsaker said, "where Elaine can monitor you."

Padilla shook his head. "I can't lie to her."

"I thought you lied to her all the time."

"Yeah, I do. What I meant was, I can't lie to her and get away with it. She asks, I lie, and then she says she can tell I'm lying and that I'd better start drinking this crap again. She says it's for my own good."

"She must love you for some reason I can't begin to fathom," Hunnsaker said.

"She has a funny way of showing it," Padilla said as he took two deep breaths, then began chugging more of what looked increasingly to Hunnsaker like hazardous waste. Padilla's features contorted and Hunnsaker grimaced in sympathy. Padilla finished swallowing—not without obvious effort—and looked forlornly at the half-full cup on his desk.

"She'll know if you don't finish it?" Hunnsaker asked.

"God only knows how, but she will."

Padilla seemed to have recovered from his last sip, so she asked, "You done going through the tips so far?"

Padilla looked down at the report on his desk. "Four more to go."

"How's it looking to you?"

"Eight yellows and ten blues. The rest is the usual garbage."

"That's close to what I have. Probably mostly the same ones. I've got a few calls to make, then we should head out and follow up on the more promising leads, see if we get lucky."

She was getting frustrated with the case. They just didn't have much to go on so far. Without an identity for the victim, they were unable to run down the kinds of leads that were often so valuable in homicides—family, friends, coworkers, and acquaintances, as well as lifestyle, habits, hangouts, and the like. Forensic investigation had turned up virtually nothing of value. No DNA or trace evidence on the body that didn't belong to the victim. And the immediate area of the warehouse surrounding the body had been traversed so many times over the years—by employees while the building was in oper-ation and by vagrants, hookers, druggies, kids, and thrill-seekers after it had been abandoned—that the odds of finding anything useful were longer than those of winning the Powerball lottery.

All of which, for the moment, left Hunnsaker with the results of the tip hotline. She scanned the blue- and yellow-highlighted text on her copy of the report. It looked like they'd be visiting three apartment buildings, a pharmacy, a local gym, a hospital, and—after they opened—five eating establishments and six bars or nightclubs. If they won the lottery today, someone at one of these places would turn out *not* to be a crackpot and would actually have useful information about their victim or the redhead. As frustrated as Hunnsaker was becoming, as much as she disliked having to rely for the moment on tips—most of them anonymous—she couldn't help but feel uncharacteristically optimistic that one of these leads would pan out. And if none did, more tips would trickle in throughout the day. Someone out there knew what Hunnsaker needed to know. All she had to do was find that person. And she would. Because Vic Warehouse's refusal to be identified was starting to make her angry. And she was even more pissed off at the redhead, who also refused to be identified but who didn't have the excuse of being dead. Without realizing that she had moved her eyes from the report, Hunnsaker found herself looking at the sketch on her desk of the mystery redhead.

"I'll give it five hours," she said quietly to the computer drawing, "ten at the most, before you and I are face-to-face. And if you saw who shot my buddy Vic, you're gonna tell me who it was. And if it was you, you're gonna tell me that, too. I promise you."

"Who the hell are you talking to?" Padilla called to her.

"The redhead."

After a moment, Padilla said, "You're crazy."

"Look at that sewage you're drinking," Hunnsaker said, "and you call *me* crazy?"

"Fair enough. I'm almost ready to go."

"I need ten minutes. Then we hit the streets, find out who the hell Vic is, and locate our pretty friend here."

"Sounds like a solid plan."

"I spent all morning working it out."

Despite the lightness of their banter, she intended to implement that plan and see it succeed. She was going to keep her promise to their mystery redhead.

———

"Okay, I think I have something here," Josh said.

He looked down at the news article open on the Internet browser of his tablet. He had already read it through three times, then searched with marginal success for more like it. He found only two related articles. The first, more than two decades old and only a column long, was from the online archives of the *Smithfield Beacon*, a midsize newspaper that was much smaller than the *Globe* or the *Boston Herald*.

"You going to fill in the rest of us," Bix asked, "or are you just gonna keep reading it to yourself over and over?"

Bix was behind the wheel, and they had been driving aimlessly through town while Josh had done a little Internet research from his usual place in the backseat. They hadn't decided where to go next, but they hadn't wanted to remain parked in front of Commando's in case Martha was less than true to her word and called the cops the second the three of them walked out of the place.

"Sorry," Josh said. "Just wanted to be sure." He looked at Bix. "It started with Caitlin's name in Martha's notebook at the pub. Her list of employees."

Caitlin stepped in. "At first, I was just looking for Jane Stillwood's name and number, but when I skimmed the other names, I saw my own, which had been crossed out. But it wasn't really my own. It was close, but not quite right."

"Meaning?" Bix said.

"Meaning it was spelled wrong. My first name was spelled right, or at least it was spelled the way I spelled it when I was going by Katherine, but my last name wasn't listed as Southard. It was Southern."

"So?" Bix said. "Martha probably wrote it down wrong. I'm guessing there are all sorts of errors in her books, both intentional and unintentional."

Caitlin shook her head. "No, the handwriting was mine. All the names and numbers were in different handwriting. I guess Martha had people write their own contact information in the book."

Bix looked confused again. "Why would you spell your own name wrong?"

"Because it's not her real name, remember?" Josh asked.

"We're hoping it means something," Caitlin said.

"And I think it does," Josh said. "Are you ready, hon?"

She frowned. "Why wouldn't I be ready?"

"It . . . it's not very pleasant."

After a moment, she nodded.

He took a breath and began. "Okay, so I had already searched the Internet for Katherine Southard, the name Caitlin was using around here, the one on her car registration and fake driver's license. I had started by focusing my search on this town, then broadened it to include all of Massachusetts, and finally the Northeast. I got nothing that seemed to work. Next I tried changing the spelling of 'Katherine,' using every possible spelling I could think of. I even shortened it to Kathy with a *K*, Cathy with a *C*, and Katie. Still nothing. But after seeing the name in Martha's address book, I tried the same geographical searches with the name Katherine *Southern*. Again, I started locally and then widened my search."

"And?" Caitlin said.

"And still nothing."

"Impressive," Bix said. "You're definitely onto something, Sherlock."

Josh ignored that and continued. "But then I tried the same alternate spellings of Katherine but with the last name Southern. And that's how I found it."

"Found what?" Caitlin asked.

"Using the name Kathryn Southern," he said, spelling the first name for them, "and combining it with 'Massachusetts,' I found an online article from the *Boston Beacon* from twenty-two years ago. About a suspected pedophile who lived two towns over. It's also about two little girls—one missing and one . . . 'damaged from the experience' is how they say it in the article."

Josh watched Caitlin carefully to see how she was handling this. "Let me guess," she said. "Kathryn Southern is one of those little girls."

Josh nodded. "The missing one."

"So was that you, then?" Bix asked. "The missing girl? Kathryn Southern?"

"No," Caitlin said. "That was never my name back then. The police and the media wouldn't have called me that."

"So why did you take that name now?"

Caitlin shook her head. "I have no idea, but there's just no reason for me to have been identified by that name, especially not by the authorities who presumably would check their facts before releasing the name of a missing girl." She turned to Josh. "What's the name of the . . . what did you call her? The 'damaged' little girl?"

"The article doesn't say. I guess because she survived her ordeal, they kept her name out of the papers to protect her identity."

"Am I mentioned in the article?"

"Not by name, no."

Caitlin was quiet a moment. "So, theoretically, that abused girl could be me?"

"Well . . ." Josh began, "theoretically, I suppose."

Caitlin nodded. "Did they ever find the girl who was missing?"

Josh had read two more articles that appeared over the two years following the suspect's arrest, the only related articles he could find. One was about the suspect's conviction, and one was about his sentencing. Josh shook his head. "She hadn't been found by the time the pedophile was convicted a year and a half later. I Googled her and didn't find anything saying she'd ever turned up, either alive or . . . not. It doesn't mean she never did, of course, just that I didn't find it on the Internet."

"Do you remember anything like that happening when you were a kid, Katie?" Bix asked.

Bix hadn't spoken for so long that, for a few moments, Josh had been able to forget that he was even there. Unfortunately, those moments were over.

Caitlin shook her head. "No, nothing like that at all."

"So maybe this story has nothing to do with you," Bix said.

"Well . . ." Josh began, but he didn't need to continue because Caitlin stepped in.

"Maybe I just forgot, Bix," she said. "It certainly wouldn't be out of the question for me, as we all know. Think about it. Why else would I be here? If I wasn't involved in any of that, why would I just happen to take on the name of a little girl who went missing all those years ago? Why would I travel from New Hampshire all the way to Massachusetts, to this particular area? That crime took place two decades ago. I was five years old at the time. How would I have known about any of this?"

Bix shrugged. "Maybe you heard your parents talking about it as a kid, back when it happened."

Caitlin shook her head. "I doubt it. I'm not sure exactly where I was at the time, what home I was in." Bix looked confused. "I was raised in foster homes, Bix. I never knew my biological parents. I'd had two homes by the time I was five or so, then my next foster parents formally adopted me. But I don't remember any of the people I lived with talking about this crime."

"I didn't find many articles on it, Bix," Josh said. "Just a few. It doesn't seem to have been a big story back then, so I'm not sure how likely it is that many people were talking about it at the time."

"But if Katie's the other girl in that story," Bix said, "the one who . . . didn't go missing, wouldn't she remember something about it? I mean, I have memories from when I was five."

"I'm not sure," Josh said. He wanted to be delicate here for Caitlin's sake. "If people go through traumatic things, they can block them out. You hear about kids blocking out stuff like that all the time. And remember why we're here in the first place right now."

"My memory loss," Caitlin said. "My 'dissociative fugue,' which Josh's research says can be triggered by traumatic events."

Bix said nothing more for the moment, for which Josh was grateful. Caitlin fell silent, too. Josh kept his eyes on her. She seemed to be thinking hard. To Josh's relief, though—and to Caitlin's credit—she didn't seem to be allowing herself to become overly upset about all of this. Rather, she seemed merely to be processing what she had heard so far and trying hard to remember if she'd ever experienced anything like what Josh had described. She was tougher than he'd thought, he realized.

"So," she finally said, "you find out anything else?"

———

Approximately thirty-four thousand feet above Utah—or maybe they were still over Nevada—Chops was unhappy. He hated flying. It wasn't that he was frightened to do it; he just hated everything about it, other than the obvious convenience of stepping into a huge machine in Los Angeles and, after mere hours in the air, stepping out again in Boston. Everything else, though, was lousy. At six-five, he could never get comfortable on an airplane. And because he'd bought his ticket just that morning, the only available seat on the entire plane was a center seat, where he struggled in vain to find a position that wasn't torture—he had already lost the feeling in his legs twice, and they'd been in the air barely more than an hour.

And in that short time, he'd grown to despise the passenger to his left. She kept adjusting her seat belt and neck pillow, and taking things out of her carry-on bag. As soon as the plane's wheels lifted off the runway, she'd slid a white paper bag from under the seat in front of her and pulled out a Styrofoam container that, when opened, released an overpowering miasma of odor of some unidentifiable pungent, spicy foreign dish. Chops didn't know what it was but knew it wasn't something he ever wanted to try himself, and he certainly didn't want to sit next to it for the next half hour while this woman took annoying little bites and smacked her lips wetly after each one. And for the record, the guy in the aisle seat to Chops's right wasn't much better—already asleep with his head tipped back, his mouth open and snoring. Every little snuffle or grunt irritated Chops to the point that it felt like someone was sticking him in the neck with a pin every time he heard it. Chops elbowed the guy, who woke with a nasty look that disappeared as soon as he saw and remembered who was sitting beside him. Chops hoped the guy would think twice about falling asleep again on this flight.

Chops was cranky, and he still had at least five more hours in the air before he changed planes in Baltimore. He hoped he would make it that long without killing one of his fellow passengers. The guy on his right was already snoring again. The woman on his left sucked something off one of her fingers and took another bite of her aggressively foul-smelling food.

He allowed his terrible mood to fester. What he was feeling might come in handy later if he found out there was, in fact, trouble back east. If he had to injure someone, maybe even kill someone, it never hurt to keep a little rage bottled up so he could pop the top off it if he needed to. As he closed his eyes and prayed for the strength to keep from snapping one of the necks in the seats beside him, he wondered if he would indeed have to kill someone tonight. And if so, with only mild curiosity, he wondered who that might be.

CHAPTER TWENTY-TWO

CAITLIN WAS IN THE PASSENGER seat of Bix's Explorer, where she'd taken to sitting; Bix was behind the wheel; and Josh was in his usual place in the backseat. Caitlin knew her husband wasn't happy about the seating arrangement, but it was Bix's car, so he did the driving, and she could only imagine how uncomfortable Bix and Josh would be riding up front together.

A few minutes ago, Bix announced that they needed to stop for gas. They pulled into a Shell station, and while Bix pumped, Josh stepped away to use his cell phone. Once they were all back in the car, in their assigned places, Josh gave Bix an address toward which to head. It was twenty-six miles away in a town called Hyattville. When Caitlin asked Josh where he came up with it, he promised to let them know when it made sense to do so as he told the story. Because they apparently had forty minutes or so ahead of them before they reached their destination, wherever it was, she was willing to be patient.

"Okay, so here's the whole story," Josh began. "Twenty-two years ago, this pedophile abducted a couple of little girls from a playground and took them to his shack at the edge of a junkyard he owned. Somehow the cops found out about him, but when they got to his place, one of the girls was already missing and the other was . . ."

"Damaged," Caitlin said.

"Right. So, they question the guy but he won't talk. He refuses to show them where the missing little girl is."

"Kathryn Southern," Caitlin said.

"Right, Kathryn Southern," Josh said. "Apparently, the cops tore that junkyard apart but they never found her. The place was also adjacent to a town garbage dump, and they searched that, too, and came up empty."

Caitlin shuddered at the all-too-familiar story of a lost child left in a ditch or dumpster or shallow grave in the woods, disposed of like garbage.

"The first of the other two articles I found talked about the suspect being found guilty of kidnapping and sexual assault."

"Not murder?" Caitlin asked. "What about the missing girl?"

"No body," Bix said. "Without it, it's hard to prove murder."

Josh nodded. "The last article was about sentencing. He got thirty-two years in Walpole State Prison, with no possibility of parole."

"So he's got about ten years left, then," Bix said. "If he's even still alive. How old was he back then?"

After a pause, during which Josh scanned one of the articles, he said, "Forty-two when he was arrested."

Bix said, "That puts him in his sixties now. That's not young for a place like Walpole," he added, referring to the notoriously tough prison by its former name, the one that had been used in the article. Though it had since been renamed Massachusetts Correctional Institution–Cedar Junction, it was still Walpole to most people. "Hopefully, the sonofabitch is dead," Bix said. "Life's hard in prison."

"Speaking from experience?" Josh asked.

"Not my own."

"What's his name?" Caitlin asked. "You keep calling him the suspect, but what's his name?"

"Darryl Bookerman," Josh said.

Caitlin snapped her head around and stared at him. "What did you say?"

He nodded slightly and repeated the name.

"Hmm," Bix said, "Bookerman . . . that sounds a little like—"

"Bogeyman," Caitlin finished for him.

"And I imagine it would sound even more like Bogeyman to a five-year-old girl," Josh said. He flashed Caitlin a sympathetic look and said quietly, "There's more, hon."

Caitlin waited.

"There's a photo with the article about Bookerman being convicted," he said. "It's a bit grainy, but . . . well, take a look, Caitlin."

He handed her his tablet. She turned it around, looked at the black-and-white photograph on the screen, and couldn't stifle a gasp. The image was small, so she clicked on it to enlarge it. Her heart thundered in her chest and she took a deep breath, then another, and forced herself to remain calm.

In the photo, two law-enforcement officers flanked a man in handcuffs. He was rail-thin and tall, at least a head taller than either man beside him. His skin was far paler than theirs, his bald head looking almost like a white oval in the photo. His eyes, unusually far apart on his head, were dark holes in the stark whiteness of his complexion.

Caitlin had recognized him at once, though she'd never gotten this long of a look at him. She was always fleeing from him through the dark, stealing terrified glances over her shoulder as he raced toward her on his long, spindly, spidery legs, his thin arms out in front of him, his white hands reaching for her . . .

Darryl Bookerman was the man who had chased her for more than twenty years through her nightmares.

He was the Bogeyman.

"It's him, isn't it?" Josh asked.

Caitlin nodded. "So I'm really the one," she said. "The little girl they found in his shack. The damaged one."

"We don't know that, hon," Josh said. Caitlin gave him a look intended to say, *Thanks for trying, but I'm not buying*. "Are you okay?" he asked.

She wasn't sure. It was strange to learn after all these years that her Bogeyman wasn't merely the stuff of nightmares. He was flesh and blood. He walked the earth. She honestly didn't know if that made her feel better or worse.

"Caitlin?" Josh said.

"I'm okay," she said, because she had to tell him something.

After a few moments passed in silence, Bix asked, "So where are we headed now, then?"

"The lead detective on the case was named Jeff Bigelson," Josh said. "I figured that if anyone could tell us more about all of this, it would be him."

Good idea, Caitlin thought, *but* . . . "It's been a long time," she said. "Two decades. You think he'd even remember?"

Bix joined the conversation again. "I've known a cop or two. Some cases they don't forget, especially the ones involving kids. But is he even on the force anymore?"

"He's retired," Josh said. "I called the North Smithfield Police Department. Then I called directory assistance and got an address and phone number for a Jeffrey Bigelson in the area. They had one in Huntington, not that far from here."

"Maybe forty minutes away," Bix said. "Could be the same guy, I guess. But how do we know he's even still alive?"

"Because I spoke with his wife. Jeff was sleeping, which may mean that he's not in great shape these days. Maybe he's old, maybe he's infirm, or maybe he rolled in at three in the morning after a night of hard drinking. Whatever it is, he's alive."

"Will he see us?" Caitlin asked.

"I told her it was about one of his old cases," Josh said. "When she asked which one and I told her, she said he'd see me. She didn't even have to check with him first."

Caitlin nodded. She thought about what Bix just said . . . some cases they don't forget, especially the ones involving kids. Whatever made the Bookerman case too disturbing for Caitlin to remember apparently made it hard for Bigelson to forget. She wondered briefly whether she would be better off letting the past stay in the past where it belonged. But it was too late now. Bigelson . . . along with whatever answers he might have . . . was waiting for her.

CHAPTER TWENTY-THREE

FROM THE OUTSIDE, THE BIGELSON house could not have looked more charming and cheerful if it had sprung from the imagination of Walt Disney. Sitting in the car in front of the house, Caitlin took in the roses intertwined through the white pickets of the fence along the front of the property; the big tree with a peaceful verdigris bench in the shade beneath it; and the curving, cobbled walkway that led up to the small stone house—almost a cottage, really—with ivy-covered walls, a wood-shingle roof, and a chimney that Caitlin was mildly surprised to see wasn't emitting gentle wisps of smoke. She half expected to see little Disney-animated bluebirds fluttering around the birdbath by the wildflower garden on one side of the property.

"I think we just drove into a greeting card," Bix said.

"Looks like the Bigelsons are into gardening," Josh said.

"And fairy tales," Caitlin added. "It's wonderful."

She looked to the houses on either side of the Bigelsons' and saw homes that would be considered attractive in nearly any other neighborhood in the country, but that looked dull next to their neighbors' idyllic home.

Caitlin began to feel bad about being there. The people inside that beautiful house had probably put the ugliness of the Bookerman case—perhaps of all of Bigelson's old cases—behind them for good. Irrationally, Caitlin feared that her being there to talk about what they were there to talk about would only bring unhappiness to those inside that house, that setting one foot on the property would break the spell enveloping it and would allow evil to find its way in.

"You ready, hon?" Josh asked.

"Not really," she said as she opened her door and walked to the gate in the picket fence. She heard car doors open and close, then the men were beside her. She lifted the latch; pushed open the gate; and, after a brief hesitation, stepped onto the cobblestone path. When they reached the front stoop, Caitlin pressed the doorbell and heard a pleasant jingling of bells inside.

"That must be Tinker Bell," Bix said.

The door opened and Caitlin took a small, involuntary step back when she saw the woman who opened it. She looked far less like, say, a fairy godmother than . . . well, maybe not an evil queen or witch, but certainly an evil stepmother. Put plainly, she was unattractive. Thin and round-shouldered, with bags under her eyes, a sharp nose, and a hard line for a mouth. When she saw them, though, she smiled warmly and genuinely in welcome, and whatever illusion of ugliness had been there a moment ago disappeared.

"Please," she said, still smiling, "come in."

She stepped aside and Caitlin walked past her, followed by the others. One glance told Caitlin that the inside of the house perfectly matched what she'd seen outside.

"I'm Dolores, Jeff's wife," the woman said.

"Nice to meet you," Caitlin said. "I'm Caitlin Dearborn."

Dearborn was her maiden name. They had discussed this on the drive here. She had to use that name, the one she'd had as a child, in order to see if Jeff Bigelson had ever heard it. But there was no reason to reveal Josh's and Bix's real names, so they chose Mark Dunlay and Archie Galvin, respectively—names of boys whom each had known in high school.

After they had all introduced themselves, Caitlin said, "You have a truly lovely home. And the flowers outside are gorgeous."

Dolores waved away the compliment with a modest flick of her hand. "Gardening is my little hobby. Would you like something to drink? Tea, maybe?"

They politely declined, though Caitlin almost accepted just to see if the teapot could sing.

"So, you're here to see Jeff," Dolores said.

"We are," Caitlin replied. "I hope we're not troubling you."

"No trouble at all. We enjoy visitors. And when you said what it was you wanted to talk about, I knew Jeff would agree to speak with you. He remembers that case . . . most of the time, anyway. He remembers a lot of cases, though not as well as he used to, of course."

Dolores looked lost in thought for a brief moment, then smiled again, though less brightly than when she'd first greeted them.

"Before I take you to him, I should tell you," she said, "he isn't quite the man he used to be. He's forgetting a lot these days."

"Alzheimer's?" Caitlin asked gently.

Dolores nodded. "Early stages, but yes. Most of the time, he's sharp as a tack still, but now and then he'll forget the littlest things, things we had discussed just yesterday. Last week he couldn't remember his sister's name. It didn't come to him until a few minutes later."

Caitlin wondered how much the man would remember about the Bookerman case after all, but then, as if reading her thoughts, Dolores said, "Before you worry whether you made this trip for nothing, I can tell you that he's had a good day so far. Hasn't forgotten a thing today."

"Thanks for letting us know," Caitlin said. "May we see him?"

"There's one more thing," Dolores said. "Last week he had a tumor removed from his back, near his spine."

"Oh, I'm so sorry," Caitlin said. "Maybe we shouldn't—"

"Not malignant, thank God, but not small, either. It was painful, and Jeff's on some pretty good painkillers. He was past due for a dose when you called, but he made me hold off so that he'd be clearheaded when he spoke with you."

"I'm terribly sorry this is such a difficult time for you," Caitlin said.

"Between the painkillers and the sleeping pills, we'll get through it. Just wanted you to know." Caitlin nodded and Dolores nodded back. "Well, I'll take you to him. We've got him set up in the spare bedroom right now so I won't disturb his rest, when he's able to get it. I can't say he's looking forward to your visit, but he's definitely curious about why you want to talk with him about that old case."

Dolores paused, as though waiting for Caitlin to let her in on it, but Caitlin said, "It's so good of him to see us, especially at a time like this."

Dolores hesitated only a moment more, then smiled sweetly and led them through what could have been Snow White's living room, then down a short hallway before stopping outside a door that was ajar.

"I'm hoping you won't need to stay too long," she said quietly. "He acts like such a tough guy, but . . ."

"We won't overstay, I promise," Caitlin said.

Dolores smiled again and knocked softly on the door. Caitlin heard a throat clear, then a voice say, "Come on in."

CHAPTER TWENTY-FOUR

JEFF BIGELSON LOOKED LIKE A man who had a knife sticking out of his back and was trying to pretend it wasn't there. The pain was evident on his face as he lay in bed, propped up by pillows, gritting his teeth while somehow smiling a cheerless but brave smile. Dolores had assured Caitlin and the others that her husband wanted to speak with them, but looking at him now, Caitlin felt guilty for having come.

Bigelson was a big man—not terribly overweight, just large. Given that he was lying down, Caitlin couldn't tell how tall he was, but he filled the twin bed. It was plain that he had been strong once, and she could imagine that as soon as he recovered from his recent surgery, he might be strong again, at least for someone his age. She thought that probably very few people had given him trouble in his day. Maybe that toughness was why he had insisted on pushing past the pain he was obviously in and meeting with them.

"Come on over," Bigelson said. "I don't have anything that's catching."

They stepped into the middle of the room and introduced themselves, using the names they had given Dolores.

"I'm sure my wonderful wife here offered you something," Bigelson said.

"What kind of a gal do you think I am? Of course I did," Dolores replied in a playfully scolding voice.

"Looks like a gorgeous day out there, Dolores," Bigelson said. "You going to be out gardening?" Caitlin took that to mean that he wanted some privacy with his guests. His wife seemed to take it the same way because she said, "Well, I do have some hyacinth bulbs that need planting. I'll be back to check on you in a bit," she added, which Caitlin figured was a reminder not to stay longer than necessary. Dolores closed the door behind her as she left.

As soon as she was gone, Bigelson said, "You look like decent people. Probably feel like you have to make small talk for a bit, ask how I am, tell me how sorry you are for disturbing me—"

"We really are so sorry to bother you, Mr. Bigelson," Caitlin said. "This seems like such a terrible time for us to have come."

"What I was going to say was, you don't need to do any of that. To be honest, and not to be rude, the fact is I don't need to hear it. You got things you want to ask, or talk about, or whatever it is you're here for, and I think we'll all be better off just getting down to it."

Bigelson shifted, and the pain was once again plain on his face.

"I understand," she said. "Just please know that we appreciate your time."

Bigelson nodded. "So Dolores told me you're here about that piece of filth Darryl Bookerman."

Caitlin nodded.

"That case was a long time ago," he said. "The guy's been in prison for two decades. And unless someone killed him there, which he deserves, he's got at least another ten to go, if I'm not mistaken."

"That's right," Caitlin said.

"Can't imagine why you're here about him now, then."

His eyes flicked to Josh, then Bix, then returned to Caitlin and stayed on her face. She knew that those weren't the eyes of an old man looking at her now; they were the eyes of a detective.

After a long moment, Bigelson said, "You're not the girl who disappeared. Kathryn . . . something or other."

"Southern."

"Right, Southern. She was a redhead, too, as I recall, but she was the genuine article, according to her parents and the pictures we had. And I hope you won't take offense, but your red comes from a bottle, if I'm not mistaken."

Caitlin nodded. Bigelson had confirmed what they had already known, but what about—

Bigelson continued. "Are you . . ." His voice trailed off, then he asked softly, "Are you the girl we found there that day?"

That was the question of the moment, wasn't it? Now that it was out there, now that it had been asked and there was a good chance it would be answered, Caitlin wanted nothing more than to leave without hearing another word. If she was that "damaged" little girl, what good did it do to find that out now? She'd gotten along fine most of her life without knowing it. She had repressed it well enough, for more than twenty years, anyway. Why force herself to face it now? Bigelson studied her face a moment longer, and Caitlin was debating whether to apologize for their intrusion and make a run for the door when he said, "But no . . . I don't think so. You're not her."

For a moment, Caitlin feared that she hadn't heard him correctly.

"She had darker eyes and darker skin, like there was some other ethnicity or race in her blood not far back."

Caitlin suddenly felt almost weightless.

Bigelson said, "You're far more fair-skinned . . . lighter eyes . . . no offense, but you're very Caucasian."

Caitlin couldn't help but chuckle.

For the first time since introducing himself, Josh spoke. "So if she's not either of those girls . . ."

"You said your name is Dearborn?" Bigelson asked. Caitlin nodded. "Is that the surname you were born with or a married name?"

"It's the name my parents gave me."

"Dearborn," Bigelson repeated quietly to himself. "Doesn't ring a bell." He squinted at her face for a few seconds, and then his eyes widened.

"I know who you are," he said, and his voice was tinged with something that sounded a little to Caitlin like wonder.

"You do?" she asked.

"Sure. I never thought I'd meet you. Never thought you'd surface again. But it's you, isn't it? I know it is. You're the prettiest one, aren't you? The one who escaped?"

"The prettiest one?" Josh asked.

"Come on," Bigelson said. "You didn't come all the way to see me just to deny that, did you?"

Caitlin didn't know how to respond. "I . . . well . . . the prettiest one? The one who escaped?"

Bigelson frowned at her. "Miss Dearborn . . ."

"Caitlin, please."

"Okay, Caitlin, then. Let's do this differently. You came to see an old police detective about an old case. Why? What does that case mean to you? What are you hoping to learn here?"

Again, he had asked exactly the right questions. One had apparently been answered. If Bigelson was right, Caitlin was neither the missing girl, Kathryn Southern, nor the damaged little girl the police found in a dirty junkyard shack. But if that were so, then what connection did she have to the case? How did she know the name of the missing girl, Kathryn Southern? Why had she been having nightmares for more than two decades about a monster she'd instantly recognized as Darryl Bookerman as soon as she saw his photograph?

"Who is the prettiest one?" she asked.

"Isn't it you?" Bigelson replied. "Aren't you the one who escaped? Maybe I'm wrong, but it sure seems to fit."

"This is going to sound a bit strange, Mr. Bigelson—"

"Call me Jeff. Fair's fair, Caitlin."

She nodded. "Okay, Jeff. This is going to sound strange, but I've had some memory issues."

She explained in the vaguest possible detail about suffering lapses of memory and the possibility that she had blocked out some traumatic events. To his credit, Bigelson—who had probably heard numerous claims of amnesia during his years of law enforcement—listened patiently and managed to keep his face from expressing doubt. As she spoke, she felt the old retired detective sizing her up, gauging her veracity.

"Well, those were certainly traumatic events," he said.

"So," Caitlin said, "can you tell us what you were talking about? You thought I might be the one who escaped. The 'prettiest one,' you said."

After a brief hesitation, Bigelson gave a short nod, as if deciding that he would choose to believe her. "That sick bastard Bookerman grabbed those girls off that playground when no one was looking. By the time their parents realized they were missing, he was long gone. Drove them a couple dozen miles back to his filthy place. Cops were out looking, but they never had a chance because they didn't have a description of him or his vehicle."

"So how did they find him?"

"The next day, somebody called the cops. See, this guy was walking his dog on the street and sees this little blonde girl come around the corner. She's dirty and looks lost. He asks her if she's okay, and she tells him that the Bogeyman had stolen her and two other girls she had been playing with off a playground, that he'd taken them to a garbage dump. At first, the guy doesn't believe her. I mean, why would he? But then, according to the guy, he could smell garbage on her, like she'd just waded through a dump. So he called the cops and told them what he knew. We went out there and found Bookerman passed out drunk. The door was wide open when we got there. There was only one little girl inside that shack, though. It looked like the girl who got away just walked right out after the dirtbag passed out. The little girl in the shack, she could have walked right out, too, if she'd thought to do it. But she was in a bad way. She had been . . . abused. I think she was in shock."

"The little blonde girl who escaped said the man who took them was the Bogeyman?" Caitlin asked.

"She called him that. We always assumed she'd heard his actual name somehow. Bookerman . . . Bogeyman . . . they're close. But it's also possible that she . . ." He paused. "You've seen a picture of him, I assume?"

Caitlin nodded.

Bigelson said, "Given his appearance, and the fact that he snatched that little girl and the others, maybe she believed he actually was a Bogeyman. There was no way for us to know for sure."

"We read an old news story about the case," Josh said. "It didn't mention a girl escaping."

"We never knew who she was," Bigelson said. "When the guy hung up with the cops and turned around, the girl was gone. He looked for her, or said he did, and I believed him, but she was gone."

Bix joined the conversation. "Why didn't you assume the girl on the street was Kathryn Southern, that she was the one who had escaped from the shack?"

"Because the girl who got away was pale blonde, and Kathryn Southern had unmistakably red hair. Also, we showed Kathryn's picture to the witness and he said it wasn't the girl he saw."

"Didn't you look for her, for the blonde girl?"

"Of course we did. But all we knew was that she was a little girl of about five with blonde hair." He looked at Caitlin again. "Bet that hair's blonde under that bottled red."

Caitlin nodded.

"But wasn't there a missing persons report or something on the blonde girl?" Bix asked. "Hadn't her parents called the cops when she didn't come home the night before?"

"That's the thing," Bigelson said. "They didn't. No one was reported missing but the two girls . . . the one we never found and the one we did. So we had nothing else to go on. We asked around, but no one knew anything. We talked to the girl we found there, or we tried to, anyway, but she wasn't in any shape to be talking . . . at least not yet. I don't think she talked for a while, to tell you the truth . . . definitely not until sometime after the trial. But by that time, Bookerman was already in prison and there didn't seem to be a reason any longer to look for the girl who had escaped. Like I said, no one else was looking for her, so we figured she must have just found her way home." He looked directly at Caitlin. "Or should I say, *you* found your way home?"

She shrugged as if she wasn't sure, but she was. It was her. She had no doubt. She had been abducted as a child. She had been in that shack, in that junkyard. She had walked through that garbage dump. She had been . . .

"Why wouldn't you have been reported missing, Katie?" Bix asked.

Caitlin didn't respond. It was another mystery, maybe, but one more than she needed at the moment.

"You really don't remember any of this, do you?" Bigelson asked.

"I don't."

He grimaced suddenly, as though someone had twisted that invisible knife in his back. "Sorry," he said. "I'm a bit overdue for my painkiller," he added, waving his hand at his bedside table, on which sat a few prescription pill bottles, a pitcher of water with an empty glass, and a copy of the *Boston Globe*.

"You want something?" Caitlin asked. "We can help you."

"Not just yet." After a deep breath, he said, "I don't know what you do or don't remember, Caitlin, but if it makes you feel any better, I don't think he touched you."

"What?"

"I don't think he got the chance to . . . to hurt you."

"Why do you say that?"

"Because when we arrested him, he was still so drunk he was babbling like an idiot. When he saw you were gone, he said—and I can still hear the sonofabitch's words—he said, 'Damn it, I never got to the prettiest one. I was saving her for last.'"

"That's why you keep calling me 'the prettiest one.' Because he did."

She shuddered at the thought of the horror she had barely escaped. A moment later, though, an immense wave of relief washed over her because she *did* escape it. Then the emotional roller coaster she was riding sent her down another steep drop when she realized that she had walked out of that shack and left an abused girl behind. She thanked God that the girl apparently suffered no more abuse after Caitlin left to find help. If Bookerman had continued his depravity with her or, God forbid, killed her as he likely did Kathryn Southern, well . . . Caitlin didn't know if she would have been able to live with herself.

As if sensing what she was thinking, Bix said, "Looks like you saved that girl's life, Katie."

Caitlin nodded but didn't feel much like a hero. "For what, though? Sounds like she was completely traumatized by the experience. We don't even know her name. Who knows if she ever fully recovered?"

"She recovered all right," Bigelson said. "Took a while, I can't lie to you, but we followed up now and then over the years, and by the time the girl hit high school, she was doing okay, I think."

"I don't suppose you remember her name," Caitlin said.

"I do."

"Any chance you'd share it with us? I'd love to find her and see for myself that she's doing all right."

Bigelson shook his head slowly. "You'll just have to take my word for it. She has a right to her privacy, and to whatever peace she's been able to find."

Caitlin couldn't argue with that. She was about to ask another question when she saw that Bigelson's eyes had closed. He looked like he might fall right to sleep, then he winced all of a sudden as, presumably, a stab of pain lanced through him. Caitlin started toward him, but he opened his eyes and held up a hand to stop her.

"I'm okay," he said.

"Is it getting bad?" Caitlin asked.

He forced a smile but shrugged in a way that told her it had passed "getting bad" a few miles back and was steaming toward "excruciating." Caitlin was startled by a knock at the window. Dolores stood on the other side of the glass, a wide-brimmed gardening hat shading her face. Bigelson nodded to her and waved. Message received. The visit was running a little long now.

"Anything else I can do for you here?" Bigelson asked them. His voice was getting weaker.

"I think you've done enough," Caitlin said.

Bigelson nodded. He hesitated. "You seem like a nice girl. A nice woman, I mean. So before you go, I want to give you . . . well, let's call it fair warning."

Caitlin frowned.

"Remember when I said I know who you are?"

She nodded. "The one who escaped, you said."

It was the old man's turn to nod. "Well, there was that, sure. But as we talked, I realized there was more." He nodded to the newspaper on the bedside table. "You seen the paper today?"

Caitlin said nothing. Neither did Josh or Bix.

"There's a story in there about a murder in a warehouse over in North Smithfield. Got a couple of police sketches with it."

Caitlin remained silent.

"One sketch looks a heck of a lot like you, Caitlin," Bigelson said, then screwed his face up in pain.

When it passed a few seconds later, Bix asked, "And what if it does?"

Bigelson looked at Bix. "I don't know what happened in that warehouse," and Caitlin thought, *Join the club*. "I don't know if she was there or what she might or might not have done if she *was* there. But I was a cop, son. I have to call the police, tell them you three were here. I have no choice. I can wait an hour or so before making the call, maybe, if that'll help you, but I do have to call. I'm sorry, Caitlin."

He was breathing differently now. The slightest movement seemed to cause him pain.

"Can you get my wife in here from the garden?" he asked.

"You need something?" Caitlin asked, alarmed.

He squeezed his eyes shut. "My pain pills. I waited too long."

Bix was closest to the table, and he moved quickly. He picked up first one prescription bottle, then two others. Finally, he popped the top from one, then another, and shook a few pills into his palm. Eyes still closed, Bigelson held out his hands and Bix placed the pills in one and a glass of water from the table in the other.

"Which are these?" Bigelson asked without opening his eyes.

"The Oxycodone," Bix said. "Is that right?"

Bigelson nodded as he put the pills in his mouth. He took a long sip of water, struggled for a moment to choke down the pills, then let his head lay back against the pillow.

"Sometimes tough to swallow those things," he said weakly.

Josh leaned close to Caitlin and whispered, "We should go. He's going to call the cops."

Caitlin nodded. Josh was right. They needed to leave now.

"Mr. Bigelson?" she said. Bigelson's eyes fluttered open. "Thank you."

Bigelson smiled tiredly and closed his eyes again.

CHAPTER TWENTY-FIVE

DETECTIVE HUNNSAKER FLASHED HER SHIELD to a good-looking bartender who would have been just her type twenty years ago. She smiled and he smiled back, and she remembered a couple of mistakes she had made in her youth with guys like this one. She held out the sketch of the redhead.

"You know this girl?"

He hesitated. He could have been thinking or he could have been stalling. He shook his head.

"Manager in?" Hunnsaker asked.

"Martha," the bartender called to a medium-size, medium-age woman who had just come through a door from a back room. "Can you come here?"

Hunnsaker identified herself to the woman—Martha, apparently—then showed her the computer sketch.

"She look familiar?" Hunnsaker asked.

Martha looked at the sketch closely and frowned.

"I don't think so," she said. "But a lot of people come through here. It's possible she came in here, had a bite to eat or a few drinks, but I don't remember her."

Hunnsaker nodded as though that made perfect sense. "Yeah, but we got a tip that maybe she works here."

Martha's frown deepened and she shook her head. "Nah, that girl doesn't work here."

"You sure?"

"I think I know my employees, Detective."

Hunnsaker nodded. "Mind if I ask around?"

Martha hesitated only slightly, then said, "Knock yourself out."

"Thanks for your cooperation."

Hunnsaker surveyed the room. Three servers. Probably a cook or two in the back. Only seven patrons at the moment. Maybe one of them would recognize the redhead even though Martha hadn't . . . or claimed that she hadn't.

Ten minutes later, the employees present had given Hunnsaker nothing. Either this was a tight-knit group and they were covering for her, or they truly didn't recognize her.

Hunnsaker looked at the patrons. The odds of one of the seven of them recognizing the redhead were slim, but Hunnsaker asked each of them anyway. She came up empty again. From behind the bar, Martha watched while pretending not to. Hunnsaker walked back over to her.

"Guess that's it, then," Hunnsaker said. "Except for your list of employees. I'd like to see that."

Martha nodded slowly, as if considering the request. "You got a warrant?"

Hunnsaker smiled. "See, that's why I don't like TV cop shows. Everyone thinks they're smart because of those shows. Criminals think they know how to get away with crimes. Witnesses who don't want to be helpful ask for warrants. All because they see stuff like that on TV."

Martha said, "I'm not—"

"But if you watch those shows," Hunnsaker said, "then you know what would come next . . . in one of those shows, I mean. The cop would threaten to bring the Board of Health down here, and if everything's not totally up to snuff, the place gets shut down for a while."

"This place is right up to code," Martha said defensively.

"Of course it is, but then the TV cop would say something like, 'Hope you haven't served alcohol to any minors here,' and then the bar owner would say, 'We don't serve minors,' and then here's where the cop crosses the line, because tough cops don't always play by the rules, do they?" Martha said nothing, so Hunnsaker continued. "The cop would say, 'Well, I bet we could find a couple of minors, maybe one we picked up holding a few dozen Oxy pills, and another who got nabbed shoplifting, and I bet they'd say that you served them alcohol. That is, if we asked them right.' Now, I don't play those games, of course, but that's what they would probably say on TV."

Hunnsaker watched Martha's jaw muscles clench a few times. "All you want is a list of employees?"

"For now."

Martha sighed and pulled a spiral-ring notebook from behind the bar. She flipped it open and turned the book around for Hunnsaker to see. There were maybe fifteen names. One of them was crossed out. Hunnsaker felt a tingle of excitement.

"Who's that?" Hunnsaker asked. "It says Katherine Southern."

"She used to work here."

"Used to?"

"Till about two weeks ago."

"She fit the redhead's description by any chance?"

Martha scratched her chin. Hunnsaker saw a few random hairs poking out of it. "I don't really remember her."

"Got addresses for these people?"

"Not all of them."

"Really? Sounds like shoddy record keeping. Makes me wonder if everything is on the up-and-up here. Maybe some people are getting paid off the books. How about Katherine Southern? You have her address?"

Martha shook her head.

"How about if we go through your employee files? Would I find it there?"

After a brief hesitation, Martha said, "You wouldn't. I swear."

"And you don't happen to know where she lives, do you?"

"I don't. Really."

Hunnsaker nodded as she took out her smartphone and used it to snap a picture of the list.

"What are the folks on this list going to tell me when I ask them about Katherine Southern?"

Martha shrugged. "You'll have to ask them. I barely knew her. I don't know where she lives. All I had was that phone number."

Hunnsaker pocketed her phone. Martha had obviously been trying to hide something, and Hunnsaker didn't think it was simply that Southern was being paid under the table. Was it the fact that the redhead in the sketch was Katherine Southern?

"If you were me," Hunnsaker said, "which of these names would you start with? Who would you call first?"

After a long hesitation, Martha said, "You might want to start at the bottom."

Hunnsaker looked down at the notebook on the bar. The last name on the list was Jane Stillwood.

"Well," Hunnsaker said, "you see? In real life, these situations don't have to end like they do on TV. There's no reason to call the Board of Health here, and I don't see any evidence that you've been serving alcohol to minors. This went really well, I think."

Martha said nothing.

Walking to her car outside, Hunnsaker took out her phone again. She texted the photo of Martha's employee list to Padilla, then called him.

"What's this?" he asked.

"Employee list of Commando's, a bar on Chestnut Street. I've got a pretty good feeling that's where our mystery redhead worked till two weeks ago. I think I've got a name, too."

"Yeah?"

"Yeah. I think she goes by Katherine Southern. And that's her phone number on the list. I'll call it, but she won't answer. I'm also going to call the other names on this list and see who knows what about her. Someone knows something. I was advised to start with the last name."

"Want me to make some of the calls?"

"No," Hunnsaker said. "Where are you?"

"At the apartment building on Loring Avenue. The super here said the redhead—Southern, I guess—doesn't live here. She didn't live at the other two apartment buildings from the tip list, either."

"If that's the last of the apartments, then forget the rest of the list. We know where she worked. Now we have to find where she lives. Look into Katherine Southern. She has a phone number, which means she gets a bill, which means that someone has her address. But I doubt anyone's at her cell phone company right now who can give us an address, and I'd rather not wait till morning, so let's hope you find something before then. Check motor vehicles, property records, the usual. In the meantime, I'll be getting in touch with her former coworkers, starting with Jane Stillwood."

"Got it," Padilla said.

"We're getting close, Javy. I can feel it."

———

Caitlin's visit with Jeff Bigelson had yielded several answers, including one she hadn't ever expected to find—the reason for her nearly lifelong struggle with nightmares about the Bogeyman. She knew exactly what kind of monster he was now. She knew his real name. She knew her place in the events that gave birth to those nightmares. Still, there were so many questions left to be answered. Why had Caitlin come to Smithfield seven months ago? Why did she stop going to work two weeks ago? What was the significance of the names and the address on the list she'd kept hidden in her closet? And what the heck was she doing at that warehouse the other night? Most importantly, did she kill that man from the newspaper sketch, the man whose face she saw in her dream with a bullet hole in it? And if so, why?

The drive from Hyattville to Lewiston took just over twenty minutes. This wasn't a stop that was directly related to the more important aspects of Caitlin's investigation, but she had returned to Massachusetts in search of answers, so she might as well get as many as she could. Where they were going wasn't far out of the way, and though she didn't remember the exact address, she knew the street and she believed she'd recognize the house, even if she hadn't seen it in more than twenty years.

When she'd told the guys where she wanted to go, Josh had said, "Caitlin, I can't imagine how you're feeling, and I know you want answers, but I'm not sure we have time for detours right now. There may be time for this visit later, but right now, we have to keep moving. Bigelson recognized your face. He told us he's going to call the cops in an hour, if he even waits that long. Maybe he was lying. Maybe he called them the second we walked out the door."

"He'll wait," Bix said confidently, "and longer than an hour."

"He will?" Caitlin asked.

"He will. And I'm not a doctor, but I'd say we have at least a few hours."

"Why do you say that?"

"Because when I gave him his pain pills, I threw in a few of his sleeping pills. The bottle said to take one as needed for sleep."

"And you gave him one?" Josh asked.

"I gave him four."

"Along with his Oxycodone?"

"Yeah, but just one of those."

"Hell, Bix, you might have killed him," Josh said.

"That's 'glass is half-empty' kind of thinking," Bix said. "I also might *not* have killed him. I like to think of it that way."

"Damn it, Bix, if the police find out we drugged—"

"Relax. I don't take drugs, never have, but I have friends who used to, and I know a thing or two."

"There's a huge shock."

"Four isn't gonna kill the guy, not even with an Oxycodone. He'll sleep for a few hours and wake up nice and rested. With any luck, he'll forget to even call the cops when he does."

Josh shook his head. "Still," he said, "we're getting short on time, Caitlin. You should keep things short if you can."

"Understood."

———

Bix turned the Explorer onto Attleburn Road and, with Caitlin scrutinizing every house they passed on both sides of the street, eased the car along until she finally pointed to a small house and said, "There it is."

Bix pulled to a stop. The Bigelson cottage, it was not. It wasn't in complete disrepair, but it was ten years past needing a paint job, and the lawn was in urgent need of attention.

"You sure?" Bix asked.

"It was light blue when I lived here, but that's definitely it," Caitlin said.

"That house *is* light blue," Josh said from the backseat. "Or it used to be, anyway. It's faded to almost nothing now."

"Think anyone's home?" Caitlin asked.

"I know a great way to find out," Bix said.

Caitlin nodded. "I'll do this by myself, okay, guys?" She knew they would protest, so she added, "If anyone's home, they'll be more likely to talk if it's just me."

Without waiting for them to agree, she stepped out of the car. She stood for a moment looking at the house where she'd lived for just two years. She remembered it a little, remembered playing with a ball in the front yard. There were far fewer weeds back then, and a few more flowers. And as is always the case when one visits a place from one's youth, everything looked far smaller than Caitlin remembered it being. She walked up the uneven brick walk trying to remember if she had been happy here. She honestly couldn't remember any truly happy times, but neither did she have specific bad memories of this place. She was okay with that balance.

She rang the bell and waited. She rang again and the door opened to reveal a small, thin woman in stained sweatpants, a faded floral top, and cheap sneakers. She had a beverage in a glass in one hand, and Caitlin couldn't tell if it was alcoholic but wouldn't have been shocked to learn that it was. The woman looked vaguely familiar.

"Yes?" she said, and the harshness of her smoker's voice was startling.

"My name is Caitlin. I used to live here."

It took a little convincing, but the woman eventually allowed Caitlin to come inside. Caitlin gave a quick wave to the guys in the car and followed her host through a house that reeked of decades of stale cigarette smoke. The interior was dark, as every shade and curtain was drawn mostly closed. Caitlin wondered why anyone would choose darkness over the light but knew that this woman may have had very good reasons. As they walked through the hallway, past the living room, past a bathroom, and into the kitchen, Caitlin tried to remember living in these rooms. They were marginally familiar, but her memories of that time were as dim as the light inside that house.

They sat at a table with a scratched Formica surface, a half-full ashtray in the center. The woman didn't offer anything to Caitlin, for which Caitlin was thankful. She also didn't light up a cigarette, for which Caitlin was also grateful.

Without bothering with small talk, Caitlin told the woman who she was and why she was there. She explained that this had been her foster home from the time she was three years old until she was five. Mrs. Goldsmith—that was her name, and it definitely sounded familiar to Caitlin—had been listening fairly attentively, but now, something changed in her eyes.

"You said your name is Caitlin?"

"That's right."

Mrs. Goldsmith nodded to herself, and Caitlin knew that the older woman recognized her, or at least realized now who she was.

Though the house held little in the way of memories for Caitlin, either good or bad, it was nonetheless not a pleasant place to be. Caitlin wanted answers to some very specific questions, and then she wanted out of there.

She told Mrs. Goldsmith about Darryl Bookerman. The woman said she recalled something about that story, but it was a long time ago. Caitlin agreed that it was. She said she had come to ask just one question: Why hadn't Mrs. Goldsmith and her husband—Caitlin's foster father at the time—called the police when Caitlin went missing? According to retired detective Jeff Bigelson, Caitlin had been missing overnight, yet the police never received a missing person report on any child matching her description.

Mrs. Goldsmith looked away. Then she stood and walked to the kitchen counter and picked up a pack of Marlboros from beside the telephone. She shook out a cigarette and lit it with a disposable lighter. She stood there flicking her ash into an ashtray she kept on the counter despite keeping another one on the table just a few feet away. Finally, the woman spoke.

"I wanted to call the police," she said in her throaty smoker's growl. "But Harold wouldn't have it. He figured you had just run away, like so many kids do. He said he did it when he was a kid and he found his way back home. He said you would, too. That you'd be fine. And it looked like he was right. You look okay to me."

Caitlin didn't want to be confrontational because the woman could ask her to leave at any moment, but that wasn't enough for her. Not nearly.

"I was only five years old, Mrs. Goldsmith. A five-year-old girl alone, away from home."

"Like I said, things came out okay. You look fine now, anyway . . . though I remember you as a blonde."

"Darryl Bookerman abducted me. Took me and those other two girls. He kept us for an entire day. One of them, he abused. The other . . . well, they never found her."

The woman took a long drag on her cigarette. "I guess you were pretty lucky, then," she said, though her tone was less harsh than it had been.

"I was. The thing is, I can't understand why you wouldn't have called the police. Sure, I was just a foster child, but you were supposed to take care of me."

Mrs. Goldsmith looked out through a crack in the curtains over the sink for a while, then turned to face Caitlin. "Like I said, I wanted to call, but Harold, my husband—he died eight years ago— he didn't want to. He figured that if the police found out we lost you, they might come and take our other foster kids away. We had a few at that time, you see, and we needed every one of them just to get by. We were worried they'd take them all away and not let us have any more, either. So Harold figured we should wait a couple of days, see if you turned up, and if you did, no harm, right?"

"And if I didn't?"

"We'd call the police then."

Caitlin took a moment to process that. She had been little more than a commodity to this couple.

"We never mistreated you or anything," Mrs. Goldsmith said.

That, at least, was true.

"So what happened?" Caitlin asked. "I just showed up here again after being gone for a night?"

The woman hesitated. "Actually, you were gone for a few days."

"A few? How many?"

"Four or five, I think. Probably just four."

"Just four?" Caitlin echoed.

Mrs. Goldsmith shrugged her bony shoulders and ground out her cigarette in the ashtray. Immediately, she lit another. Caitlin had never been a smoker, but she thought it probably would have been easier if the woman had lit the second one directly from the first, but perhaps this way she was able to fool herself into thinking that she wasn't a chain-smoker. She seemed good at fooling herself.

Mrs. Goldsmith said, "We got a call from someone at some church or something. They had an orphanage there. They said that someone had brought a little girl to them a couple of days earlier. The girl said her name was Mary or Sue or something, I can't remember what it was. They began to process her or whatever they did back then, but suddenly, on the second or third day, the girl changed her story. Said her name was Caitlin Goldsmith and she lived on Attleburn Road. They looked us up and called us. But when Harold got there to pick you up, people from the foster-care program were waiting."

As they should have been, Caitlin thought but resisted the urge to say.

"We lost you," Mrs. Goldsmith said. "We lost all of you. You never came back again, and they came and took the others away. It worked out just the way Harold was afraid it would."

Caitlin wouldn't swear to it, but it sure looked to her like Mrs. Goldsmith was glaring at her accusatorily, as though all of that were Caitlin's fault.

"They said they'd find you new homes and that we were through as foster parents."

Caitlin nodded.

"We never mistreated you," Mrs. Goldsmith said again. "You or any of the others."

Caitlin nodded again and stood. She thanked the older woman and said that she would be able to find her own way out. As she passed one last time through the dark house, she couldn't help but recall the sunny times she'd spent in her next home, with her next foster parents, the ones who ultimately adopted her and gave her their name and loved her the way parents are supposed to love their daughters, right up until their untimely deaths in a car accident when Caitlin was twenty.

Caitlin opened the front door and didn't bother to turn to take a last look at the place as she closed the door behind her and breathed in the clean air outside. She walked back toward the car. Even though she didn't yet know why the Bogeyman . . . or was it Bookerman? . . . was on her list or who One-Eyed Jack or Bob were, she had to admit that she was starting to get some answers. So far, though, she didn't like the ones she was getting. Not at all.

CHAPTER TWENTY-SIX

ON THE WAY BACK TO Smithfield, Bix listened while Caitlin filled Josh and him in on her conversation with her foster mother from years ago. Bix hadn't even known that she had lived in foster homes. Then he reminded himself that he didn't really know that much about her at all, at least not the real her.

Caitlin said, "After I escaped from Bookerman's house, and after I told the story to the guy who called the cops, why didn't I go back to my . . . to the Goldsmiths' house? How did I end up in an orphanage? And why did I give them a fake name at first, before finally giving them my real name a few days later?"

"You know what I think?" Bix said.

"I can guess what you think," Caitlin said. "And I bet Josh is thinking the same thing. Because that's what I think, too." After a pause, she added, "It sounds like I might have had a little dissociative fugue way back then."

"It seems to fit," Josh agreed. "If they really can be triggered by traumatic events, I'd certainly say that what you experienced qualifies. You don't remember anything from Bookerman's house or the days in the orphanage, so the amnesia is there."

"And it seems I established a new identity for a while," Caitlin said, "calling myself by a different name for a few days before apparently coming out of the fugue and giving them my real name and the street where I lived." She paused. "So, it looks like this is something of an issue for me," she said sadly. "I wonder if there have been any other instances of fugue states during my life. I don't remember any."

"Well," Bix said gently, "I'm not sure you would, Katie."

"I mean, I don't ever remember waking up in a strange city or learning that months had gone by without my knowing it. No gaps in time that I can't account for."

"Even if you've experienced them before," Josh said, "they're still quite rare. You may have had only the two. They're probably only triggered in you by really, really traumatic events."

"Which makes me wonder what sent me into a fugue state seven months ago."

They fell silent until Bix said, "I keep wondering how you ended up in Smithfield."

"Yeah," Caitlin said. "Why would I want to come back here, of all places?"

"It's hard to say why you would have fixated on such a terrible event from your life," Josh said, looking at Caitlin, "but maybe after experiencing something truly traumatic seven months ago after you left our house—whatever it was that threw you into a fugue state—you found your way back here because it's a place you subconsciously associate with traumatic events."

"Armchair analysis," Bix said.

"Got a better theory?"

"That's possible, I suppose," Caitlin said. "We're filling in some of the blanks, anyway, even if I'm not actually remembering anything. We know now where the red hair comes from, and the name Katherine Southern/Southard, though I confused the spelling."

"Well," Bix said, "we may know where those things *come from*, but not *why* you took the name or *why* you dyed your hair red."

Caitlin was nodding her head slowly, as though working something through. "I must have heard Kathryn's name back then, either while we were in that shack or before, on the playground. And because of what we shared, what we . . . went through, it makes sense that I might feel some deep connection to her. And if Josh is right and I somehow . . . tapped into feelings about this place, maybe her name and hair color bubbled to the surface. As for why I would go so far as to take that name and dye my hair, though . . . I can't even guess."

"I doubt it was a conscious decision," Josh said. "More likely you were operating on autopilot for a while, doing those things without necessarily knowing why. Hell, you'd lost your whole identity. Bix asked your name, and for whatever reason, it was Kathryn's that came to mind."

"And then, what, once I said I was her, I remembered on some deep level that I should be a redhead?"

They were quiet for a moment, giving this thought.

"I guess that makes as much sense as the rest of this," Caitlin said. "We're just blowing bubbles here. Until we know more, we can't be sure about any of this—why I came here and why I subconsciously tried to become Kathryn Southern. Did I have a plan? Did I just get lost, end up here, and pick her name out of a mental hat?" She paused. "Why would I choose to bring all of this back into my life after I'd so successfully blocked it out decades ago?"

Bix opened his mouth to speak, but before he could say a word, his cell phone rang. With one hand on the steering wheel, he pulled the phone from his pocket and looked at the caller ID. "It's Janie."

After leaving Commando's earlier, they had discussed how best to approach Jane Stillwood. One option was for Caitlin to call her and pretend that she remembered Stillwood, which would be difficult given that they were supposed to be BFFs and all, and would therefore likely have an established rhythm to their interactions that Caitlin was unlikely to be able to fake convincingly. More importantly, it would be difficult for her to ask questions about what Caitlin had been doing lately and why she was doing those things. Wouldn't she already know? A second option was for Caitlin to call and give Stillwood the same story they had tried on Martha, the one in which Caitlin said she'd recently suffered a head injury and was having issues with her memory. The problem was that, though somewhat true, it was nonetheless a difficult story to believe.

After a short debate, they decided on a third approach. Bix would call Stillwood and tell her that he suspected Caitlin had gotten herself mixed up in something potentially dangerous and Bix wanted to help her get out of it. The problem with option number three was that Stillwood's loyalties would no doubt lie with Caitlin—or Katie, as Stillwood knew her. She would likely decide that if Katie was keeping things from her boyfriend, it was Stillwood's job to help keep those things secret. She might doubt that Bix had good intentions. Maybe he was merely suspicious of his girlfriend and was checking up on her. Still, they all agreed that Bix being the one to make the call made the most sense. So, on the way to the Bigelsons' house earlier, he had done so. Stillwood hadn't answered, so he left a message asking her to call him back. He'd said it was important.

And now she was calling back. Bix had no idea how this conversation was going to go. He had met Stillwood a few times, but they hadn't spent much time together. He certainly had never called her before.

He said hello and they forced a few pleasantries, neither of them putting much effort into the exchange, before Bix got down to it.

"Janie, I'm worried about Katie."

"Why?"

"I think she might be in trouble."

Cautiously, Stillwood said, "Yeah?"

"Yeah. And I'm hoping you can help me."

"Help you what?"

"Help me get her out of it." Stillwood said nothing. "Janie? You still there?"

"Yeah. Where's Katie now?"

"She's out somewhere. That's why I called you."

"Yeah?"

And so it went, much the way they expected it might. Stillwood was cagey and not the least bit forthcoming. At first she played dumb, but finally she came right out and said that Katie's business was her own, even if she lived with Bix, and that Stillwood wasn't about to get her friend into trouble.

"But that's just it, Janie . . . I'm trying to keep her *out* of trouble."

They went around a few more times, and once or twice Bix thought she might just hang up. Finally, he said, "Goddamn it, Janie, I love the hell out of Katie . . . more than most people love the people they love, you understand? I'm not going to let anything happen to her. And I don't think she's sneaking around behind my back, if that's what you think I'm thinking. She wouldn't do that to me, and even if she did, if that's what makes her happy, then she should be happy."

Bix sensed Caitlin listening with interest beside him. Josh, too. He hoped they thought he was just playacting for Stillwood's benefit—at least he hoped Josh thought so—but he was on a roll and he wasn't about to dial it back, not when he thought he might be getting somewhere.

"But I think it's something else," he continued, "and I think maybe you think so, too. So I need you to tell me everything you know that she was up to. And I'll get the ball rolling for you, okay? I know that this started about two weeks ago, right around when she stopped going to work."

"You . . . know about that?" Stillwood asked. "Katie told me she wasn't gonna tell you."

"She didn't, but I found out. And thinking back on it, I sort of remember her acting a little different with me starting right around then. I wasn't sure at the time, but now I think so. Not angry with me, or less in love with me, just . . . like she had something on her mind."

Bix thought he heard a mumble on Stillwood's end of the line, as though she had quietly said "mm hmm" in agreement.

"What do you say, Janie? Will you help me help the woman I love, who just happens to be your closest friend?"

Stillwood fell silent. Finally, she said, "Did you hear that somebody got himself murdered at a warehouse over in North Smithfield?"

"Yeah."

"Don't suppose you saw the drawings of the victim and some woman who's supposedly connected to the case?"

"I did."

"Is that a drawing of Katie, Bix?"

"I don't know, Janie, not for sure. But maybe now you have some idea of why I'm worried about her, worried that she somehow got herself into trouble. Maybe you can see why I need you to tell me everything you know. For Katie's sake."

———

As it turned out, Jane Stillwood knew a lot about what Caitlin had been up to lately. Not everything they needed to know, which was a disappointment to Caitlin, but a good amount nonetheless.

Bix had looked pointedly at her and then at Josh, then held a finger to his lips and said, "I'm gonna put you on speakerphone, Janie. I hate driving with a phone to my ear." Without giving her a chance to object, he pushed a button on his phone. "You there?" he asked.

Stillwood's voice came through the phone's little speaker. "I'm here," she said, and Caitlin had no trouble hearing her.

There were questions and answers, reluctance and prodding, doubt by Stillwood that she was doing the right thing, and reassurance by Bix that she was. Eventually, she shared what she knew.

Things had been fine, Stillwood said—Katie had been the same old Katie—up until one night a couple of weeks ago. They were working the same shift at Commando's, and it was a busy night. Todd, an unreliable prick who called in sick every time there was a big basketball game on or something, had begged off work again, and Stillwood and Katie were doing extra duty. So Janie definitely noticed when Katie sort of just . . . stopped working. Stopped even moving. People were buzzing all around her—customers, waitresses—and Katie had just stood there by the bar, staring straight ahead. Maybe she was looking at someone in particular, but it kind of seemed like she was just zoning out. Stillwood took a quick look around but didn't see anything out of the ordinary, nobody staring back at Katie or, alternatively, trying not to be seen. But Katie had sure seen something or someone. As Stillwood had said, though, it was a busy night and Martha was barking at everyone, so Stillwood gave Katie a nudge. Katie said something really weird then. "Did you see him?" she asked. When Stillwood asked who, Katie didn't answer directly but said, "He was with that guy with one eye."

At that, Caitlin, Josh, and Bix had exchanged glances. *One-Eyed Jack.*

Stillwood continued her story. She had told Katie that she didn't see anybody with one eye, and Katie said he had just left. They both had. Again, Stillwood asked her *who* had just left with a one-eyed guy, but after another moment in a daze, Katie shook her head and wouldn't talk about it. But according to Stillwood, Katie wasn't the same after that.

A few days later, she'd finally admitted that she was trying to find the two guys who had been to the pub the other night—a one-eyed man with long blond hair, and the guy he was with, both probably in their thirties. It turned out she had been asking most of the regulars if they knew the guys. She described them, focusing on the blond guy with one eye, presumably because he was the more memorable of the two. Katie had tried to be casual about it, as though she were just making conversation, but Stillwood said it was starting to get weird. Finally, according to what Katie told Stillwood later, somebody said he knew of a guy like that. Eye patch, long yellow hair. Katie asked how she could find him, but the guy shut down. Probably didn't want to get involved. But Stillwood reminded Bix that Katie has a way with people, so the guy finally admitted that he'd seen the one-eyed guy one night at Bob's.

Caitlin caught Josh's and Bix's eyes again. Bob? Another name from Caitlin's secret list.

"Bob who?" Bix asked.

"Not Bob who," Stillwood said. "Bob what. It's a place, a bar. The Barrel O' Beer. Everyone calls it Bob's because of the initials," she added in a tone that implied that Bix was a halfwit.

Bix nodded, then shook his head slowly, as though he felt he should have thought of that.

"Never been there," Bix said, "but I know of the place."

Stillwood said, "So the next thing I know, Katie starts calling in sick at work, then finally just stops coming altogether. Martha fired her, though she never actually told Katie, I think. Just announced to everyone else that Katie was fired."

"And what was Katie doing all that time?" Bix asked. "Now that she had stopped going to work?"

Caitlin could practically hear Stillwood shrug. "Looking for the guy with one eye, I guess . . . though I think it was the other guy she was really looking for, the one-eyed guy's friend."

"She tell you she was doing that?" Bix asked.

"She did, without actually saying it, if you know what I mean. She didn't want to talk about it, whatever it was. I pushed her on it a few times but she wouldn't give me anything. She started calling me less often, and she didn't answer a lot of my calls. She was a woman on a mission."

"To find the one-eyed guy and his buddy."

"I'm pretty sure," Stillwood said.

"Exactly where was she looking?"

"She wouldn't tell me. I doubt she would actually go inside Bob's—that place is just dangerous—but maybe she staked it out or something. Maybe she looked for them in other bars, too. I don't know. Like I said, she started shutting me out."

"Anything else?" Bix asked.

"Hold on . . ." A moment later, Stillwood said, "Sorry, another call is coming in. I'll ignore it. Oh, I've got a message, too. Didn't see it."

"Janie?" Bix prompted.

"Oh, yeah, sorry. What were you saying?"

"I was asking if there's anything else you can think of, anything I should know."

"That's about it," Stillwood said. "Except . . ."

"Yeah?"

"If she's in trouble, Bix . . . get her out of it."

"That's the plan."

He disconnected the call.

Caitlin summarized the situation for them. "So, according to Janie, a few weeks ago I saw a one-eyed blond man and his friend, and it freaked me out or something. I asked around and finally found out that he sometimes goes to a bar that everyone calls Bob's. I spent less and less time at work until finally I stopped going altogether, apparently to find those two guys."

"So who are they?" Josh asked.

Caitlin shrugged. "No idea. The one-eyed man is obviously not the guy I shot in the warehouse."

"You didn't shoot anyone, Caitlin," Josh said.

"Whatever," Caitlin said. "The warehouse victim had two eyes, according to his sketch." And, Caitlin knew, according to her nightmare in which she shot him to death. "So it's not One-Eyed Jack. But maybe the other guy, whoever he is . . . maybe that's the guy I shot."

"Come on," Josh said. "You didn't shoot anyone."

"We may find out soon enough," she said.

"Looks like we're going to Bob's," Bix said. "Like Janie said, that place can be dangerous, so fasten your seat belts."

CHAPTER TWENTY-SEVEN

THE BARREL O' BEER—or Bob's, as it was apparently known to the locals—was in a nasty part of town, not far from the equally nasty part of town where they had been just hours earlier when they visited the empty store that used to be called the King of Pawns. Josh saw similar graffiti on the walls and iron bars on the first-floor windows.

The entrance to Bob's was a black door in an otherwise featureless brick wall—well, featureless in the way of architecture. It was covered with spray-painted tags, gang signs, and random profane words. Affixed to the brick above the door was a wooden barrel, sawed in half, with the name of the establishment carved into it.

Josh, Caitlin, and Bix were sitting in the car, staring at the black door across the street, and Josh was about to suggest that they walk over and go inside when two guys rounded the corner and swaggered toward the bar. They looked like they could have literally come straight from prison. Josh wouldn't have been surprised to see them each dragging an iron ball by an ankle chain. The men opened the black door and pushed their way past a similar-looking guy on his way out. The guy leaving the bar was rubbing his forehead, as though he had a terrible headache . . . or had just been hit on the head with a barstool.

"Have you actually been here, hon?" Josh asked.

"I don't know," Caitlin said.

Josh couldn't imagine Caitlin would actually go inside a place like that. If she had been there, she must have waited in a car outside, watching, hoping to catch sight of One-Eyed Jack or his friend.

"Listen," Bix said, "I've never been here, but this place has a reputation, and it ain't a good one. It's in the news a lot because someone's always getting stabbed here, sometimes inside but more often out on the sidewalk in front. Shots have been fired here, too. Can't remember if anyone died. The point is, it could be dangerous in there. It's not a place for you. Maybe you should wait in the car. I'm worried about you."

"Thanks, but I need to go in," Caitlin said.

"I was talking to Josh."

"Knock that shit off, will you?" Josh said. He was getting really tired of Bix. Then again, he'd been tired of Bix the moment he first met him. "Let's go inside," he said without hesitation, and in a steady voice that belied his anxiety about entering the Barrel O' Beer. When he let Bix take the lead as they crossed the street, it was only so he could bring up the rear and keep Caitlin between them.

When they reached the black door, Bix grasped the handle and, before he pulled, looked at them and said, "Try to act like you belong here."

He opened the door and they stepped into the dark bar.

The bouncer sitting on a stool just inside the door had a head like a chunk of cement sitting directly atop his burly shoulders. No neck that Josh could see. He was chewing something that might have been gum but was equally likely to have been chewable ste-roids. They walked up to him, and before any of them could speak, the bouncer said, "These guys with you, Katie?"

Josh looked at Caitlin. So did Bix. Remarkably, Caitlin hesitated only a moment before saying, "For now they are. No promises they'll leave with me, though."

She winked at the bouncer and sauntered past. Stunned, Josh followed. Bix looked equally surprised as they pushed through a set of black velvet curtains and into a big room full of big men and big-haired women. Music thumped from a low-quality speaker system. Billiard balls clacked. People argued. A glass pitcher shattered. A bartender yelled in the face of a drunk slumped over the bar with his head on the scarred wooden surface.

"What the heck was that back there with the bouncer?" Josh asked Caitlin, just loud enough to be heard over the music.

Caitlin shrugged. "He recognized me. I've obviously been here before. I can't imagine I would have survived here if I didn't play it tough."

"I can't believe you've been inside this place before," Josh said. He also couldn't believe how easily Caitlin could turn on her wilder side when she needed it.

"Katie girl!" someone called. Josh turned to see an oak tree walking toward them, every square inch of his arms covered in tattoos of skulls. Nothing else, just skulls of various sizes.

"Hey, there," Caitlin replied in a voice that wasn't her own, again tapping into whatever persona she had channeled to get them past the bartender.

"Missed you last night," the guy said. Which confirmed that Caitlin had actually become something of a regular lately. "I was bringing one of these to my lady," the man said, holding up a bottle of Budweiser in each hand, "but she can get off her ass and get her own beer." He handed one of the Buds to Caitlin, then took a swig of his own and waited until Caitlin tipped her bottle up and took a deep draw on it. The guy smiled at her, then looked at Josh and Bix and the smile disappeared, his face hardening as though it had been slathered in quick-drying cement.

"Who are these guys?"

"Friends," Caitlin said.

The guy eyed them with suspicion and naked loathing. "They're with you?"

"They are."

The guy frowned before turning to Caitlin again. "You owe me a dance, Katie. The other night, you promised me another one, and then you were gone."

Had Josh heard that right? His wife had danced with Mad Max here?

"Not sure I'm gonna be here long tonight," Caitlin said. "Just came in for a drink with my friends. Rain check?"

The guy glowered at Josh and Bix again before nodding and lumbering off.

"Should we head to the bar?" Caitlin asked. "That's where they always start in the movies when they need information."

She headed for the bar across the room. On the way . . .

"Whassup, Katie?"

"Yo, Katie."

"Didn't see you in here last night, Katie."

"Katie, check out my new tattoo."

Finally, they reached the bar. It wasn't a long walk. The place wasn't that big. But it seemed as though every guy they passed had words of greeting for Caitlin and distrustful glares for Josh and Bix. To Josh, passing through the bar felt like walking through the jungle-cat section of a zoo with the cage doors all left open.

"Guess there's no doubt that I was a regular here, too," Caitlin said.

"Looks that way," Bix said.

When the bartender saw Caitlin, there was a perceptible brightening to the scowl on his face. He came over, ignoring several guys at the bar who didn't look used to being ignored, and said, "The usual, I assume." He smiled, exposing a nearly complete set of teeth.

Caitlin smiled back, and Josh saw that it was a smile different from her real one. This one was friendly but contained an element of mischief. As the bartender stepped away to fill a glass with beer from a tap, Josh said to her quietly, "You're getting good at this."

"Trying to fit in," she replied just as quietly. "I'm scared out of my mind."

"Don't worry," Josh said. "I'm right here." Reluctantly, he added, "So is Bix." He felt a bit silly, to be honest. It was pure bravado on his part, because while he knew that he would die to protect Caitlin, he also knew that a confrontation with anyone here was unlikely to end any other way.

The bartender returned and slid a beer in front of Caitlin. Josh opened his mouth to order one for himself, but the bartender leaned his brawny arms on the bar and ignored him, just like he ignored everyone else looking for drinks.

"You didn't show last night, Katie," he said. "I got worried about you." He smiled again. It was a smile that only a mother could love . . . and even that would require a very special kind of mother.

"Worried about me, huh?" Caitlin said.

"Sure. You come in every night for a couple of weeks, then you don't show. We were wondering what happened to you."

"We?"

"Sure, me and some of the guys," the bartender said, jerking his head to one side to indicate a group of toughs sitting a few feet away. Josh saw them each give a nod to Katie when she briefly turned their way. What the hell had she been doing here?

Caitlin smiled that mischievous smile again and said, "Nice to know you care, but I'm fine."

"Never said you weren't fine, Katie," the bartender said with another smile. "Give me a second, will you?"

He turned and yelled something loud and profane at the patrons who had been impatiently trying to get his attention. One by one he gave them drinks, along with an insult, and took their money.

"Looks like you've been making a lot of friends lately," Bix said quietly. He seemed amused. Josh was not. Katie coming here alone could have ended very badly for her.

She shrugged.

"You seemed to figure out how to fit in," Bix said, obviously impressed. "Guess there's a wild child in her after all, huh, Josh?"

Josh found that ignoring Bix was often preferable to acknowledging him. He also ignored the constant contact of the guy to his left, who kept bumping Josh and acting as though he held the deed to the tiny spot of real estate on which Josh was standing. Josh looked around the dark bar and tried to look inconspicuous doing it. He was searching for a blond guy with an eye patch.

Quietly, he said to Caitlin and Bix, "Anyone see One-Eyed Jack?"

Bix, who had also been scoping out the place, said, "No."

Caitlin shook her head, too, and they all continued to survey the people in the room. As Josh scanned the faces at the bar, his gaze caught a pair of eyes that seemed to be looking at Caitlin. They belonged to a guy with a scraggly, thin goatee in desperate need of a trim—or better yet, Josh thought, a total shave. The man was sitting by himself at the other end of the bar, apparently squinting at Caitlin. When he noticed Josh looking at him, he quickly dropped his eyes to the beer in front of him. *Probably just another guy who likes the way Caitlin looks*, Josh thought.

A bruiser walked past, zipping up his fly for some reason with one hand and carrying a pool cue in his other. As he passed, he said, "Gonna give me a chance to get even tonight, Katie?"

She turned on that Katie-in-the-Barrel-O'-Beer smile and said with a sexy wink, "Don't have the time tonight. You're too far in the hole. Maybe next time."

The guy snorted and lumbered on.

"You're a little too good at this, Caitlin," Josh said quietly.

"You're a natural," Bix added.

Caitlin shrugged. "Maybe I really have had some of this party girl inside me all along."

"That's what I've been saying, Katie," Bix said with a grin. Then he looked over Josh's shoulder and said, "I'll be right back."

———

Bix shouldered through some lugs slouching at the edge of the dance floor, watching other lugs dancing awkwardly with their she-lugs. He zeroed in on a big guy leaning over the pool table, lining up a shot. On the table in front of him was a small stack of bills. Bix stopped short of the table and watched the guy sink his shot and snatch up the money with a cocky grin.

"You almost scratched," Bix said.

"But I didn't," the guy said, then extended a fist, which Bix bumped with one of his own.

"Hey, Bix," the guy said.

"Hey, Longo."

The guy's name was Davey Longordo, and Bix knew him from when they'd worked construction together a few years back. Longo fit right in at the Barrel O' Beer. He took shit from nobody. But Bix and he had always gotten along. They'd even fought together, side by side. They were jumped one night behind a bar after a day of hard work followed by a night of hard drinking. Four against Longo and Bix. Davey took care of three of the guys and Bix took care of the fourth one, although—as Bix made clear to everyone who heard the story—his guy was the biggest. Anyway, a night like that . . . a fight like that . . . creates a bond between guys. He hadn't seen Longo for at least a year, but neither doubted that he had the other's respect.

"Never seen you in here before," Longo said.

"Never been here before. It kind of sucks, doesn't it?"

Longo laughed. "Sure does. Terrible vibe. But that's exactly why these guys come here. They're looking for trouble, hoping like hell they'll find it, or at least be around to watch when it happens."

"Why do the women come here?"

"Because they like the kind of guys who come here. Go figure, right?"

"How about you, Longo? Why do you come?"

Longo shrugged his thick shoulders. "I like the energy, I guess. You never know what's going to happen, but something just about always does."

"You a regular?"

"I'm here most nights, so I'm as much a regular as anybody here, I'd say." He paused, then added, "Except for that chick over there. The hot little redhead by the bar." Bix followed Longo's eyes to Caitlin, who looked perfectly comfortable in this hellhole of a bar. Beside her stood Josh, who didn't. Longo added, "Other than last night, maybe, she's been here every single night for the past few weeks, I think."

Bix nodded. "She is hot, isn't she?"

Longo shook his head. "Forget about it, bro. Katie's way out of your league. Besides, every guy in this place has hit on her multiple times and she's rejected every single one, every time."

Bix was relieved to hear it. "Isn't that pissing everyone off?"

"You know," Longo said, frowning as though the thought hadn't occurred to him, "you'd think it would. Something about her, though . . . somehow she does it in a way that seems all right. She's just a really cool chick."

It was time to fess up . . . or brag a little. "She's with me, Longo."

"Bullshit."

"No, seriously. She's been living with me for months. We're engaged."

"Bullshit."

"No bullshit."

Longo squinted at Bix for a long moment. "Hell, bro, you're doing something wrong then, 'cause she's spending every night here."

Bix replied, "That's a long story. I'll tell you about it sometime over beers."

"You buying?"

"I'll arm wrestle you for it." Which they both knew meant that Bix would be buying.

Longo nodded. "Who's the dweeb with Katie?" he asked.

Bix glanced at Josh, who, though clearly out of his element here, was doing an admirable job of not wetting himself in fear.

"That's part of the long story. We'll talk about him over our second beer."

They stood together awkwardly for another moment, and Bix sensed that Longo was about to walk away, so he quickly said, "To be honest, Longo, I'm not too thrilled that Katie's been coming here. I didn't know about it until tonight. I thought she was working."

Longo gave a low whistle. "Oh, boy. Well, listen, if it makes you feel any better, I was telling you the truth. She hasn't left with anyone or even gotten close to anyone, as far as us guys can tell.

Sure, she's a world-class flirter . . . but that's it. And it's not like she's a tease or anything. Nothing like that. She just chats you up, lets you buy her drinks, listens while you talk her up right back." He shook his head with a wry grin. "It's like she's a social worker or something, like it's her job to make you feel good about yourself. Like if a chick like that'll spend time with you, well, hell, maybe you aren't as bad as you think."

Bix nodded to himself.

"So don't worry, man," Longo said. "She ain't been naughty. And like I said, everyone seems to . . . I don't know, respect her, I guess."

Bix nodded again. He needed more. "So . . . what? She just comes in, flirts with guys, then leaves?"

"Flirts, dances a little, shoots pool . . . Hey, she's pretty good, too."

"And there's nobody she got close to? Nobody she talked about?"

Longo frowned. "Talked about?"

Bix sighed, as though this were hard for him. "Well, maybe you didn't see her with anyone in particular, but maybe you heard her talking about some other guy? Somebody I should be worried about?"

Longo said nothing.

"She ever talk about anyone in particular, Longo?"

Longo shifted his eyes over toward Caitlin again, then back to Bix. "Well, she did ask me about a couple of guys she said she was looking for. A few other guys in here told me later that she's asked them, too."

"Let me guess," Bix said. "One of them's a blond guy with one eye?"

"So you know them?"

"I heard about them. She ever find them?"

"I'm not sure, but a few nights ago, or maybe it was last week, some guy told her that he knew the guys she was talking about. He'd seen them someplace a few times. She left right after that."

"Where did he send her?"

Longo shrugged loosely, as though he could not possibly have cared less. And he very likely couldn't have. "I don't know," he said.

"How do you know that some guy told her that?" Bix asked.

"I was shooting pool with the guy."

"Didn't you hear where he told her he'd seen those guys?"

"We were shooting pool, Bix. They were talking but I walked away when it was my shot. I didn't hear the rest of what they said. As I recall, I went on a good run, sank five or six balls, and when I was done, Katie was gone."

"The guy you were playing, the guy who told Katie where she might find those other guys . . . is he here tonight?"

Longo gave a cursory glance around the bar, then shook his head. "Don't see him."

"Does he have a name?"

"It would be weird if he didn't, right? But I don't know it. I've seen him here two, maybe three times before. He's not a regular. Just some guy."

Bix exhaled in frustration and rubbed the stubble on his chin as he thought.

"Can I make a suggestion, Bix?" Longo said. Without waiting for a reply, he continued. "If you and Katie really are together, why the hell don't you just ask her these questions yourself?"

It was a fair question.

"Maybe I'll do that, Longo. Thanks."

Longo held his fist up for a good-bye bump and Bix complied.

"Don't forget those beers you owe me," Longo said.

"I don't owe you yet. We're arm wrestling for them, aren't we?"

Longo looked at him with amusement for a moment, then laughed as he turned back to the pool table and said loudly, "Okay, so whose turn is it to lose money to me?"

Bix wended his way through the bar, back to Caitlin and Josh, who reported that they hadn't learned anything of value. Josh said he would tell them what little he discovered when they were back in the Explorer, assuming it was where they'd left it, which wasn't a given in this neighborhood. They all agreed it was past time to leave.

———

As soon as the cute redhead left the bar with the men she was with, a guy with a scruffy goatee named Richie Janzen left his stool at the bar and made his way to the pool table. He put a ten-dollar bill on the edge of the table, reserving his place to play the winner. Two shots later, one of the players scratched on the eight ball and said, "Damn it, Longo, you got lucky that time."

"Seems like I get luckier every time I play you, Chet," Longo said with a laugh.

Janzen starting racking the balls. "Longo, right?" he asked.

"Do I know you?" Longordo asked.

"We shot stick a few weeks ago," Janzen lied. "You took me for twenty bucks. I'm back to get even," he added with a smile.

Longo shrugged and scattered the balls with a thunderous break.

Janzen waited through a few shots before casually asking, "Hey, I think I saw you a few minutes ago talking to a guy I used to work with. He left with that sweet little redhead."

"Bix?" Longo asked.

"Bix . . ." Janzen repeated, frowning, as if that didn't sound right. "Are you sure that's his name?"

Longo sank two balls, then said, "Last name's Bixby. First name is something weird, like Delbert or Desmond."

Janzen snapped his fingers. "Now I got it. Everyone calls him Bix, right?" Which, of course, Longo had called him a few seconds ago. "What's the deal with him and that redhead?"

"Katie? I guess she lives with him, the lucky bastard."

Janzen nodded, as if he once knew that but had temporarily forgotten. "I can't remember Katie's last name," he said.

Longo was leaning forward for a shot. He looked sideways at Janzen for a moment. "I never caught her last name. How did you say you know Bix?"

"Worked with him, I think."

"Doing what?" Another ball dropped.

Janzen had no idea. "Landscaping," he said.

"Didn't know Bix ever landscaped."

Longo lined up a shot on the eight ball.

"I think he was only with the company a few months. I was there less than a year myself."

The eight ball settled into a corner pocket. Janzen hadn't taken a shot. That was fine with him, though. He left the table a winner.

On the street outside, he took out his wallet and removed a folded cocktail napkin from it. He read the phone number written on it and dialed it on his cell phone. A moment later, his call connected.

"It's Janzen," he said into the phone. "Yeah, I'm down at Bob's. The redhead you were looking for the other night, Katie, she was in tonight. Just left . . . Swear to Christ, she was . . . No, I didn't get her last name, but I got something almost as good . . . The name of the guy she lives with. That's gotta be worth the hundred you promised, right? . . . Well, fifty, then, at least . . . Yeah, okay, next time I see you."

Janzen gave up the name and ended the call. It had cost him ten bucks to get the information from Longo, but he'd make forty bucks in profit. Not a bad return on twenty minutes of his time.

———

Martin Donnello slipped his cell phone back into his pocket and gave a quick scratch to the skin under his eye patch. He was a little surprised to have heard from Janzen. Sure, the guy spent his every waking hour in that dump, so if the redhead ever returned, he was likely to see her, but Donnello hadn't expected her to return so soon after what happened the other night at the warehouse.

Donnello knew she'd been there that night. Not her, necessarily, but someone. When bullets started buzzing and Donnello saw her in the shadows, he and his partner, Mike, gave chase, but even though they split to cover more ground, they lost her. Then when Donnello saw the woman's face in the police sketch, he remembered where he'd seen her—at the Barrel O' Beer two nights ago, the night things went to shit just hours later at the warehouse. It was only the second time Donnello had been to Bob's, so he didn't know who the woman was, but when he went back today shortly after the place opened at three this afternoon, he asked around and everybody seemed to know her. But no, that wasn't really true. They all flirted with her, they said, and she flirted back, but nobody actually knew who she was. And given what had gone down the other night, Donnello had doubted that she'd ever show up there again. More likely, he'd thought, she was on a Greyhound at the moment just outside of San Antonio or somewhere equally far away. So when Donnello gave that pathetic boozehound Janzen his number and asked him to call if the redhead ever came back, he didn't really expect to hear from him. But Janzen had called.

Donnello dialed his phone and waited. Damn voice mail again. Where the hell was Mike? Donnello thought he might have been shot the other night, but he figured it was only a flesh wound. But maybe Donnello was wrong. Maybe it was much worse.

When Mike's outgoing message ended, Donnello said, "I don't know where the hell you are or what the hell you've been doing, but I've been busy looking for the girl from the warehouse, like you should have been doing. And I found her. Well, almost. I've got her first name and the name of the guy she lives with. As soon as I have his address, I'll call you. Pick up next time, would you?"

Donnello hadn't talked to Mike since the warehouse. When things go to shit like they did that night, you stay the hell away from the people you were involved with for a little while. But things were different this time. This time, that damn redhead got involved. The cops would find her eventually. Donnello planned to get to her first.

Fortunately, he had a name now. Delbert or Desmond Bixby. Couldn't be too many of those around. Shouldn't be hard to find him. And when he did, he'd find her.

CHAPTER TWENTY-EIGHT

CAITLIN SAT LOW IN HER seat, her back to the rest of the diner behind her. She hoped the high seat backs of the booth would keep people from seeing and recognizing her. For good measure, she was wearing a worn Red Sox baseball hat Josh had found on the floor of Bix's car.

"Relax a little, Katie," Bix said. "No one's going to recognize you. And if they do, no one in this place is gonna call the cops on you."

"How can you be so sure?" Caitlin asked.

"Because there's no reward in it for them. If the cops ever put a dollar figure on you, then we'll have to be careful."

"What about someone seeing me and calling the police just to do his or her civic duty?"

"We're in the wrong part of town for something like that."

When they'd left the Barrel O' Beer a couple of minutes ago, they'd driven a few blocks until spotting a hole-in-the-wall with the no-frills name of "Diner." They were hungry, not having eaten since breakfast, so when they saw the diner, Bix slowed down the SUV and they looked in the windows as they passed. There were only a few customers, so they decided to chance it. Once inside, Caitlin walked with her head down to a booth in the back. Josh slid in beside her and Bix sat across from her.

"I like what I see here," Bix had said.

"What's that?" Josh had asked.

"That nobody gave a shit about us when we came in. Nobody looked up, not even the waitresses."

Bix's observation was borne out over the next several minutes when nobody came to take their orders. As much as they craved anonymity, they also wanted food, so Bix finally whistled for a waitress, who shuffled over and took their orders without looking up from her little notepad.

While they waited for their food, Bix finished telling them what Longo had said, that he overheard someone telling Caitlin where he'd seen the one-eyed blond guy once or twice.

"But he didn't say where?" Josh asked.

"He didn't know."

"So we still don't know where the hell to go."

"Maybe we do," Caitlin said. "I think we should go back to the King of Pawns."

"The shop was closed," Josh said.

"It's the only address on my list. It has to be there for a reason. The Barrel O' Beer was on the list, too, and that panned out."

"It did?"

"Well, we know I hung out there, right? Looking for One-Eyed Jack and his friend. And apparently I got a lead on him there, too. So why should we assume that the address on my list isn't relevant?"

"Well," Josh said, "because, like I said, it's closed . . . it's closed down."

Caitlin nodded. "Remember the hours I wrote on my list, next to the address?"

"Sure, ten to four."

"We assumed that was ten a.m. to four p.m. But what if it was ten p.m. to four a.m.?"

"Who stays open till four a.m.?" Josh asked. "And besides, the place was empty. Closed for years, by the look of it. I doubt they'll be up and running again"—he looked at his watch—"in half an hour."

"The pawnshop won't be. But maybe there's more there than just an empty pawnshop."

Bix nodded, looking impressed. "It's worth checking out."

"We don't have anything else to go on," Josh said with a shrug. "Might as well go back to the worst part of town."

"We're already in the worst part of town," Bix said. "That's just a different street in the worst part of town."

Their food arrived and it wasn't terribly good, but it was filling. Caitlin ate her spaghetti as she thought things through. Finally, she said, "How does the Bogeyman fit into all this?"

The guys looked up from their meals.

"The Bogeyman was on my list," she said. "Why? One-Eyed Jack makes sense now. So does Bob. If we're right about the address, then that makes sense, too. But what about the Bogeyman?"

"He can't be One-Eyed Jack's buddy," Bix said. "Bookerman's still in prison, right? Has another ten years to go?"

"That's what we read online," Josh said, "and Bigelson confirmed it. And I didn't see any article about him being released. Besides, we don't even know if he's still alive. Like Bigelson said, maybe he died in prison."

"And let's not forget," Bix said, "you were telling people One-Eyed Jack and his buddy are both in their thirties. Bookerman would be in his sixties by now."

"The Bogeyman—the Bookerman I thought I was shooting in my dream—was young," Caitlin said. "Younger than he'd ever been before."

"Bogeyman Junior," Bix said. "Maybe Bookerman has a son."

"If he does, I couldn't find him," Josh said. "After we learned about Bookerman, I searched for any sign of that name and got nothing but the old news items we already saw. There are no other Bookermans in the area."

"Who owns the junkyard he used to run?" Bix asked. "The one next to the town dump."

"I looked for that junkyard. I don't think it's there anymore. The dump is still there, but none of the junkyards in the local Yellow Pages had addresses near it."

"I don't think the guy I shot in the warehouse could be a Bookerman," Caitlin said.

"Caitlin," Josh said, "will you please stop saying that?"

"Whatever. The murder victim in the warehouse? I don't think he's related to Bookerman."

"Why not?"

"No resemblance." She knew that the guys were thinking of the man in the police sketch. Caitlin, though, was remembering the face from her dream, lying on the cement floor with a bullet hole in it. "Bookerman was one of the ugliest people I've ever seen. Very distinctive and ugly features. The dead guy in the warehouse looked too . . . normal. He was really average-looking. It's hard for me to believe that Darryl Bookerman could be that guy's father. I just can't see it."

They were just about finished with their meals. For her part, Caitlin was relieved about that. She had needed the sustenance, but the food had ended up being pretty lousy.

Josh looked at his watch. "Ten after ten," he announced. "If you're right, hon, the pawnshop, or whatever is at that address now, should be open."

"So let's head back there," Bix said.

Josh nodded, looking pretty brave, Caitlin thought . . . certainly braver than she felt.

Hunnsaker had left two messages for Jane Stillwood, the person who Martha at Commando's recommended she call first. Hunnsaker had also left messages for a few other employees and had managed to speak with three of Katherine Southern's coworkers. They all liked Katherine—quite a lot, actually—but none of them knew her well. No one knew where she lived. No one knew who her friends were outside of work. Every one of them recommended that Hunnsaker call Jane Stillwood, though. So while she continued calling other Commando's employees in case one of them knew Southern better than those Hunnsaker had reached by phone so far, Hunnsaker was heading to Jane Stillwood's home address to have a chat.

She had just finished leaving a message for yet another person on the list when Padilla called her.

"What's up, Javy?"

"I can't find her," he said.

"What do you mean?"

"I mean that I can't find any Katherine Southern. She doesn't exist anywhere that I could find. Motor vehicle, Social Security, property, tax, nothing."

"Damn," Hunnsaker said. "False identity?"

"That's what I'm thinking."

"So what does Katherine Southern, or whoever she really is, have to hide, other than the fact that she may or may not have shot our victim in the warehouse the other night?"

"I don't know, but there's something else, something interesting."

Hunnsaker liked the sound of that. She liked interesting.

"A call came in through the tip line from a guy who says he used to be on the job. Jeff Bigelson. Retired from the North Smithfield PD nine years ago."

Wow, an honest-to-God tip that wasn't anonymous. And from a former cop, no less. "You check him out?"

"He could be lying about being Jeff Bigelson, of course, but there was definitely a Detective Jeffrey Bigelson who retired nine years ago from the North Smithfield PD."

"And he called about this case?"

"Yeah. Says he spoke with our redhead—that is, with Katherine Southern."

"He *spoke* with her? About what?"

"He didn't say, but he wants the lead detective on the case to call him. That would be you."

Padilla was right. This was interesting.

"Give me his number."

———

Not surprisingly, Greendale Boulevard, where the King of Pawns was located, was even scarier at night. Looking up and down the street from the relative safety of Bix's car, Caitlin saw a collection of frightening characters similar to but slightly different from the ones who had populated the street when Caitlin was there that morning. It was almost as if the night shift had shown up and relieved the day shift.

As Caitlin, Josh, and Bix watched the long-shuttered pawn-shop, looking for signs of life that would indicate the place saw nighttime activity despite being closed for business, they talked about whether Caitlin could really have come here by herself. Josh hoped that if she did, she had sat in the car like they were doing now and watched from afar, waiting for One-Eyed Jack and his buddy, rather than going inside. If not, Josh said, she must have been crazy. Bix reminded them that apparently Caitlin had visited the Barrel O' Beer every night for the past few weeks and survived, and that place wasn't exactly a Friendly's. Caitlin promptly noted that she was, in fact, crazy, hence the fugue state. Josh stepped in to reassure her that experiencing a fugue state didn't mean she was crazy. While they were debating, a couple of guys walking along the other side of the street slowed down in front of the former pawnshop, then pushed open the doors and went inside.

"There was a padlock on those doors earlier," Josh said.

"Looks like Caitlin might have been right about this place, whatever it is," Bix said. "You two ready?"

"Not really," Caitlin said.

Josh said, "I'd like to say that I am, but . . ."

Bix nodded. "I hear you. Let's go."

They crossed the street, ignoring the cold stares from the denizens of Greendale Boulevard, and Caitlin turned a deaf ear to the low wolf whistle that she figured was more likely aimed at her than either Josh or Bix. When they reached the doors to the shop, they saw that the chain that had secured them earlier in the day was hanging loosely through one of the door handles, and the big padlock hung open from one of the chain's links.

"Looks like you nailed this one, Katie," Bix said. Without hesitation, he pushed open the doors and stepped into what had been the King of Pawns shop. The shelves were empty, as were the display cases that held nothing but broken glass. Dust covered most of the surfaces in the place, except for a wide path across the floor that cut through the center of the store, around the end of a display case, and over to a closed door toward the back of the shop. Caitlin didn't need a magnifying glass and deerstalker cap to deduce where to go. They started across the room and Caitlin noticed a thrumming in the floor and rhythmic vibrations from below, and as they neared the door she began to hear muffled calls and cries that sounded almost primal.

They were at the door now. Bix grasped the knob. Caitlin took a deep breath. And the door suddenly swung open toward them, pushed from the other side, letting a blast of raised voices escape from the basement below. Through the door staggered a shirtless man with blood covering his mouth and running down his neck and bare chest. A raised purple knot above his right eye looked ready to burst like a huge tick. He headed for the exit to the street, stopped for a moment just short of them to vomit, then lumbered out through the glass doors.

Caitlin, Josh, and Bix exchanged glances.

"If you're nervous, we can leave," Bix said.

Caitlin shook her head. "I have to keep going."

"I was talking to Josh," Bix said, then winked at Caitlin before stepping through the door and starting down the basement stairs toward the bloodthirsty cheers below.

"Stay close to me," Josh said, then followed Bix.

The first thing Caitlin noticed on the way down the steps was the smell of violence—men, stale sweat, stale beer, and the tangy scent of blood . . . though she might have been imagining the blood after seeing the bleeding man vomiting upstairs. They were in the basement of the old pawnshop, a large square-shaped space packed wall-to-wall with screaming people, nearly every one of them facing in toward the center of the room, forming a big circle several rows deep. Bix, who was taller than either Caitlin or Josh, craned his neck up and said loudly but still barely loud enough to be heard over the raucous cries of the crowd, "Looks like some kind of fight club."

A cheer went up, followed by another, then half the crowd was screaming things like "Finish him off" and "He's done," while the other half cried variations on "Get back up, you loser." Another cheer erupted, making Caitlin think that the loser had probably gotten back up. Somehow, even over the cries of the throng watching the fight, Caitlin could hear the meat-slapping, fist-on-bone sounds of a bare-knuckles fight. She had never heard one before, not in person, and though the noises weren't as dramatic as the sound effects in movie fight scenes, they were somehow far more nauseating.

Caitlin stared at the backs of the people ringing the contest. A shifting of bodies allowed her a brief glimpse of one of the fighters . . . bare-chested, bloody, and exhausted. A fist came out of nowhere, dropping the guy to the concrete floor. The cheering reached a crescendo, and Caitlin heard a voice amplified through cheap speakers say, "It's over. Winner . . . Dan Driscoll!" More cheers and more than a few jeers. "Next fight in twenty minutes. Place your bets."

The crowd dispersed. One of the men near Caitlin backed into her and turned aggressively. Both Bix and Josh stiffened, but the man just smiled and said, "Sorry, Katie. Didn't see you there."

He waited, almost expectantly, so Caitlin flashed a smile and said, "Oh, come on now, you know you can bump into me anytime."

The guy smiled and turned away.

Josh looked at Caitlin and shook his head. "Guess they know you here, too. Why am I not surprised?"

Caitlin merely shrugged.

Some of the people milled about, but most were lining up in front of three folding card tables. Behind each sat a sweaty guy with a metal strongbox on the table in front of him. Standing beside each sweaty guy was a bigger sweaty guy with his thick arms folded over his chest. Slips of paper were passed back and forth. Money changed hands. Caitlin followed Bix as he meandered through the room. Josh followed close behind. As they moved slowly through the place, every now and then someone nodded at Caitlin or said, "Hey, Katie," as they passed. It was like being back in the Barrel O' Beer, only with fewer women and more blood. Realizing that whenever she had come here, she was probably in her "Katie the Wild Thing" persona, she touched each man on the shoulder or arm and gave out winks and sly grins as though they were candy she was tossing from a parade float. From the men's reactions, she was acting as expected. The ease with which she slipped into her "Wild Thing" persona still surprised her a little. It was almost like stepping into an unfamiliar costume only to find that it had been tailored specifically for her.

"Okay," Josh said, "so I think we established that you've been coming here a lot lately, too. Probably every night, after spending the early part of the night at Bob's."

It looked that way to Caitlin, too.

Bix shook his head. "You told me Martha asked you to work more closing shifts at Commando's for a few weeks. I thought you were working late all those nights."

"Sorry," Caitlin said.

Josh said, "I can't believe you came to these places by yourself, hon. Do you realize how dangerous that was? How incredibly lucky you were not to have been hurt or killed . . . or worse?"

She did. She couldn't believe she'd had the courage—or was it the stupidity?—to come here. Then again, she seemed to be fitting in just fine.

"A little attitude goes a long way," Bix said. "She acted like she belonged, so she did."

With his swagger, Bix did, too, Caitlin noticed. Josh . . . well, less so, but he was trying. As they passed near the money tables, Caitlin asked, "So what do we do? Start asking around to see if anyone knows One-Eyed Jack?"

Before they could answer, someone called, "There you are, Katie."

Caitlin turned to see one of the sweaty guys behind a table beckoning her over. She glanced at Josh and then Bix, then walked over to the table. The guy behind it took paper slips from bettors and, after glancing at them, paid out money, or he took money and wrote on slips of paper, which he handed back. Without missing a beat in his work, he said to Caitlin, "I wasn't sure you were coming in tonight."

Caitlin had heard this tune before. She'd been coming in lately, didn't make it in last night, yadda yadda.

"Yeah," she said cautiously. She knew that she was probably talking with someone who was likely pretty dangerous, but she also knew what the guys around here expected from her. So she gave the guy a sexy grin and said, "I've been busy. Besides, who wants to be predictable?"

The money guy chuckled, then glanced up and saw Bix and Josh hovering just inches behind her. His eyes narrowed. Still looking at Bix and Josh, he said, "You betting tonight, Katie?"

"I hadn't planned on it."

"Come on now. You've got me for more than a grand over the last week, I think. You gotta give me a chance to win it back. And you know what they say . . . you can't win if you don't play."

"Yeah," Caitlin said with a wink, "but you can't lose, either."

"What are you doing here, then?" he asked, eyeing Bix and Josh again.

"Thought I'd just watch a bit."

Money Man frowned. "Come on," he said again. "You owe me."

"She does?" Josh asked. "Why?"

The man slid his eyes over to Josh and chewed his lip for a moment. Caitlin didn't like the look in his eyes, and she doubted Josh thought much of it, either.

"They with you?" the guy asked Caitlin.

"Yeah."

The man chewed his lip for another moment, then nodded, as if deciding something. The fact that no one came to drag Josh away told Caitlin that Money Man had decided not to have someone come and drag Josh away. Instead, the guy ignored him and looked back at Caitlin.

"Like I was saying," he said, "you owe me."

"Yeah? Why's that?" Caitlin asked.

The voice over the speakers said, "Five minutes."

Money Man kept handing money and paper slips back and forth with the fight-club patrons. He jerked his head to the side, signaling Caitlin to come closer. She leaned down and was overwhelmed by the smell of far too much cheap cologne.

"I called you like you asked me to, didn't I?" he asked her.

Caitlin figured that if he said he called, he must have called, but she had no memory of it, so she said nothing.

"You're playing dumb? When that one-eyed dude you were looking for came back the other night with his ugly-ass buddy, I called you like I promised, didn't I?"

"What did the buddy look like?" Bix asked.

Money Man looked over Caitlin's shoulder and said, "I don't know you. Never seen you here before. Never taken a bet from you. You're here with Katie, and I trust her, so I'm willing to let you stand there while I talk to her, but don't interrupt us. Got it?"

Bix said nothing.

Caitlin said, "Remind me . . . what did the buddy look like?"

The money guy squinted at her. "For a week, maybe two, you're looking for those guys, and suddenly you don't remember what one of them looks like?"

Caitlin gave the man her cockiest, sexiest grin. "Humor me, will you?"

After a moment, Money Man said, "Tall, bald, and skinny. Pale and ugly. My age, maybe a bit younger. That's about it."

Bogeyman Junior.

The next customer in line started to complain about something, grabbed his little slip of paper back from Money Man, and pointed emphatically at it. Caitlin didn't catch the bettor's words, but the money guy said calmly, "That's a four, not a nine, you idiot. So you're all paid up. Now move aside."

While they disputed payment, Caitlin turned to Josh and said quietly, "You looked online for other Bookermans in the area?"

"Yeah," Josh said. "Checked everything I could access—phone records, public land and tax records, anything I could think of. Came up empty."

Money Man turned back to Caitlin. "Let's go, Katie. Window's closing. Last chance to make a bet."

Caitlin dug into her front pocket and pulled out the twelve hundred dollars. "You know where I can find the ugly-ass guy?"

The guy glanced at the thick wad of bills in her hand, then regarded her coolly for a moment. "Why?"

"Just wondering."

"It's possible I might have had to ask around a bit a few months ago so I could send a couple of guys over there to get him to get his account up to date."

"You have an address?"

"You gonna make a bet?"

"Is there a good bet tonight? A sure thing?"

Money Man consulted a list on a piece of paper beside his strongbox. "Long odds in the next fight. Between you and me, the underdog doesn't have a chance."

Caitlin handed him the money. "Put twelve hundred on the underdog." The man raised his eyebrows and nodded appreciatively as he began filling out a slip of paper. "Don't bother," Caitlin said. "It's such a long shot, there's no need for me to stick around to see how it comes out. After you give me that address, I won't be back here."

The money guy turned to his right, and the bruiser beside him leaned down. They whispered back and forth, then the big guy pulled a small notebook from his back pocket and consulted it. A few seconds later, he whispered to Money Man, who wrote something on a slip of paper and slid it across the table to Caitlin. "Thanks for your bet. Guess I won't be seeing you around anymore, Katie."

She looked at what was scrawled on the paper. "Nope. Thanks."

CHAPTER TWENTY-NINE

TWENTY MINUTES AFTER LEAVING THE basement fight club, they were on the outskirts of North Smithfield. Bix told them that the warehouse where the murder had taken place, where Caitlin said she had come out of her seven-month fog, was only a mile or two up the road, which Josh knew—and the others must have known—could not have been a coincidence.

Using the GPS feature on Josh's tablet to guide them, they had nearly reached the address the money guy at the club had given them. Bix pulled the Explorer to a stop along the shoulder of a quiet, wooded road. If Money Man had been straight with Caitlin, the driveway they were looking for was just ahead. Bix backed up the vehicle a hundred yards or so, then pulled into a gap between two trees and eased to a stop twenty feet into the woods.

"Let's walk from here," he said. "We might not want to announce our presence."

Bix reached over to the glove box, opened it, and withdrew a handgun.

"Whoa," Caitlin said. "We don't need that."

"A gun?" Josh said. "That's just asking for trouble, I think."

Bix checked the magazine, saw that it was full, and snapped it back into place. "Actually," he said, "I think we could be asking for trouble if we *don't* have this with us. Just in case."

"I'm not sure about this," Josh said.

"I've never had to fire this in my life. Ever. But if I need to, I'd rather have it with me. So stop arguing because I'm bringing it."

Josh shook his head and Caitlin sighed, but neither protested further.

They left the truck and walked along the road, ready to dart into the trees the moment they saw headlights.

"You really think One-Eyed Jack's buddy is Bookerman's son?" Josh asked.

Caitlin replied, "The description the guy at the fight club gave us is so close to Darryl Bookerman's, it can't be a coincidence."

"It wasn't the most detailed description, hon."

"It was close enough."

"There are no Bookermans in the area. I checked."

"He changed his name," Bix said. "Wouldn't you, if your dad was put away for abusing and possibly even murdering little girls?"

That made sense to Josh. "Or maybe he was adopted after his father went to prison," he said. "He must have been just a kid. He had to live somewhere, with someone."

Caitlin said, "It's obvious that the guy I shot at the warehouse isn't Bookerman, though, or whatever he calls himself now—"

"Would you stop saying that, Caitlin?" Josh said. "You didn't shoot anybody."

"Yeah, and that wasn't really blood all over me the other night. And that gun was a toy." Josh said nothing, so Caitlin forged ahead. "Anyway, the guy in the warehouse wasn't bad-looking. And he had hair. So he's not the guy I followed from the fight club. He's not Darryl Bookerman's son. So who is he, then, and why did I shoot him?"

Josh sighed loudly and dramatically and Caitlin ignored him.

"And what is young Bookerman's connection, if it really is him?" Bix asked.

Josh had been considering the facts they knew. It would actually fit if the house to which they were heading did belong to Darryl Bookerman's son. Many questions had been answered so far. Things had become clearer. Seven months ago, something happened to send Caitlin into a fugue state, something probably traumatic. Josh had been forced to consider the possibility that it was their last argument that was the cause, but he truly didn't believe that could be the case. Maybe it was a guilty mind rationalizing, but she hadn't seemed on the verge of snapping when she walked out. It had to have been something that occurred, something terrible, after she left their house. After all, when she apparently first suffered a fugue more than two decades ago—though it lasted only a few days—it was the result of having been abducted by Darryl Bookerman and possibly having witnessed abuse, maybe even murder. A truly traumatic experience if ever there was one.

Josh continued to run the facts through his mind. When Caitlin fell into her more recent fugue, she somehow ended up with keys to a car almost certainly belonging to someone who lived in the Smithfield/North Smithfield area, because on the seat she'd found a menu for the Fish Place, where she must have driven that night. There, she met Bix and introduced herself as Katherine Southard, which was remarkably close to the name Kathryn Southern, who happened to be the little girl who went missing from Bookerman's junkyard shack. Caitlin also later dyed her hair red, which had been the color of that poor missing girl. With the help of Bix and one of his apparent legion of shady friends, she'd established a new identity as Katherine Southard and began working at Commando's, where, one night, this younger Bogeyman—Darryl Bookerman's son?— walked in with his one-eyed friend. Caitlin must have recognized him—maybe not consciously, but at least subconsciously—and she felt compelled to find him. She had asked around, learned that the one-eyed guy spent time at the Barrel O' Beer, where she subsequently learned that he sometimes went to the fight club in the basement of the closed-down pawnshop. She quit her job and spent her evenings, unbeknownst to Bix, at Bob's and later at the fight club, too, until she received a call one night from the guy at the fight club telling her that this Bookerman double and One-Eyed Jack were there. Caitlin said she remembered none of this, of course. The first thing she said she remembered was walking through that warehouse parking lot, then driving home, where Josh had noticed that she was covered in blood.

So what the hell happened between the fight club and the warehouse parking lot?

"I think you probably followed Bookerman and Jack from the fight club to the warehouse," Bix said as they walked along the dark road.

"Where I shot someone?" Caitlin said. "Someone who wasn't even Bookerman or One-Eye? Why?"

"That's what we're going to ask Bookerman," Bix said. "He must have been there. Let's knock on his door and see what he has to say."

"It's not his door," Josh said. "I mean, he doesn't own it. I checked the online property records again on the way here. The place is owned by someone named Michael Maggert."

"All right, then. So now we know what Bookerman Junior changed his name to," Bix said. "So let's see what Michael Maggert knows. Something tells me he has the answers we need."

Caitlin was quiet. Josh couldn't imagine how she was feeling. He knew she wanted answers, but she couldn't have been looking forward to talking to what seemed likely to be the son of the monster who had abducted her as a child, the man who had abused little girls and probably murdered at least one.

"How do you know he'll talk?" Josh asked.

"He'll talk," Bix assured them, and Josh thought about the gun tucked into the back of Bix's belt.

———

Retired police detective Jeff Bigelson had been a font of interesting information. Hunnsaker had been on the phone with him for only a few minutes and she'd been surprised several times already.

"And you're sure she's the redhead from the sketch?" Hunnsaker asked.

"No doubt about it. After I showed my wife the picture, she agreed, too."

"Remind me why you waited several hours after she left your house to call us?"

"I fell asleep," Bigelson said. He sounded embarrassed, or maybe frustrated. "I've been on post-surgery painkillers and they knocked me out."

"I see. And she called herself Caitlin Dearborn?"

"That's right."

Bigelson went on to say how Caitlin Dearborn had been accompanied by two men who called themselves Galvin and Dunlay, though Bigelson couldn't recall their first names. Hunnsaker didn't care, because they had to be fake names anyway. For that matter, so was Katherine Southern or Caitlin Dearborn, or both.

"And they came to see you about a twenty-year-old case of yours?"

"Twenty-two."

Bigelson described the case in broad strokes and then opined as to the redhead's likely role in it. He also noted that she was probably not a natural redhead but was actually a blonde. Hunnsaker tried to imagine what any of this had to do with the murder of the warehouse victim. Why the hell would the redhead/former blonde, whatever her real name was, seek out Bigelson now, in the middle of everything that was going on, to talk about that old case?

"Did you hear the name Katherine Southern?" Hunnsaker asked.

"That's the name of the little girl Bookerman made disappear all those years ago."

Interesting, she thought, but all it did was raise more questions. Could the redhead running around as Katherine Southern be the same girl who disappeared twenty-two years ago? Or was she really Caitlin Dearborn? Or could it be that her real identity was still undiscovered?

Hunnsaker took down a more detailed description of the redhead, and then descriptions of her companions, and wrung out of Bigelson everything else he knew, which wasn't much. Then she did it all again with Bigelson's wife in case she remembered something differently. She wasn't a retired detective, but she also wasn't doped up on painkillers. As it turned out, she didn't have anything to add, though she did corroborate the names their three visitors had given, as well as their physical descriptions.

As soon as she hung up with the Bigelsons, Hunnsaker called Padilla.

"Javy? I have another name for you to run. See what you can find on a Caitlin Dearborn." She gave him her best guess at the spelling and told him to check every variation he could think of if that didn't get him anywhere.

"I'm on it. That's our redhead, huh?"

"With any luck."

When they neared the driveway, Caitlin, Josh, and Bix cut into the trees, deciding to approach through the woods. Caitlin's mouth was dry and her legs were far from steady. She was breathing loudly but she couldn't help herself.

After a few short minutes, they were at the tree line looking at a neglected ranch house that looked dirty gray in the dim moonlight and, Caitlin suspected, would look just as dirty gray in the bright light of day. There were lights on inside.

"Anyone see signs of a dog anywhere?" Bix asked. "A chain or water bowl?"

"It's almost like you've done this kind of thing before," Josh observed.

"I don't see anything," Caitlin said.

"I don't, either," Bix said. "Let's get closer."

The waxing moon had grown since the other night, when Caitlin had found herself at the warehouse a few miles from there, but not by much. It was still a small crescent that left the world below substantially in darkness. That made Caitlin feel a little better about crossing the open space to the house beyond, though her knees were still weak and her heart still pounded.

As they neared the house, which was set far back from the road, up a curving driveway, Caitlin saw a dark car parked in front of the house, its trunk open. Caitlin tapped on Bix's shoulder and pointed to it. He slowed his steps and whispered to them, "Looks like he's home. We got lucky."

Caitlin didn't feel lucky. She wasn't so sure his being home was a good thing.

They reached the house. Bix motioned for them to stay put at the corner while he slunk to a dark window along the front of the house and peered inside. He turned back to them and shook his head, then moved along to the next window, which was lit by lamplight inside. He took a long look, then moved quietly toward the front door.

Caitlin and Josh followed and Caitlin almost looked through the window, but Bix was already at the door, so she hurried over to it. She now saw that it was ajar, though she knew that Bix hadn't touched it.

"What did you see through the window?" Caitlin whispered.

"A body," Bix replied quietly.

Caitlin didn't know what to make of that. In her nightmare, she'd shot the warehouse victim, not the Bogeyman. Or had she? Actually, she remembered shooting the Bogeyman—or was it Bookerman—but when she'd looked at him on the floor, he had become the fair-haired victim whose sketch had been in the paper. Had she shot them both? Was she a double murderer?

"Is it Bookerman?" she asked, still whispering.

By way of answer, Bix said, "I gotta be honest. It isn't pretty in there. Try to stay calm, okay?"

Caitlin nodded. "Okay."

"I was talking to Josh."

Josh shook his head. "Damn it, Bix—"

"Sorry," Bix said. "Just trying to ease the tension."

He nudged the door open farther. Caitlin could not think of a thing in this world she would rather do *less* than walk into that house. But she had to.

She followed Bix over the threshold and into the house that might have possibly belonged to Darryl Bookerman's son. The first thing she noticed was an unpleasant smell, not overpowering, but strong enough to hit her as soon as she stepped inside. Something was rotting somewhere. Caitlin saw that Bix had his gun in his hand.

They were in some sort of a den. Stained wall-to-wall carpet. Mismatched furniture, some of which probably had come from a dumpster, while the better pieces looked to be yard-sale bargains.

An ashtray overflowed on a cheap end table. Most of this Caitlin registered in the blink of an eye, without even realizing she had done so . . . because what really snagged her attention was what she saw on the floor of the next room. It was a hand, attached to an arm, which was presumably attached to a body that she couldn't see from her angle.

"Stay here," Bix said quietly as he started for the next room.

"Wait up," Josh whispered. "I'm coming with you."

"*Muy macho*, but if anything happens to me, you should be here with Caitlin to help her deal with whatever I wasn't able to deal with myself."

After a moment, to Caitlin's relief, Josh nodded.

Bix walked across the den and disappeared into the room where the body was. A moment later, gun still at the ready, he passed by the doorway again and headed in the other direction. After several tense seconds that seemed like half an hour, he returned.

"We're alone," he said. "Well, if you don't count him," he added with a nod toward the dead body. Josh walked into the next room, and Caitlin hesitated before following.

The smell was much stronger near the body. It wasn't overwhelming, but it was strong. And unpleasant. In the movies, people gag at the smell of dead bodies. *Perhaps this body simply hasn't reached that level of decomposition yet,* Caitlin thought in a more clinical fashion than she would have expected of herself in a situation like this. Was she detaching herself emotionally as a means of self-preservation? Was she in some sort of a state of shock? She didn't feel like she was.

She didn't want to look at the body, at least not right away. Instead, she let her eyes roam around the room. It was a living room. There was more faded wall-to-wall carpet in here, covered with stains, though in this room one of those stains was a huge bloodstain, which she saw out of the corner of her eye. The room clearly had the same decorator as the den. It held the same hodge-podge collection of furniture, though the threadbare sofa in here was a pullout, which was, at that moment, pulled out, exposing a bare mattress on which Caitlin saw numerous stains, including a few small ones that could have been left by a spray of blood.

On top of a sagging pressboard bookshelf sat two photos in frames. She looked at the first one, a black-and-white picture, and gasped. There he was, the Bogeyman from her nightmares. Skinny and tall, sickly pale, lumpy bald head. His dark eyes, which were spaced too far apart on his face, were the eyes that had haunted Caitlin for decades. At his side stood a small boy, maybe five years old. The boy's light-colored hair was wispy and short, and the black-and-white photography almost gave it the appearance of a bald head. The same was true of the other child in the picture, a toddler sitting on the ground at Bookerman's feet wearing only a diaper. Both boys were the spitting image of their ugly father. Neither was smiling. Given the eldest Bookerman's apparent age in the photo, Caitlin assumed it had been taken shortly before Bookerman was sent to prison for more than three decades.

In the second picture frame was a color photograph that looked to be only a few years old at most. Caitlin's heart stopped. The subject of the photo was obviously one of the Bookerman sons. He stood with a rifle resting on his left hip, the barrel pointed toward the sky. His face displayed no expression. Dangling from his raised right hand was a dead animal. It was brown and Caitlin saw mostly its back, but the shape of it reminded her too much of a dog. She saw immediately why she would have been rocked to the core upon seeing this man a few weeks ago. Despite having been in a fugue for months, during which a person is evidently highly unlikely to remember anything about life before entering that state, Caitlin had still suffered nightmares about the Bogeyman—at least according to Bix. And if the man in this photograph had walked into

Commando's, as he evidently had done, then Caitlin—even though she was Katie at the time—couldn't have failed to recognize him as her nightly nightmare tormentor. The resemblance was uncanny. How could she not have felt compelled to find him? The man in the picture had grown up to look almost exactly like his father. Maybe his brother had, too, wherever he was.

———

Chops walked through Baltimore–Washington International Airport, cursing himself for choosing Skyway Airlines for today's cross-country trip. The first leg of his three-flight journey—from LA to Chicago—had been almost unbearable. And a passenger with an incessant, hacking cough in the row behind him hadn't made his connecting flight to Baltimore a hell of a lot better. Chops had considered complaining and trying to move, even though he knew there weren't any available seats, but given that he was traveling under a false identity—albeit with a top-notch, high-quality fake passport—he didn't want to draw too much attention to himself. So now, after two seemingly endless flights, he still had another hour and twenty-two minutes in the air to Boston.

He looked at his watch and remembered to set it ahead three hours to make up for the time difference between the coasts. He'd be at his gate in another minute or two, and wheels up in less than an hour, which would put him in Boston in two and a half hours. And, he knew, he'd be pissed off at the world when he got there. He almost felt sorry for any poor bastard unfortunate enough to cross his path.

CHAPTER THIRTY

CAITLIN STOOD IN THE LIVING room of the house belonging to Michael Maggert, whose real last name was Bookerman. The time had finally come for her to look at the body. When she did, her heart skipped a few beats. Other than a reddish-green hue to the skin, which she could see had probably been very pale when he was alive, the dead man looked remarkably like he did in the photos Caitlin had just seen of him. In death, his eyes were open and dark and expressionless, just as they had been in the picture of him as a small child, as well as the one in which he was a grown man who had just shot a dog. She had no doubt. This was Darryl Bookerman's son.

Though she'd had some idea what she was going to see when she looked at him, Caitlin was still unprepared to see someone in person, someone *right there*, who looked so much like the monster from her nightmares. She felt as though she were in a slasher film, when the psycho killer finally lies dead at the heroine's feet after terrorizing her in the dark, from the shadows, for two hours . . . Only here, Caitlin had been terrorized almost every night for two decades. And now there he was on the floor in front of her. She couldn't believe it. Couldn't believe it was really him. That he was real.

She stopped herself. This wasn't Darryl Bookerman, the man who had abducted her so long ago. No, this was that monster's son. And he was dead. Caitlin probably had killed him.

"Two bullet wounds in him that we can see," Bix said as he stood near the shirtless body. "One in the shoulder that looks like it wasn't too bad, and one in the gut that was very, very bad."

Caitlin looked at the man's bloody stomach, then looked away.

"Unless there are other holes in him somewhere, I'd say the shot in his stomach is what killed him."

Caitlin nodded. She was numb, she realized. She had no doubt that she had put that hole in his stomach. Bullets she had fired had made all of this blood pool onto the carpet. She was the reason his eyes were open and staring yet seeing nothing.

"Got a couple of bullet holes in the wall over there, too," Bix said, pointing to a pair of holes in the far wall, spaced a few feet apart.

Caitlin looked at them blankly.

"By the way, guys," Bix said, "I probably don't have to tell you not to touch anything, but in case I do, don't touch anything. And if you already have, wipe it down with your shirt. I'm sure we're leaving all sorts of shit anyway, stuff from our shoes, flakes of skin, whatever, but why make things any easier for the cops whenever they finally get here?"

Caitlin nodded. She didn't remember touching anything. Then again, she had certainly been here two nights ago, and for all she knew she had touched every surface in the place, either before or after she shot Bookerman Junior.

"There's some mail on the table here," Bix said. "Addressed to Michael Maggert."

Caitlin looked over at Josh, who was a few feet away, leaning down close to the pullout sofa.

"What are you looking at?" Caitlin asked.

He stood too quickly, as though he'd been caught being sneaky, which made Caitlin walk over. She looked down. Secured to the metal frame of the pullout, next to the thin, stained mattress, was a pair of handcuffs. The dangling end was open, a key still in the keyhole. Caitlin took an involuntary step backward.

"We don't know what those are for, Caitlin," Josh said, "or why they're here, or whether anyone had been . . ."

He didn't finish. He didn't have to.

"Katie," Bix said, "is that your cell phone?" He pointed to a phone lying on the dirty carpet, not far from the body.

"Is it?" she asked.

"That doesn't look like yours," Josh said as he knelt close to it. "That's not your brand. And your phone case was black."

"That may not have been the phone she had when she was with you," Bix said, "but she didn't have a phone at all when I met her, and that looks just like the one we got her. Bet the back of the case has one of those Wild Things on it, just like her tattoo. I bought it for her. We used it for the tattoo guy to copy. Turn it over."

"I thought I wasn't supposed to touch anything," Josh said.

"If it's not hers, wipe it down after."

Josh turned over the phone. Same Wild Thing as her tattoo. He stood and handed the phone to Caitlin. Without thinking, she tried to turn it on, but it was dead.

"I guess there's no doubt now that I was here," Caitlin said.

She looked around the room—at the body again, at the blood on the floor and on the mattress, at the handcuffs, at a small table that had been knocked askew, and at the lamp that had fallen over on top of it. A mostly empty bottle of Budweiser lay on its side on the floor beside the table. Caitlin wasn't sure exactly what had transpired here, but the most important fact was clear to her.

"I killed him," she said.

She looked over at Josh who, for the first time, didn't object to her saying something like that. Finally, he said, "If you did, I'm sure you had a good reason."

"Really, Josh? Isn't it obvious what happened?"

Josh didn't reply. Caitlin sensed Bix watching her.

"I saw this guy come into the pub and I decided to get revenge for what happened to me when I was a kid, and what happened to those other girls. Maybe I confused him with his father, or maybe I didn't care that he wasn't the same Bookerman who abducted me as long as I got my revenge. I don't know. But I followed him home from the fight club the other night and I shot him to death." She wasn't sure how the handcuffs factored in, but she was sure about the rest of it. "But he wasn't his father," she added. "I shot an innocent man."

No one said anything for a long moment.

"I'm not sure how innocent he was," Bix said. "Look at the handcuffs."

"So he deserved to die?" Caitlin asked.

Another moment passed in silence before Josh said, "I'm not sure it's as simple as you make it sound, Caitlin. Remember, your car was at the warehouse. You didn't follow this guy here, at least not in your car."

Caitlin nodded. "That's right, thanks for reminding me. I probably went to the warehouse first, shot someone else there—the light-haired guy in the papers—then came here and shot Bookerman Junior . . . Mike, I guess his name probably is." He may have called himself Maggert, but he was a Bookerman, and that's how Caitlin thought of him.

Josh didn't reply. Caitlin knew there was little he could say.

"It's time for me to turn myself in, guys."

Josh protested, of course, and Bix shook his head. Caitlin knew that they didn't agree with her decision, but it was *her* decision to make, not theirs.

"Before you run to the cops, Katie," Bix said, "let's take a minute to look around here."

"Why?"

"Why not? You in a hurry to go to jail?"

Caitlin shrugged.

"Let's check things out a little, just to see if there's something useful we can learn here. Maybe it will help you with the cops. And remember, don't touch anything."

"I assume we're not worried about the police showing up while we're looking," Josh said.

"Two days and no one's found the body yet," Bix replied. "Our boy here wasn't exactly Mr. Popularity. I'd say we have a few minutes."

"Okay, I'll check out the kitchen," Josh said.

Bix said, "And I'll poke around a bit in here. Katie, why don't you see what's down that hall?"

He nodded to a hallway. Caitlin figured that Bix knew she wasn't keen on hanging around her murder victim longer than necessary, so she started down the hall. She didn't see much point in this exercise but, though she knew that turning herself in to the authorities was the right thing to do, she had to admit she wasn't looking forward to doing it. Might as well look around a little, just in case there was something to find.

She passed a bedroom on the right. Its door was open. From the hallway she saw an unmade bed and an open closet with clothes spilling off hangers. With nothing that bore scrutiny jumping out at her, she decided to move down to the next door, see what was in there, and work her way back toward the living room. But when she reached the second door, which was also open, and looked into the room, her heart stopped beating. It just stopped. It took her a moment to find her voice, and when she did, she called to the others.

"Guys . . . ?"

She thought she sounded remarkably calm under the circumstances.

———

Either Jane Stillwood wasn't home and hadn't yet listened to Hunnsaker's phone messages, which was certainly possible despite the late hour, or she was home and ignoring Hunnsaker's calls and messages, which was equally possible. Hunnsaker knocked, then knocked more loudly, then added, "Open up, it's the police." When no one answered, Hunnsaker tried the same thing at the next-door neighbor's door, which eventually opened to reveal a man wearing loose-fitting sweatpants and a Felix the Cat T-shirt and holding an open bag of Cheetos with orange-tinted fingers. Hunnsaker questioned him and he admitted to being marginally friendly with Jane Stillwood. She worked at Commando's a lot of nights, he said, but also waited tables at a strip club on Thatcher Boulevard. Hunnsaker knew it had to be a place called the Sugar Factory, which was the only such club on Thatcher. And no, Cheetos Guy didn't know the redhead in the sketch but thought she might have visited Janie a couple of times.

As Hunnsaker walked back to her car, her phone rang.

"Hey, Javy."

"This is really weird, Charlotte."

"What is?"

"Our redhead. Caitlin Dearborn."

"So that's her real name, then."

"Not anymore. I dug for a while and finally got a hit. I think that was her maiden name."

"And now?"

"Her name now is Caitlin Sommers."

Hunnsaker slowed as she reached her car. She stood with her remote in her hand but didn't press the unlock button. She just stood there.

"I recognize that name," she said. "Help me out."

Padilla paused—dramatically, Hunnsaker thought—and said, "There was a woman who disappeared in New Hampshire back in March. It was on the news for a while. They found her car in a shopping plaza parking lot or something, but she was gone without a trace."

"Yeah . . . I remember that. Everyone figured the husband must have killed her, but there was no evidence, if I recall. They tried to say he was cheating on her and killed her to get her out of the way, but nothing came of that angle, right? I don't think she was ever found."

"Until now," Padilla said.

"Are you sure?"

"I'm texting you a picture of Caitlin Sommers. It's the one they kept showing on the news back then."

Hunnsaker's phone vibrated in her hand. She put the call on speakerphone and checked her texts. She opened Padilla's, then enlarged the attached picture.

"Holy shit," Hunnsaker said. "Swap out her blonde hair for shorter red hair and that's her."

"I'm sending you another picture."

"What is it?"

"I used Photoshop to swap out her blonde hair for shorter red hair."

"You don't know how to use Photoshop," Hunnsaker said.

"All right, I had someone do it for me. But take a look."

Hunnsaker's phone vibrated again and she opened the picture. It was their mystery redhead. No doubt.

"You want me to call the husband in New Hampshire?" Padilla asked.

She thought about it. "Not yet. There's still too much we don't know. Maybe she's running from something and he knew it all along, maybe even took the heat over her disappearance to help her."

"If I remember right, that was a hell of a lot of heat."

"Maybe he loves her. Anyway, if that's the case, he could tip her off."

"Okay. What are you doing now?"

"Heading to a strip club. Place called the Sugar Factory."

"I've driven by there. Need backup?"

"No, I got it. Going to talk to Jane Stillwood."

"Really sounds like you need backup."

Now Hunnsaker understood. "I can handle it, Javy, but thanks for the offer."

"No problem. You go to the strip club. I'll just stay here at my desk and watch Fusillo clipping his toenails at his desk across the room. It's lovely."

Hunnsaker ended the call. She couldn't remember the last time a case had taken such a hairpin turn on her. As she recalled from the news stories, Caitlin Sommers had been an unremarkable woman when she went missing. Married, suburban house, suburban friends, worked in some local small business. Joan Nobody. Could she disappear only to turn up in North Smithfield seven months later and kill a guy in a warehouse?

———

Josh peered over Caitlin's shoulder into the bedroom beyond the doorway. Bix was looking over her other shoulder. It took Josh a second to see why Caitlin had called for them. At first glance, the room was nothing but a second bedroom converted to a small office. A clunky, outdated laptop computer sat on a cheap wooden desk. Above the desk on the wall hung a cork bulletin board. On the bulletin board was . . .

A photograph of Caitlin on plain copy paper. The picture wasn't sharp, as though it was a detail that had been cropped from a larger photograph, then enlarged to five inches by seven. Though the image was grainy, it was unmistakably a picture of Caitlin before she'd cut and dyed her hair. Beside the five-by-seven was an eight-by-ten copy of a photograph of several people standing in front of a building. Josh recognized it.

"I don't understand," Caitlin said. "While I was out looking for him, he was . . . what? Watching me?"

Josh slid past Caitlin into the room and over to the desk, where he leaned toward the photo on the corkboard. The caption listed the names of the people in the photograph, including Caitlin Sommers.

"This was in the newspaper last winter," Josh said, "when the new real-estate office opened."

"He's been watching me for that long?" Caitlin asked. Josh thought she sounded less scared than she had a moment ago, less scared and more . . . angry.

"Not necessarily," Bix said. "He might have gotten that off the web three days ago, for all we know."

"But why?" Caitlin asked. "How did he know me when *I* didn't even know me?"

Bix said something to Caitlin but Josh didn't hear what it was. Caitlin responded and Josh didn't hear that, either. He was focused on something else, something he saw sticking out from the bottom of a pile of papers and magazines. It was a manila folder with the name *Caitlin Sommers* written on the tab. The magazines and papers on top of the folder told Josh that it probably had not been opened in a while. He slid the folder out and flipped it open to find, inside, pages of writing, as well as more photos on cheap copy paper. There were also news articles printed from the Internet. Josh skimmed the items at first but quickly realized that he had to go back to the beginning and read more carefully. After a few minutes, he realized that Caitlin was standing close to him, looking at the folder's contents as well. Bix was looking around the room.

"What do you think all that is?" Caitlin asked, and again, Josh marveled at how strong she seemed. He wasn't sure how many people would find something like what they had found in this room and not been completely freaked out. But not Caitlin.

Josh said, "I've looked these over pretty quickly, but . . . well, it seems that Bookerman Junior has been following you for a while . . . or at least your story."

"What do you mean?" Bix asked. In his hand was a small stack of photographs he'd found on top of a dented metal file cabinet.

"First of all," Josh said, "he knew your real name, Caitlin, which nobody else in this town did."

"How?" Caitlin asked.

Josh referred to Bookerman's notes, skimmed for a few seconds, and said, "He actually has a few names for you here, Caitlin. Let me see . . . Goldsmith? Isn't that the name of—"

"The foster parents I was living with when I was abducted. Yes. But I never took their name, at least not legally."

"Well, he has that name in here," Josh said. "Could you have told your name to Darryl Bookerman all those years ago, back when . . ."

Caitlin shrugged. "It's possible." She thought about how the Bogeyman of her nightmares would call her by name. "Yes, I probably did."

Josh nodded. "He also has Caitlin Dearborn in here."

"My name after my parents adopted me."

"And then Caitlin Sommers," Josh said, reading. His eyes skipped through the pages some more. "There are notes in here referring to a private investigator named Larry Seger. Gives his phone number, too. It's after that that the names appear. It looks to me like Mike Bookerman started with Darryl's memory of your name and hired someone to find you."

"But why?"

"Because his father remembered you," Bix said as he looked through the pictures in his hand. "Remembered that you escaped. He probably knew that you were the reason he was caught and sent to prison for more than thirty years."

Josh said, "With Daddy in prison, Junior essentially grew up without a father. We have no idea what his life was like for the last twenty-two years. No idea how he was raised or by whom. But it can't have been easy being the son of a convicted pedophile. He might have had a hard life and, irrational as it might be, he may have blamed you for it."

"And then what?" Caitlin asked. "He wanted revenge for that? His father was the guilty one here, not me. I was just a kid."

"This guy was probably one screwed-up individual," Bix said, "like his old man. Can't expect him to think rationally. He probably thought you ruined his life."

Josh continued flipping through the folder.

"So why didn't he ever do anything about it?" Caitlin asked. "He obviously found out who I was. Easy to find out where I lived."

Under the section where Junior had apparently written notes as he spoke with the private investigator, Josh had already seen the address of his and Caitlin's home in New Hampshire. "Maybe he did try to do something about it," Josh said.

Caitlin and Bix looked at him.

"Maybe he went after you seven months ago. Maybe when you left our house that night, he was already watching it."

Bix added, "And he followed you to the strip mall where Josh said your car was found, and he tried to abduct you. But somehow, you got away."

They all took a moment to think about that scenario.

Josh nodded and said, "Somehow you got away from him, but the experience, as traumatic as it was, triggered a fugue state . . . just like when his father abducted you twenty years ago . . . and when you escaped from Junior, you got into the nearest car: Junior's."

"Yup, that's what happened," Bix said without a trace of doubt in his voice. "Check this out."

He held up a four-by-six photograph of Bookerman's son leaning against a car.

"That's the piece-of-shit Dodge Charger Caitlin drove into town the night we met," he said. "The one we ended up trading in. I recognize this dent in the hood."

"So we're right," Caitlin said. "I got into Bookerman's car that night. And I must have found the takeout menu from the Fish Place and drove there, without any real idea what I was doing . . . or even who I was."

"And I was there that night when you arrived," Bix said. "You came home with me and we didn't step foot out of my place till we left to sell the Charger a couple of days later, so it's not like Bookerman would have seen you driving around town in it."

"But why did he just give up on me after that night?" Caitlin said.

"He didn't," Josh said. "There are articles from the Internet in here about your disappearance that night, and articles over the months that followed detailing how the authorities couldn't find you. Mike knew you were gone but had no idea where you'd gone to. According to these notes, he had his investigator try to find you for a little while, but you were just . . . gone."

Caitlin shook her head. "Little did he know that I'd driven back to his stomping grounds in his car."

Bix said, "Must have surprised the hell out of him when you showed up here and—" He cut himself off.

"And shot him," Caitlin finished for him. Her voice was harder than the previous times she had talked about the possibility of her having killed someone. She certainly didn't seem happy to have done so, and Josh knew she probably regretted it, but she also didn't seem as torn up about it as she had before they pieced together their theory.

"I'm not the world's biggest cop fan," Bix said, "but if you insist on turning yourself in, the fact that Junior was stalking you is bound to help your case with the police."

Josh thought about it. The police would investigate and find out, at a minimum, what *they* already knew—that for some reason, Caitlin had searched for Mike Bookerman, and when she found him, she had killed him. Sounded a lot like premeditated murder. So maybe the stalking angle might help a little, possibly with sentencing, but he doubted it would keep Caitlin from going to prison.

"Anything on the computer?" Bix asked.

"I don't know," Josh said.

"Aren't you a computer whiz or something?"

"No."

"I assumed you were. You're always playing with your tablet thing."

Josh looked at the screen of Bookerman's laptop. He wasn't sure how much he would be able to get off the device, which he could see by its little green light was already on. "I can use a computer as well as most people can," he said, "but it's not like I'm some kind of forensic cyber tech or anything. If this thing is locked with a password, I won't be able to get into it unless we find it written down somewhere."

He sat in the chair in front of the desk and reached for the laptop's mouse. He paused and looked questioningly over his shoulder at Bix.

"We'll wipe it down after," Bix said.

Josh turned back to the screen and gave the mouse a nudge. The screen crackled itself awake.

Josh involuntarily pushed his chair back. Caitlin gasped. No password was required, which was stupid of Bookerman, considering what they saw pop up on the screen. Bix said quietly, "Shit."

On the screen was a still image of Mike Bookerman engaged in sexual intercourse with a naked woman. She was on her hands and knees on the mattress of a pullout sofa—the same sofa, no doubt, as the one in the living room down the hall. Bookerman was behind her, and the look frozen on her face made it difficult to believe that this act was consensual. Josh's suspicion was confirmed when he saw a handcuff around one of the woman's wrists.

"It's a video," Josh said. "On pause."

He looked at the video's progress bar at the top of the screen. The scene had been paused eighteen minutes into a ninety-two-minute video.

"Close that out, Josh," Bix said.

Damn it. He was an idiot. He used the mouse to shut down the video player. When he did, a list of numerous video files appeared on the screen. Realizing immediately what the files were, he exited the video program entirely.

"No," Caitlin said quietly. "I need to know."

"Caitlin . . ." Josh said.

"I won't watch, but I need to know. Bring them back up."

Josh sighed and opened the program again, then clicked on the File tab. The video icons reappeared. They were all labeled. Josh saw file names like "Blonde With Big Tits" and "Tall, Skinny Girl" and "Older But Great Ass." He quickly scanned the file names, looking for any reference that could be applicable to Caitlin. He knew the others were doing the same thing. A quick count revealed that there were eleven videos, but none of their titles immediately stood out as referencing Caitlin. They were arranged chronologically, by the dates they had been created, with the older files toward the bottom of the screen. The earliest video had been created fifteen months ago. A little mental math told Josh that Bookerman had averaged nearly one video every month and a half during that time. Josh quickly looked at the most recent file and saw that it was titled simply "Curly Hair, Long Legs" and had been created almost a month ago. According to everything they had learned, that would have been before Caitlin had found him, and presumably before he knew that Caitlin was in town. Thank God. Josh shared his thoughts with the others, who were obviously as relieved as he was . . . Caitlin even more so, of course. But she didn't look relieved.

She said, "Do you think he killed these woman after . . ."

"No," Bix said. "It would have been in the news if almost a dozen women went missing or turned up dead over the last fifteen months. And I didn't hear anything like that."

That made sense to Josh.

Caitlin nodded. "How had he been getting away with this for so long?" she asked.

"He drugged them, right?" Josh said. "Some of the women may not remember anything. And even if they do, maybe they're too embarrassed to come forward."

Bix added, "And maybe he threatened the hell out of the ones who did remember. Also, maybe some or even all of the women are hookers. I'm not sure how many of them would be anxious to go to the cops about something like this."

"It's disgusting," Caitlin said.

Bix nodded. "No argument from me. Time to go now, though, I think."

"We can't just leave those videos on there," Caitlin said. "It's not fair to the poor women in them."

"It's evidence," Josh said.

"Evidence that might end up helping you," Bix added, "if I can't talk you out of your plan to go to the cops."

Caitlin shook her head. "I don't like it."

"It's the smart thing, hon," Josh said. Caitlin sighed, which Josh took to mean that she would relent on the issue. "I guess we leave this folder behind for the cops, too, right?" he asked.

"Leave it," Caitlin said. "We need them to find it. If we miraculously produce it later, it could look suspicious, right?"

Josh nodded in agreement and Bix didn't object.

One by one, they headed back down the hall and through the living room. As they walked, Josh noticed that Caitlin kept her head up when she passed Bookerman's corpse.

———

At Boston's Logan International Airport, Chops Maggert snatched his small suitcase from the baggage-claim conveyor belt. It was almost the last one down the chute, as always. Someone's bag had to come down first. Why had that bag never belonged to Chops in his entire life? He wouldn't have checked his bag for this trip except that he wanted to bring a couple of his favorite knives with him—just in case—and he couldn't have done so in a carry-on bag.

He looked for signs to the ground transportation area. He'd have to take a shuttle bus to the car rental company and pick up the midsize sedan he was renting, then drive out to Smithfield, which he could probably do in an hour and twenty minutes. As he walked, he took his phone out of his pocket and dialed his brother's number for what felt like the twentieth time since yesterday. If he got lucky, Mike would answer and Chops could turn around and head right back to Los Angeles. He hated Massachusetts. Blood was blood, of course, so if Mike were in trouble, Chops would be there for him, but if he didn't have to be . . . well, even better. He waited as the phone rang. Finally, the call connected and was routed to his brother's voice mail.

"Mike," Chops said, "that was your last chance to answer your goddamn phone. Now I have to come and find you. And you'd better be dead, because if you're just coked up or strung out or whatever the hell you do, you're gonna *wish* you were dead."

He ended the call and stepped into the Boston night just in time to see the doors to the Hertz shuttle bus close and the bus pull away. He looked at his watch. Another would be along in a few minutes. Still, he was pissed that he'd missed it. Which went with his mood perfectly, because he was pissed that he'd had to leave his wife and daughter behind, and miss the circus, and fly thousands of miles just because his brother wouldn't answer his damn phone.

He hoped Mike wasn't dead because if he was, Chops wasn't sure there was much he could do about it. But if, on the other hand, he was still alive, then Chops might have to kick his ass a little, and right now, he was in the mood for a little violence.

CHAPTER THIRTY-ONE

AFTER LEAVING THE HOUSE OF Mike Bookerman—who still wasn't and would never be Mike Maggert to Caitlin—Caitlin wanted to go straight to the police. She had wanted answers? Well, she'd found them. And she believed she now knew enough of the facts to assure her that she belonged behind bars. The guys, on the other hand, had their own opinions. Bix proposed that Caitlin let him visit his shady friend, the one who had already set her up with a false identity once, and have him do so again. He reiterated his offer to accompany her on the lam, if Josh were opposed to the idea of joining her. By contrast, Josh knew her well enough to know that if Caitlin wanted to go to the police, he wouldn't be able to dissuade her. He proposed that she wait until morning at least and decide with a clear mind. Because Caitlin was exhausted, she agreed to Josh's proposal. She did not agree to Bix's. In the morning, she would march herself into the nearest police station. So tonight, she might as well get a good night's sleep. It might be the last good one of her life.

Bix pulled his Explorer into his driveway and they got out of the car. Caitlin's legs were lead as she tramped up the cracked cement walkway to the porch, then up the stairs to the front door. Using his key, Bix unlocked two dead bolts.

"Ladies first," he said as he pushed the door open for Caitlin. She wondered if he was also referring to Josh, needling him the way he had done several times already today. When she turned to see if Josh was annoyed, she saw that he wasn't on the porch but was walking back to the car. Must have forgotten something.

Caitlin walked into the apartment with Bix right behind her.

Immediately, she sensed that something wasn't right in the dark living room, but she didn't know what it was. Then she saw it. A shadow in the armchair. Bix saw it, too, because he said loudly, "Who the hell are you?"

"Don't do anything stupid," a voice said in the darkness. "I have a gun."

Bix said, "Take it easy," as he shut the door behind them. That left Josh outside . . . which Caitlin realized was the point.

"Where's the other guy?" the voice asked.

"What other guy?"

"See, you're already doing something stupid. You're lying. I heard there was another guy with you tonight."

"We dropped him at his place," Bix said, no doubt hoping, as Caitlin was, that Josh had heard Bix say, "Who the hell are you?" and realized there was trouble. Caitlin further hoped that Josh was on the phone with the police at that very moment.

———

Josh had been on his way back to the Explorer to retrieve his tablet, which he had left on Bix's backseat, when he heard Bix say, "Who the hell are you?" Someone had broken in and was waiting for them. Josh forgot about his tablet and hurried into the shadow of the building. His first instinct was to call the police. It was probably the safest thing to do. It would be what Caitlin wanted. Josh wasn't quite as ready as she was for her to turn herself in just yet, but for all he knew, her life could be in immediate jeopardy, so he had no choice. He reached into his back pocket for his phone and found nothing but an empty pocket. He checked his others. No phone. With a quick glance at the still-dark living room window near the front door, he dashed to the rear door of the Explorer and peered through the window. There was his cell phone, on the backseat right next to his tablet. He tugged on the door handle quietly . . . and without success. Bix must have used a remote to lock the car.

That changed everything. Josh couldn't afford to waste the time it would take to knock quietly on neighbors' doors until he found one willing to call the police for him. In this neighborhood, that could take hours. In fact, in this neighborhood, he was likely to be shot for sneaking around their houses at night. Or one of the neighborhood dogs would start barking at him, alerting the intruder in Bix's house, who might then act rashly.

Josh had to move fast. For all he knew, the intruder intended to kill Caitlin in the next few seconds. And Bix, too, though Josh wasn't terribly focused on that aspect of the situation. He hurried around the side of the house toward the back of the building. Thankfully, the mangy pit bull that lived next door must have been inside the neighbor's house, because it didn't bark its ugly square head off as Josh made his way around to the backyard and over to the window he had left cracked open that morning. He pulled over a plastic lawn chair, stood on it, and slid the window farther up as silently as he could. He slipped quietly through it and into the bedroom where he and Caitlin had spent last night, then moved through the dark room over to the closet and eased open the door. Right where he'd seen it that morning, leaning in one corner of the closet, was a black wooden baseball bat.

The shadow in the chair reached up and turned on a light on the end table beside him, which illuminated the intruder. Though Bix had never seen the man before, he knew him at once. It wasn't difficult. How many men with long blond hair and an eye patch could there be running around Smithfield? One-Eyed Jack hadn't lied; he had a gun in his hand, which rested in his lap. Bix had one, too, which rested in the glove compartment of his truck, where he'd left it like an idiot.

"I guess we found Jack," Bix said to Caitlin.

"My name's not Jack," the guy said as he stood and, with a wave of his gun, motioned them toward the sofa.

"It'll be okay, Katie," Bix said as he took Caitlin's hand and together they walked to the sofa and sat. Bix was mildly surprised that her hand wasn't trembling. Nor did she grip his hand tightly with panic. No, her hand was cool and calm, like she seemed to be.

The man had remained standing. He looked at them. The room was still only dimly lit, but Bix could see his one eye going back and forth between them, before settling on Caitlin.

"I recognize you," he said. "And you recognize me, don't you?"

Caitlin didn't respond.

"I remember you from the bar the other night. And maybe from the fight club, too, I think. It's hard to forget seeing a face like yours in places like those."

Still, Caitlin said nothing.

"Most importantly, you were at the warehouse, weren't you?"

Bix thought that Caitlin should probably say something soon . . . anything . . . or the guy with the gun was going to get mad. He might get mad enough to shoot somebody, and even if he intended only to wound one of them—probably Bix—in order to make Caitlin talk, who knew how good his aim was with just the one eye? He might aim for a knee and put his bullet in a heart or, worse, a crotch. Bix hoped when Josh had called 911, he was able to convince the cops that they should probably hurry. Bix had been opposed to the notion of involving the police, but at the moment, it seemed like a fantastic idea. He had no doubt that Josh would see it as the safest course of action, too.

"You really need to start talking," the guy said. "What did you see at the warehouse the other night?"

Finally, Caitlin spoke. Her answer surprised Bix.

"What did *you* see?" she asked.

It looked like One-Eye was even more shocked than Bix. His eye widened in surprise. Then their surprise multiplied tenfold as a shadow raced from the hallway. The man heard or sensed the movement and turned as Josh charged at him with a baseball bat cocked. The guy threw an arm up to block his head as Josh swung and the bat connected with his shoulder, eliciting a howl but apparently doing little in the way of serious damage, because not only did the man remain standing, but he immediately lowered the shoulder that had been struck and rammed into Josh, knocking him back against a wall and overturning a table and knocking the lamp to the floor, where it flickered before going out. Josh's head smacked off the plaster behind him and he dropped the bat. Unfortunately, the other guy didn't drop his gun. He pointed it down at Josh and looked as though he was debating pulling the trigger.

"No!" Caitlin cried.

The single eye stared down at Josh a moment longer, and then the guy kicked him.

"Get over onto the sofa, next to them."

Josh climbed to his feet, touching the back of his head gingerly, and sat on one end of the couch, next to Caitlin. His eyes were down. Bix followed them to Caitlin's lap, where his own hand was still holding Caitlin's. He withdrew it.

"Please tell me you called the cops before you came charging in here," Bix said.

After the slightest hesitation, Josh said, "Of course. You think I'm stupid?"

After a slight hesitation of his own, One-Eye said, "You're lying. If you called the cops, you would have waited outside for them. Lie to me again and I'll shoot out your knees."

The man was right, Bix knew. For some reason Bix couldn't fathom, Josh hadn't called the cops. Instead, he'd snuck into the house and, armed only with a baseball bat, attacked a guy with a gun. Stupid. But ballsy, too. Bix had to give him that.

"And don't think I don't know that you lied to me, too," One-Eye said to Bix. "You said you dropped this guy off at his place."

"I did," Bix said. "He's been staying here. That makes *this* his place."

The man squinted his eye menacingly. "I should blow out your knee just for being a dick."

"I'd rather you didn't," Bix said.

The guy seemed to be considering it for a moment that felt far too long to Bix. Finally, he said, "Turn on that light."

Bix turned on the lamp on the end table beside him. The bad guy looked at Caitlin. "I'll ask you again. What did you see at the warehouse?"

"And I'll ask *you* again," Caitlin said. "What did *you* see?"

One-Eye seemed just as surprised by Caitlin's response this time as he had the first time. Then he looked angry. "Last chance to tell me what you saw before I hurt someone."

"She can't," Josh said.

"Shut up," One-Eye snapped.

"You don't get it. She can't tell you what she saw. She can't remember."

With the gun still in his hand, the man turned his palms up as though asking the others, *Am I the crazy one here?*

"She has amnesia," Josh said. "If she saw something the other night, she can't remember it. She can't remember anything."

"Seriously?" One-Eye said. "That's what you want to go with here?"

"It's the truth," Josh said.

"It is," Bix confirmed.

The man took a deep breath and pointed his gun toward them, at knee level, and swept it back and forth. "Who gets it first?" he asked Caitlin. "How many knees have to die before you talk?"

"They're telling you the truth," Caitlin said. "I can't remember the other night. I can't remember anything from the last seven months."

"What, we're in a soap opera? You expect me to believe that bullshit?"

Caitlin shrugged. "I can't make you believe it, but it's the truth. Just out of curiosity, though, what is it you think I saw?"

Bix couldn't believe the balls on this girl. If the situation weren't so serious, he would have laughed at her brazenness. One-Eye looked as though he had no clue how to handle her.

"Why do you keep asking me that?" he said.

"Because I don't remember what happened at the warehouse and I . . . need to remember. Did I . . . kill someone there?"

The blond man blinked a few times. "Did you—?"

"Did you see me kill someone?"

One-Eye shook his head. "Is she for real?" he asked, looking at Bix.

Bix nodded. "We're telling you, she doesn't remember a thing from that night."

The man scratched his head with his free hand, frowning. It looked to Bix like a debate was raging inside that blond head. Finally, he said, "I can't take the chance. I can't go back to prison. Besides, this sounds like total bullshit."

"It's not," Bix said.

The guy frowned for another few seconds, then shook his head emphatically. "I can't do it. I can't believe you. I'd like to, but I can't. I can't go back to prison. No way."

To Bix, it sounded as though the man's voice had cycled from cocky to unsure to frightened. Bix wondered if it was time to make his move. He might be shot, but he was probably going to be shot anyway. Taking a run at the guy might be their only chance.

"I can't go back," One-Eye said. "Not after what they did to me there."

"She's telling you the truth," Josh said.

The man shook his head again. "I won't go back. I won't. I won't let them take my other eye. I'd rather die."

"Your other eye?" Caitlin said.

When she spoke, the man stopped shaking his head and glared at her for a moment. Then he lifted the eye patch, exposing lids that had been sewn together. The skin was unnaturally flat. The eyeball was gone completely, leaving behind an empty socket covered by taut skin.

"They took it out with a spoon," he said. "I'm never going back to prison." He let the patch fall back into place and shook his head, sadly this time, it seemed. "I think I have to kill you all. I don't want to. I really don't. But I just can't take the chance. Besides, that amnesia story sounds like bullshit."

"I killed someone," Caitlin said abruptly.

He narrowed his eye. "A second ago you were asking me if you did. And what, you suddenly remembered?"

"Not him. I killed somebody else."

He chuckled. "Right. Okay, who'd you kill?"

"Michael Bookerman," Caitlin said. "I shot him to death at his house."

"Who's Michael Bookerman?"

"You probably know him as Michael Maggert."

If Caitlin had wanted to convince One-Eye not to shoot them, Bix doubted the wisdom of admitting that she had killed his bald buddy. But the guy said, "Yeah? Seriously?"

"Seriously," Caitlin said.

After a moment of thought, One-Eye said, "I never liked him."

"I thought you two were pals," Bix said.

One-Eye said, "We hung out some, did a few jobs, but he was an asshole. Always pushed me to take jobs I didn't want to take. Made me do things I didn't want to do. He's the reason this happened," he said, pointing to his eye. "I never should have been caught. We never should have pulled that job. But Mike pushed me. Then I took the fall for it. Cost me my eye and three years of my life. It was his fault."

"I killed him," Caitlin repeated. "I shot him. Twice, I think. First in the shoulder, then in the stomach. Left him dead on his living room floor."

"Why are you telling me this?"

"So that you know. It's a confession. You have a cell phone on you? One with a voice recorder? I'll confess again. Then you'll have that over me, and I wouldn't be able to go to the cops even if I wanted to."

Not bad, Bix thought, especially considering that she was planning to go to the cops anyway, so a confession wouldn't matter. The man looked lost in thought as he chewed on that for a bit. Bix again considered making a move but decided to hold off a little longer. Quietly, almost to himself, One-Eye said, "I never liked him. I don't really want to kill you. I'd like to trust you. I won't go back to prison, though." Finally, he looked up at them. "You really killed Mike?"

Caitlin said, "I did. You don't believe me, go to his house. He's still there. We just left him."

"I thought you killed him two nights ago."

"I did. We went back."

"Why?"

Caitlin shrugged. "Looking for answers. Like I said, I don't remember doing it."

The man reached up, slipped a finger under his eye patch, and scratched. Bix felt himself grimacing as he watched. "And he's still there?" the man said. "The cops haven't found him?"

"Not as of forty-five minutes ago."

"What about the money?"

"What money?" Caitlin asked.

"You know what money. You saw it at the warehouse."

Caitlin shook her head. "You're forgetting—I don't remember that night. And we didn't see any money at Bookerman's house, though we weren't looking for anything like that, so maybe it's there."

After what seemed like another minute or two of internal debate, One-Eye pulled a cell phone from his pocket, fiddled around with it, then turned it toward them. He looked almost relieved as he did it. Apparently, he was telling the truth about not wanting to kill them.

"I'm taking a video of this," he said. "Just in case. So tell me again for the record."

Caitlin stated her name, her real name, and for the record confessed to shooting Michael Maggert, whose real name was Bookerman. She said she shot him twice, killing him. She provided his address and added whatever detail she could recall, such as the room where he died and the position of his body. For motive, Caitlin said that he had been stalking her, which seemed to come as a mild surprise to One-Eye. Apparently, Bookerman and his one-eyed buddy weren't as close as Bix and the others had thought, as Bookerman had never shared his pet project with his friend, nor had he invited him into his spare bedroom where Caitlin's photo was pinned to a corkboard. Caitlin wrapped up her confession, and Bix had no idea if it would ever be heard in court, but he knew it would be enough to cause Caitlin serious trouble if it were. The man gave a satisfied nod and pocketed his phone.

"Okay, then, that's it," he said as he started for the door. Halfway there, he paused. "And you really don't remember the other night?"

"I really don't," Caitlin said. "Any chance you'd tell me what happened? I really want to know."

One-Eye just laughed. Then he was gone. Bix stepped over and closed the door behind him, locking it. He turned back to Caitlin, wondering how she was holding up. She looked thoughtful for a moment, then said, "I need a beer."

———

Following a bartender's direction, Hunnsaker found Jane Stillwood in stiletto heels and a red corset with matching panties, serving beers to a table of rambunctious businessmen in starched white shirts that were open at the collar, their ties hanging loosely. Hunnsaker thought Stillwood was attractive, but the men had eyes only for the topless woman in a shiny gold G-string squatting on the low stage in front of them, her knees spread, her boobs jiggling for dollar bills.

Drinks delivered, Stillwood headed back toward the bar with her empty serving tray, and Hunnsaker caught her attention. For the waitress's sake, Hunnsaker didn't want to show her detective shield, if she could avoid it, and draw unnecessary attention to the woman. Managers in places like this had enough trouble with the law; they might not take kindly to an employee who led a cop to their door.

"Jane Stillwood?" Hunnsaker said. "My name is Detective Charlotte Hunnsaker. I left you a few messages."

Stillwood tried to look confused, but she made her attempt a fraction of a second too late, and Hunnsaker saw something in her eyes that told her that Stillwood had listened to but chosen to ignore Hunnsaker's messages.

"What's this about?" Stillwood asked, looking around nervously.

Hunnsaker walked to a relatively quiet corner and took a seat at a tiny table. Stillwood followed but balked at sitting down.

"This won't take long. You know this woman?" Hunnsaker showed her the picture on her phone of Caitlin Sommers, the one that had been tweaked to give her short red hair.

Stillwood frowned and pretended to be thinking. She was a terrible actress.

"I don't think I do," Stillwood said.

"It wasn't really a question, Janie. You know this woman. I know you do. I've spoken with just about everyone you know, and they all told me that you do. They said you two are pretty close, in fact."

Stillwood didn't respond, which was probably smart. Hunnsaker changed the photograph on her phone to the undoctored one from months ago, before Sommers disappeared, when she had her shoulder-length blonde hair.

"How about this woman? You know her?"

This time, Stillwood's confused look was convincing. "Who's she? She looks like . . ."

"Yeah," Hunnsaker said. "Same woman. This woman with the blonde hair is named Caitlin Sommers. She disappeared without a trace seven months ago. This," she said as she switched back to the photo of Sommers as a redhead, "is the same woman. You know anything about that?"

Stillwood shook her head slowly, looking befuddled. Hunnsaker believed that she didn't know anything about the identity change. She didn't know Caitlin Sommers the blonde. But she sure as hell knew Katherine Southern, the redhead.

"Something strange is going on here," Hunnsaker said. "I don't know what it is, but I need to know where to find this woman. And I know you can tell me. So tell me."

Stillwood stared at the picture of her friend, probably a bit shocked to learn how little she really knew her.

"You seem reluctant to help me, Janie," Hunnsaker said. "Look, I get it. You two are besties, probably get together to paint each other's toenails, drink wine coolers, and talk about boys, but I think you can see now that you don't really know this woman. She was never honest with you. So how much can you possibly owe her?"

Stillwood looked up from the phone.

Hunnsaker said, "And if you two aren't quite as tight as you thought you were, is she really worth facing obstruction charges, maybe aiding and abetting?"

Stillwood's eyes widened just a bit. That struck home. Finally, she spoke. "I think she might be in trouble."

"Really? You think?"

"I don't want Katie to get hurt or anything."

"I know you don't. And you're right. She's in trouble. So tell me how to find her so I can keep her from doing something stupid, something that might get her hurt or worse. Where does she live?"

Stillwood shook her head. "I don't actually know where she lives."

"Janie . . ."

"No, it's true," she added quickly. "I've only been there once, maybe twice. And Katie always drove. I never paid attention to the turns we took or to the street names."

"You're telling me that even though everyone I spoke with told me that you and Katherine Southern, as you've known her, are pals, you don't even know where she lives?"

Stillwood looked confused again, and now it was starting to piss off Hunnsaker. Before she could voice her displeasure, though, Stillwood said, "You mean Southard."

"What?"

"You said Katherine Southern. You mean Southard, don't you?"

Hunnsaker still had her phone in her hand. She flipped back past the two photos of Caitlin/Katherine, to the list of employees who worked at Commando's. Even though there was a line through Katherine's name, Hunnsaker could read the last name clearly. Southern.

"Her name is Southard?" she asked Stillwood, who nodded. "And you're sure about that?" Stillwood nodded again.

Hunnsaker left the Sugar Factory in a hurry. If Caitlin Sommers had been going by Katherine Southard lately—and not Katherine Southern, as they had thought—perhaps another records search would be more fruitful than their last one. She dialed Padilla's number.

"Got yet another name for our redhead, Javy, and I've got a good feeling about this one."

CHAPTER THIRTY-TWO

MIKE MAGGERT WAS DEAD AND Martin Donnello was okay with that. Or maybe his name was Bookerman, or whatever the redhead had said it was. Either way, according to her, she had shot him two nights ago, after the warehouse, which made sense because Donnello hadn't been able to reach Mike since then. Donnello had looked for the redhead and assumed Mike had been doing the same, but he hadn't been sure because the guy wasn't answering his damn phone. Now Donnello knew why.

He and Mike had made some money together over the years, but they'd lost some, too. They'd had a few good times, but plenty of bad ones, ones that were far worse for Donnello than for Mike. So, yeah, all in all, Donnello was all right with Mike's death. An eye for an eye, as they say, right?

But given that the two of them had been involved together in plenty of things over the years that Donnello wouldn't want the cops to know about, he thought it would be wise to get to Mike's house before the cops found out about his murder and tore the place apart. Who knew what the guy had lying around the house that could tie Donnello to illegal activities? Besides, Mike had left the warehouse with five thousand bucks, which they had planned to use to pay for the stolen smartphones that had turned out to be a bag of fake hands instead—which was what had led to the storm of shit that started at the warehouse and apparently ended when the redhead killed Mike at his place. Presumably, the money was still at Mike's, if the girl wasn't lying when she said they hadn't taken it, so Donnello figured he might as well retrieve it while he was there.

He pulled his motorcycle into Mike's driveway and up around the bend toward the house. He saw Mike's car and wondered idly why the trunk was open as he pulled his bike to the side of the house. He doubted that anyone saw him pull in, and the house was secluded enough that no neighbors would see his motorcycle, but still . . . can't be too careful. He trotted around the house to the front door. There was no need to hurry on Mike's account; he wasn't going anywhere. But again, better safe than sorry. Get in, find whatever there was to find, grab the money, and get the hell out.

The front door was unlocked. The place smelled rank, which wasn't surprising given the dead body he now saw on the living room floor. Two bullet wounds, one to the shoulder and a kill shot to the gut. It looked like the redhead and her friends had been telling the truth. Donnello had taken a hell of a chance that they were, but he really hadn't wanted to kill them. Mike would have murdered them without a second thought. But he wasn't Mike. He'd never killed anyone and wouldn't unless it was absolutely necessary. And Mike could no longer tell him what to do.

Donnello looked at Mike's dead face and still felt nothing close to sentimentality. The guy had been a prick, and the world was probably a better place with him dead. Just ask any of the women he'd brought here. Donnello had never taken part in any of that, and he'd turned down Mike's only offer to watch one of the videos, but he knew that there had been quite a few women Mike had drugged and "entertained" here, as he used to put it. Prick.

Enough time spent on reflection. Time to look for anything the cops could use to tie him to Mike, along with the cash. He turned away from the body to find someone standing close behind him. Donnello hadn't even heard him. The man didn't move. He stared down at Donnello from just two feet away. The guy looked a *hell* of a lot like Mike Maggert—bald, pale, and ugly—though this man was at least half a foot taller and a little less thin, and where Mike's dark eyes had always seemed almost completely lifeless, even during moments of excitement, there was something down in the darkness of this guy's eyes . . . a deeper darkness that somehow seemed to be a separate living thing. Then Donnello noticed the knife. His thoughts immediately flicked to the gun at the small of his back.

"Did you kill my brother?" the man asked.

This guy's brother was dead on the floor and he showed no emotion . . . just the slightest squirming of whatever it was that lived in the darkness of his eyes. *God, what a creepy thought,* Donnello realized. He struggled to speak. "No . . . I didn't . . . I wouldn't . . . we were friends."

"Not good enough friends to call the cops, though. He's been dead a while. Why are you here?"

"I'm . . . looking for something," Donnello said as he backed up a step. The other man moved forward, staying close to him.

"Money?"

"No," Donnello lied.

"What, then?"

"Something that might . . . incriminate me."

"In my brother's death?"

"No," Donnello said quickly, "I swear to God. Something . . . anything . . . you see, the thing is, your brother and I used to . . . well, we did some things together, illegal things, and I wanted to make sure there wasn't anything the cops would find here to point them to me. You see?"

Mike Maggert's awful brother looked down at him. "How did you know he was dead?"

"Because I just talked to the person who killed him. She told me."

"She?"

"Yeah. It was a woman. A redhead."

"I'm sure there are a lot of women who had a good reason to kill my brother, but did this one tell you why she did?"

"She said he was stalking her."

Maggert frowned as he considered that. "Where can I find this woman?"

Donnello quickly told him the address. "She lives there with her boyfriend. I left her there just a half hour ago."

"Was she alive when you left her?"

"Yeah."

"Some friend you are," the man said. "Now, I'm going to give you a choice."

Donnello allowed himself to feel the slightest sense of relief, the smallest glimmer of hope. He hadn't wanted to find out if his draw was quicker than a knife thrust, and it looked like he might not have to. If Mike's brother were planning to kill him, why would he bother letting him choose anything?

The brother said, "Would you rather I cut your throat or slice your stomach open? The first way ends you quick. The second is more painful but gives you a few more seconds of life. You probably have less than a hundred left, at most, so every one is precious."

Donnello backed up a step, his gun hand inching behind his back. The guy stayed with him, knife in hand.

"But why?" Donnello said. "I told you I didn't kill Mike. And I told you who did."

"Because when people start finding the various pieces of the woman who killed my brother, you'll know it was me who chopped her up. And I can't have that."

Seconds later, as Donnello lay on the floor next to Mike, spilling his life on the faded carpet, he knew two things: his draw hadn't been quick enough, and he'd made the wrong decision. As soon as he'd hit the floor with his gut torn open, he'd been given another chance to have his throat cut, to end it quickly. He should have taken it. He'd hoped the few extra seconds his choice bought him would be filled with a sense of relief that his miserable time on Earth was over, a sense of peace that he'd be moving on to whatever new life waited for him beyond this one. Instead, he'd merely had more time for sadness and regret and pain.

Detective Charlotte Hunnsaker stood in the living room that Caitlin Sommers shared with Desmond Bixby, her boyfriend. Hunnsaker had no warrant and no one had answered the door, so under normal circumstances she shouldn't have been standing inside the apartment, but through the window near the front door they had seen the over-turned table and broken lamp, and because good cops are interested in the welfare of the community, Hunnsaker felt she had an obliga-tion to enter the premises to ensure the safety of anyone who might be inside and possibly be injured. Anyway, that was how she'd spin it if she were ever questioned about it. The door had been unlocked, which was stupid in this neighborhood, but it made things easier for Hunnsaker.

Nobody was home, which annoyed Hunnsaker. Then again, that would have been too easy. It never seemed to work out that way.

They searched for additional evidence that a crime had been committed here—further justifying their entry into the home— while also looking for anything that would help in their investigation of the warehouse murder. They couldn't touch anything without a warrant, but things in plain sight were fair game. Hunnsaker's eye fell on an open cardboard box with several random items inside, including bits of trash, a wrinkled takeout menu from a restaurant called the Fish Place, duct tape, and a pack of cigarettes. Nothing terribly helpful at first glance, but something here might turn out to be significant if they came back later with a warrant. What she most wanted to find, though, was something telling her where Caitlin Sommers was right now. She let her eyes drift around the room, then across the hall, into the kitchen, where they fell on a phone book lying open on the table. She walked over to it and saw that a page had been roughly torn out. The page on the left side of the book had listings for horses, hospice care, and hospitals. The page on the right, the one that came after the one that had been ripped out, listed hotels—alphabetically, of course, starting with the Lullaby Inn Motel. Apparently, motels didn't get their own section but were instead listed in the hotel section. Hunnsaker used her cell phone to snap a picture of the book and called out, "They're renting a room in the area, Javy."

Padilla walked into the kitchen from the bedroom down the hall.

"Any idea which one?" he asked.

"Not sure. Probably a motel, but we can't rule out hotels, either. We need to get some of our people to start calling them alphabetically, but stopping at the Lullaby Inn." She pointed to the open phone book. "And let's see if there are some uniforms on patrol who can pop into a few, too."

"Want me to start a warrant application for this scene?" Padilla asked.

"I don't think that's a priority at the moment. Let's find Sommers and Bixby, then we'll get our warrant and come back and take the place apart, see if anything here ties them to the warehouse or the victim. For now, though, I need a copy of the page that's missing from this phone book."

"Gotcha. Want to post someone down the block?"

"Yeah, let's get an unmarked car out there in case we're wrong about the motel."

"Are we wrong?" Padilla asked.

"No."

"And what's next on our agenda?"

"We're going to hit a few motels ourselves," Hunnsaker said. "What do you say, Javy? You, me, cheap motels?"

"I've been waiting years for you to ask, but what will Elaine say?"

"I think she'll be happy for us," Hunnsaker said. The truth was, it was Hunnsaker who was happy, or at least getting closer to it. They now had a name for the redhead, they knew where she lived, and now they knew generally where to find her. It shouldn't be long now.

———

Caitlin looked down at the page Bix had torn from his phone book.

"How about the Deluxe Motel on Larchmont Avenue?" she asked.

They had decided to spend the night in a motel. The police were looking for them. Who knew who else might be doing the same? They certainly hadn't known that One-Eyed Jack had been. And if he had been able to find them, someone else could, too. Bix had argued that they should just keep driving, get the hell away from Smithfield and out of Massachusetts altogether. But Caitlin still intended to turn herself in to the local police, though both Bix and Josh had convinced her to sleep on it and make sure it was what she wanted to do, at least so soon. She knew she wasn't going to change her mind, but the thought of spending one more night a free woman sounded appealing. Either way, though, if Caitlin wanted to go to the Smithfield police in the morning, they had to stay in the area, which led to their search for a nearby motel.

"Deluxe Motel?" Josh said. "Simple name, gets right to the point, but is there such a thing as a deluxe motel?"

"Larchmont Avenue's a little close to our place," Bix said. "I mean, my place. What else you got?"

Caitlin scanned the list. "This only goes through most of the *L*s."

"We were in a hurry. I figured there had to be a good one for us on that page. It's two-sided, you know."

"I'm looking," Caitlin said. "How about the Eagle Inn Motel on Rossdale Boulevard?"

Bix nodded. "Sounds good."

Caitlin gave the address to Josh, who typed it into the GPS application on his tablet. The feminine robotic voice had just given its first direction when Bix's cell phone rang. He looked at the screen and said, "It's my cousin."

He answered and listened for a moment. "No shit? Hang on, Terry, I need to put you on speaker . . . Because I'm in the car, that's why. Hang on." He shot a *Be quiet* look at Caitlin and Josh, then switched the call to speakerphone. "Terry?"

"I'm here," a voice said.

"Okay," Bix said, "so you were saying that the woman in the paper who the cops are looking for—the one who's a dead ringer for Katie—saved the life of one of your girls?"

"Thanks for bringing me up to speed on what I just told you, Bix."

"Just making sure I heard you right."

"Yeah, that's what I said. So, the other night my girl Evangeline gets in this dude's car; it was only supposed to be a blow, but instead of pulling around the block, he keeps driving."

Caitlin realized that the man on the phone, Bix's cousin, was a pimp.

"Then he offers her a bottle of water," the pimp said, "which was already open, and he gets really angry when she won't drink it. Evangeline gets scared and asks to be dropped off at the next corner, and the guy hits her. The next thing she knows, they're going too fast for her to get out of the car."

"When was all this, by the way?"

"Tuesday."

Three days ago. The day before Caitlin killed Mike Bookerman.

As Caitlin listened, Terry the pimp told Bix how the guy took Evangeline to his house, where he made her drink the water that obviously contained a drug. Then he handcuffed her and spent a day raping her every few hours. Finally, he said he had something he had to do, so he made her take another drink that knocked her out for a while, though she had no idea how long. All she knew was that it was daytime when she took the drink and it was night when she came to and found him standing over her. He was really pissed off about something and seemed to want to take it out on someone, and Evangeline said she knew it was going to be her.

"He drank himself a beer," Terry said, "talking to himself the whole time, all angry and crazy-sounding, and Evangeline was scared to death. She was still pretty loopy, she says, still kind of drugged up, but he looked like he was going to hurt her, and then she thought he'd kill her."

"And then what?" Bix asked.

"Then some girl came in and saved her."

"How?"

Caitlin's heart was beating fast. This was it.

"Walked right in and shot the guy. He fell down and died, and the girl stared at him for a minute. Now remember, Evangeline wasn't exactly thinking clearly, but she thought the girl looked confused about what she'd done, like she'd suddenly forgotten that she'd walked in and shot the guy and was only just then realizing she'd done it. I don't know what the hell she's talking about . . . Shut up, Evangeline, would you? I'm telling it the way you told me, aren't I? Besides, you were high at the time, remember?"

Caitlin heard a faint voice in the background but couldn't make out what it said.

Terry continued. "The girl looks at Evangeline for the first time, then she looks around the room and sees the handcuff key, which she tosses to Evangeline. Then she just walks out of the house, still carrying the gun."

Caitlin closed her eyes. She'd just heard a recounting of her murdering someone. The man may have been a vile rapist, but did that justify cold-blooded murder?

"Anyway, Bix, just thought you'd want to know," Terry said. "I recognized the redhead right away, of course, as soon as I saw the paper this morning. Knew it was Katie. But it wasn't until Evangeline saw the paper and told me that the girl in the drawing saved her life that I decided to call you. I thought it might help somehow . . . though I don't know how, I guess. It's not like Evangeline's gonna come out and talk about what that guy did to her. But maybe you'd feel better knowing that your girlfriend might've saved someone's life."

"We were there tonight," Bix said. "We saw the handcuffs. Didn't know who'd been in them."

"We? You mean she's with you? Thought she'd have tried to disappear by now. What the hell are you—Wait, never mind. I don't want to know. But you were there *tonight*? This shit all happened days ago."

"Cops still hadn't been there yet."

"Shut up, Evangeline . . . What? . . . Say that again . . . You sure? . . . Well, why the hell didn't you tell me about that before? . . . Bix, Evangeline wants to know if you found a video camera. Says your girl didn't hang to look around after she popped the guy, just turned and walked out, and Evangeline was too drugged up and freaked out to do so herself before she got the hell out of there and thumbed a ride."

"She knows about the camera?" Bix said.

"*You* know about it?"

"Yeah, we saw recordings on his laptop. You're saying he had the camera running with Evangeline?"

"That's what she says. He kept it in a closet in the living room." According to Terry the pimp, between his numerous attacks on Evangeline, he would take the camera out of the closet to download the videos onto his laptop. "Must be a hole in the wall or something," Terry added, "for the camera to shoot through. Evangeline says a couple of times that asshole even sat with her on the bed, the laptop between them, and made her watch a video of him forcing himself on another woman. Then he'd do the same shit to Evangeline."

Bix asked, "And she thinks he turned it on that last time with her the other night? When the redhead came in?"

"Well, again, she was loopy as hell, but she thinks so."

"Thanks, Terry."

"You going back for the tape, Bix?"

"Yeah. Why?"

"Evangeline would rather it not be seen by too many people, you understand?"

"Of course. We need the tape, but given what's on it, I can't imagine wanting to show it to anyone."

Bix disconnected the call.

Josh said to Bix, "Why aren't I surprised that you have a cousin who's a pimp?"

"Hey, it's not like I approve of what he does. Besides, according to him, he keeps them safe. Without him, the girls would be doing the same thing they're doing, only without any protection. Well . . . without his kind of protection. Anyway, if it makes you feel better, he's also a CPA, though I have to admit, he's been doing less accounting and more pimping the last couple of years. To tell you the truth, I don't like the guy, but I'm glad he called."

Bix swung the car into a U-turn.

"Looks like we're heading back to Mike's house," he said.

Wonderful, Caitlin thought. *Let's have another visit with the man I killed, then watch a video of me killing him.*

CHAPTER THIRTY-THREE

HUNNSAKER LAID OUT THREE PHOTOGRAPHS on the counter in front of the desk clerk of the Bed-E-Bye Motel. The first was the doctored photograph of Caitlin Sommers, the one Padilla had found on the Internet and had Photoshopped to replace her blonde hair with shorter red hair so that it reflected the way she looked now, unless she had changed her appearance again. The second picture was of Caitlin Sommers's husband, Josh Sommers, taken from the database of the New Hampshire Division of Motor Vehicles. The third photo was of her boyfriend, Desmond Bixby, pulled from the Massachusetts Registry of Motor Vehicles. The motel clerk scanned the pictures with disinterested, sleepy eyes. He shrugged.

"Nope," the clerk said. "Haven't seen them."

"You sure?" Hunnsaker said.

The clerk shrugged. "I think so."

"Good, because I'm assuming you wouldn't want to be sitting at this desk knowing there's a suspected murderer on the premises."

That wiped the sleep from the clerk's eyes.

"You got a copier here?" she asked. "Preferably a color one."

He nodded.

"You mind putting these next to one another and running me fifty copies? I'd appreciate it."

"I'm not allowed to use the copier for personal stuff. It's only for official use."

"This is official police business. Does that help?"

"Manager says toner's expensive."

Hunnsaker smiled. "Like I said, I'd appreciate it." She handed her business card to the clerk. "And put my card next to them so it shows up on the copies, okay? Thanks."

The clerk hesitated a moment, then scooped up the photos, took Hunnsaker's business card, and disappeared into an office behind the desk. Hunnsaker heard the rhythmic whirring of a copier doing its job. A minute later, the clerk was back with a stack of copies, which he handed across the counter.

"So I'm hoping you'll give me a call if you see any of these people," Hunnsaker said, handing him back one of the copies. "And don't do anything stupid. Don't act suspicious. Just check them in, and once they've gone to their rooms, call 911 and tell them you have a person of interest in a murder investigation staying here, and tell them to call me. Then when you hang up, call me yourself using the number on that card. Got it?"

The clerk nodded.

"What's your name?" she asked.

"Jerry."

"Thanks, Jerry."

Outside, Hunnsaker slipped behind the wheel of her car. She dialed Padilla's number.

When he answered, she asked, "Anything going on?"

"I sent the three photos in a blast text to patrol units, with instructions to check motels on their routes if they can, even if the place has a name that comes later in the alphabet. I figured the suspects might not stick to the phone book if they passed a motel that looked good to them."

"Good thinking. Anything so far?"

"Two units called in already and said they'd checked motels, shown the photos, and left instructions to call 911 if the suspects showed up."

Hunnsaker took the names of the two motels and crossed them off her list.

"Where are you, Javy?"

"Just left my first fleabag joint."

The page that had been torn from Bixby's phone book listed several dozen hotels that came alphabetically before the Lullaby Inn Motel. Hunnsaker and Padilla had divided the list in half, with Hunnsaker taking the first part. They would each drive to the motels on their list, starting with the closest, while also calling the other places on their list while driving. Fortunately, Hunnsaker was a good multitasker.

Between the two of them and the various officers on patrol, there were a lot of eyes looking for Caitlin Sommers and whoever might be with her. There were only so many motels in the area. It was just a matter of time.

———

It was getting late as they neared Bookerman's house. They had passed only one other car on this quiet stretch of road, a sedan traveling in the opposite direction. Otherwise, nothing, which was just as well considering that they were heading back to the scene of a murder that one of them had committed. Bix couldn't imagine what was going through Caitlin's mind right now. He wished she would let him get them both new identities, then run off with him. But she insisted on doing what she thought was the right thing. He admired that a little, but only a little, because he also thought it was a really lousy idea.

He pulled up Bookerman's curving driveway and saw the same car that had been there before, with the trunk still open, just as it had been when they were there not long ago. They hurried to the front door, which was closed but unlocked, just as they'd left it. They went inside, and from where they stood they could see that everything in the next room looked as it had when they were here two hours ago, except for the addition of the dead guy on the floor with blond hair, one eye, and a huge slit in his belly. One-Eye was lying beside the corpse of Mike Bookerman, or Mike Maggert, or whatever the dead dirtbag would rather be called in whatever part of hell he was now roasting in.

"Shit," Bix whispered as he reached into the back of his waistband and drew his gun. "You guys know the drill."

Caitlin and Josh nodded and stood beside each other while Bix walked softly to the kitchen and peered around the door. He moved quietly down the hall, checking Bookerman's bedroom first; then the bathroom; then finally, the second bedroom that Bookerman had used as the base for his Caitlin-stalking operation—the same search he had conducted just half an hour ago. They were alone in the house.

Bix returned and led them into the living room. With the overall tension level a little lower now that they knew One-Eye's killer wasn't still in the house—but still fairly high because sometime within the past thirty minutes or so someone had killed One-Eye pretty much right where they were standing—they opened the door to the only closet in the room. On the shelf, Bix found the camera.

"I looked in this closet last time," he said as he took down the camera, "and I saw this in here, but I thought it was just sitting there in the corner. It didn't occur to me that it could have been carefully positioned there in front of a peephole. That last video would still be on here, right? Not somehow already on the laptop?"

"That's right," Josh said. "He'd have to have transferred it."

"Yeah, well, he didn't get the chance to do that." Also on the shelf, Bix found the box the camera had come in. He closed the door and handed the camera and the box to Josh. He looked at the hole in the wall. It was big enough for the lens to see through clearly but still wasn't easy to see in the shadow of a picture frame on the wall.

"One more thing to do," he said as he stepped over to the blond man's corpse and knelt down, being careful to stay away from the blood. He saw a rectangular bulge in the guy's front pocket, slipped his fingers in, and withdrew the cell phone with Caitlin's recorded confession. Then he stood. "Ready to go?"

He needn't have asked. The looks on their faces said it all. He had to admit that he was looking forward to leaving this place for good, too. There was the smell, of course. But for Bix, it was more the fact that people kept dying here. It was time to put the Bookermans behind them. And with Daddy Darryl in prison for the next ten years and his son dead for eternity, Bix figured they should be able to do just that, at least until the cops started interrogating them.

———

Chops knew he would have to go back to Mikey's house and clean things up before he flew back to LA, but at the moment he had other work to do. The woman could decide to run at any moment.

He cruised down Jasmine Street. Desmond Bixby's building looked quiet—no lights on that Chops could see in either Bixby's first-floor place or the upstairs residence—but there was a cop in an unmarked car down the block, which might have meant that Bixby and the girl were inside and the cops wanted to keep an eye on them in case they left. Maybe the police thought they would lead them to someone else or something. Another option, though, was that Bixby and the girl weren't inside, and the cop was watching the place in case they returned home.

Chops turned left at the next corner and then left again. He drove halfway down the block until he could see the back of Bixby's building on the next street over. He pulled to the curb and thought about how to play this. The girl had to die, that was certain. She'd killed Mikey, and even though he and Mikey weren't close, they were brothers. So she was a dead woman. The question was, how to go about it? Only a sliver of a moon tonight with clouds occasionally obscuring even that, so Chops thought he could break into the place from the back without being seen. If the girl and Bixby were home, he'd kill them. If they weren't, he'd wait for them inside and kill them when they got home. He wouldn't have long to act. The cops might knock as soon as the couple closed the door. The problem would be if the cops nabbed them before they entered the house, which was a possibility. But Chops had spied only one car out there, so the cop inside was probably just surveilling the place and would report in if the suspects made an appearance.

Chops slipped through the shadows of the yard abutting Bixby's backyard, quietly scaled a short and rusted chain-link fence, and moved quickly to a window on the back of the building that someone had conveniently left open for him. Even more conveniently, someone had left a lawn chair under the window, perfect for using to climb into the apartment. Strange. But it was too weird and obvious to be a trap of some kind, so Chops stepped onto the chair and pulled himself into the apartment.

He slipped a knife out of a sheath in his boot and walked quietly through the dark rooms, hoping to find someone to kill. He realized soon that he was alone. On a bedside table he found a photograph of a pretty redhead. And he recognized her. It was the same woman from the picture tacked to the bulletin board in his brother's house. Different hair but the same face.

Very interesting.

He had been planning to kill his brother's murderer, but now that he knew who she was, things were different.

Where were they now? Before he died, the one-eyed guy had said he had spoken with them not long before, so they hadn't gone on the run or into hiding by that time, despite the fact that the girl had killed Mike two days ago. Had they finally done so only in the last two hours?

With nothing else to do but wait for now, Chops went to the kitchen. He was thirsty. He wanted to look for a beer but worried that someone would see the refrigerator light, so he decided to drink water right from the tap. That's when he saw the phone book with the missing page.

He took a few moments and used his cell phone to snap pictures from photographs in frames around the apartment, photos of the redhead and the guy she lived with here. Two minutes later, Chops was on the street where he'd left his car. He strode up the nearest front walk and pushed a door buzzer. He pushed it again. It was late. The occupants would be home. He leaned into the button and heard a constant buzz inside. Finally, the curtains in the window beside the door parted, and a round, cautious face peeked out at him. Chops released the buzzer. He didn't expect the man to open the door. Who would be that stupid these days? But he smiled and said, "I know, I'm a scary-looking guy. And to be honest, I'm armed."

At that, the man's eyes widened.

"But I need to be quick here," Chops said. "You see this phone book?"

He held up the directory he'd taken from Bixby's apartment. The man in the window nodded.

"I'm betting you have the same one, right? And don't lie, okay?" The man nodded again.

"I need you to get it for me. And don't call the cops, all right? If you take more than one minute, I'm coming through this door and gutting you like a deer, you got me?"

The man looked like he was about to cry.

"All I want is your phone book, you understand?"

Finally, the man spoke in a shaky voice. "But you already have the same phone book."

"Yes, but I want yours," Chops said. "And I want it now. You can just hand it to me through the window if you want. Better yet, I'll stand back and you can toss it out. Sound good?"

The man was obviously confused, perhaps wondering if he'd read anything in the papers lately about a phone-book bandit.

"I need to get going here, buddy," Chops said. "What's it gonna be? You going to get me the phone book, or am I coming in to get it myself?"

"I'll get it," the man said. "I'll be right back."

Chops looked at his watch. Thirty-nine seconds later, the man was at the window again, too soon to have called the cops. Chops took two steps back, and the man opened the window two and a half inches and shoved the two-inch-thick book out and onto the porch. The window shut quickly and the man watched Chops from behind the glass.

"Thanks," Chops said as he picked up the book and walked away.

In his car, he turned to page 118, the page missing from Bixby's phone book. Chops took a moment to study the list of hotels and motels. He'd ignore hotels completely and start with the closest motels. He'd drive to the nearest one and call others on the way. In his experience, the average person wasn't above taking a bribe, even if it meant screwing someone over. And people were more likely to screw over someone they didn't know. And motel clerks were among those most willing to pocket some cash in exchange for information. Equipped with his list of motels and a couple of photographs of the redhead and Bixby, Chops began making calls and visits, offers and threats.

———

Bix paid for two rooms at the Eagle Inn Motel. A perky young woman with a ponytail smiled brightly as she took his cash and handed him two keys on rings with big plastic tags displaying the room numbers. Then Bix went back out to his SUV, which was one of only eight vehicles in the lot. He wished there were more.

"All done?" Bix asked.

Josh nodded and handed him the screwdriver Bix had given him from his trunk. He'd advised Caitlin to keep her increasingly familiar-looking face in the car while Josh found a set of license plates to steal from another car and put on Bix's Explorer. It wasn't much of a trick, especially when the plates came from a car parked in the same lot, but at least it was something.

They walked up exterior stairs to the second level and stopped outside room 206.

"This is your room, Josh," Bix said, handing him the key. "Caitlin and I will be right next door in 207 if you need us."

"Funny," Josh said. He unlocked the door and they all went inside, as they had planned to do. Bix locked the door behind them. He would spend the night next door, but for now, there was something they had to do. No one was particularly eager to do it, especially not Caitlin, but they had to . . . especially Caitlin.

Bix placed a box on the bed and sat beside it. It was the box the video camera had come in. He flipped open a little screen on the side of the camera and found the power button. The screen stayed dark for a moment, then the word *Sony* appeared before soon being replaced by an image of the motel room.

Bix said, "If it was recording when Caitlin got there, it should have kept recording until the tape was full, right? So we'll have to rewind."

"It looks like that camera has a hard drive," Josh said.

Bix looked at him.

"So no tape," Josh said. "It records right onto an internal drive. Here, let me see."

Josh sat on the other side of the bed and Bix handed him the camera.

"Looks like there's not a lot of battery left," Josh said. He peered into the box and pulled out a black power cord. Then he removed another cord with several wires attached.

"This should make it easier to see what's on here," he said, taking the cord over to the television on the dresser. He pulled the TV away from the wall and fiddled around behind it. Then, he plugged one end of the power cord into the camera and the other into a wall outlet. Using a remote, he turned on the TV and scrolled through input settings until they saw some kind of menu on the screen.

"That's the camera's menu," Josh said. Using buttons on the camera itself, he navigated through it. "There are several files on here, but we're only interested in the last one, if it's the one we think it might be. Hmm," he said. "Okay, looks like the . . . uh, the prostitute . . . Evangeline . . . she might have been right that Bookerman had turned on the camera before Caitlin got there the other night."

"How can you tell?" Caitlin asked as she sat on the bed beside Bix, facing the TV.

"The size of the last file is a lot bigger than any of the other files."

"As though the camera was left running for a long time," Caitlin said, "after I . . ."

Bix reached over and held her hand.

"You ready?" Josh asked.

"Not really," Caitlin said, "but play it anyway."

Josh hit the "Play" button and joined the others on the bed. Bix figured he would object to another man holding Caitlin's hand—especially Bix—but instead, Josh sat on the other side of her and held her other hand.

The video began to play.

CHAPTER THIRTY-FOUR

THE SCREEN ON THE TELEVISION in the motel room faded up from black to an extreme close-up of Mike Bookerman's face—eyes dead and black and too far apart, like his father's, the skin the same sickly white. Caitlin gasped. It was the Bogeyman's face, or close enough, and it wasn't some nightmare vision or half-buried memory. It was alive this time, or at least alive in the video . . . though his eyes somehow still looked dead.

The face disappeared from the screen, and the view swung around a room, went dark for a moment, and then the point of view changed to what was obviously from the camera's hidden position in the closet, looking through the large peephole. In the center of the screen was the pullout sofa, on which lay a naked woman wearing only a handcuff on one wrist. The angle of the camera allowed a view beyond the sofa; in the background was the doorway to the den, where the front door to the house was.

"Why does he bother hiding the camera if he drugs the women?" Josh asked.

"Maybe he doesn't always drug them," Bix said. "Maybe some go back to his house willingly for whatever reason and have sex with him, and he tapes them without them knowing."

On the TV, a shirtless Bookerman walked back into view, his pale, thin, hairless upper body on full display. He took a swig from the bottle of beer in his hand.

"Is that blood on his arm, just below his shoulder?" Josh asked.

"Looks like it," Bix said.

"He'd already been shot in the arm, then," Caitlin said. "I must have only shot him in the stomach," she added, though a tiny little hope flickered inside her that maybe, just maybe, she hadn't fired the fatal bullet, either.

Bookerman's voice came from the TV's speakers. It chilled Caitlin. "Did you miss me?" he asked the girl on the bed, who was looking at him through glazed eyes under heavy lids. To Caitlin, she looked mostly out of it, thankfully. Caitlin wanted to close her own eyes but couldn't. She had to see this. They all did. But did they have to watch everything? As if reading her mind, Bix said, "Maybe we can skip ahead, huh?"

Josh hurried to the camera, hit a button, and the screen jumped and flickered as the action moved quickly. Caitlin didn't want to see more than she had to, so she looked away from the screen. She saw Josh position his body in front of it as he fast-forwarded. Soon, though, he said, "Whoa, wait a second. Here we go. Looks like he didn't have time to . . . do anything to her before . . . Let me back up a bit . . . Okay, here we go."

He returned to the bed. Caitlin looked back at the TV and saw the action moving at normal speed.

On the screen . . .

Bookerman said, "No? You don't want to watch a quick video of me with another of my girlfriends?" He waited and the woman on the bed said nothing. "How about one of you and me from this morning? No? You must want to get right down to it, I guess. Well, that works for me. I've had a hell of a night, and my arm hurts like a sonofabitch, so I'm fine with just moving things along."

Bookerman took a gulp of his beer, then reached down to place the bottle on the table in the foreground, wincing suddenly as he did. He looked at the short, angry red track along the outside of his arm, just below the shoulder joint—a little furrow obviously left by a bullet. He tipped the bottle up and poured beer onto the wound, wincing again. Then he put the beer on the table and sat on the mattress beside the woman. He reached out and touched her thigh. She barely moved. Her eyes were half-closed.

In the doorway in the background, Caitlin appeared, wearing jeans and a tight, low-cut maroon sweater. She was holding a gun. Bookerman stood quickly.

Caitlin squeezed Josh's hand. "That's the gun I brought home the other night," she said.

Bookerman said, "Who the hell are you?"

Caitlin said nothing.

"Is that my gun?"

"Found it on a table near the front door," Caitlin said.

Bookerman took a step toward her and Caitlin fired a bullet past him.

"Holy shit, are you crazy?"

"Maybe. But I'm not a great shot. It was lucky I didn't put that right through you. Take another step and you may not be so lucky."

Listening to her voice on the TV, Caitlin barely recognized it. It was strong and clear, but that wasn't what made it seem different to her. She couldn't put her finger on what it was; it was just . . . different, almost like that of a tough TV cop.

"I'll ask you again," Bookerman said. "Who the hell are you?"

Again, Caitlin said nothing.

"All right, then, what do you want?" he asked.

"Let her go."

He looked at the naked woman handcuffed to his sofa.

"No. Shoot me."

Caitlin seemed to be considering it. Instead, she took a cell phone out of her back pocket.

"I'm calling the police."

"No, you're not."

"Why not?"

"Because you would have already done it if you were going to. I know who you are now."

"Yeah? Who am I?" Caitlin asked.

"You're the girl from the warehouse tonight. You're the reason everything went to shit. Why the hell were you there, anyway?"

After a hesitation, Caitlin said, "I followed you from the fight club."

"Why? Who am I to you?"

"You're nobody."

After a moment, he said, "All right, then who are you?"

"The one holding the gun. So you're saying I'm *the reason things happened the way they did at the warehouse. It was* my *fault?"*

"Sure," Bookerman said. "I got shot because of you. You were hiding and watching and you made a noise. When I turned, that scumbag pulled a piece and shot me."

"You already had a gun on him," Caitlin said. "You were going to kill him."

"Yeah, but if it wasn't for you, I wouldn't have gotten shot, too."

"Why were you going to kill him?"

"Because he tried to sell me fake hands. Fake hands, for Christ's sake."

"What are you talking about?"

"What do you care? And anyway, you were there."

Without warning, Caitlin fired another bullet past him.

"Jesus Christ! Stop that."

"Answer my questions, then. Why were you going to kill that guy?"

"Okay. No more shooting, all right? Shit. So the guy comes from out of town. Martin says he knows him or his family or something. He tells

Martin that he has a crate of stolen smartphones to sell. Martin brings him to the warehouse and he doesn't have any goddamn smartphones. Says he had them but found a higher bidder this morning. But he wants to sell us what he's got, which is—now get this—a bag of fake hands."

"Fake hands?"

"Seriously. Fake human hands. Says they're robotic or something. He read online that they can sell for ten thousand bucks each, maybe more. He had six in his bag. Why the hell he had them in a bag and not in whatever boxes they probably came in is beyond me. Anyway, he says that's at least sixty grand, but he's willing to give them to us for the five grand we were gonna pay him for the phones."

"So you decided to kill him?"

"Smartphones I can sell. What the hell am I gonna do with fake hands? Got the bag right over there." He nodded his head toward a black canvas bag on a table near the sofa. "No idea what I can do with the things. I'll probably just dump them. Anyway, the idiot tried to put one over on me. Of course I was gonna kill him. Wouldn't have mattered. He was from out of town, didn't know anybody here except other lowlifes like him and me, and people like us, we don't care if one of us disappears. Nobody would miss him. Then you made noise or something from wherever you were hiding and watching, I turned, and the sonofabitch pulled a gun and shot me in the shoulder, goddamn it. So, shit yeah, I shot him."

Caitlin heard those words and felt relief that, at the very least, she wasn't a double murderer. She hadn't killed the guy at the warehouse, after all. She'd only witnessed his murder.

"What I want to know is," Bookerman said, "where the hell you went. Me and Martin split up and covered a lot of ground pretty quick, but you must have been flying, girl. I probably got a bit cocky," he added with a grin, "wasting time yelling about all the things we were gonna do to you when we caught you." He shook his head.

"My God, Caitlin," Josh said. "That must have been terrifying for you."

"Sure sounds like it," she replied, relieved that she didn't remember it. It did indeed sound frightening.

"*But you disappeared into thin air,*" Bookerman said, "*and now, somehow, you found me here.*" He seemed truly impressed. "*You must have waited us out while we were looking for you, then followed me here, but I can't figure where you were. We looked everywhere.*"

Caitlin shook her head. "*I was in your trunk. When I ran outside, I saw your car, so I popped the trunk, climbed in, and held the lid closed until you got in and drove home.*"

"*Seriously? You've got balls, girl.*"

"*I didn't want to lose you. Plus, I figured you wouldn't look in your trunk when you left.*"

Caitlin sensed Josh and Bix looking at her and not at the screen.

"My God, Caitlin," Josh said.

"Bookerman's right, Katie," Bix said. "That took balls."

Caitlin kept her eyes on the screen.

Bookerman was shaking his head. "I gotta hand it to you. You're something else. I actually drove around a bit looking for you, then my arm started hurting and I figured I'd leave the rest of the looking to Martin so I could get home and clean this bullet wound."

He looked down at the superficial wound on his shoulder. "*Yeah,*" Bookerman added, "*you're crazy but brave. Not too smart, though.*"

He took another step toward Caitlin and she raised the gun. Bookerman stopped.

"*So now what?*" Bookerman asked. "*You followed me to the warehouse for some reason. You working with that cheating scumbag I killed? Were you two planning on double-crossing us?*" He paused for a moment. "*Hey, maybe it wasn't me you followed from the fight club. Maybe you followed Martin's car and were there when he picked up the idiot with the goddamn fake hands, then followed them to the warehouse. Is that it? Who is he, your boyfriend?*"

"*I'm not working with anyone. And I followed you, not the other guy.*"

"And so you came here to what? Shoot me? You didn't even bring a gun of your own."

After a pause, Caitlin said, "I'm not actually sure why I followed you here. But when I looked in your window, I saw her," she said, nodding to the naked woman. "And I saw the gun on the table, so . . ."

"You're not sure why you followed me?" Bookerman seemed confused by that.

Caitlin shrugged. "Not really. I'm not sure why I followed you here tonight. Or even why I've been looking for you at all. But when I saw you a couple of weeks ago . . ."

Caitlin trailed off. She looked uncertain about what to do. She had the gun in one hand and her phone in the other. While she seemed to be debating her next move, Bookerman snapped his fingers. "Holy shit," he said. "It's you. How the hell . . . ?" He sounded even more perplexed than before. "Different hair, so it took me a minute, but it's the same face. It's really you. The one that got away. The prettiest one. That's what he used to call you, you know. My father went on about you all the time. From behind bars . . . all those years, he never forgot you. And I had you, goddamn it, I actually had you for a little while. But I lost you, you slippery little bitch. That was a hell of a bump you gave me." He pointed to his head, just above his hairline. "I should have remembered I kept a tire iron on the floor. I was only out for a few seconds, but you'd already taken my car."

He shook his head. "I looked for you ever since March, and then you show up here all on your own. Unbelievable." He chuckled. "I don't know how the hell you found me," he said, no longer chuckling, "but I guess you want your revenge, huh?"

"I want to know what happened next," she said.

"What?"

"Tell me what happened after I took your car."

"What? Why?"

"Because I have a gun, that's why."

He shrugged. "After you got away, I figured you'd go right to the cops, so I stole someone else's car and took off. I would have gone back and taken yours, but I didn't know if anyone had seen us."

He paused again.

Caitlin raised the gun an inch. Bookerman shrugged again and said, "I drove like hell back here and planned to split, right? Pack a few things and take off. But then they started saying on the news that you disappeared. They found your car but not you. So I realized you didn't go to the cops after all. Who the hell knew why, but you didn't. So I kept my eye on the news for a while, and the days went by, and you were just . . . gone. You went missing. Weird. So I had to forget about you . . . but I couldn't." He smiled. "I didn't. But after all that, it's you who finds me."

Caitlin looked lost in thought. Bookerman moved a little closer.

"So why didn't you go to the cops?" he asked.

Caitlin looked up. "Why did you grab me?"

"You don't know?"

A step closer. Caitlin didn't seem to notice. She looked caught up in the story.

"Because you're the one that got away. The prettiest one."

He took two sudden steps toward her and she quickly raised the gun, which had lowered an inch or two. She pointed it at his midsection. Bookerman, just three feet from her now, hesitated. Caitlin watched him. Something changed in her face then. Bookerman made a quick move and Caitlin pulled the trigger. The woman on the sofa bed screamed. Bookerman staggered back, holding his stomach.

"Holy shit," he said as he fell out of frame.

Caitlin watched herself on the TV screen, watched herself shoot a man dead. A horrible man who did horrible things to women. A man who had stalked Caitlin and even tried to abduct her. And she had killed him. She wished she hadn't, but she'd had to do it, right? He'd been about to rush her . . . hadn't he?

On the screen, Caitlin let the gun hang at her side. She stared down for a few moments at the body that lay on the floor below the camera's line of sight. Something changed in her face. Her features went . . . slack. Her eyes, which had been hard just moments ago when she had stared down Mike Bookerman, looked empty now, as though awareness had leaked out of them through tiny cracks. Almost mechanically, she turned her head toward the naked woman handcuffed to the bed frame, then her eyes roamed slowly around the room for a moment before settling on the table in the foreground. She walked across the room, giving the body a wide berth, and picked up something small from the table and tossed it toward the woman. It jingled when it hit the mattress. The handcuff key on a metal ring.

Caitlin walked around the body again. Seemingly without thinking, she dropped the gun into the black canvas bag on the table by the sofa; grabbed the bag by its straps; and, without a backward glance, walked slowly out of the room. A moment later, a door opened and closed offscreen.

Josh crossed to the TV and turned it off. He shut off the camera, too; disconnected its cable and cord; and stuffed it all back into its box. Caitlin watched him, unsure how to feel. Now she knew. They all did. Josh sat beside her again and took her hand. Bix had never let go of her other one.

"You rode to Bookerman's house in his trunk, right?" Bix said. Without waiting for a response, he said, "You left your car at the warehouse. Did you walk back to your car?"

Caitlin shrugged. "I don't know. I guess."

"That's almost three miles."

That explained why Caitlin's feet had been so tired when she got there.

"You okay, hon?" Josh asked.

"You had to do it, Katie," Bix said.

"Did I?" she asked. She wasn't being argumentative. She genuinely wondered.

"He was making his move on you," Bix said.

"Are you sure?" she asked. "I mean, maybe it looked that way. He definitely moved. But maybe he was trying to raise his hands. Maybe he was going to back away from me."

Bix shook his head. "He was going for you. No doubt. Right, Josh?"

Josh didn't hesitate. "He was, Caitlin. You saw it. We all did."

Caitlin wondered how a jury was going to see it. They would probably be sympathetic. The man was heinous, and the fact that he was stalking Caitlin, and had even admitted to trying to abduct her, would certainly play in her favor. But a prosecutor would argue that instead of going to the police, Caitlin had gone to see Bookerman. And instead of calling the police when she had the phone in one of her hands, she shot him with the gun she had in her other.

"I'm tired," Caitlin said. "You guys must be, too." She stood. "Let's get some sleep. Tomorrow's probably going to be a long day."

Bix walked to the door and opened it. Then he turned and looked back at her. "This may not make you feel any better, Katie, but this world is a far better place without Mike Bookerman walking around in it." Then he closed the door behind him.

Maybe Bix is right about that, Caitlin thought, but she couldn't convince herself that it had been her place to correct the problem. If she had been acting in self-defense, maybe she could live with her actions. Maybe. If not . . . well, she was going to have to live with herself anyway, but it would be a lot harder.

Life was going to get hard soon either way, though. She'd be behind bars tomorrow. In the morning she was taking herself and the video camera to the nearest police station.

CHAPTER THIRTY-FIVE

CHOPS RAPPED HIS KNUCKLES ON the reservation counter of the Eagle Inn Motel. He heard movement in the small back office, then a young woman came through the door sporting a smile far brighter than Chops expected from a motel night clerk, though it faltered slightly when she saw Chops. He wasn't offended. He wasn't a good-looking man and he knew it. In fact, some considered him creepy-looking, and that was undoubtedly how the young woman viewed him. He smiled, knowing it wasn't a great smile, but he hoped it would disarm her. It seemed to work, because her smile regained its former brightness, and she asked, "Looking for a room?"

"Actually, I'm looking for some friends of mine," Chops said.

"Oh, are they guests here?"

Chops tried for a sheepish look. "I feel like an idiot, but I can't remember where they said they're staying. I'm supposed to meet them but I forgot the name of the motel." He pulled out his cell phone. "I have pictures of them, if you . . ." He trailed off.

"Oh, well, I'm sorry," the clerk said. "I'm not really sure I can help you. We have to respect the privacy . . . sir, are you okay?"

Chops was fine. He was staring at a piece of paper among other sheets of paper and flyers tacked to a bulletin board on the wall behind the counter. The piece of paper that had drawn his interest was pinned on top of several others, indicating that it had been put there fairly recently. Chops could see the three photos clearly. Two of the faces unmistakably belonged to the redhead and her boyfriend. The third man must be the one the one-eyed guy said was with them. Above the pictures, someone had written in black marker, *Police are interested in these people. Call 911.* Chops pointed to the flyer.

"When did the police leave that?" he asked.

"What?" She turned. "Hmm, I don't know. It wasn't here yesterday, though. Maybe it came in earlier today, or tonight before I got on. I only came in half an hour ago."

As she looked at the flyer, her eyes went wide. And then Chops knew. They were here. He'd found them on his third try. He casually looked around the lobby and saw no security cameras.

"What's your name?" he asked her.

She turned, her eyes still wide.

"Your name?" he prompted.

"Betsy."

"They're here, aren't they, Betsy? They checked in within the last half hour."

She nodded. "That one guy did. He rented two rooms."

"But you didn't call the police, did you? Because you didn't see that flyer until just now, am I right?"

"Yeah. I need to call now."

She started to pick up the phone, but Chops reached over the counter and put his big, pale hand over hers. Gently. She pulled her hand away.

"I'm afraid I lied to you before, Betsy," he said. "I'm not here looking for friends of mine. I'm a bounty hunter. You know what that is?"

"I think so."

"I get paid to find certain people the police are looking for. But if the police find them first, I don't get paid. I need to be the one to bring them in, you understand?"

She nodded.

"Good, that's good," he said. He took out his wallet and put five twenties on the counter. "Here's a hundred dollars. I'll make a lot more than that when I hand them over to the cops, so I can spare it. All I need you to do is not call the cops."

Betsy frowned. "Won't I get into trouble if I don't call?"

"Oh, you misunderstand. It's okay for you to call the cops. I just need you to wait until after I get these three suspects into hand-cuffs. Once I do that, I'll give you the go-ahead to call the police. All I need is a few minutes. And when the cops get here, I'll tell them that I followed the suspects here and captured them in their room. You can pretend we never even spoke. That way, you did your duty and called the police. The only difference is that I'll be the one who gets credit for capturing them, so I'll be able to get paid. Sound okay to you?" He smiled again and hoped it didn't creep her out.

"And I'll be able to call the police? You promise?"

"I *want* you to call them. That way I won't have to. I'll be able to keep my eye on my prisoners while you call and tell the cops to meet me here."

Betsy chewed her lower lip. Chops nudged the money toward her.

"You promise you'll let me know when I can call them?" she asked.

"If you promise to wait until I give you the word, I promise to let you know when to make the call. It will be just a few minutes, Betsy. I'm really good at what I do."

After another moment of hesitation, she picked up the money. Chops smiled again.

"What rooms are they in?" he asked.

Bix lay on his back staring at the ceiling. He hated leaving the woman he loved with another man while he went to his own room to spend the night alone. Sure, Caitlin was different than she had been before, he couldn't deny that. Nor could he deny that he didn't know Caitlin nearly as well as he knew Katie. But neither could he deny that he still loved her . . . that her departure from his world would leave a gaping wound in his life. He would have given anything for the chance to get to know Caitlin the way he'd known Katie. But that wasn't going to happen. She was married. Oh, and she was going to be behind bars tomorrow once she turned herself in. He hoped he would at least get the chance to say a proper goodbye in the morning. He wished he'd been able to say a proper good night moments ago.

He heard a soft knock on his door. He sat up, crossed to the door, and opened it. Caitlin gave him a quick, tentative smile and slipped past him into his room. He closed the door and faced her.

Bix wondered if she had sneaked out of her room while Josh was showering or something.

"Does he know you're here?"

She nodded.

"Did you come here to tell me that you're forgetting about all that 'turning yourself in to the police' nonsense and you've agreed to ditch the geek and run away with me?"

"No," she said, smiling ruefully.

"I didn't think so. Did you at least give it some thought?"

"Not really, no."

"Katie . . . Caitlin . . . I know you want to do the right thing. I know you don't want to live your life on the run. But I don't want to see you go to prison, not even for a day."

"I know," she said.

"You're gonna laugh," he said, "but I still love you."

"I know that, too."

She didn't say it back to him. He didn't expect her to, but it's not fun to say it and not hear it in return.

"Why did you come over here?" he asked.

She stepped close to him, reached up and touched his cheek, then raised herself up on her toes and touched her lips gently to his for a few wonderful seconds. When she pulled away, she kept her hand on his face a moment longer while she looked into his eyes. Then she left without a word and Bix heard the door close.

She was really gone now. Tomorrow, she'd be in police custody. And if by some miracle she was acquitted at trial months from now, it was Josh she would be going back to. And if she was *not* acquitted, it would still be her husband waiting for her at the prison gates when her time was up years down the road.

Bix was thirty-two years old and he knew without a doubt that the best days of his life were now behind him.

He returned to the bed, lay on his back, and stared at the ceiling, trying not to listen to the muffled voices coming from next door.

———

Chops looked up at the second floor of the motel from the shadows across the parking lot. The light was on in 206 and off in 207. He wasn't sure who was in which room. He didn't know exactly how this was going to work out, other than that just before he made his move, he'd have to go back to the registration desk and kill Betsy. He hadn't done it before in case someone looking for a room came in before Chops was ready to get started. He had gambled that she wouldn't call the cops before he told her she could. And even if she did, it would take her a few minutes to screw up her courage to do so and go back on her promise to Chops. She just seemed like that kind of a girl.

Now that Chops had seen the layout of the motel, the position of the rooms next to each other, and where they were located in relation to the stairwells, he was ready to go back and kill Betsy as quickly as he could—she'd seen his face, after all—but only after she had given him duplicate keys to their rooms, or a passkey, or whatever they used here. After she was dead, he would march upstairs and let himself into the dark room first. Hopefully, he'd catch someone asleep, making the kill easier and a lot quieter. Either way, he'd move fast. Before they even knew he was there, he'd kill both men.

But not the girl. No, he wanted her alive.

———

"How's Bix?" Josh asked.

Caitlin doubted that he truly cared, but she said, "He's okay. Thanks for understanding why I needed to say good night to him."

"Good night or good-bye?" Josh asked.

"Good-bye."

Caitlin stepped out of her shoes, then unsnapped her jeans. She felt a little self-conscious as she slipped out of them in the brightly lit room, leaving her wearing nothing but her shirt and a tiny little thong, because even though Caitlin had always worn underwear that was conservative yet stylish, apparently she went in for skimpy skivvies when she was Katie Southard. It was all Caitlin had found in the dresser at Bix's place. As she folded her jeans and laid them on a chair in the corner, she could feel Josh's eyes on her. Nothing creepy, nothing he hadn't done literally a thousand times during their life together, but tonight it felt different . . . and not because Josh was doing anything wrong, but because . . . well, she wasn't sure, but it felt like it might have had something to do with Bix being in the next room.

"You okay?" Josh asked.

She shrugged. "Not really. That was hard to watch a little while ago." She was deflecting, she knew.

"I'm sorry, honey. I can't imagine."

He crossed the small room and took her in his arms. Even though he was her husband, it felt strangely intimate . . . her standing there in nothing but a shirt and a thong. To Caitlin, this would have felt as natural as breathing not long ago. And she had shared the same bed with Josh just last night. But so much had changed since then. Still, Josh was her husband and she loved him, and the weirdness of this kind of contact would fade, she knew. She relaxed into the hug and Josh dropped his arms to her waist. Then his hands slid and came to rest on her nearly naked hips. He pulled back a little but kept his hands where they were. He leaned to the side and looked down.

"You know," he said, "even though that damn guy next door has a Wild Thing tattoo like you do, and I'll probably have a hard time for a while looking at yours without thinking of him . . . I have to admit, this is kind of sexy."

He traced the outlines of her Wild Thing with one finger. Caitlin didn't truly think he was trying to start something intimate with her—after all that she had been through the last few days, on the night before she'd be confessing to killing someone—but still, it felt wrong. She pulled away.

"Josh, I'm not . . . I mean, I hope you don't think I could—"

He took a step back, looking both surprised and hurt. "Oh my God, Caitlin. I'm so sorry. I didn't mean for you to . . . I would never . . ." He shook his head. "After everything you've been through lately . . . you think I'm a monster?" He looked wounded, then shook it off and smiled.

The temperature in the room dropped forty degrees. Caitlin couldn't speak. She took a step away from her husband, then another.

Dark, wide-set eyes in a fish-pale face. Long fingers reaching for her. You think I'm a monster?

A wineglass in shards on the floor, dark red wine pooled around it like blood. Caitlin rushing past Josh, his hands reaching toward her. You think I'm a monster?

White fingers digging into her arms, pulling her down . . .

Josh's hands holding her upper arms, trying to pull her down, to make her sit beside him, trying to calm her. You think I'm a monster?

Caitlin breaking free, rushing from the house, driving away, driving without thinking, wanting not to think at all.

Mike Bookerman—not the Bogeyman from Caitlin's nightmares and not Darryl Bookerman the pedophile who had abducted her twenty-two years ago, but Mike Bookerman, his son—walking up to her car in a dark parking lot, grabbing her, choking her . . . then Caitlin waking up in the passenger seat of a car that wasn't her own as it rumbled along . . . and hearing a clink of something metal, something heavy, and it bumping against her foot and her reaching down and closing her fingers around the cool, smooth metal . . . and when he pulled the car over, her swinging the tire iron with all her strength, aiming for his head . . . and there was blood and . . . that's it.

Caitlin remembered nothing after that. But she now remembered everything before it. Everything. She remembered the argument with Josh the night she disappeared, the one that had made her storm out of their house, where Mike Bookerman must have been waiting nearby, waiting and watching. He must have been so pleasantly surprised when she left her house alone, got into her car alone, and drove off down the street alone.

Caitlin took another step back, then another, until she bumped into the wall behind her. She remembered so much . . . too much.

"Caitlin?" Josh asked, clearly alarmed.

A ringing phone, an unexpected voice on the line. Accusations. Denials. Words of anger. Words of protestation and of love.

"Caitlin, what's going on? You're scaring me. Are you okay?"

She shook her head. She wasn't okay. Not at all.

Because she remembered. Not what happened the other night at the warehouse. Nothing that happened during the seven lost months in Smithfield. But Caitlin remembered everything that happened before she lost her memory, her identity. She remembered Mike Bookerman's botched abduction attempt and, before that, the fight she had with Josh, the one that occurred after Caitlin answered the phone and was told by Gretchen Sorrento, the personal assistant to Josh's boss's boss, that she and Josh had been having an affair and Gretchen was tired of sneaking around. At first he denied it.

"I love you, Caitlin," he had said. "I couldn't do that to you. God, you think I'm a monster?"

But she hadn't believed him, and she'd pressed him and he'd finally admitted the truth. He claimed it was a onetime thing, that Gretchen was lying about it being an ongoing affair; it was just the one time and she was calling now to hurt Josh because he had told her that it could never happen again. Then he told Caitlin that he had wanted to die he was so sad about what he had done, that he loved her too much to hurt her. Caitlin had told him how miserably he had failed in that regard, and after more words, and more tears, and pain that felt like a poison in her stomach, she'd pushed past Josh, grabbed her keys from a hook by the door, and left the house. She had driven and driven, circling the town, until she'd needed to pull over and just cry for a while, so she'd parked in the empty lot of a strip mall and begun to let it out . . . and then her door had been pulled open and she'd been yanked from the car and—

"The night I went missing, we didn't just fight about some small thing," Caitlin said. "You lied to me."

Josh's mouth slipped open, just a little, but he said nothing.

"You were having an affair with Gretchen," she said.

Josh suddenly looked tired and sad. He sighed.

"That's right," Caitlin said. "I remember now. We were drinking wine and the phone rang. It was Gretchen. She said she was sorry to call so late but she didn't sound it. I asked if she wanted to speak with you but she said no, she was calling me. Right then I wondered. I remember in that moment being surprised that I wondered. Didn't I trust you more than that? But the second she said she was calling for me, I had a feeling. And I was right."

Josh was looking at the carpet. "Caitlin . . ."

"Yes, Josh? What are you going to say? What *can* you say? That it was a mistake? That you still love me? That you never meant to hurt me?"

"I didn't mean to hurt you," he said softly.

"Here's a tip, Josh. You don't want to hurt someone, then don't marry her, swearing before God and everyone you know that you'll love her forever and be faithful to her forever, and then cheat on her."

Her voice had risen. She felt like a complete fool. She was afraid Bix could hear them next door, though she wasn't sure why that should matter to her.

———

Bix had given up staring at the ceiling several minutes ago and rolled onto his side so he could stare at the wall for a while. He had also given up any hope of sleep coming tonight. His thoughts swam lazy circles in his head, each drifting slowly by, teasing him as it passed, tormenting him, telling him that Caitlin was as good as gone and Bix would never see her again, never find a woman like her again. And Caitlin, the woman he loved, was probably going to jail. He knew she felt remorse for what she had done—though Bix thought she deserved a medal—and because she was in pain, and must have been scared about what lay ahead of her, Bix was in pain, too. He hurt for her. He hurt for himself. He wished he *could* sleep right now, but it was tough when he could still hear Caitlin and Josh talking next door in loud voices.

Loud voices?

Were they arguing?

———

Chops wiped the blood from the blade of his knife on Betsy's shirt, then stuffed her body beneath the desk in the office behind the registration counter. He closed the door and handwrote a sign reading: *Back in 15 minutes,* which he taped to the door.

Outside, he started for the stairs to the second level.

———

There was nothing Josh could say as Caitlin brushed past him. It *had* been a mistake. He *was* sorry. He *hadn't* meant to hurt her. He wanted to tell her all those things and more, but she didn't want to listen. He couldn't blame her. He could only blame himself. How could he have done what he did? He should never have told Gretchen that she had a nice smile. He should have stopped her flirting as soon as it started. He never should have flirted back. And as much as he would have liked to deny it, he must have known deep down that their first lunch together was something more than two colleagues having a casual midday meal. And then . . . he never should have stopped at that motel after lunch.

Caitlin was his world. How could he have forgotten that? How could he have been so stupid and thoughtless and shortsighted and cruel? How could he do what so many others had done, people whom Josh used to look upon with nothing but scorn?

And how could he say anything now that wouldn't sound like the same thing everyone else says when they get caught cheating? How could he say anything to make this situation even remotely better?

He couldn't. So he watched Caitlin step into her jeans, then into her shoes, then out the door.

She's going next door to Bix, he thought. And he couldn't blame her.

Their voices had quieted. Bix heard nothing for a moment, then the door to room 206 opened and closed a moment later . . . closed rather hard, he thought. He wondered if they had indeed had a fight. He wondered if she would knock on his door again.

He sat up.

He waited.

Seconds passed.

She should have knocked by now if she were going to.

He rolled onto his side again and stared at the wall.

Caitlin felt a powerful, painful sense of déjà vu. She now clearly recalled fighting with Josh about his infidelity seven months ago and walking out on him to get some distance to begin to process what she had learned. And here she was now, doing the same thing. That last time, she had run into Mike Bookerman, who had almost certainly been waiting for her. This time . . .

And then, *impossibly*, there he was again at the top of the stairs.

A sense of vertigo nearly toppled Caitlin.

Mike Bookerman, back from the dead, was walking toward her.

But no . . . it wasn't Mike Bookerman. It nearly was. It looked almost exactly like him. Same thin build and bald head, same sickly white pallor and dark little eyes. This new Bookerman, though, was quite a bit taller than Mike, she now saw, but the family resemblance was astonishing. But for his greater height, he could have easily passed for Mike, who was obviously his brother. And both of them were dead ringers for their father. Darryl's DNA code might as well have been tattooed on his sons' skin.

Whichever Bookerman this was smiled as he strode toward Caitlin. She had been too shocked at first to scream, and now, far too late, she tried but managed little more than a grunt as Bookerman threw a punch that caught her on the cheek. Her vision sloshed to the side and the vertigo returned as she fell but didn't lose consciousness. Bookerman bent down, threw a hand over her mouth, and whispered in her ear, "Make another sound and I snap your neck."

With his hand still over her mouth, he wrapped his other arm around her waist and hoisted her seemingly without effort and carried her under one arm back toward the stairs and down. He leaned a little to the side as he walked to counterbalance her weight, but he seemed otherwise hardly inconvenienced by the load he carried. Caitlin was groggy but had enough sense to wonder at so much strength in a man who looked so thin.

———

Chops had been ready and, he had to admit, almost eager to kill the men who had been with Caitlin Sommers. He had run it through in his head a few times before climbing the stairs, and he'd been curious to see whether it played out in real life as it had in his mind. But when he'd topped the stairs and found the woman right there in front of him, alone, he'd seized the moment and grabbed her. And it was a good thing he'd acted so quickly because it was obvious she had been about to scream. He wasn't worried that he couldn't have handled the men, but he certainly wouldn't have wanted curious faces to appear in nearby windows and see what was going on out here. So luck had been on his side tonight, and taking the woman could not have been easier.

Halfway down the stairs, she began to come to her senses. She grunted into his hand and started to struggle. Chops paused and said quietly, "Make another move, another sound, and I'll break you in half, then go upstairs and cut your boys into tiny pieces." Chops felt the woman's body go slack. Then it twitched in a rhythmic pattern that he realized meant she was crying.

He carried her across the parking lot to where his rented sedan waited in the shadows. When they reached the car, he set her on her feet and hugged her tightly against him, her back to him, his hand clamped over her mouth. He fished his car keys from his pocket and handed them to the woman.

"Hold these for a sec, will you?"

She took the keys. Chops raised his knee and slipped a knife out of his boot. He put the knife into the hand that had been over her mouth, then held the knife tight against the soft skin of her throat. He leaned down and whispered in her ear from behind, "Remember what happens if you make a sound?"

She nodded.

"Good girl," he said.

With his free hand, he took the car keys from her and used the remote to open the trunk. He pushed the blade harder against her throat, hard enough to draw blood.

"Okay, in you go."

She shook her head but didn't make a sound.

"Last chance before I get mad," Chops said.

She hesitated, then nodded and let him guide her into the dark, open trunk, no doubt afraid that Chops would kill her boyfriends or whoever they were if she didn't—and she was right about that; he would have. She stared up at him from the dark trunk with the wild white eyes of a panicked mare, but she still didn't make a sound.

"Very good girl," he said.

She watched him, tears in her eyes. As he started to close the lid, he said, "My father's gonna be so glad to see you again. He's been thinking about it for the last twenty years."

Caitlin's scream was cut off by the *thunk* of the trunk lid.

———

Josh sat on the edge of the bed, his head in his hands.

He'd ruined everything. He had deeply hurt the kindest woman he'd ever known, the only woman he'd ever—

He lifted his head. What was that sound?

It hadn't been loud and it hadn't been clear, but there was something about it . . .

He walked to the window and looked out at the parking lot below. Nothing but cars and . . . *there*, in the far corner of the lot . . . a tall, thin man at the trunk of a car. As he walked around toward the driver's door he looked up . . . and straight at Josh's window . . . no, straight at *Josh*.

Josh's heart shot into his throat.

The thin build, pale skin, bald head . . . It could only be a Bookerman. But Mike was dead. Could there be another? There *had* to be. The resemblance was too strong.

Where was Caitlin?

And then he knew . . .

The trunk.

The driver's door closed, the sedan's engine turned over, and the car screeched across the lot and out of sight around the corner of the building toward Rossdale Boulevard.

Josh threw open the door and screamed for Bix, but Bix had already burst from his room and was heading for the stairs, five steps ahead of Josh. He called over his shoulder, "I know, I heard her, too. *I saw him.* Come on."

Josh followed Bix down the stairs, which they took two at a time. They flew to the Explorer and leaped inside. Bix gunned the engine and they roared across the lot and around the corner of the motel. At the street, Josh swept his eyes back and forth, looking desperately for Bookerman's dark sedan. The street was straight and flat and the car was nowhere in sight. Bookerman had plainly done the smartest thing he could do, which was to turn off the main drag at his first opportunity. That left Josh and Bix without the slightest clue which way he'd gone. They had no choice but to pick a direction at random and hope for a miracle.

———

Chops had lost them before the chase had even begun. He was sure of it. He'd taken his first right turn off of Rossdale, and the men who were certainly in pursuit were stuck having to guess where he'd gone, and they'd plainly guessed incorrectly. There would be no catching him now.

He hated running. It wasn't something he had done often before, if ever. But to hell with the men. This wasn't about them. This was about the girl in his trunk.

The one who had killed his brother.

The one who had escaped his father.

The prettiest one.

———

Caitlin screamed until her throat felt torn.

His *father?*

The man couldn't possibly be taking her to his father. Darryl Bookerman was in prison. He had ten more years to go on his sentence.

Didn't he?

But God, the cold look in the man's eyes when he'd said it . . .

My father's gonna be so glad to see you again. He's been thinking about it for the last twenty years.

Caitlin shuddered.

She tried to calm down, which wasn't easy in the suffocating dark of the trunk. Was it possible that Darryl Bookerman was already out of prison? How could that be? Had he escaped? No, that couldn't be it. They would have heard about that. And retired detective Bigelson would have mentioned that. And hadn't Bookerman been sentenced without the possibility of parole? If he were truly out of prison, however it happened, wouldn't there have been some news story about a monster like him being released early?

Caitlin dared to hope. Was her abductor—Bookerman's son—lying, just to torment her?

But that look on his face . . .

Calm down, Caitlin.

But she couldn't. According to the brother of the man Caitlin had recently killed, he was taking her to see his father, the Bogeyman, who had abducted her more than twenty years ago, abused a little girl, and very likely molested and killed another. Also according to Darryl Bookerman's son, his father had been waiting for twenty years to see her again.

Alone in the dark, Caitlin screamed through her tattered throat and kicked at the walls of her prison.

CHAPTER THIRTY-SIX

CHOPS WAITED WITH HIS CELL phone at his ear, listening to the ringing on the other end of the line. He let it ring and ring. He knew there was no machine to answer his call. And he knew for a fact that the person he was calling was at home. He had to be. If he wasn't, his ankle bracelet would alert the authorities that he had left the premises in violation of his release agreement and he'd be back behind bars for the rest of his life inside of two hours.

Finally, the ringing stopped and Chops heard the old man say, "Yeah?"

"It's me, Dad. George."

His father cleared his throat. It took several tries. "You here in Massachusetts?"

"Yeah. I'm right in Smithfield."

"When'd you get in?"

"Little while ago."

"Your brother still hasn't answered his phone," Darryl Bookerman said. "Two days now."

"Yeah, I know."

"You out looking for him now?"

This was the tough part.

"You want the good news or the bad news, Dad?"

After a pause, "The good news."

"Come to think of it, I think I'd better start with the bad news."

"Then why the hell'd you ask me?"

"Mikey's dead, Dad."

Maybe there was a better way to break the news, but Chops couldn't imagine what it would have been. There was just no good way to say something like that. After a few seconds of nothing but labored breathing on the line, his father said, "You sure?"

"I saw him, Dad."

More breathing, then, "How'd he go?"

"He was shot. In his house."

Silence now. Not even the breathing. Finally, "You said you had good news?"

"Well, I'm not sure how good it is, not when Mikey's dead and all, but anyway . . . I've got the person who killed him."

"You got him? What does that mean? You killed him?"

"No. First of all, it's a her, not a him."

After the briefest of pauses, Bookerman said, "Can't say I'm surprised."

"And second," Chops said, "she's in the trunk of my car."

His father was quiet a moment while he appeared to be processing that. "What are you gonna do with her?"

"I'm bringing her to you."

"What the hell for? I don't want her. Give me a little time to mourn for my son, for Christ's sake. I don't want to see whoever killed him. Just do whatever the hell you want to do with her. I'm too tired. It's been a bad day today. Real bad. I feel like shit. And now this. My son's dead. I'm tired, George. You can come over in the morning and tell me all the bad things you did to your brother's killer if you want, how you made her suffer, but right now, I'm going to bed."

"Wait up for me," Chops insisted. "I'll be there soon."

"I'm not waiting, George."

"Listen, Dad. Trust me on this. You've been waiting a long, long time for this. A few more minutes aren't going to kill you."

A long pause. "What the hell are you talking about?"

"Wait up and you'll see. I'll be there soon."

He couldn't wait to see his father's face when he opened the door. It would be like Christmas morning.

———

Bix and Josh had crisscrossed the entire city of Smithfield, or so it seemed to Josh. And while they were forced to drive in random circles, hoping for a glimpse of the dark sedan, Darryl Bookerman's son was driving straight to wherever he was planning to go. For all they knew, he was already there and had already started doing whatever he planned to do with Caitlin.

"Damn it," Josh said, pounding his thigh with a fist. "Where is he?"

"What is it with these damn Bookermans?" Bix asked. "This is the third time one of them has tried to take Katie. Bunch of twisted freaks."

"He's the one who killed One-Eyed Jack," Josh said. "He has to be."

"No shit. We need to find him fast and get Caitlin the hell away from him. Where was she going, by the way?" he asked. "When she left your room?"

"Don't worry about it," Josh said. "Listen, I know you have a thing against the police, but it's time to call them. Caitlin was going to turn herself in tomorrow anyway. And we need them *right now*."

"Hey, I'm all for that now. We do need them. But what are you going to tell them? Be on the lookout for a dark sedan?"

"If I tell them that a woman has been abducted, and it happens to be the woman whose picture was in the news today, the woman

wanted in connection with the warehouse murder, they'll pay attention. They'll tell the cops that are out on patrol to look for the car."

"Even if he hasn't holed up somewhere yet, we still have no
description other than 'dark sedan.' You know how many cars fit
that description? We don't even know what direction he went."

"I'm calling them," Josh said as he pulled out his phone.

"Like I said, it's fine with me. But I don't know where you're
gonna tell them to start looking."

Josh dialed a nine. "If only we had some clue about where he
might take her."

He dialed a one.

Bix said, "The only places we know that are connected to that
family are the junkyard from twenty-two years ago—and you said
that's no longer even there—and Mike's house, which is full of bodies. I don't know if he would take her back there, with his brother's
corpse just lying there, but he knows that we know about that place.
He'd want to take her somewhere we don't know about."

Josh dialed another one, the final digit . . . then disconnected.
An idea had come to him.

Acutely aware—almost painfully so—of the seconds ticking by,
Josh brought up the Internet browser on his smartphone.

"I thought you were calling the cops," Bix said.

"In a minute. Shut up, will you?"

Josh revisited the public property records database for
Hampshire County, Massachusetts. He typed as quickly as he could
without making mistakes. He couldn't afford mistakes. Caitlin
didn't have time for them.

That morning, Josh had learned that no one named
Bookerman owned property in the area. That evening, he had
searched for the address where they had found Mike Bookerman
and learned that he was going by "Michael Maggert" now and
owned the property in that name. But Josh had never looked

for more properties owned by Mike Maggert. He did so now but found only the one. Searching by name again, though, rather than by address, Josh now saw that there were two other Maggerts who owned property in or around Smithfield. A Leonard Maggert and a George Maggert. Could one of them be Darryl Bookerman's other son?

"What are we doing, Josh?" Bix asked. "We're losing time."

"Damn it, shut up."

A quick search for "Leonard Maggert" combined with "Smithfield, Massachusetts" produced an article about a sixty-eight-year-old Smithfield resident who rolled a perfect game in a local seniors bowling league. That obviously wasn't the man who took Katie. The same search with "George" substituted for "Leonard" produced no results at all, so Josh couldn't rule out the possibility that George Maggert was really George Bookerman. Maybe a family of Maggerts had adopted both boys when Darryl went to prison. Josh went back to the property records and found it quickly.

"1320 Linden Road," Josh said. "You know where that is?"

Bix nodded. "Is that where they are?"

"There's no way I can know for sure, but other than Mike Bookerman's house, which has two dead bodies in it, it's all we have."

"Linden is pretty close," Bix said as he banged a sudden, hard left. "We caught a break. We've been driving in circles. You could have figured this out when we were on the other side of town and added fifteen minutes."

Bix gunned the Explorer without regard for the speed limit, traffic lights, or safety—all of which was fine with Josh. Maybe they'd even attract a police escort and they could lead the cops right to the door of George Maggert . . . who hopefully was really George Bookerman.

Josh called 911 and explained that a woman had been abducted and that he was in pursuit. The operator asked his name. He gave it.

And he gave Caitlin's name. And knowing this would get the cops' interest, he said that the woman in the trunk of the kidnapper's car was the same woman whose picture had been on the news and in the papers all day. He begged the operator to get cars to 1320 Linden Road as soon as possible. And in case he and Bix were wrong and Bookerman *was* taking Caitlin back to Mike's house, and knowing that it no longer mattered, Josh also gave the cops that address and said they'd find two dead bodies there. Then he hung up, willed the truck to move faster . . . and prayed.

The car eased to a stop. Caitlin huddled in the dark and waited for the trunk to open. She gripped the tire iron she'd found in the blackness—once she had stopped panicking—and prepared to come out swinging the second the lid began to rise. She thought of the tire iron she'd used to escape from Mike Bookerman seven months ago and hoped she would have the same luck with his brother. A car door closed. Footsteps crunched in gravel, getting closer to the trunk. The latch disengaged and the lid popped up a little and . . .

Caitlin rose to her knees, shouldering the lid the rest of the way open, and swung wildly in front of her with the tire iron and connected with . . . nothing. There was no one there. Suddenly, the trunk lid banged hard against the back of her head, sending her sprawling forward and knocking the tire iron from her hands. Too late she realized that Bookerman's son had stood to the side of the trunk in case Caitlin tried to pull something like the stunt she had just attempted, and when she took her swing, he'd slammed the lid back down on her.

"Nice try," the man said as he pulled her from the trunk by her hair. Caitlin screamed and tried to hold her scalp to keep it from tearing away from her skull. "People call me Chops," the man said.

"You don't want to know why." She landed on her face on the gravel, and he dragged her roughly across it for several feet. "Remind me what your name is again."

The calm way he was able to speak to her while at the same time brutalizing her was chilling. He yanked her to her feet.

"Your name?" he said.

"Caitlin Sommers."

"Caitlin, that's right." He pulled her away from the car, across uneven slate pavers, toward a big house that looked like an unmade bed. Peeling paint. Missing shutters. A gutter hanging loose at one end. The yard had been neglected for years; the grass was sparse, and where it still managed to grow, it was too long. There was no garage and no other car in the driveway. Caitlin hoped that meant that no one was home . . . and by no one, she meant no Darryl Bookerman.

They were at the front door now, and Chops opened it without knocking.

"Dad," he called. "I have a surprise for you."

"I'm back here, in the living room."

The voice was that of an older man who needed to clear his throat in the worst way. And even though it had aged, it was also instantly recognizable to Caitlin, though she hadn't heard it in person in more than two decades. Then again, why shouldn't she remember it? She'd heard it in her nightmares nearly every night since then.

The man who called himself Chops gave her a small shove and she started walking. Then a strange thing happened. Her steps became extraordinarily slow. Her breaths seemed to come once a minute. Time had slowed to a glacial crawl and a fog began to envelop the room.

Hunnsaker had finally learned the identity of the man who had been killed at the warehouse two nights ago. Padilla called to inform her that he was Peter Brennan, a loser from Philadelphia who was a suspect in the hijacking of an eighteen-wheeler on a run from Nevada to Philly eleven days ago. Brennan and his partner had made their move at a truck stop, putting a serious dent in the driver's head on his way back from taking a leak. The thing was, the idiots had hit the truck after it had delivered most of its goods. According to Brennan's partner, who was in custody, all they got was a box of smartphones, which wouldn't be too difficult to fence, and a box containing half a dozen prosthetic human hands, which would be a lot harder to move. A quick check by Padilla revealed that some company in Michigan that made bionic human hands had filed a report about the loss of six of their robotic prosthetics that had been custom-made for specific patients on the East Coast. Hunnsaker wondered why the hands hadn't been shipped FedEx or UPS, but Padilla said something about the shipper knowing the trucker personally. Anyway, Peter Brennan apparently had some pretty big outstanding gambling debts with some people who wouldn't take kindly to missed payments, so he screwed over his partner and skipped town with the phones and the fake hands. The cops tracked down his partner in crime, who was only too happy to finger Brennan.

So, that was one mystery solved. But they already had another. Someone had found the body of a young woman crammed into the knee well of a desk behind the reception counter of the Eagle Inn Motel. It could be a coincidence, Hunnsaker realized, but when Padilla informed her of the murder and told her that there hadn't been a robbery or any signs of a sexual assault, Hunnsaker knew there was a connection. The strange thing was that the woman had been killed with a knife. If Caitlin Sommers was involved, that was odd. The victim at the warehouse had been killed with a gun. What little Padilla had been able to learn about Sommers in the past hour made it hard to believe that she was capable of stabbing someone to death. It didn't seem to fit. Then again, maybe either the husband or boyfriend who was running with her had done it. Either way, Hunnsaker was certain it was connected.

"Javy," Hunnsaker said, "have the cops on the scene—"

Padilla interrupted her. "Hold on, Charlotte." She could hear him talking with someone else for a moment, then he was back on the line. "You're not gonna believe this."

"Try me."

"Someone claiming to be Josh Sommers just called 911 to report that someone named Caitlin Sommers has been abducted in a dark sedan and is probably being taken to one of two addresses."

What the hell?

"Have you run the addresses yet?" Hunnsaker asked.

"No, I just got them."

"Send units to both places. Tell them that the suspects are probably armed and dangerous."

"Which suspects? Sommers? She's apparently in a trunk, and the husband is in pursuit."

"Everyone. Tell them everyone is a suspect. What are the addresses?"

Padilla relayed them to her.

"I'll take Linden Road. It's closer for me. You head to the other one. Let's go find out what the hell's going on here."

The street was clear, so Hunnsaker whipped a U-turn and gunned the engine. Every fact she'd learned sent this case spinning in another direction. Why would a happily married suburban real-estate agent disappear for more than half a year, then turn up a suspect in a murder case in another state? What was this all about?

Who the hell was Caitlin Sommers, really? Was she a bad guy or an innocent woman in the wrong place at the wrong time? How had she ended up in the trunk of a car? And what was going to happen to her if someone didn't find her soon?

CHAPTER THIRTY-SEVEN

CAITLIN WALKED IN A DREAM. Time meant nothing. Each step was a slog through quicksand. Gauzy curtains of mist hung in her mind.

Who was pushing her from behind? Who was . . . she?

Her name was . . . Katherine? No, that didn't sound right.

Katie? No . . .

Caitlin, she thought. *I'm Caitlin.* She stopped and said it again, out loud this time. "I'm Caitlin."

"Yeah, we already talked about that," a man said from behind her. "Keep moving."

"I'm Caitlin," she repeated. "I live at 41 Ivy Street in Bristol, New Hampshire."

"Yeah?" the man said. "I don't give a shit. Now move."

As she was pushed forward, Caitlin recited her Social Security number in her mind. Then her address again. Then her phone number, followed by her Social Security number again, and her address, and she repeated them until she knew who she was—really *knew*—and the curtains lifted and her breathing felt right and time resumed at its normal speed.

She had been on the verge of another fugue state, she realized, yet she had fought it off this time. She knew who she was. A hand pushed her through a doorway, into a living room, and she suddenly remembered exactly *where* she was . . . and then she saw him there, in the flesh, after so many years and so many nightmares, and wondered if she would have been better off if she had just let herself slip away.

Sitting in a La-Z-Boy was Darryl Bookerman.

There was no doubt about it. He looked like his sons. He looked like the Bogeyman from decades of nightmares. Bald, lumpy head. Deathly pale. Disturbing little doll eyes spread too wide on his skinny face. Though he was instantly recognizable, he looked older now, far older than could be accounted for by the twenty-two years that had passed since he had burned his image into Caitlin's five-year-old mind. He had always been skinny, but he was even skinnier now, almost impossibly so. The years hadn't been kind to him, for which Caitlin was unable to work up any sympathy. Prison probably hadn't done him any favors, either. And it was plain that God or Nature or whoever was running the big show had probably been the cruelest of all to him. A plastic tube ran under his nose and over each ear, then down to an oxygen tank on the floor beside his chair. His face, which had always been thin, was caving in on itself. His cheeks were hollow. His eyes were black pits. And they were studying her. After several long seconds, he managed a smile. It turned Caitlin's stomach.

"It's you, isn't it," Bookerman said in a wet, sickly voice. "It's really you. The one that got away from me so long ago. My pretty little one. And now I have you back."

He slid a dry tongue over cracked lips.

"You were right, George," Bookerman said. "This is a nice surprise. It doesn't make up for Mikey, of course, but it's nice anyway."

His dead little eyes were still fixed on Caitlin. He just stared at her, looking her up and down. Gooseflesh rose on her skin. She felt small and naked. After he'd had his fill of gazing at her, after he'd feasted on the sight of her, he said, "It's been twenty-two years, Caitlin. Like what you see?" He paused. "Yes, I'm dying. Unfortunately for you, though, I'm not dying fast enough, because I don't need long with you. The docs say I've got maybe three months left. More than enough time, don't you think? All I need are a few good minutes and I can die happy."

The man who had identified himself as Chops, but whom his father had called George, said, "Don't talk like that, Dad."

"Shut up, George. I'm dying, and I'm dying hard. This cancer is a bitch. An hour ago, I was bitter as hell. I felt cheated. But now that my little Caitlin is here, somehow it doesn't seem to matter. She's prettier than ever. Totally worth the wait. You have no idea how happy you've made me, George. And you, too, Caitlin. Come closer."

Caitlin didn't move until Chops pushed her. She took a few steps forward, then Bookerman said, "Stop there. I want to be able to see all of you. I want to take you all in before . . ." He trailed off. It looked to Caitlin like he had become lost in a reverie. Finally, he said, "You killed my son Mikey?"

Caitlin said nothing.

Bookerman frowned. "This isn't going to be a pleasant night for you, pretty Caitlin, but it will be a lot less pleasant if you don't start getting with the goddamn program, understand?" He coughed and hacked and raised a paper cup and spit something thick into it. "Now answer me," he said.

Caitlin took a deep breath, then regretted it. The air tasted like sickness and decay. She said, "He was about to rape a woman and take a video of himself doing it."

"Sounds like Mikey."

"He tried to abduct me seven months ago."

"I know. He did that for me." Bookerman's mouth contorted into something resembling a grin, though it bore a greater resemblance to the grimace of a long-dead corpse. "I thought of you every day, Caitlin. Every day I was in prison. Maybe even every hour. For twenty-two years. I dreamed about you every night. My pretty one. The one who got away before I got the chance to . . ."

Caitlin was relieved that he didn't finish the thought. She couldn't help but see the terrible synchronicity. While Bookerman was dreaming of her every night for all those years, she was having nightmares about him.

"I asked Mikey to find you, to keep track of you. When I got out of prison, I asked him to bring you to me. He told me that he tried but somehow you escaped from him. But then you just disappeared, Mikey said. Even the cops didn't know where you were." Bookerman shook his head. "I have to admit, that was a bad time for me. I thought you were gone for good, that I'd never see you again. How the hell did you end up here?"

"No," Caitlin said, "how did *you* end up here? Didn't they sentence you to thirty years? Without a possibility of parole, I thought. So why aren't you dying in prison where you belong instead of dying a free man? Did you escape?"

Bookerman stared hard at her for a moment. She thought he might have been angry, but it was hard to tell because his eyes were so emotionless. The eyes of a mannequin. Or a shark. Finally, he said, "In a manner of speaking, I guess. Worked out a deal."

"What kind of a deal would they give a murdering pedophile?"

He stared again but said, "There was never any evidence that I killed that little girl."

"How about the pedophile part, then?" Caitlin asked.

Bookerman nodded. "That one's tougher to argue with."

"So why would they cut you a deal? How long have you been out?"

"Ten months," Bookerman said. And then he told her how it happened. Several factors had contributed to an agreement for his release. First, he had been a model prisoner. He never even retaliated whenever other prisoners or the occasional guard abused him, sexually or otherwise. Second, and far more importantly, he had learned valuable information from a fellow prisoner, a kindred spirit—the whereabouts of the body of a missing boy who happened to be the son of a senator. Bookerman had nothing to do with that crime, but he knew enough of the details to convince the authorities that he could help them find the boy's remains, which he eventually did. Third, he was dying now and dying fast. He was deemed to no longer be a threat to society . . . or at least, he wouldn't be for long. And besides, the senator really, really wanted closure. So knowing that he had but months to live, and given that he had agreed to spend the rest of his life in the house his son from California would buy for him, and that he agreed to wear an ankle bracelet that would alert the cops if he stepped one foot outside of it, the authorities agreed to his release in exchange for the information they sought. Of course, the good guys must not have been terribly proud of their deal because they kept it all very quiet. And the second he was free, Darryl Bookerman instructed his son Mikey to bring Caitlin Sommers to him.

"And here you are," Bookerman said, smiling that terrible smile again, though it ended at his thin lips and never came close to touching his eyes. He coughed and spit into his cup. "Thanks to my sons. They're good boys."

"The hell they are," Caitlin said.

"Well, they've been good to me. George bought me this house. It's crappy, but it's home. And he flew out from LA just to see if Mikey was okay. And Mikey . . . he brought me food and stuff I needed, twice a week. Called me every night . . . right up until the day you killed him."

Bookerman's eyes were still dead, still emotionless, even when he talked about his son's murder.

"Dad," George said, "I don't want to rush you, but I'm not sure how long you have."

"Three months at the most," Bookerman said. "We've been through this."

"No, I mean tonight. With her. I doubt the guys she was with will find this house, but you never know. And maybe they'll call the cops and the cops will find us somehow."

"They won't call the cops," Bookerman said. "This girl here's a killer. The last thing they'll want is to bring in the cops, right? So I'm not worried about them. And I'm not worried about any guys she was with, either, because you're here, George, and if they show up, you'll take care of them."

George nodded.

"And now, Caitlin," Bookerman said with another flick of his tongue across his bottom lip, "it's time for me to show you some of the things I've been thinking about doing for the last twenty-two years."

———

Bix killed the headlights and slowed the Explorer to a stop at the end of the driveway of 1320 Linden Road. It looked a lot like the driveway to Mike Bookerman's house—long, winding, leading to a secluded house. It was a perfect place for doing bad things if you wanted privacy.

Bix reached over in front of Josh, opened the glove compartment, and removed a 9mm handgun. He checked the magazine, then locked it back in place. Reaching up, he switched off the truck's dome light so it wouldn't turn on when the doors opened. He doubted anyone was watching—he didn't think Bookerman, aka George Maggert, expected them to find this house—but it would have been stupid not to be careful. After walking for a few yards, they came to the first gentle bend in the driveway and saw the house . . . and the dark sedan parked in front of it. The ranch house sat on maybe half an acre of scraggly grass, with the yard surrounded by trees. They decided to circle around the building at a distance, along the edges of the dark yard, and approach it from the back. Bix silently thanked the thin crescent moon and gray clouds enshrouding it.

There was a light on in two windows on the near side of the house, and Bix made straight for them rather than continue around back. He knew how difficult it was to see out into darkness from inside a lighted room. To anyone inside, the windows would look like black squares. Bix didn't think they'd be seen unless they put their faces right up to the glass. And as it turned out, they didn't need to. They were still fifteen feet away when Bix saw very clearly into the living room, where George Maggert/Bookerman was sitting on a sofa beside Caitlin. He had a knife against her throat. They were both looking straight ahead of them. Then someone else walked into Bix's view. Someone thin and tall but stooped by age, and possibly more than merely age because he carried an oxygen tank in his hand as he shuffled slowly toward Caitlin.

Josh said, "My God, is that . . . ?"

"Yeah," Bix said. "I don't know how the hell it's possible, but Darryl Bookerman has Katie again."

CHAPTER THIRTY-EIGHT

CAITLIN FELT THE KNIFE AGAINST her throat. She felt the tears rolling down her cheeks. She felt fear and despair. She felt sad that her life would end in this terrible way, at the hands of a pathetic, twisted old man. She felt a searing hatred for Darryl Bookerman . . . for what he had done to the little girl he had abused decades ago, and to Kathryn Southern, who was never found. She hated him for supplying his sons with the defective DNA that made them grow up into soulless creatures like him. Or maybe they'd been adopted long ago by a decent family and had been given every chance to lead normal lives one day, but their father's legacy had been impossible for them to escape. Either way, Caitlin blamed Darryl Bookerman for what his sons became. But she also hated the sons for what they had done for their father. She wondered if Darryl had abused them. If so, that was sad, but it didn't excuse their behavior.

Mostly, she hated Darryl Bookerman simply for being a monster.

And that monster was shambling toward her on his long, weak, stick-figure legs, carrying an oxygen tank in a hand so thin the veins stuck out like blue interstate lines on a map, wheezing as he came, grinning as he came, looking at her with eyes as dull and black as empty windows.

"Don't worry, my pretty little one," Bookerman said. "George isn't here to participate. I didn't wait all those years to share you with someone else."

"He's just here to watch, then?" Caitlin asked. "You must be so proud."

"Well, he can watch if he wants, but no, he's here to hold the knife. To keep you under control. You may have noticed that I'm not quite the man I used to be."

"You're not a man at all," Caitlin said.

"Well, we'll see about that, I guess," Bookerman replied as he lowered himself to the couch beside her, putting a hand high up on her leg for support and leaving it there.

Caitlin was trapped. A sociopath to her right. A sick, murdering pedophile to her left. A knife at her throat. A bony hand on her thigh, moving higher . . .

She closed her eyes and again regretted having willed herself earlier not to fade away into another identity, another person, someone who might not remember this one day.

But who was she kidding? She wouldn't be alive long enough to remember this anyway.

———

Hunnsaker was getting close to the address on Linden Road. Two black-and-whites weren't far behind. She had learned that the house belonged to a George Maggert, which was interesting because the house from which Padilla had just called was in the name of a Michael Maggert, who had owned the place right up until someone had shot him to death recently . . . though apparently not as recently as the one-eyed man who someone had gutted and left lying next to Maggert. Forgetting about the guy with one eye for a moment, that left them with two houses and two Maggerts. Interesting. Also interesting was what Padilla found in Michael Maggert's house. Apparently, the man had been stalking Caitlin Sommers. He had photos on the wall and a file of information on her. When the police eventually combed through that house, they were bound to find a lot of answers. And as Hunnsaker sped toward George Maggert's house, she knew that even more answers awaited her there. She just hoped that Caitlin Sommers would be alive to provide them.

———

Chops had no desire to watch his father do whatever the hell he was planning to do to Caitlin Sommers, but he liked seeing the old man so excited and animated. He'd had a rough time of it for so long now. Twenty-two hard years in prison. On top of that, he'd been in nearly constant pain for almost a year, so much so that he kept saying he was looking forward to death. But now, at least for the moment, he was happy. So Chops could look away while his father sucked a bit of joy from what little time he had left to him.

When he turned his head, his eyes drifted to the window . . . where he saw a flash of movement, something less dark than the deeper darkness around it. It was fleeting, but it was there, and then it was gone.

Instinct and the quick glimpse he'd caught told him it wasn't the cops out there. The guys who had been running around with Caitlin must have somehow found this place after all. Chops thought for a moment, then remembered that he hadn't locked the front door.

What to do? He knew he couldn't give his father the knife and hope he'd be able to keep Caitlin in check. He could barely lift his own arms; he couldn't be expected to hold a healthy young woman captive with a knife. No, Chops had to keep Caitlin with him.

"Hang on a sec, Dad," he said. He stood and yanked Caitlin to her feet.

"What the hell are you doing?" Bookerman asked. "I finally have my—"

"Shhhh."

Keeping the knife at Caitlin's throat, Chops dragged her across the living room, over to a short stretch of wall beside the wide doorway between the hall and the living room. They'd be coming through here. They had no choice. It was the only entrance to the room. They were obviously hoping they still had surprise on their side. They didn't.

Chops hugged Caitlin tightly from behind. He clamped one hand over her mouth. With the other, he held his knife against her neck. He heard her moan as the barest tip of it pierced her skin. He put his mouth right beside her ear and whispered, "Not a sound or I'll rape you after my father does, and your men will watch it all, then I'll carve them up and make them swallow the pieces until there's nothing left of either of them. Understand?"

She nodded.

Chops waited.

The faintest footfall in the hall.

Then a sudden rush of movement and Caitlin grunted loudly in warning, goddamn it, and the men must have heard her because the one who came through the doorway ducked suddenly, and the knife Chops had taken from Caitlin's throat and swung neck-high at him sliced through the air an inch above his head. The man's momentum carried him to the center of the room, where he spun and pointed a gun at Chops.

Damn.

Chops hugged Caitlin even more tightly and held the tip of his knife against the soft skin of her neck again.

"Let her go," the man with the gun said.

"No," Chops said.

"I have a gun."

"And I have a knife at your girl's throat. I promise you, if you shoot me, unless you can put a bullet in my brain in a place that instantly stops all motor activity, I'll be able to jam this knife through her neck before I die. Count on it. Where's the other guy?"

"What other guy?"

Rather than play that game, Chops sliced downward with the knife, opening a painful but nonlethal slice vertically between her larynx and her carotid artery. Caitlin cried out.

"Don't make me ask you again," Chops said.

The barrel of the handgun never wavered as the man said, "Come on in, Josh."

An unarmed man stepped slowly into the room. He looked from the guy with the gun, to Chops's father on the sofa, and finally to Chops and Caitlin. When he saw the blood on Caitlin's neck, his eyes widened.

"Are you okay?" he asked.

She nodded very carefully, which was smart when she had a knife at her throat.

"Drop the gun," Chops said.

"No chance," the gunman said. "Drop the knife."

"I don't think so. You can't hit me without hitting her at this range. I don't know you, but I know you aren't that good."

"I'll shoot," the man warned.

Chops just laughed. Then he tugged Caitlin with him as he walked slowly sideways, his eyes never leaving the barrel of the gun, until he was standing in front of his father. The man with the gun turned slowly, tracking their movement, but he didn't pull the trigger.

———

Hunnsaker's car crept up the first part of what looked to be a long, winding driveway. She reached a curve where it started to bend back on itself and shut off her headlights, keeping her engine running. A moment later, two black-and-whites pulled up behind her and did the same. Padilla had left cops at Michael Maggert's house with the dead bodies and was on his way here, but he was several minutes away still and Hunnsaker didn't feel as though she could wait. Quietly, she opened her car door and slipped out of the vehicle, leaving the door open. The officers in the patrol cars did the same.

She spoke in a soft voice. "We're going on foot from here, quietly." She pointed at two of the officers. "You, head around the right side of the house and watch the back. You two," she said, pointing to the remaining cops, "split up and watch the sides of the house and make sure no one comes out a side door or window. You're with me," she said to the last cop. She looked at the first two again and said, "I'll let you know when we're about to go in. Everyone got it?"

They nodded.

"Good. Let's move."

———

Chops had seen headlights through the window, stretching for just a split second across the dark yard before they snapped off, and in that instant everything changed for him.

"I gotta admit, I didn't think you'd call the cops," he said. "Guess you don't care if your girl here goes to jail for killing my brother."

"We were more worried about you than the cops," the guy without the gun said.

"You were right to be more worried about me," Chops said, while never taking his eyes off the other guy and his handgun.

Chops was frustrated and saddened by this development. His mind raced. There was no way now that his wife wouldn't find out just what kind of person he really was. He wasn't looking forward to seeing the disappointment on her face, if indeed he lived to see it. And he wasn't certain he would even want to live, knowing that his daughter would grow up with a father behind bars. Chops knew what that was like. Knew the shame of it. Knew the things the other kids would say about her family, and about her.

No, he couldn't allow that to happen. Which meant that he couldn't be arrested, no matter what. He didn't think it likely that he'd be able to kill everyone in the room, and then every cop that was about to storm the house. That left him with three possible outcomes. Either Chops would be killed, which he didn't intend to let happen, or he could use Caitlin and the others as hostages, but that rarely worked out for the bad guy. Or finally, he could escape out the back before the cops got the rear covered, which meant leaving almost immediately and not leaving witnesses. He had to escape and call Rachel right away and tell her to take Julia to a location where he would meet them once he found a way to get back to them . . . and it was critical that he make that call before the police discovered his involvement in all of this and put the clamps on his family. Rachel wouldn't understand why she had to run, but if she loved him enough, she'd do what he asked; if she loved him enough, she'd understand who he was, what he'd done, and why they now had to go on the run and start over somewhere. And that was the big question, of course: Did she love him enough? He had to find out, which meant that everyone in the room—including his father—had to die and do so quickly. Since Chops had traveled under a false name, if he could get out of this house clean, it should take the cops a good while to figure out that he was involved, which should give him time to get in touch with Rachel . . . unless someone in the room told the cops about him. Which meant that Chops had to make sure that no one could.

"My problem," Chops said, "is that I don't want to be arrested tonight. Which means this has to end now."

Chops's plan was to kill the woman and shove her toward the guy with the gun. That should distract him enough for Chops to disarm him. Then he would shoot both of the boyfriends or whatever they were, fire a few rounds out the window to slow down the cops, let them think this could turn into a standoff. Finally, he'd kill his father. Then he'd leave through the back door—while the cops were thinking about trying to negotiate with him—and hope like hell he made it to safety before they caught up to him.

It was a lousy plan, almost certainly destined for failure, but it was all he had. He wasn't going to prison. He couldn't allow that. He couldn't live with what that would do to his family.

"Close your eyes, Katie," the guy with the gun said to Caitlin.

Chops understood. The man cared for her and didn't want her to see her own blood spilling out in buckets. Better for her to die without that image in her mind. Chops respected that. Still, he didn't have time to waste.

"Trust me, Katie," the man added. "Close your eyes."

———

Josh watched events unfolding and felt impotent. There was simply nothing he could do but observe. He didn't have a weapon. One move on his or Bix's part could make Bookerman's son cut Caitlin's throat. This was a standoff with Caitlin in the middle. And now it sounded as though Bookerman's son was about to bring this to a close. He looked ready to use the knife. Why didn't Bix *do* something? He had a gun. Time was running out. And all he could think to do was tell Caitlin to close her eyes, like he had when he wanted her to remember how to shoot pool . . .

Could that be it?

"Close your eyes, Katie," Bix said calmly.

Caitlin looked into Bix's eyes for a moment, then closed her own. Bix raised his gun an inch. "You can do it, Katie," he said.

"Sorry it has to end this way, Dad," Bookerman's son said, "but I've got to finish this right now. Say good-bye to pretty Caitlin."

"No!" Darryl Bookerman cried in a broken voice.

And then it all happened fast . . .

Caitlin opened her eyes and swung her leg far out in front of her, then brought it back hard and fast, her heel connecting with George Maggert's shin with enough force to sound like a Louisville Slugger crushing a fastball. Maggert cried out and released his grip both on his knife, which dropped from his hand, and on Caitlin, who fell to the floor. For a second, Maggert had no one in front of him to take a bullet for him, which must have been Bix's plan because the instant Caitlin was clear, he pulled the trigger and . . .

He missed. The bullet sizzled past Maggert and shattered a window behind him while Maggert lowered his shoulder and charged, reaching Bix in three long strides, slamming into him before he could fire another shot. The two crashed into the far wall. Maggert clamped one hand on Bix's throat and the other on his gun hand, and somehow, despite Bix's own considerable strength, wrenched the weapon from his grip and was turning it on him as Josh darted forward and threw a punch as hard as he could, with all the force of his momentum behind it. The blow caught Maggert on the ear and his head snapped to the side and he released his hold on Bix and staggered a few steps to the side. Josh looked for the gun in Maggert's hand, but his punch must have knocked it loose.

Hunnsaker had heard the report of the gun.

"Gunshot," she cried. "Go, go, *go.*"

She pulled her own piece and ran toward the house fifty yards away, with four cops in uniform at her sides.

———

Josh thought that the good guys might have actually won the fight. George Maggert was both outnumbered and unarmed now . . . until he reached down into his boot and drew out a second knife. He slashed at Bix, who jumped back, narrowly avoiding having his midsection sliced open, but as he dodged, he stumbled and fell backward. Instead of finishing off Bix, though, Maggert went after the only man still on his feet . . . which was his mistake, because as he bore down on Josh, covering the distance between them in four long strides, knife raised and ready to strike, Josh saw Caitlin streaking toward him from his right side, swinging the knife Maggert had dropped when Caitlin kicked him. Just before Maggert reached Josh, Caitlin drove the blade up to its hilt in the side of Maggert's neck. Maggert stood for a moment, tottering unsteadily, blood flowing from his mouth.

———

Chops dropped to his knees, then fell on his side. He couldn't believe how fast it had all come apart. He couldn't believe it would end like this for him. He wondered if his wife and daughter had gone to the circus that evening without him. Then his last thoughts were of little Julia's face and how disappointed Rachel was going to be with him.

———

Caitlin looked down at the second Bookerman she'd killed in two days, then turned to face the only one still alive. He had risen from the couch, leaving his oxygen tank behind, and was shuffling quickly away across the room on his frail, spindly legs. At first she thought he was heading for the doorway to the hall and she marveled that he thought he would be able to run away. Then she saw the gun lying against the wall and realized that reaching it was his objective. She flew after him, over Bix, who had just started to rise from where he'd fallen. Bookerman was closer to the gun but Caitlin was far faster, and as he bent to pick up the weapon, she grabbed his shoulder and yanked back, spinning the old man around. He staggered backward, losing his footing, and dropped to the floor where he lay with his long limbs stretched out, looking like a spider dying on its back. Caitlin calmly picked up the gun.

"Finish him, Katie," Bix said.

Bookerman looked up at her. Even now there was nothing in his eyes. Somehow, despite the tear rolling down from one of those black stones, there was still no emotion in them. But there was something in his voice, something pathetic, when he said, "I was so close . . . after so long, I had you again . . . the prettiest one . . ."

"Do it, Katie," Bix urged.

"Caitlin?" Josh said.

Caitlin stared down at a man who deserved death as much as any man did. She heard footsteps and someone shouted, "Police." A woman's voice. "Raise your hands, take two steps backward, and kneel on the floor with your hands above your head."

On the floor, Bookerman was still mumbling to himself. "H-how could she get away again . . . my pretty little Caitlin . . . after so long, so many years . . . I was so close . . ."

"Caitlin Sommers," the cop said again. "Raise your hands right *now*."

Caitlin was still pointing the gun at Bookerman, who was still lamenting the fact that he had lost her again. And even now she saw nothing, nothing at all in his eyes. Was he even human? Would killing him even be a sin?

"Caitlin," the cop said again, "don't move anything but your head, but I want you to look at me."

Caitlin turned her head, just her head, and saw a woman in plainclothes pointing a gun at her. Two police officers in uniform stood behind her doing the same.

"My name is Charlotte Hunnsaker, and I don't know you, and I don't know what the hell happened here or what this man may have done to you, but I know one thing for certain . . . he's not worth it."

Caitlin looked into the woman's eyes for a long, long moment, then without another glance at Bookerman, she took her finger off the trigger, raised her hands over her head, and lowered herself to her knees. One of the uniformed officers walked over quickly and took the gun from her.

"Good decision," the woman said as she stepped up, took Caitlin's hands one by one, and snapped cuffs on them.

Caitlin looked over at Bix. He was rubbing the back of his head, but he seemed to be okay. She remembered him calmly saying, *Close your eyes.*

She said, "I guess you taught me a little self-defense, too."

"I taught you a lot of things," he said with a half smile.

Josh also seemed fine. Caitlin met his eyes and nodded tiredly. It was over.

"Caitlin Sommers," Hunnsaker began, "you're under arrest for . . ."

CHAPTER THIRTY-NINE

JOSH WAS WAITING FOR CAITLIN outside of Bridgewater State Hospital, a Massachusetts state mental-health facility tasked with housing and treating the criminally insane, as well as evaluating individuals for purposes of the criminal justice system. Among other issues, the experts at Bridgewater helped shed light on numerous important questions, including a patient's competency to stand trial or, as in the case of Caitlin Sommers, her criminal responsibility. After forty days of comprehensive evaluation, a team of doctors and psychologists eventually came to several conclusions about Caitlin. First, even though it was not uncommon for patients and inmates to try to evade responsibility for their actions by claiming to have suffered amnesia, it was their opinion that Caitlin had indeed experienced a protracted fugue state, probably for at least the second time in her life. She had no memory of the seven-month period during which she had lived in Smithfield or of the events that had occurred during that time, nor was she likely ever to recall them. Second, given that she had adopted an entirely different personality during that time, it was almost as though a different person had participated in those events . . . and had shot Michael Maggert/ Bookerman. Third, given that she had likely entered the fugue state as a reaction to the extremely traumatic abduction attempt by the man she eventually killed, a man who was the son of the pedophile who had abducted her when she was a child and who bore a striking resemblance to his father, and also given that she was almost certainly never going to find herself in a similar set of circumstances, it was highly doubtful that she posed a danger to others, even in the unlikely event that she entered another fugue state in the future. So, after having her mind dissected for almost a month and a half, Caitlin was deemed fit for release from the hospital's custody.

While medical professionals had been evaluating Caitlin's mind, law enforcement and legal authorities had been examining the facts of her case. There was no doubt that Caitlin Sommers had been a victim. But there was also no doubt that she had killed not just one man, but two. The second could be justified easily under the circumstances. She had been abducted and been forced to stab a man to protect her husband. The accounts of two of the witnesses supported that. And even though both witnesses had reason to lie to protect her, seeing as they were her husband and boyfriend, respectively, the facts supported their statements.

The death of the first man Caitlin had killed, though—Michael Maggert, aka Michael Bookerman—had proven to be more troublesome for the authorities. They had it all on video, which Sommers herself had urged her boyfriend and husband to give to the police—along with half a dozen robotic prosthetic hands. Despite the fact that her victim had been a rapist who had stalked her and tried to abduct her, there was considerable doubt as to whether she had committed premeditated murder. And Sommers, unable to recall the incident, couldn't give a statement shedding light on her frame of mind or her intentions. Though the naked woman in the video looked glassy-eyed and all but unaware of the events unfolding around her, she gave a statement to the police in which she claimed to have believed at the time that Maggert was about to attack Caitlin. Of the officials who viewed the video, some believed

Caitlin shot Michael Maggert in cold blood. Others seeing the same footage swore that Maggert had started to make a move toward Caitlin and she'd had to pull the trigger to protect herself and the naked woman handcuffed to the sofa bed. Still others had no idea whether Caitlin had been forced to pull the trigger but didn't blame her one iota either way for doing so.

For what it was worth, Detective Hunnsaker, who had worked the case and made the arrest, wasn't anxious to see Caitlin prosecuted after learning all the facts. What Hunnsaker didn't know, though, what no one but Caitlin knew—though she wondered if Bix suspected—was that Hunnsaker was the main reason Caitlin wasn't going to spend most of the rest of her life in prison . . . because Caitlin had indeed decided to kill Darryl Bookerman. She was going to shoot him where he was, lying on the floor. It might have been morally wrong, but Caitlin wasn't even positive about that. He wasn't human. But with the clarity of hindsight, she knew that under the circumstances, if she had shot an unarmed man to death with three cops as witnesses, a jury would have had a difficult time not convicting her.

But because Hunnsaker had arrived in time to stop her from killing him, Caitlin wasn't going to stand trial at all. In the end, the prosecutor who drew the case decided not to file charges against her. The suspect was sympathetic, the victim was far from it, and his and his entire family's history and recent criminal activity involving her would have made it a tough case for the prosecution. So when Caitlin was released from the hospital, she was allowed to go wherever she wanted.

Darryl Bookerman wasn't so lucky. He may have had only two months left to live now, but because he had violated the terms of his release agreement by conspiring to kidnap Caitlin Sommers, he was going to spend every last second of that time in prison. Caitlin wondered what was the worst thing for Bookerman—his cancer, being back behind bars, his sons being dead, or Caitlin escaping from him again. She knew it didn't matter, though. They would all make what little remained of his life a living hell, and she couldn't make herself give a damn. And if millions of people in the world were right, he'd be in an even far greater hell before long.

With a small bag of her clothes and toiletries hanging over her shoulder, Caitlin walked to the parking lot to where her husband was leaning against the door of his car, which he had parked near the main entrance in a no-parking zone. Once Josh had been allowed to see her, he had visited almost every day.

As she approached, he smiled, though sadly. She thought her smile probably mirrored his.

"I've been looking forward to seeing you walk out of there," Josh said.

"It feels good."

"You're a free woman. In more ways than one."

She nodded, thinking about the divorce that would be final in a few months.

Josh looked at his shoes for a moment, then raised his eyes. "And that's it, then? Nothing I can say?"

"No, Josh."

"Seven years together, six years married, one mistake, and it's over?"

"It was a big mistake," Caitlin said, and Josh seemed unable to argue with that. He had tears in his eyes. Caitlin felt tears threatening in her own. It hadn't been an easy decision for her. The doctors weren't the only ones examining her mind over the last forty days; she'd been doing the same thing, trying to determine how she felt about everything. She'd searched every inch of her soul, and with respect to Josh, she kept coming back to a few thoughts. First, she doubted she could ever truly trust him again. She could forgive him, maybe, but she could never trust him. More importantly, if he could cheat on her, even one time, he just wasn't the person Caitlin had thought he was. And equally important, Caitlin had learned that she wasn't the person she'd thought *she* was, either. She had changed. And the new Caitlin, whoever she was, would never fit with Josh the way the old one did.

"Your neck's looking pretty good," he said.

"Thanks," she replied, touching the two-and-a-half-inch scar where George Maggert/Bookerman had sliced her. The stitches were out, though the scar was still a bit bumpy. But she was alive.

After a moment of silence, Josh said, "I'm so sorry."

"I know."

He looked back down at his shoes for a second, then raised his eyes again. "Thanks for saving my life."

She smiled wistfully. "Thanks for saving mine."

"Bye, Caitlin."

He turned and opened his car door. He slipped inside, started the engine, and drove away. Caitlin watched him go. She thought she saw his eyes in the rearview mirror, looking at her all the way until his car was out of sight.

She walked toward a black Ford Explorer parked in the lot's first row. Bix was behind the wheel. His window was down and his elbow rested casually on the door frame.

"Hey, there," he said. "Looking for a ride?"

While Caitlin had been locked up and sorting things out in her mind, she had reflected on numerous topics besides her relationship with Josh. She thought about all that had happened. And about Bix. And about who she used to be and how different she was now. She recalled how easily she had slipped into the persona of Katie Southard. How simple it had been for her to show a wilder side when she'd had to, almost as if that person had been inside her all along, hoping to step out of the shadows and into the light. She came to realize that not only was that person a part of who she was, but it might have been just as much the "real her" as the woman she had always thought she was.

All of her soul-searching made Caitlin certain of two things. First, it was time to figure out just who she was going to be. Not who she had been a year ago, or a month ago, but who she would be moving forward. She was starting a new life. And it wasn't going to be in Smithfield. Or New Hampshire. No, wherever she was heading, it would be someplace she'd never been. And the second thing she knew was that as she embarked on the journey to discover just who and where she should be, she wanted Bix along for the ride. He may have some questionable acquaintances and a somewhat murky past, but she knew he was a good man at heart. He loved her. She knew that for certain, too. And she felt pretty good about her chances of one day loving him back.

"So what do you say?" Bix asked with a killer smile. "Need a lift?"

"Sure," Caitlin said.

"Where to?"

Rather than walk around to the Explorer's passenger side, Caitlin opened the driver's door.

"I don't know," she said, "but move over. I'm driving."

ACKNOWLEDGMENTS

I can't do this alone, and I wouldn't want to try. My first thank-you, as always, goes to my wife, Colleen, for just about everything. Thanks also to my sons for inspiring me and giving me time to write when I need it. I'm also grateful for the advice of criminal lawyers Susan Hankins and Brian Cullen. John Hankins earned my thanks by reading an early draft of the book and sharing his thoughts on it. I owe gratitude to my agent, Michael Bourret of Dystel & Goderich Literary Management, for everything he does for me. Thanks to sharp-eyed editor David Downing, who makes the editorial process enjoyable. I am deeply thankful to Alison Dasho for bringing me to Thomas & Mercer and for her steadfast support, and to Jacque BenZekry, Tiffany Pokorny, Gracie Doyle, and the rest of the T&M team for all the hard work they do for me and for my books. My final thanks goes to my family, my friends far and wide, and my wonderful readers, whose kind and unswerving support allows me to continue to do what I love to do. Thank you all. One final note: I invented Smithfield, Massachusetts, so I think I got the facts about it right, but if there are any other errors in this book, the blame is mine.

SHADY CROSS

A THRILLER

JAMES HANKINS

An excerpt from *Shady Cross* by James Hankins, available now.

In one hand, small-time crook Stokes holds a backpack stuffed with someone else's money—three hundred and fifty thousand dollars of it.

In the other hand, Stokes has a cell phone, which he found with the money. On the line, a little girl he doesn't know asks, "Daddy? Are you coming to get me? They say if you give them the money they'll let you take me home."

From bestselling author James Hankins comes a wrenching story of an unscrupulous man torn between his survival instincts and the plight of a true innocent. Faced with the choice, Stokes discovers his conscience might not be as corroded as he thought.

ONE

"YOU JUST GOT OUT OF jail? Seriously?"

Stokes heard nothing but curiosity in the guy's voice. No judgment, no fear, just curiosity and maybe a little slur from the alcohol.

"Didn't say I was *in* jail," Stokes said. He took a sip of Budweiser and wiped his mouth with the back of his hand, the one that held the bottle. "Said I was *at* the jail. They had me in for questioning. No big deal."

The guy looked at him in drunk-eyed wonder, like he was a rare species of lizard. "Wow. In jail." He took a sip of his manhattan. "I guess you must not have done whatever they thought you did, though, or they wouldn't have let you go."

Stokes knew it didn't always work like that, but why get into it?

"Like I said, no big deal." He looked at the guy's tailored suit again, the suit that had led Stokes to the bar stool next to him in the first place. "So what's your deal?"

"Tom."

"What?"

"My name's Tom," the guy said.

Stokes nodded, waited for an answer to his question, didn't get it, so he asked again, "So what's your deal, Tom? You from Shady Cross?"

"What's Shady Cross?"

Stokes smiled amiably. "This little city you're in."

"Shady Cross?" the guy repeated as if he'd never heard of the place, like a few drinks had erased the name from his mind.

"They say it was built up a long time ago around the crossroads at the center of town," Stokes said. "Used to be shady, I guess. So anyway, what's your deal?"

"My deal? What do you mean?"

Stokes indicated the rest of the bar with a tilt of his head. It was on the seedy side, the kind of place people went to drink hard, to shoot pool, to swap bullshit stories about sexual conquests, to bitch about their blue-collar jobs or their bosses or their wives. Sometimes they went looking for a fight. Sometimes they went just to be left alone. And more often than not, whatever reason they were there, they also went wondering whether they might meet someone drunk enough, lonely enough, and tolerably attractive enough to spend a little time with after last call.

"You sort of stick out around here, Tom," Stokes said. "Nice suit, polished shoes. Your hair's all combed. So what's your deal? I told you about jail, you can tell me your story."

Tom turned his head to face Stokes. His glassy eyes caught up a fraction of a second later.

"Not much of a story. In town on business. Staying at a motel just down the road."

"The Rest Stop?"

"Yeah, that might be what it's called. You know it?"

Stokes did. He'd spent a few hours there two Saturdays ago with the waitress across the room. He nodded.

"Finished my business here this morning," the guy said, "but can't get a flight back to Pittsburgh till tomorrow. Just killing time now. Stopped in here for an early lunch, but, well, I met you instead and my lunch, uh . . ."

"Turned liquid?"

Tom looked at Stokes for a long moment, then laughed loosely. Stokes could have asked what business the guy was in. It was probably expected of him. But he didn't think Tom was tracking the conversation very closely any longer. He was tottering on his stool now, his vacant eyes staring sightlessly at the mirror behind the bar. Stokes could have looked at that mirror, too, but he didn't.

"You a cowboy?" Tom asked, chuckling like he'd made a joke.

"A what?"

"You're wearing a cowboy shirt."

Stokes looked down at his Western-style shirt, black with white stitching near the shoulders, which he wore over a black T-shirt.

"Nope," he said. "Not a cowboy. Not even close. I don't even like country music. It's just a shirt I found in a thrift store. So what do you say, Tom? One more for the road?"

The guy said nothing for a moment, the words seeming to wander aimlessly through the fog in his mind for a while before finally finding their way. He looked at Stokes.

"Another? No way, man. Thanks, but I've prob'ly had enough. Thanks again, though, for buying all these drinks for me. Nice to find someone friendly in a strange place."

Tom's eyelids were sagging over tired, empty eyes.

"Yeah," Stokes said, "you've had enough. You drive here this afternoon?"

"Drive? Yeah, I did. My rental."

"Yeah, well, you're not driving back to the motel. I'll call you a cab, OK? You can come back for the car in the morning, on your way to the airport."

"Cab?" He shook his head, looking like he was about to protest as he stood. Then his foot caught a leg of his stool and he just barely managed to grab the bar in time to save himself from a tumble onto the grimy, beer-stained cement floor. "Yeah, maybe a cab's good idea."

Stokes had called for a taxi ten minutes ago. He figured it would be pulling up outside just about now.

"I'll help you," he said, grabbing the guy by the arm, guiding him across the bar. Halfway to the door, he caught the eye of the waitress, Annie, the one he'd spent a few decent hours with a couple of Saturdays ago. She rolled her eyes at him before turning her attention back to her customers.

The taxi was idling in front of the bar. Stokes reached into the guy's suit jacket, into the inner breast pocket, and removed a soft leather wallet. He opened the back door of the cab, helped Tom inside, and took out one of the guy's twenties. He gave it to the cabbie and told him to take Tom back to the Rest Stop. Stokes counted the rest of the money, put forty bucks back into the wallet, and slipped $230 into his own pocket before leaning into the cab and returning the wallet to Tom's jacket.

"See you, Tom," Stokes said as he closed the door.

The taxi pulled away and Stokes walked back inside, heading to the bar without looking Annie's way.

"What was it?" Stokes asked the bartender, money in hand. "Four manhattans for my friend Tom and two Buds for me? What's that come to?"

The bartender frowned, turned his back to Stokes, and punched a few buttons on the cash register. He turned around again. "It was three Buds. Forty-four bucks."

Stokes peeled off two twenties and a ten and put the bills on the bar. "Keep it."

"What a guy, Stokes," the bartender said. "Hard to believe the cops could ever question the character of a saint like you."

"Hey, feel free to give me that tip back, Chuck."

The bartender put the money into the register, took out the change and stuck it into the tip jar beside the bottles of hard liquor.

Stokes smiled. "Maybe I'll be in again later. We could shoot some stick, if it's quiet. I could try to win that tip back, huh?"

The bartender shrugged. Stokes grabbed his leather jacket from his stool, nodded to Annie has he passed, and stepped out into the crisp fall day. In half a minute he was straddling his Yamaha SZR 660, helmet on and buckled, the motorcycle's engine ready to roar. Five minutes later, he'd left behind the county highway, with its motels and diners and gas stations and seedy bars strewn along it like litter tossed from passing cars. He was flying along a wooded back road. The early-October leaves were nearing their fall peak, the last of the green having given way to fiery reds and glowing golds, but summer wasn't so far behind that the leaves had started dropping in great number yet.

Stokes was feeling all right. His night in jail was behind him, and even though the sun wouldn't set for hours yet, he was surrounded by trees full of sunset colors whipping by in a kaleidoscopic blur as he gunned his bike, sailing through the straightaways, leaning into lazy turns. He'd head back to his trailer, relax for a few hours, and maybe after dinner—

Leaning to his left, Stokes took the next curve way too tight, well over the centerline. He was halfway around the bend when a dark car appeared, was suddenly right on him, and there he was, leaning into the turn, leaning toward the car, *speeding* toward it, horribly exposed, nothing but soft flesh covering brittle bone, and he knew it was over, *oh shit*, it was over for him . . .

He was barely aware of the car lurching toward the far shoulder of the road as he jerked the handlebars of his motorcycle to the right, trying to wrestle the bike back into his own lane, away from the car. He watched the vehicle's glittering headlight assembly sail toward his face, then zip just under his ear, his helmet nearly brushing the front quarter panel. He felt the huge metallic bulk of the car, throbbing with deadly power, blast past him, just inches away from him. And then, incredibly, he was beyond it, beyond the car, with nothing in front of him but road and trees, his bike cutting sharply across his lane, his front wheel turning now, seemingly on its own, beyond his power to control it, and in a deafening, bone-shaking, world-tilting moment, his bike slammed into a guardrail and he was flying, twisting, spinning through the air. Everything went unnaturally silent for the briefest of moments, and then he heard a violent, metallic crash from somewhere, just before he slammed to earth and his breath and consciousness exploded out of him.

———

The guy was dead. No doubt about it. Somehow Stokes wasn't, but the driver of the car sure as hell was.

Stokes had come to rest near the bottom of a gentle incline sloping away from the road, on a thin blanket of dead leaves over a mattress of soft, moist ground. He'd lain for a moment, staring up at the trees all around him, at first wondering where he was and how he'd gotten there, but remembering soon enough, then wondering how the hell he'd flown fifteen feet into the woods and rolled down the hill without hitting a single tree. And, apparently, without breaking any bones.

He left his helmet by his mangled bike and climbed the little slope back up to the road. He stepped from the woods and looked for the car that had come so close to sending him elsewhere, either hell or purgatory or somewhere like that—certainly not heaven, if such a place existed. The car was nowhere in sight. For a moment Stokes thought it might have simply swerved around him and kept going wherever the hell it had been going when their paths had crossed . . . and then he saw them. Across the road, ten yards farther along, parallel grooves running through the gravel on the side of the road, grooves leading off the shoulder and down the hill on the other side, into the trees.

Stokes looked in both directions. Not a car in sight. He walked over to the tracks in the gravel. No skid marks on the road that he could see. The driver hadn't even had time to hit his brakes, at least not before he hit the gravel on the shoulder. Stokes squinted into the woods, where the still-thick canopy of leaves dropped dense shadows to the forest floor. He looked down at the tire tracks in the gravel, where they led onto the soft earth by the road. He followed them with his eyes, down the gentle slope, through the first trees. And there it was. Maybe thirty feet in. A black car accordioned against a thick tree. Stokes looked down again at the tire marks in the gravel, then slid the sole of his boot over the marks, obliterating them. After one more look for cars on the road, he stepped into the woods.

And now there he was, staring into the car, staring through a spiderwebbed window at the bloody face of a body slumped over the steering wheel. Either this car didn't have an air bag or it had been defective and hadn't deployed. Or maybe the dead guy had unwisely deactivated it. The poor bastard's eyes were open. Open and staring and totally lifeless.

Stokes took a step back. The woods were silent but for the ticking of the cooling engine. Most people would have called 911 by then, he knew. Then again, most people wouldn't have spent the last night being interrogated by the cops about a burglary. Nor would they have been arguably at fault for this accident—and therefore this man's death. And the fact that Stokes had recently had a couple of beers would surely complicate matters. No, Stokes wasn't going to be calling the cops. Instead, he decided to hide his twisted wreck of a motorcycle as best he could, then leave as fast as possible. Maybe he'd come back after things died down around here and dispose of the bike properly, if no one had found it by then. Or maybe he wouldn't—fortunately, it wasn't registered in his name.

He was just about to implement his plan, such as it was, when something caught his eye through the window of the rear door. He leaned closer to the glass, careful not to touch the car, and peered inside. He blinked. He blinked again. He reached up under his shirt, gripped the door handle through the fabric, and tried the door. It swung open.

On the floor of the car, behind the passenger's seat, was a backpack. But that wasn't really what had snagged his attention. Rather, it was the bundles of money spilling out of the bag that had caught his notice.

Thousands of dollars.

Stokes swiped a hand across his forehead. It came away wet with sweat despite the cool autumn air in the shadowy woods.

That was a hell of a lot of money lying there. And that was merely what had spilled from the bag. If there was more inside, which there looked to be, it would be more than Stokes had made in years, maybe a decade—certainly far more than he had made honestly. And it was just lying there.

He saw two options: leave the money, knowing it would probably wind up under somebody else's mattress—maybe whoever found the car, maybe the first cop on the scene—or take the money. The dead guy sure didn't need it. Stokes sure did. The decision wasn't a tough one for him.

ABOUT THE AUTHOR

Bestselling author James Hankins pursued writing at an early age. While attending NYU's Tisch School of the Arts, he received the Chris Columbus Screenwriting Award. After career detours into screenwriting and the law, Hankins recommitted himself to writing fiction. Since then, he has written four popular thrillers—*Shady Cross*, *Brothers and Bones*, *Jack of Spades*, and *Drawn*—each of which became Amazon #1 bestsellers. Additionally, *Brothers and Bones* received a starred review from *Kirkus Reviews* and was named to its list of Best Books of 2013. Hankins lives with his wife and twin sons just north of Boston. He can be reached through his website, www.jameshankinsbooks.com.